CU00865962

A Salient in Flanders

Alan R. M. Thrush

Though based on factual historical events, *A Salient in Flanders* is a work of fiction. All incidents and dialogue, and all characters with the exception of some well-known historical figures, are products of the author's imagination and are not to be construed as real. Where real-life historical persons appear, the situations, incidents and dialogues concerning those persons are entirely fictional and are not intended to depict actual events or to change the entirely fictional nature of the work. In all other respects, any resemblance to persons living or dead is entirely coincidental.

© Alan Thrush

First published 2022

Transition Publishing Limited

.

Blessed Michael, archangel,
defend us in the hour of conflict.

Extract from Leonine prayer to the Archangel Michael, in biblical teachings the leader of Heaven's armies in their triumph over the powers of Hell.

One is worth ten thousand to me, if he is the best. — Heraclitus

CHAPTER ONE

The sergeant was weeping.

It was 1917. October's final days. Private Peake had been training for twelve weeks. In just a few more he'd be heading to war. But today, the luck of temporary reprieve: a brief leave – a twelve-hour pass. It allowed him to quit the barracks of Brocton Camp.

Peake's training might have been incomplete, but the weeks endured had already toughened him. They'd made him strong and fit, so he'd walked the four miles to nearby Stafford through the natural forest surrounding Cannock Chase, now home to recently built Brocton which occupied the high ground. Throughout his training, Peake had relied on camp views across this forest to calm and soothe, reminding him as they did that there was still a normal world, albeit rural, beyond the perpetual, wearying rigours of the army, an army that was still hammering, forging and refashioning his young mind and body into what was needed for the task ahead. Whenever he looked at this forest, he thought it served well as a foil to the ant-like military busyness brought to the vast clearing that was Brocton by the thousands vacuumed up by the recruiting arm of Kitchener's New Army: volunteers all, until conscription started in January 1916. Those gentle forest views were a foil, too, to the toughened hardness of the NCOs – the staff sergeants, sergeants and corporals – who trained them.

Now, after those four miles, he was in Stafford by the River Sow, in England's West Midlands.

The weather was fair for his pass, unusual for this time of year. There was birdsong instead of threat of rain or drizzle. The sigh of a gentle breeze whispered through the trees as he approached the town. Peake had no plans for Stafford, thinking to explore a little before finding an inn to serve ale and a lunch – a proper lunch, a meal carefully prepared and flavoursome, akin to home cooking even. Whatever he found, he hoped for contrast to the routine dreariness that was camp food, solid but plain: Brocton cuisine was something to suffer, not enjoy.

He had not been in Stafford before. When he reached the town, he looked about with a keen eye as he meandered through lanes and roads leading toward the town centre, enjoying the simple peace as people went about their daily work, and welcoming the absence of barked command and regimented regularity. The borough's arrangement and architecture offered a haphazard contrast to the drab, disciplined order of Brocton's lines and squares of prefabricated timber and asbestos. As he neared the town centre and turned a corner, he came upon a small square with a large tree, old and gnarled, rising from patchy grass as the focus of a quadrangle. Three wooden benches were set upon flagstones in the shade of this tree as rest for the weary, or simply as places to sit and ponder. Two of the benches were empty, but on the third sat a man, a soldier in the same uniform as that worn by the young man on pass: peaked cloth cap, thick woollen tunic with large buttons fastened to the neck and featuring prominent collar and even more prominent breast pockets, a broad belt, trousers that disappeared into puttees wound tightly about the lower leg, and boots. The men were two strangers, drably identical in army brown, save for protruding hands and faces, the latter their last vestige of individuality.

Something about this man on the bench – the cut and fleshy angle of his face, his solid stature with its promise of strength – or perhaps just the way he sat leaning forward with forearms on knees and looking directly ahead … something was somehow familiar to the young man from Brocton. He had seen this soldier on the bench before. But the general bearing of the seated fellow radiated authority and experience, so the newcomer kept an eye on him in case he was required to salute or brace up to show respect for higher rank. Wise, because as the distance narrowed, three broad chevrons and the coloured insignia above them showed the stranger to be a sergeant of the Lancashire Fusiliers, a regiment very likely to become the young man's own, a vast brotherhood comprising more than a score of battalions with training camps at Catterick, Brocton and elsewhere, and with some ten thousand men already committed to the trenches of France and Belgium, and Gallipoli before that.

Realising his path would carry him into the sergeant's peripheral vision, Peake could have altered direction, but did not. Confidence and a directness of manner instilled by training prevented any possibility of shirking an open display of respect from entering his mind. He knew that he would do it – he would respect the sergeant – whereas three months before he might have considered evasion. So, as he came within range of expected greeting, and knowing that the sergeant would be aware of his approach, the young man further squared an already erect bearing and stride, braced his arms stiffly to his sides, and sang out in a strong, confident voice:

'Good morning, Sergeant!'

The man on the bench did not change posture even slightly, which was unusual and not at all what the young man expected. Neither did the sergeant return the greeting, which was something required of him by military dictate in recognition of the private soldier's essential presence and value on the battlefield. The sergeant did, however, move his head to glance sideways at the young man, and that was when he revealed the tears on his cheeks.

There are times in military life when unthinking, instinctive humanity breaks through even the most rigid discipline, or perhaps combines with it to deliver something stronger than regimented reason. This was one such moment. This, and the sudden recognition by the young conscript of the sergeant on the bench, for they had been at school together, down in London.

'Winterman! What on earth is wrong?' asked the conscript, ignoring rank and with much concern in his voice as he moved quickly to sit beside the covertly weeping sergeant, now wiping at his eyes with the heels of his palms.

The reply was a mumble, terse and gruff, an attempt at regaining self-control and re-establishing authority despite the tears:

'That'll be "sergeant" to you, Peake. This isn't Camden Secondary.'

'Yes, Sergeant! Sorry, Sergeant!' came the newcomer's immediately disciplined response, though not in the same loud, firm, Brocton-drilled voice of his greeting, and he neither stood up at the reprimand nor braced to seated attention as he would have done within the camp. Instead he faced his front, stared ahead and fell silent to allow the other, older man, two years his senior in unfashionable Camden, time to compose himself.

The sergeant – Winterman – sighed audibly. It was an uneven, broken sound in the quietness of the little square. Then he said:

'I've set a bad example ... I'm sorry.'

Finding himself at a loss for words because of the shock of what he had seen, the conscript – Peake – said nothing.

'When did they get you?' asked the sergeant at length.

'Get me, Sergeant?'

'Yes. Get you – call you up.'

'Late July. I got here August.'

'I see. You're almost through, then.'

'Yes. Almost through.' Peake paused, gathering himself. He wanted to know the reason for the sergeant's weeping, but of course could not ask it. Careful to inject respect into his tone, he ventured:

'And you, Sergeant? When was your call-up?'

'I wasn't. Didn't wait for conscription. I volunteered.' For a few seconds Winterman seemed to be considering that fact. Then he added quietly: 'Been in close to three years now. It was still the thing to do back then, volunteering. Popular … attracted the ladies. There were more volunteers than the army could train. Madness.'

There was a trace of resentment in this quiet observation. Together with the tears, it underlined experience of something bad, but Peake did not venture to enquire after detail because Sergeant Winterman's elevated rank, something not usually attained in so short a time, hinted quite clearly that most of his months had been spent in the trenches, a probability underlined by his gruff manner. Gruffness had not been the man's way while still at Camden Secondary.

Peake observed:

'I don't think you're based at Brocton, Sergeant. I would have seen you about.'

'No, I'm not. I'm on home leave. There were papers for me at Brocton. Regimental affairs to sort out.'

'From France, then?'

'Yes … from France.'

Peake, the conscript, summoned enough courage to ask:

'What's it like over there, Sergeant? Really. We hear rumours, but of course we don't know.'

For the first time, the sergeant turned his head so that he could look directly at the newcomer.

'How's your bayonet work, Peake? Your drills?'

'My bayonet drills, Sergeant? We have rifles.'

A flash of irritation crossed Winterman's face, his dark eyebrows furrowing in a frown over grey eyes. His retort was quick:

'Well of course you have rifles, man. All of us have those … All right, then, tell me about your marksmanship. How's your shooting?'

'I can hit the target, Sergeant. Not like at first … I was always wide.'

'Good. Hone that skill. Get as good at hitting the target as you can. But I still want to know about your work with the bayonet, Peake. Tell me, can you do it? Have they taught you to stick a man? From above and below him?

Straight on, too, of course. You'll need your bayonet over there as much as you'll need to shoot straight. And you'll need to be quick with it, too.'

'We do quite a bit of bayonet training. I'm not sure how I rate – there's no way of measuring it, no way of telling how you've done. It's more like physical training than anything.'

Sergeant Winterman grunted, assessing the conscript from Brocton sitting beside him on the bench, this young man he could remember as a schoolboy when Winterman himself had still been at school, three years before, and whom Winterman could have had doing a fag's work, as indeed had been the case on many occasions. Abruptly, he stood up to leave.

'Where're you going, Sergeant? Thought we might eat together.'

'I've a train to catch. Embarkation port. We go back tonight. Stand up, please, Peake.'

The conscript did so, snapping smartly to attention before this sergeant probably back from battle, though he had made no mention of its fact.

Winterman examined Peake keenly from cap to toe, and then back up again, assessing the young man's general turnout and alignment, his bearing, demeanour and probable level of fitness, and gauging from these his state of discipline, the stage of his training – his readiness – and weighing all against what would be required of him in a few weeks' time.

'You'll receive more training when you get over there, Peake,' said Winterman evenly and in a not unfriendly manner. '… when you get over to France. They'll put you in a base depot to start with: Étaples. Or perhaps Calais. If you're lucky you'll have as much as another two months there before they move you up the line. Or unlucky, depending on your point of view. So, remember what I've told you: Hone your marksmanship by all means, but focus equally on your skills with the steel.'

And without another word Sergeant Winterman, grey eyes now dry and calm, turned back to the bench, stooped to retrieve his small pack beside it, then walked quickly away from Peake to leave the square with its tree and grass and benches, making for the railway station and, beyond that, embarkation.

Peake trained at Brocton for three more weeks. It was rigorous, difficult training lasting ten hours a day and sometimes longer. Much of the work was practical in nature, out of doors in rain and mud. Parts were physically brutal. Nevertheless, the lessons were absorbed with fierce concentration by all under the whip of instruction, for the men knew that the battlefields ahead held real possibility of death. They understood the need to master every skill offered. So Peake and his mates stayed positive as they followed the intricacies of their classes through these final days, confronting squarely and cheerfully all physical tasks – wet or not – paying close attention to theory, and undertaking every practical exercise and drill with enthusiasm and vigour.

At the end there was leave. All were granted a final pass from Brocton Camp: ten November days free to do as they wished before the time came to re-assemble and move as a single body of trained soldiers to their embarkation port.

Peake, like most of the others, went home, which for him was the plain brick terrace house in which he had been raised by uncle and aunt, his guardians. They lived in a lower middle-class street on the outskirts of Camden, their small home one among many hundreds of almost identical dwellings covering like a blanket the featureless ground of this part of London. These two and three-storey rows of dull brown, plain brick dwellings shared common walls and were densely packed one upon the other, all externally quite similar as they lined both sides of the meandering streets – some cobbled but many still of plain, packed earth – and rising or falling with the slight undulations of the land. At night, the place was lit by occasional gas lamps dotted here and there to supply cones of dim light, but these were few and far between, so that the greater parts of all streets remained places of cold, unwelcoming darkness. Even during the day, the streets were grey, narrow places which sunlight struggled to penetrate. Edged by their multi-storey dwellings, the streets and alleys snaked and intersected endlessly across the land, the homes buttressed one to another, lit within by oil lamp and heated by coal – a Dickensian holdover.

On the third day of his ten days of leave, Peake met a woman. She was older, but only by two years; the same age as Winterman, then, being twenty, or so he guessed at the time of their introduction. Peake himself was barely eighteen, having passed through that anniversary of his birth within the confines of Brocton. To young eyes untrained in women's fashion, she seemed correctly and unostentatiously presented for their arranged meeting. He could not know that the woman had taken considerable care in her preparations, choosing her most elegant garments which, though second-hand, showed her at her best. A long-sleeved afternoon dress of darkish crinoline flowed from high vee-neck down to brown, low-heeled boots of well-worn leather, tightly laced to disappear upwards into the flounce above. Peake imagined them to be of calf length as he admired fleeting glimpses of a pale pink petticoat. At the woman's waist, a wide band of the same dark colour and material gathered the garment to her body, though not too tightly, gently showing off the natural curve and flow of her figure from breast to hip. She seemed to Peake slimly generous in build, pleasing to the eye yet with somewhat plain looks that ran no risk of running to beauty. Across the bust of her dress, beneath artificial lapels sewn to give the appearance of a jacket, the woman's garment showed a second, narrower band which was darker and edged with a line of bright thread, the petals of a single flower sewn into the motif at its centre. As with Peake, who was in uniform for their meeting, only the hands and head of this young woman were bare of clothing. Unlike Peake, her neck and a tiny vee of the smooth, pale skin of her breast remained naked save for a narrow necklace of modest metal. She neither carried nor wore any hat, proudly displaying her pleasant features and the natural lustre of her pinned up fair hair.

Peake wanted her. He had met this woman through deliberate and formal introduction, and he experienced the usual, instinctive reaction of any young male confronted by an attractive female. He was accustomed to this feeling, but had learned to suppress and control it, a skill he had mastered on account of his guardians, and especially his uncle. He understood that he should not act upon this straightforward physical urge. Indeed, Peake at this point of his life was not sure that he would know *how* to act on it, even were he to be presented with open opportunity. The only woman who had ever touched Peake, or awarded an affectionate kiss, had been his aunt.

Tea and biscuits had been prepared for the introduction of this uniformed soldier to the woman in flowing crinoline. These were set on a tray in the home of Penelope Brooke, a friend of Peake's aunt and a woman who had known Peake since the time when his mother had died giving birth to him, at which point the aunt and uncle had become Peake's guardians. Nobody knew who the father might have been.

Christine – for that was her name – had arrived ahead of Peake and was already seated in her host's modestly furnished lounge, ready for the introduction. She felt an excitement similar to Peake's own when the young soldier was shown into the room by Penelope, who had answered his knock at her door. Christine hoped that her quickening pulse would not carry through to any noticeable flush of cheek or neck. She sat calmly forward on the cushion of her chair, knees together beneath the crinoline and hands resting modestly in her lap, lightly smiling.

'Simon, I want you to meet Christine. She is the daughter of a close friend and feeling rather alone at the moment, aren't you, Christine?'

7

At this, Christine felt herself blush. Promised to another, she was no stranger to men. Yet the engagement was strained and her fiancé absent, a hardship made worse by the distant coldness her partner had projected when last together. She had felt used, objectified and emotionally betrayed during their reunion, and had shared her consequent confusion and worry with Penelope. This teatime introduction to Peake was the outcome of that conversation: Penelope Brooke did not believe in fidelity for its own sake, and especially not in one so young as Christine. Time to explore another relationship – that was the required medicine in Penelope's opinion. Christine agreed. Now, though, hearing herself described as feeling alone caused Christine embarrassment.

'Young Simon here is equally alone, I think. He's been away training in Stafford for a long time, haven't you, Simon? Three months, is it?' This while examining her uniformed guest. 'Seems to have filled you out a bit since you left us all to go soldiering – well, to my eye at any rate. Such a change since I last saw you as a schoolboy, Simon! How is that possible?'

It was now Peake's turn to feel embarrassment as the eyes of both women roamed over and about him. Christine seemed to take particular delight in this opportunity for frank inspection of his height and build.

'Christine has a brother over in France,' Penelope announced. 'In the artillery, Christine, isn't he?'

'No, Mrs Brooke. He's with the infantry.'

'Ah, yes … Of course. How silly of me. Well, perhaps you'll meet him, Simon, being a foot-soldier yourself and all. How do you take your tea? One sugar or two?'

Peake indicated two. He placed the service cap which had been under one arm throughout this introduction carefully on the sideboard, savouring the spark of delight he'd felt at the touch of Christine's gentle handshake. Now he crossed the small, wallpapered room with its modest furniture to accept the cup proffered by Penelope, who had placed a small biscuit on its saucer. She had already added milk.

Peake sat.

Opposite him, Christine gauged her newly introduced acquaintance calmly but eagerly. Lean and tallish (but not too tall) Peake's stature pleased her, though something stubborn and determined in the set of mouth and chin unsettled her. She hoped it did not signal any reserve in his attitude to women. Her wish was that beneath the guarded manner of his exterior he might be making a similarly interested appraisal of her. She wondered what she might say as she raised her cup to sip. All were silent for a while, the atmosphere awkward. Eventually, Penelope Brooke, her tea only half finished, positioned her cup centrally on its saucer and placed both on the table beside her. She stood.

'Well,' she said, 'I've things to do and you two are not children. I'll be going and leaving you to yourselves to get acquainted. Is the rain still holding off, Simon?'

'It is, Mrs Brooke. There'll be none for a good few hours, I think.'

'Good. I'll see you later, then. Close the door if you decide to go out, please. No need to lock.'

And with that, Penelope Brooke smiled brightly at her guests and left the room in a brush and rustle of stiff cloth and even stiffer petticoats. They heard the front door close behind her.

Peake, feeling an obligation to fill the ensuing silence, opened:

'And how have you come to be acquainted with Mrs Brooke, Christine?'

He looked straight at her as he asked, taking in the curve of her cheek and the delicacy of lips still lightly smiling above the smooth skin of her rounded chin. No makeup, he saw.

Christine repeated Penelope's explanation: her mother and Penelope Brooke were friends. She kept her manner light and open, careful to avoid any hint of rebuke in the way she delivered this reiteration, but in spite of her care the young man's face fell a little because of his error. She pressed on, anxious to please him:

'But never mind that. I'm ever so pleased to meet you, Simon.' She giggled at her next thought, gave voice to it: 'Whatever do you suppose she meant by excusing herself so soon? I mean, "and you're not children" … What do you suppose Penelope meant?'

Christine's giggle was a happy sound to Peake's ears, and he laughed with her.

Pressing her advantage, she said:

'Well, shall we take some air? The day is quite good. We could stroll. The park is not far. Shall we?'

She stood, unsure of her mood beyond happiness at the presence of this boy in soldier's uniform, but clear in her mind that the park would offer opportunity to better know him.

'Why not?' was his reply.

Peake found himself surprised at the young woman's confident manner, but also pleasantly encouraged. He felt enchantment at her light smile and the easy grace with which she rose from her chair. Hastening to the front door, he opened it before standing aside so that Christine could pass through. Then, on the street, military training made him pause to don and adjust his service cap. Usually the headdress bestowed confidence, but now it somehow failed. Complete uncertainty threatened to overwhelm him, for this was the first time Peake had strolled with any woman other than his aunt and her friends. He realised he did not know what to do with his hands. Christine saved him, taking his arm firmly as though he had already offered it and, smiling encouragement up at him, tugged gently in the direction of the park. After that, Peake took the lead as he felt he ought, so that they walked in the natural and unhurried manner of any couple of those days, strolling along the narrow way between the twin ranks of buttressed two- and three-storey homes, somewhat grim in appearance though presented more fairly to them in the moment because of their happy mood.

What luck to meet this girl! How wonderful to be walking with her beside him! Peake thought Christine quite lovely in her simple plainness. Her cheerful, somewhat forward manner and bright smile seemed to him the perfect foil for his own awkward hesitancy. He experienced an uplifting happiness at their physical closeness as they strolled. The feel of her arm in his, her light chatter, the rustle of her dress and click of her heels on the cobbles blended perfectly with the sounds of daily life on the street, modifying them to appear less overpowering. He thought that he could hear the occasional bird chancing the dull sky above the narrow band of open view afforded by the walls and roofs either side, and he felt that the combination of all these sights and sounds might well be framing the happiest moment of his life.

For Christine, too, what luck! What luck that her acquaintance with Penelope Brooke had brought her this young man at a time when she was experiencing such confused loneliness and need. How fortunate that Penelope should understand and empathise with the natural desires and appetites of a healthy young woman for a man of similar age and background; that she should view as an almost perfect opportunity for the satisfaction of these drives the return to London from Brocton of this newly trained soldier now strolling with increasing confidence beside her on the cobblestones as they headed to the park. What luck that Penelope should contrive to construct for Christine a route to overcoming the asphyxiating obstacles presented by the social mores of the day. At last, here was opportunity for release and outlet.

Next morning, that stroll through the park with Christine at his side, her light chatter and electric physical closeness – all were still warm in Peake's memory.

It was Sunday. After breakfast, the family – uncle, aunt and ward – moved from kitchen to sitting room, a simply furnished space similar in both small size and ordinary style to that of Penelope Brooke, the place where Peake had experienced his magical introduction to Christine. It could have been the sitting room of any one of the myriad homes along their suburb's narrow streets.

Uncle glanced up from his morning daily to peer over reading glasses. He took out his pipe and said:

'I must tell you, I really do approve of that new uniform of yours, Simon. Best thing for the British Army since we beat the Boers, eh? Need to blend in with the earth these days … More practical than scarlet and white. They give you a tin hat yet? At Brocton? No? Haven't seen one myself, but we could do with a few, what with the bombing and all.'

'Well, they're not bombing this suburb yet, dear, and we've not seen one of those horrible Zeppelins. Rather let our lads in France have the helmets.'

This was Wainwright's wife, a short, plump woman with round face, ready smile and happy, positive disposition, attributes that Wainwright considered essential to his own contentment. Given to plain, high-necked, full-length dresses of dark colour, she was in her mid-forties, and her hair was beginning to grey. She swept it always to the back of her head, and pinned it in a tight bun.

'Hmmm …' Wainwright grunted agreement. He loved his wife, faithful companion through years made quite difficult by the responsibility of raising her sister's boy, Simon. The couple themselves had no children. 'Well,' he observed, 'they may've stopped with the Zeppelins for now, but they still have their aeroplanes – these new bombers of theirs. Hope we never do see one.'

Peake's uncle – Wainwright – was spruce for church: pressed trousers, white shirt and tie. A well-worn waistcoat was the best he had. There was no fob and he had decided to wear a flat cap, not possessing a bowler and knowing that probably he would not feel comfortable in one even if he did. Peake and his aunt, too, were dressed for the Sunday service, though Peake wore uniform as always. This was standard practice and obligatory even when off duty, sparing soldiers the barbed taunts and white feathers that many young women had taken to pressing upon shirkers to shame them into taking up arms. Wainwright's wife had chosen a dress of ordinary cut, dark as always, and shoes that Peake had only ever seen her wear to church.

Now, leaning back with eyes closed in happy memory of the park, Peake opened them again, smiled and replied:

11

'They'll issue us helmets in France, I suspect, Uncle. They're quite scarce and Brocton has hardly any. I'm told everyone has them at the front now, though – they're not trench stores anymore. On general issue these days, so we've been told.'

The aunt, eyeing Peake's uniform and replying to her husband's comment on it, said:

'It may well be practical, dear, but I'll miss the colour and sparkle of the bright parades. England's a poorer place for this new style, without a doubt.'

'Yes, well perhaps they'll bring them back when this mess is over. The scarlet and white, I mean. After they've brought the army home.'

Peake looked at his uncle in wonder, thinking this observation less than correct. The uniforms were there to stay. As for the war, it seemed endless despite the entry of the Americans in April; they had yet to reach the front in any strength. Uncle, returning to his newspaper, shared tidbits from time to time:

'Casualty list not too bad today.' He drew steadily on his pipe, the tobacco crackling softly with the draw and glow. 'Numbers're well down on those dreadful pages of last year. My oath, but that was a bad do.'

'Seems we had to do it, Uncle. Somme's been a big topic at Brocton because of the changes it forced. We've been taught things the old sweats were not. Some of our instructors were there. They went through it, and they keep emphasising particular aspects of what they saw – keep telling us how necessary it is that we learn the lessons.'

'Hmmm … Our obligation to the French, if you ask me, and nothing less.' Wainwright did not remove the pipe from between his teeth, so that the words emerged framed by wisps of smoke. 'Enormous pressure on them there at Verdun. Our do at the Somme made the Hun draw off some of his troops. Russia attacked at the same time as well, I remember, in the east. We had to do it. Russia was still solid back then …'

'Agreed, dear, of course,' soothed Peake's aunt, though with a worried tone, 'but there are many families who might not … Mrs Smith two doors down still has her curtains drawn. She's not over it and it's been more than a year. Lost both her boys and will only wear black when she's about. It's rumoured she's considered taking her life. Padre Burke talked her out of it.'

'Yes. I remember.' This from Peake.

'Well, of course you do, Simon,' said the aunt. 'You were still here at home with us, and still at school, too. We were happier for that, your uncle and I. Will you be looking up any of your masters, then?'

'I might, Aunt, if I'm at a loss for things to do.'

12

Peake felt great discomfort at this topic and its direction. He turned his eyes to the ceiling by way of evasion, certain he would be forced to experience many of the realities of battle just a few months from now, and wondering how he would cope in the moment; whether he would pass what all considered such a critical test of manhood and mettle, perhaps its ultimate test.

Some of the Brocton instructors had been at the Battle of the Somme. Not many, but a handful had been part of that great offensive. One of the sergeants instructing Peake's platoon had been wounded on the first day and invalided back to recuperate. Probably he had needed to recover his nerve as well. Though he never gave specifics, he'd once observed that the battle had changed the way the British Army approached the war, and especially the practicalities of attacking with massed infantry. For him, all discussion of the war could be divided into two distinct timelines: before the Somme, and after it. Peake could remember one particularly nasty episode bearing clear relation to the sergeant's experiences there. They had been exercising in that part of Brocton where they spent so much of their time: the trench-training area. It was the only occasion that Peake had heard the sergeant express real anger:

"Cold steel, Farmer? Is that what you said?"

The sergeant had been countering a muttered quip from the squad's joker.

"Charge, Farmer? That it – cold steel and charge?"

A pause, then the tirade:

"Well, sod you, Farmer, you cocky little runt! D'you think the charge is some kind of joke? You have absolutely no idea – you can't imagine what it means, what it's like – but you'll certainly rue the day you have to walk forward with fixed bayonet when they order you to do it, by God, if ever they do!"

The sergeant's voice was level. He had not raised it to the bellow of the barrack room inspection, but his tone held such a cold and vicious anger that the words carried to every man in the squad standing at his post along the trench, and it was all the more frightening for that.

"Charge?" continued the sergeant, his ire mounting. *"Charge, you say? Hah! We lost more men on the first fucking day of that lot than this army's ever lost in any battle before in history. Did you know that, Farmer? Did you?"*

All were silent before the tirade, initial grins and chuckles brought about by Farmer's humour now vanished. The sergeant instructor was poised on the parapet of the trench, hunched forward and grim-faced as he glared down at Farmer. There was a snarl upon his lips. The man was only three years older than the eighteen-year-old conscripts in the trench, but he had the manner of a man of thirty.

"Did you know that, Farmer?" he repeated. *"Did you? Answer me, man!"*

"No, Sergeant! Sorry, Sergeant!"

"Brace up when you address me, Farmer! Stand to attention when you even mention the Somme! Damn your useless hide! My battalion lost more than five hundred good men in that attack. Did you know that?"

"No, Sergeant!"

Farmer was now standing rigidly to attention within the trench, blond schoolboy curls peeping out from beneath the brim of his helmet. His eyes were wide with fear of his instructor, and he was sweating.

"Five hundred down in the first thirty minutes, Farmer. Thirty minutes. And we were only seven hundred and fifty strong when we went over the top. At the Somme there were dead and wounded everywhere. Everywhere, by God. I can still hear the screaming. Fuck your cold steel! You have no idea at all! By Christ, Farmer, I get so weary of your jokes! Well, God help you if ever they make you move forward in a charge like that – you'll probably never make one of your rotten, snide remarks ever again, should you survive it, because you'll have forgotten how to laugh. Completely. And you'll not sleep easily at nights, afterwards."

And it was true. They had never seen their sergeant instructor laugh. The man rarely even smiled. After his tirade that day, Peake and the others had made an effort to find details of the battle. The facts were sobering: 19,000 British dead and another 39,000 wounded on the first day. Instead of overwhelming the German defences and breaking through, no advance had been achieved at all. Four months after the offensive began, the British were still fighting to take some of the objectives set for Day One. Some were saying the Battle of the Somme eventually cost the British Army one million casualties.

In the comfort of the family sitting room, Peake wondered: had Sergeant Winterman been there? He remembered the NCO's grey eyes, wet with his public weeping. Had Winterman experienced that awful battle? Peake had not forgotten their encounter one month before in the streets of Stafford; it still shook him to think of it. He had discussed the episode with no one, not even others within his Brocton platoon, so troubled had he been by Winterman's tears – it was unheard of for an NCO to display weakness, for all soldiers looked to them in faith and expectation of strength and courage. Ensconced in his sitting room chair, Peake now stretched his long legs out before him and folded his hands behind his head in deliberately relaxed pose to disguise his thoughts. He asked quietly:

'Have you seen anything of the Wintermans? He's a sergeant now, I think.'

'A sergeant?' exclaimed the aunt. 'Who? Tom Winterman? Can't be. Still runs the tavern three streets down! And with his wife every night …'

'No, Aunt – not Mister Winterman. John. Their son. He was two years ahead of me at school. Played a good game of football. He's in the army now, like everyone.'

'Well,' said the uncle, 'We'll see for ourselves. I'll take you down to The Duke after work tomorrow. We can ask after John over a pint.'

There was a pause, affording Peake chance to reflect on these two – his uncle and aunt – who had raised him with much care and affection, and never a word of complaint. He loved them dearly. They were as parents to him, his only family, for Peake had no siblings and there was never mention of close relatives other than a grandparent on his aunt's side. One day a long time before, while still a small boy, he had questioned the form of address that they had taught him – Uncle, Aunt – and they had gently revealed to Peake that his mother had died during childbirth. 'What of my father?' had been his instinctive and immediate question, but they had avoided any explanation. Later, Peake had discovered that nobody had known who his father was.

Uncomfortable at the silence and wanting to change tack from thoughts of the Somme and bereaved mothers who darkened their homes and wore only black, Uncle said:

'There's no doubt you're doing the right thing, Simon. No doubt at all. Everyone must do his patriotic duty in this war. And especially young men. King and country, y'know – it may be hackneyed and glib, but it's true. You must do it. We must whip Germany, and soundly too. Your aunt and I are very proud of you. I want you to know that.'

'We are, Simon.' There was emphasis in the aunt's expansion. 'We're proud. But you take good care of yourself when you're sent across, d'you hear me? Your uncle and I … We'll … we'll need you here when we get older.' Then, to rescue a mood which had become sombre, she asked:

'Tell us, Simon, how was tea at Mrs Brooke's yesterday? I believe she wanted you to meet a certain young lady?'

The aunt looked at her ward kindly, waiting for his reply. Returning her steady stare, Peake thought that his aunt's eyes, always frank in their examination of him, appeared somewhat keener than usual in that particular moment of observation and enquiry. There seemed a lively sparkle of slightly wicked enthusiasm about them.

* * *

Christine contrived to meet Peake a second time. She achieved this simply by asking for the meeting when they parted after their unhurried walk through the park. During that stroll, she had made sure to bump him gently from time to time with shoulder and hip, linked as they were by their arms, and sometimes she granted him the slight press of bosom, softly firm and enticing enough for Peake; this was her wish. Christine was conscious that her actions were something of a deliberate tease, but it was one she hoped would prove effective. She found that her time with Peake helped her forget the coldness of her fiancé's last visit, easing for a while the ache he had caused. She was grateful, and when they parted she awarded Peake a delicate brush of her lips across the razored skin of his cheek, almost a kiss.

For Peake, this display of affection was received with delighted surprise. He had not previously experienced a kiss from anyone bar his aunt, and he lost for a moment all awareness of his surroundings, Christine's lips blanking out everything beyond the woman who had delivered it. Though there were other strollers in the park, some of them openly admiring the obvious attraction between these two young people, Peake's world closed in to focus solely on Christine. He shuffled awkwardly, striving to control reaction and hold it within the limits of publicly tolerated displays of affection. Christine took a graceful step back. She recognised the impulse of desire in his eyes.

'May I see you tomorrow please, Simon?'

'Of course,' he managed to stammer, happily surprised and unsure of what might be required of him. 'But I have to go to the late morning service with my aunt and uncle. Before, I mean. After … after that – well, of course I would be delighted.'

So next day – after attending with his guardians the Sunday service – they met where they had parted, at the gated entrance to the park with its trees stripped almost bare of leaves by the season, so that they might again walk along pathways that would lead them around the natural pond and through open spaces of greyish grass wet from earlier drizzle, escaping the press of buttressed building and narrow street, and particularly its many people. Peake made sure to arrive at the gate before the appointed time. He sat down on a bench offering good views toward all possible directions of Christine's approach. He waited.

When she came into sight, there was joy and delight in his heart. Her coat covered all but the hem of a dress which may have been the one worn before, though Peake wouldn't have minded; he had only one set of good clothing himself, and that not used since muster.

'Christine! You look splendid! And … and happy,' he blurted, smiling widely in unabashed pleasure at her arrival, and rising from the bench. He was unsure whether to offer any kiss, but Christine shared no such uncertainty. Returning his smile with equal pleasure, she rewarded him with a second light brush of lips upon cheek, took his arm, and led the way into the park.

Around them, sparrows and pigeons pecked at the cold ground. The November afternoon was dry, though overcast and cold enough to afford excuse for a tight grip of Christine's gloved hands upon Peake's trench-coated upper arm. He wore uniform, as always. December was now only a few days away with its colder, wetter weather – and perhaps an early snow – but today the rain was holding off, and neither could stop smiling in the happiness of young affection and attraction as they proceeded. Christine let him guide her while she looked continually and contentedly up into his face.

Their first kiss of passion became inevitable during this walk.

Again, it was Christine who took the lead, necessary because of Peake's nervous inexperience. Yet she did it gently and with great sensitivity, and in such a way that allowed him to feel it might have been he who initiated it. Momentarily shielded from strollers by a curve in the path and a clump of shrubbery, they knew they were too distant for folk around the pond at the foot of the open slope ahead to observe them in any detail. Recognising the opportunity, Christine released Peake's arm and turned to face him. Their hands seemed naturally to link, gloved fingers entwining and Peake's eager thumbs caressing her palms.

For a few seconds of silence they stood facing each other in the dull, cold light, no longer awkward. Rather, it was a completely natural thing, and necessary too. Christine gave the signal with upturned chin. When the kiss came, it was instinctive to both of them, long and sweet.

Unforgettable.

CHAPTER TWO

The November night was clear and cold. Patches of thin cloud sailed across, aided by a gentle breeze. To any soldier glancing up among the many as they marched, the patches were like ghosts: transparent, phantom ships upon an upside-down sea of black that sparkled with a million stars, all of it suspended miraculously by some higher power to cover the land. Hundreds were marching beneath that ghostly cloud, guided through the darkness by twin lines of extruded steel – a railway track destroyed by Russian engineers during their retreat. The only light to help these German soldiers was watery and weak, bestowed by a quarter-moon as mysteriously suspended as the myriad pinprick stars.

The steel rails were not precisely parallel. Here and there they moved in toward one another, their wooden sleepers deliberately torn in two by a mechanical ripper dragged by the last Russian locomotive to withdraw along the route. The marching Germans – some eight hundred of them – could not see these splintered sleepers, nor could they see anything of the countryside or lie of the land, for the watery moon was not strong enough to reveal the track, nor to light their way and indicate position. No matter: whoever was leading them – the *Oberleutnant*, probably, or perhaps the *Herr Oberstleutnant* himself – would somehow chart their progress westward along this railway by dead reckoning, calculating any mistake in direction from the flickering, intermittent flashes coming from directly behind, a variable, pulsing glow which continued as a sporadic, reliable constant in terms of eastern bearing. These glimmering eruptions of light overcame the night for split seconds at a time, as would far away lightning, but their source was land-bound rather than something from the sky, the flashes momentarily throwing helmets, packs and shouldered rifles into stark silhouette as the detonating shells of German artillery – their own guns – exploded some dozen kilometres behind them to further sap what strength remained within Russia's disintegrating armies on the Eastern Front.

Nettermann's battalion was pulling back.

Clear and cold the night may have been, but it was not quiet. It was filled with noise. Nettermann registered this vaguely through his weariness. The boots of many hundreds of men crunched across light snow that covered the land, marching towards their rendezvous with wagons and horses – some trucks, too – and there was the deep crash of distant artillery as individual guns were fired, their shells exploding with a rumbling, unhappy thunder more distant still. They had passed three of these cannons – part of the gun line – ninety minutes before as they marched away from trenches left in the care of their rearguard. Now the soldiers had moved well beyond those artillery pieces booming and thumping behind them, a sporadically predictable noise that was individually definable rather than the continuous roar of an attack barrage. Between the angry bark of each gun that fired, dully loud, Nettermann could hear conversation from the men around him.

Nettermann, a *gefreiter* or private soldier, was tired. Though not exhausted, he was too tired to offer interjection or comment to the softly spoken chatter of the march, such as it was. Everyone in the column was presumably equally weary, for they had been in the line for nine consecutive days before the unexpected order to move had come. Once withdrawn to the *kompanie* rendezvous a short distance behind the line, all had been ordered even further back as part of a general withdrawal of their battalion and, unbeknown to them, their regiment and the greater division of which it was a part – all pulling back. About eight thousand men in total.

Nine days in the line was guaranteed to tire a man. Even should there be no attack by either side, time spent at the front's cutting edge meant numbing repetition and endless manual labour: twice daily stand-to at first light and last, and work parties to maintain the trenches by day, or the barbed-wire entanglements by night. Ammunition and rations had also to be carried in from the rear, and sometimes the truly unlucky were sent forward on dangerous reconnaissance patrols to chart the enemy lines or, worse, on trench raids to capture or kill. Proper sleep was impossible under these conditions. The men in the line dozed when they could, drifting off into slumber now and again for ten or fifteen minutes until some or other sound of quiescent battle startled them out of it: the shot of rifle fired by one side or the other, the thump of mortar either launched or exploding, or the occasional hammering clatter of a machine gun. Even with the line in this state of what the men themselves described as quiet, occasional, startling small-arms and mortar fire continued as an intermittent backdrop to the louder crashing of artillery shells fired from time to time by either side. These exploded with terrifying exclamation at the rate of two or three an hour, sometimes close, more often far away. Even when there was nothing obviously noteworthy to report, all this noise – completely unpredictable, dangerous and random – was effective in depriving the soldiers of real sleep. It made the men nervous and edgy. It was part of the process, part of a proven tactic employed by each side to wear down the other.

Through his trudging weariness, Nettermann noted that the battalion's withdrawal was unusually orderly and unrushed, almost like a training exercise. He could make such comparison because he had been a part of other withdrawals forced into chaos and sometimes even borderline disaster by the press of attacking enemy. During those other rushes to the rear – hasty and pressurised – the men had been under shellfire, and sometimes they had had to run, nervous and fearful, not really knowing what was happening around them. On those occasions, there had been the frequent shouts of officers and NCOs maintaining discipline, and the constant bark of rifle fire from the rearguard.

But not tonight.

Tonight the movement was calm and orderly.

The column of soldiers marched on, moving quite quickly alongside the line of broken railway. They marched out of step by arrangement, for in this way the men could relax a little, and more easily adjust individual loads that ate into shoulders and strained the muscles of their backs as they walked. Some smoked, others chatted quietly between the distant, booming thumps of their artillery. Had it been daylight, it would have been possible to see that they were a very long, steadily moving line of men in field grey, staining the grey-white carpet of light snow with their heavy steps, the men's faces creased with fatigue beneath stubble and grime, and heads bobbing up and down beneath oversized coalscuttle helmets of pressed steel which completely enveloped the skull and overhung much of the neck and shoulders, too. Behind the marching column, the dark sky continued to flash and flicker, shivering and shimmering like the living storm that it was. The slow, steady artillery fire was very effective in affording them cover.

The column's movement was not technically a withdrawal and certainly no retreat, for there was no pressure from the enemy to force it, no imminent assault in overwhelming strength to urge movement away from positions that could no longer be held. Some in the column reckoned there was no longer even any enemy from which they might reasonably be expected to withdraw. More accurately, then, it was a redeployment, a deliberate, unforced movement rearwards that lacked the haste and attempted silence and secrecy associated with real withdrawal under threat of massed attack. Indeed, their enemy – the Russians – seemed no longer capable of attack, instead undergoing themselves a cancerous political and moral disintegration that was now accelerating into military collapse, the result of a rotten political and social order which had mutated into open revolution five months before, in June of 1917 after the Tsar's abdication some time before that.

Now, the implosion of Russia's military was accelerating. Many of its soldiers were simply abandoning their weapons and trenches to go home, ignoring the orders of officers trying to maintain discipline and order, and sometimes even murdering them. There was no longer any credible Russian threat to Germany's army. As a result, its eastern divisions were being ordered westwards across the continent of Europe to the place where they were most needed – the Western Front. Enormous numbers of men were on the move in this direction, Nettermann's battalion among them. They were moving to reinforce defensive lines dug across France and Belgium three years before, and stuck there in virtual stalemate since that time. On the Western Front, the need for reinforcements was very great and very urgent, for the Americans were coming, indeed were already beginning to arrive and assemble in great strength from across the Atlantic, freshly trained and eager for the fight. They would join the battle quite soon.

Thus marched Nettermann and the others of his battalion, following the line of abandoned Russian railway on the first leg of their journey to help defeat the British and the French before the Americans could properly organise. Their initial destination was an assembly area where they would link up with the unit's stores wagons and horses to march further still. Eventually, all would be carried by snail-like train along a temporary light railway – a movable track that the army's engineers repositioned and re-laid according to need – to a proper train at one of the fixed German railheads serving the Eastern Front. From that point – the railhead – movement westward would be fast.

Marching with the others, Nettermann was experiencing a level of fatigue so great that his movements had become mechanical and took place without conscious thought. Yet there were some individuals in the column who, though equally tired, forced themselves to remain alert. One such was *Oberleutnant* Goettner, the officer whose job it was to motivate and, above all, care for Nettermann and the other thirty or forty men under his command.

Goettner was from Graudenz, a small industrial city on the River Weichsel in West Prussia. The Prussian Army was the heart and soul of Germany's military, its hard core since the German Empire had declared itself a new fact of European politics forty-six years before in 1871, an official conglomeration of the old princely states sharing common language and heritage, and destined to vigorously expand in the years after that declaration. Excellence in arms had always been deeply valued by the people of Prussia, and so it was with Goettner. Though not a soldier by profession, he took great pride in having been with the army almost since war began, donning uniform at his country's behest late in 1914, then finding himself selected for careful, thorough leadership training for commissioning as a *leutnant*. His first posting was to an infantry unit in Belgium, where the German advance was bogging down into a line of defensive trenches all the way across France to the Swiss frontier. Excited, worried and nervous all at the same time, unsure how he would manage the test of actual battle as a junior commander responsible for the lives of others, he arrived at the line of engagement only to find himself granted a stay of this trial, for his battalion had already moved east to join the counter-offensive against a Russian advance in the Austro-Hungarian province of Galicia. By the time Goettner caught up with his unit more than a thousand kilometres away from where he had expected to find them in Belgium, the fighting was all but over. Germany was temporarily victorious against the Russians, and Goettner's battalion was diverted north with the rest of the division to advance against enemy units closer to the Baltic Sea. A year later, with Warsaw occupied and the front now further east than even that Polish city, the division rested before being ordered south once again to Galicia – this time to Kraków – to help stem a second Russian push in the province.

But that second thrust into Galicia was the Bear's last gasp. The country was militarily spent, its energy dissolving into chaotic revolution. Germany's enormous effort against its eastern foe had won through, and even as a Russian plea for truce became inevitable, orders to move were being drafted for issue in November to Goettner's battalion and others, to withdraw from the line and return to the west.

As an individual, *Oberleutnant* Goettner was a special case. Like almost all the battalion officers, he was flawlessly proficient in the profession of arms. Yet Goettner somehow managed to stand out from his peers, and not merely because he was a tall man, the tallest of the unit's officers. It was also because of the way he did things as a *zugführer*. He seemed to possess a determination greater than most to do his utmost for his men as they endured the awful conditions of this war. His courage under fire and ability to make correct decisions within the tight vice of battle were greatly respected and widely known, as was his indefatigable enthusiasm for any task. These characteristics were recognised even beyond his *kompanie*, and he was generally received with confidence – even welcoming faith – by soldiers throughout the battalion's eight hundred men. Goettner's *zug* – his platoon of soldiers that included Nettermann – was glad to have him. To all for whom he was responsible, Goettner seemed by manner, bearing, intellect and conduct as somebody preordained to lead. In this assumption his men were correct, for Goettner's ancestry had indeed all but dictated his rank, his grandfather having served with distinction as an officer in the Franco-German War of 1870. Now, in the winter of 1917, Goettner's men were more than content that it was them that the grandson was leading.

In the darkness shrouding the broken Russian railway, Goettner stepped aside for a moment from the flow of the battalion to pause and weigh the morale of his men as they moved past him, greeting or encouraging those he recognised through the gloom by particular stature, gait or specialised weapon. Time together under the harsh whip of battle had given all in the *zug* an instinctive ability to recognise one another. Indeed, for some it was probably easier to recognise their fellow soldiers than it would have been to spot their own fathers, had they been present in this crowd of soldiers moving beside the track under cloak of night. Goettner, recognising the broad frame of his sergeant approaching as the shepherd of the *zug's* rear within the long line that was the marching battalion, knew immediately from the presence of this man that all were keeping pace as a cohesive whole, for any lagging or absence of his sergeant would have alerted him that it was not so. He awarded his trusted second-in-command, this sergeant and the *zug's* most important man, a friendly slap on the shoulder and words of jovial praise, then turned under his load of pack and blanket, holstered pistol, compass, binoculars and other paraphernalia of commissioned rank, to jog back up the line and reclaim his position at the front.

Such a display of energetic leadership was not strictly necessary. Probably, few of the other *zugführers* would be making similar effort. Yet it was typical of Goettner. The man went above and beyond. When others were almost too tired to continue, Goettner would somehow muster an energy and enthusiasm that was inspiring. It was one of many reasons why his men loved him. Now, identifying his *oberleutnant* by the height of his silhouette moving past at a half-jog in the darkness, Nettermann, tired though he was, managed a stubbled smile and a shouted reply to Goettner's cheerful greeting:

'All good, Nettermann? Not long now. We are close. With luck there will be coffee at the wagons.'

'All good, *Herr Oberleutnant*. I hope you are right!'

'Me too, Nettermann! Me too!'

And with a hearty guffaw, Goettner continued his jog forward along the line of his men.

The march carried on. First light began to compete with the flickering, flashing horizon behind the column, so that when the battalion reached their wagons the transport materialised as blurred, greyish silhouettes of things that had previously been completely cloaked in black. There was not yet sufficient light for the arriving men to count the battalion's twenty military carts with their strong, brawny horses already in harness, snorting or whinnying, or stamping strong, hairy hoofs upon snow now turning to slush. There were two animals to each of the four-wheeled stores wagons with their framed tarpaulins sheltering ammunition, rations, water, maintenance equipment and more. The horses and carts were assembled into parallel lines, one line for each *kompanie* and a further line for battalion headquarters with its administrative staff. All of this transport occupied most of a large field, long since disused and now rank with weeds, beyond which could be seen in outline the ruins of a farmhouse and some similarly abandoned and heavily damaged outbuildings, old victims of the war's eternal shelling. From this side of the house, the approaching men could hear the work of the cooks – the muffled, hollow clanging of lid on pot or pan – their field kitchens moved back ahead of the main body by wagon from the usual location just behind the trenches. And they could smell the cooks' work, too: food. These specialists, and others in charge of the battalion's transport, had been busy right through the night so that now, with the men approaching, this newly created assembly area was expectantly ready, neither noticeably noisy nor silent, but rather something in between, and nothing if not completely prepared for what it had to do, so that above the tramping of their boots the approaching soldiers could hear not noise so much as the occasional shouted query or acknowledgement. Not commands exactly, for these were not needed, but rather the organised, busy conversation of steady preparation accompanied by the occasional creak of impatient axle or wheel, and the tinny ringing of steel spoon against cooking vessel.

Suddenly, as if by magic, shadowy figures materialised from the gloom to meet the battalion: rear echelon men moving quickly down the column – sometimes running because of the urgency of a timetable needing to be met – to locate and guide the arriving *kompanies* to their individual kitchen areas.

The troops and their rear echelon shepherds were like a living entity that November morning, a single organism tending naturally toward order because of discipline, training and thorough organisation. Each man of the battalion's

24

eight hundred knew what needed to be done. Each had direction and task within the grand plan while, in meadows and fields out of sight and sound of this one, assembly areas for the regiment's other battalions were similarly preparing for the move west by train, and beyond these fields even more – the entire division of eight thousand soldiers.

Eight thousand. And, when these men had left on their train for France, another division of eight thousand would repeat the process.

And more after that.

The pace of the long line of soldiers slowed, the signal coming down the line all the way from the officer leading. They halted without shouted command. There was no need. They simply stopped, each man gratefully easing as much as he could his load of pack and helmet, weapon and ammunition, or hunching forward a little to lean on rifle butt-grounded on the earth, grasping the cold barrel with the same end in mind and panting short bursts of condensing breath into the chill air, for the pace had been brisk. Now, the guides moved quickly down the line to locate their individual *kompanies* and lead them off toward the kitchens.

Goettner had been right. There was hot coffee – not excellent, but certainly of better quality than those back home were being forced to endure because of shortages. More, there was for each man a thick sandwich of *würst* recently fried in proper fat and wedged between generous slices of something resembling bread; solid food to keep spirits high for a further march to the light railway that would carry them in small, open wagons borne on even smaller wheels to the railhead where lay swift passage onward by proper, covered troop train – a journey all the way across Germany's main rail network to the fighting in the west.

The troop train, when they boarded it, became a living thing too: a hissing, rattling, articulated line of wood and steel manufactured by a few to carry the many, and pulled by a locomotive that rhythmically belched smoke and black soot into the clear sky above. That steam engine was noisy but powerful. It pulled its load quickly, from time to time pitching screams of whistled warning into the silence covering this land that Germany had invaded and conquered, and which she now sought to abandon. Within the wooden carriages, the beat of steel wheel on rail, regular and rhythmic, carried through the floorboards to soothe and lull. Most of the soldiers slept.

But more than the train's sound and beat, it was the soldiers packed tightly within who made the thing live. The fittings of peace had years before been stripped from the carriages and replaced by wooden benches to maximise capacity, so that they were now more like wagons. Some sat on these benches. Others were haphazardly asleep on the floor in between, or lay balanced precariously upon the benches themselves, dozing. Personal equipment had been stuffed and crammed into whatever nooks and crannies of space remained, but there was not much to stow, for most used packs for pillows and arranged their leather webbing around them, placing their long Mauser rifles alongside, for there were never enough racks. Steel helmets they put where they could, and they wore their trench coats for warmth. The floor had become a sea of uneven grey.

Goettner was not asleep. He was one of those sitting on the benches. Occasionally he would nod, but his body's discomfort at feeling the weight of head falling forward onto chest would force consciousness upon him again, and Goettner would jerk himself erect and glance around guiltily. It was precisely because he knew that sleep was unlikely to properly claim him for as long as he remained vertical, that Goettner had chosen to sit. A combination of pride and self-discipline made him want to stay awake. At his feet was a steel helmet, his own, and all around lay the rifles and sleeping forms of his men.

Goettner knew without looking that most of the other officers would similarly be seated, and for the same reasons. Yet he did look, and by the dim, yellow light of a bulkhead lamp he could see two *hauptmanns* and three *zugführers* in a huddle on a bench at the far end of the wagon. They were not conversing – probably too tired – and one officer had already given up the fight, chin on chest, fast asleep. Perhaps the man's spine and lungs were better adapted to this unnatural posture than Goettner's own.

The route along which their train was moving was an extension of Germany's national railway network, which had been modernised and greatly expanded over two decades in anticipation of this war. "*Stop building fortresses – build no more of those! Build railways!*" – this was the watchword and order issued by successive Chiefs of the General Staff as a counter to the threat posed by France to the west and Russia to the east, both of them hostile and bound by treaty to unite as allies. The order had been diligently carried out. Even before war began, all arterial rail routes had been widened into two-track affairs that allowed trains carrying troops and equipment to pass along them in both directions at once. They were known as Germany's cannon routes, named for the speed of movement that they allowed. Unimpeded, trains could be fired along them at rapid intervals between strategic railheads incorporating platforms of two hundred metres and more in length, an aid to rapid embarkation and deployment. The general staff had on several occasions despatched multiple divisions up and down these rail routes, east and west, and they proved more effective than even their planners had imagined. When war eventually came in 1914, more than two million men and half a million horses were catapulted into position in just nine days – five hundred and sixty trains per day. Now, Goettner, Nettermann and the rest of the battalion were being moved with similar rapidity from Russia, across Germany and into France, along with the rest of their regiment and, beyond that, the division.

Goettner's gaze continued to roam, seeing without registering most of the sleeping soldiers. One man sitting up among the prone forms caught his eye. It was Nettermann, the biggish *gefreiter* possessed of that peculiar, almost dance-like gait enabling easy recognition even at night: the man seemed to bounce along as he walked. It was this odd prance and the man's solid stature that had facilitated Goettner's detection of him during last night's approach to the field kitchens, and their subsequent exchange about the coffee. Now, Nettermann was squinting to read by the carriage's dim light the pages of a letter. He seemed to be reading them over and over, holding the papers quite close. The news must either be very good or very bad, Goettner thought, for otherwise Nettermann would have been asleep like the others. Their state of fatigue was such that any of them would have slept given space, as Nettermann had been given it. Sometimes they did not even need that space, as evidenced by the sleeping officer.

Goettner ran over mentally what he knew of Nettermann, cursing himself with inward reprimand that he could not immediately bring all the facts to mind. Knowledge of the individual was difficult to acquire and even harder to recall, especially when tired, because replacements and casualties came at such a steady tick. Further, the *zug* was quite a large beast – sometimes the platoon held almost forty men – although attrition meant this number was rarely attained.

Nettermann … Nettermann …

The man was from Essen, Goettner thought. Yes, that was right – Essen. His family all worked for Krupp, the father and a brother in the steelworks and the mother in one of the armaments factories. Probably they lived with all the other tens of thousands of company employees in Krupp City, that enormous, sprawling residential complex that embraced and complemented the mass production carried out within the multiple factories themselves. Goettner had never been to Essen – didn't want to ever go. He avoided polluted skies and industrial grime, but he knew that the City was completely self-contained, with Krupp-owned and Krupp-managed hospitals, schools, sports facilities and shopping centres, everything a good Krupp worker could possibly need.

Goettner liked Nettermann, something noteworthy because Goettner did not like all in his *zug*, though he did respect them for the job they did and the efficiency with which they did it. The platoon was a good, solid team, Goettner thought. Nettermann, though, was somebody different, and Goettner had developed a genuine affinity for the man because of his steady demeanour and willingness to bear the grinding chore that was infantry life beyond its short injections of actual battle, and because of the man's evident pride in the profession of arms to which they were all currently wed. Nettermann never seemed to complain. Possessed of a taciturn manner, he maintained neutral expression and steady gaze whenever addressed, absorbing all and processing the order or instruction silently and without question, exhibiting neither acceptance nor rejection of his assignation before going about it. A member of the *zug* for almost a year now, posted in directly from muster and training, Nettermann had apparently adopted the necessary circumstances of his life as they now were, opting to adjust and choosing to embrace the grime, discomfort and general unpleasantness of trench existence, accepting it and compartmentalising its unpleasantness into some deep recess of his mind so that he could consciously focus on the more important job at hand. More than all these things, though, it was because of Nettermann's dependability that Goettner liked him. When ordered to carry out even the most mundane of tasks, he could be depended upon to execute them correctly. There was no need to check up on him. He was also an excellent man to have close by in the fight: a first-class shot who hit his target every time. Under the pressure of skirmish or the chaos of full-on assault, an order to swing his fire and eliminate a particular threat would result in exactly that – the death of the man concerned by a single round from Nettermann's carefully aimed bolt-action Mauser. Nettermann never missed his target. He was a marksman. A dead shot.

Goettner looked away from Nettermann reading his letter, switching his gaze to the helmet at his feet. Searching for reasons not to succumb to fatigue even as he recognised his exhaustion and the futility of his resistance to it, Goettner identified and examined the one thing that occupied his mind ahead of all his other responsibilities and preoccupations. It was the handwritten signal passed to him by the *Herr Hauptmann* as they withdrew through the battalion rendezvous before heading for the wagons and horses. His *kompanie* commander had already read this paper by torchlight, handing it to Goettner to scan and digest when he could, but not at that moment because their *kompanie* was taking up position within the long line of men marching on toward the waiting wagons. Pocketing the paper, Goettner knew that the instructions on the form would have been decoded and transcribed in the regimental telegraph office, then delivered by runner to the *Herr Hauptmann*. They would have been for his eyes and action. That the signal had then been personally passed to Goettner to read was therefore significant, for there was no duplicate to pass to anyone else.

The train clattered onward, an articulated steel serpent belching smoke. Behind, the sun of a new day clawed over the horizon to ease the darkness. In Breslau, Liegnitz and Frankfurt-am-Oder there were people lining the tracks, though they were few and stooped, intent on picking among the ballast for odd pieces of coal to heat their homes. They were not there to watch any passing train. Some did pause, though, straightening to wave to the soldiers. It was an effort. They were hungry and tired. Food was scarce. Enthusiasm for the war had dimmed. The possibility of starvation hung as a dark threat over all. They were predominantly children and women, those beside the tracks, some of the women wearing black to mourn husbands, sons and brothers lost to the fighting. The euphoric cheering of three years ago – that wave of national pride epitomised by serenading bands and ecstatically waving families dressed in Sunday best as they bade farewell to the brave soldiers marching away to patriotic duty – this was long forgotten. Now there was a heavy weariness, an overarching tiredness as though all had been denied sufficient sleep for too long, making them reluctant even to attempt the routine of another day. They seemed as a people going through the motions, and sometimes too exhausted to fake even these, for they were very hungry. Most were eating just half the food necessary for basic health.

When the troop train reached the marshalling yards of Berlin, it was routed into a siding to pause. The armour-plated locomotive issued a final wheeze of compressed steam before being decoupled. Armour plate, necessary in the east to protect against ambush by enemy bands operating behind the German lines, was not needed here. A different steam engine, not armoured, relieved its predecessor so that it could take on water and coal and return to the east with wagons carrying rations, ammunition and other supplies to soldiers still in Russian Poland. Hauled by its new engine, the troop train moved out of the yards to resume its westerly direction, picking up speed.

So the day passed.

29

After dark, there was a second stop, the men stepping off onto the long platform of a siding to stretch their legs and eat a hot meal prepared for their arrival by field kitchens temporarily established to aid this movement to the west. While they ate, two more troop trains, long and similar to their own, clattered past. There were sidings at many points along the line, each one built to supply coal, water and food. Movement was carefully scheduled to allow halts and replenishment without impeding the general flow of men, horses, ammunition and equipment redeploying from Russia to France – hundreds of thousands of infantry, thousands of horses, hundreds of *kompanie* wagons and dozens of motor vehicles. There were also field hospitals, doctors, nurses, cooks, armourers, mechanics, administrative personnel, tents and stores beyond number. Finally would come the artillery, when its job of covering this movement of troops away from the line was complete.

The journey's second dawn was already a broad smudge of dirty orange holding threat of later cloud when the train crossed the Rhine River. It did so on a truss bridge of riveted steel.

In his carriage, Nettermann was re-reading his letter. He'd snatched a few hours' sleep and then re-seated himself on the bench to give others a chance. There were sleeping soldiers all around him as the bridge's verticals and diagonals flashed by the carriage windows, bewildering interruptions of a night sky no longer completely black. Nettermann held the pages in grimy fingers. He was allowing the words, so carefully penned, to take him to another place in another world, imagining he could feel the presence and actually see the young woman who had written them, his sweetheart. He could still quite easily picture her, pen in hand and bottle of black ink open to recharge nib. Nettermann had not seen his love since the end of his leave – his only leave – granted almost one year ago immediately post-training.

Nettermann's sweetheart was at that moment geographically quite close – just a few hundred kilometres north of where the train was crossing the Rhine. Yet they could not meet. No leave was being granted to anyone at all, regardless of rank and irrespective of need, for there remained one final task of overriding importance: the defeat of Anglo-French forces in the west.

How Germany was going to do that had been roughly outlined to each and every man even as the battalion was withdrawing from the line. For Nettermann, the way it had been explained made sense: the Russians were done for but, alas, not the French and not the British. These armies were still clinging stubbornly to their defences and had to be attacked – attacked and defeated before the Americans could arrive in sufficient strength to make any difference to the outcome of this war which, everybody understood, Germany simply had to win in order to continue as a nation. Such were the contents of a general headquarters signal read out to Nettermann and the others by the *Herr Hauptmann* in the assembly area in front of the wagons. With their own regiment and hundreds like it rapidly reinforcing Germany's armies in the west, weight of numbers would end the stalemate and tip the scales sufficiently to grant Germany decisive victory while the Americans were still arriving and organising in France's ports.

Well, thought Nettermann, maybe after that they would let him to go home. All he had to do was stay alive until the day of victory.

Such simple reasoning was typical of Nettermann. It was the way he thought about most things, affording the future neither careful examination nor bothering to ponder possible alternative outcomes. He preferred to view life in simple black and white. No grey areas for Nettermann, no projection onto a particular problem of multiple interdependent factors with their individual complexities. Nettermann's thinking had been forged by the hard roots of the industrial heartland into which he had been born, and by the unforgiving upbringing he had endured there. The trick was to trust your leadership and obey, his father had taught him. Just obey. If you obeyed, you would generally be all right, because those in charge knew what was best for all, of course, and they'd make sure the correct thing was done. Therefore, Nettermann did not dwell on obstacle or hardship, and wasted no effort on unrewarding reason. Better to leave that to the officers.

Around him, the unsteady sway and noisy rhythm of the train was incessant, the locomotive hissing and belching its way quickly westward. Nettermann looked around at the soldiers of his *zug* – big, lanky Zimmermann now scratching absently at a leg as he awoke, a habit of his; unflappable Bauer, built like a boxer and with crooked nose to match. Bauer was the *zug's* translator because he could speak a bit of Russian, and quite a lot of English too. He was still asleep, as were the somewhat dumpy König and his counterpart Schäffer, at twenty-four the good-looking 'Old Man' of the unit. Schäffer was married, and some said this luck had come about because of those good looks, though none could now guess at them because of a grubby bandage wound around much of his head. Schäffer's scalp had been nicked by a shell splinter the previous week, yet the man had dismissed the drama of the aid-station as unnecessary. Just a scratch, he said – more blood than anything else. He had declined a strong recommendation to undergo further examination at the field hospital, instead re-joining Nettermann and the others in the line.

Nettermann scanned the sentences on the pages again. The handwriting on the cheap paper was untidy despite its author's care; almost a scrawl, reflecting an education as basic as Nettermann's own. Yet it was sufficient to communicate meaning clearly enough. The words brought worry and comfort in equal measure. They stated in simple form and outline the heartbreak of the Essen townsfolk: the burden of heavy grief hanging over all activity, any conversation and every interaction; the deep void in the communal soul caused by the loss of so many of its men; an unspoken yearning for an end to this war and all the hardship that it had brought. His sweetheart wrote that she herself felt a great burden upon her being – upon her very soul – something she admitted being unable to adequately describe. It seemed an ineffable shadow, some kind of ever-present, spectral oppression that she could escape only through sleep. Each new day brought with it this same great lack in her spirit, said the words: this thing that she could not quite identify, this thing for which she could find no description, this great emptiness.

Nettermann read and re-read the sentences, trying to gain greater understanding. She missed him so much, she said. She wanted to hold him, to feel his body and the reassuring strength that it brought to her. She needed him back. She wanted to feel him hard and urgent inside her. When, oh when, would he return to her? Nettermann looked up from the pages, startled as he met Goettner's eye and caught the *oberleutnant*'s querying glance and wry grin of weary recognition. Nettermann returned it, then looked down to the pages again. But he did not read them; Goettner's fatigued look had distracted him – the *zugführer* was clearly very tired. Yet Nettermann trusted him completely. Goettner was okay and would do his best to get them through. Nettermann valued Goettner.

Still looking at the pages, Nettermann turned his thoughts to his home town, tried to visualise its streets, dwellings and shops on the outskirts of the great Krupp industrial complex, tried to see in his mind's eye the smoke billowing from the stacks of the factories as they churned out the weapons and ammunition, tried to feel the weight of the people's pain, the stoic numbness with which ordinary folk were having to face each day; the shortages and effort required to continue the fight. Most still believed it to be absolutely necessary, this fight, the letter said. What other option was there, really? According to the newspapers it was a fight to the finish, one where no compromise was possible. The soldiers returning on brief leave or sent home permanently to adjust to loss of limb or eye – well, they seemed to agree, though these men said little or nothing, preferring silence over the effort of describing an experience of battle apparently impossible to adequately convey.

Nettermann looked up again from the pages. The *oberleutnant* was no longer watching him, his head nodding forward onto his chest. The poor bastard was probably more exhausted even than his men, thought Nettermann. Goettner had been in this mess for years before Nettermann himself had joined the *zug*.

An experience impossible to adequately convey …

Well, battle was not something indescribable or unimaginable to Nettermann. He had experience of it and reckoned he would be more than able to provide adequate description, were they to relent and allow him home. Now, reading the letter, he felt a sudden stab of jealousy that some had been allowed to return permanently to their towns and villages. However grievous their wounds, for them the daily strain, awful hardship and terrible fear that all on this train were still having to endure – these things were over.

He thought about the fighting so recently abandoned, twenty-four hours behind them now and victory finally theirs as the Russian Army collapsed inwards upon itself, giving up bit by bit the unequal four-way struggle against the Germans, against the Austro-Hungarians, against the Romanians and, worst of all, against themselves – against their own internal revolution and the overthrowing of the Tsar.

The Eastern Front …

Nettermann remembered the landscapes he had crossed on foot – always on foot once they left the trains – landscapes taken and held and lost and then retaken again. A dozen skirmishes, two heavy defences and one frantic charge – this had been his personal experience of the war thus far. How many dead? By Nettermann's reckoning, almost a third in the *zug*, and these gone in the single year since he had joined. More than half of this number had died in one awful dawn assault on the Russian positions, part of a bigger attack. He tried to recall the names of those lost on that day, but found he could not. He could remember only the noisy, terrifying chaos of it all, and his relief at being one of the lucky ones to have found the barbed wire entanglements destroyed by the artillery where his section was ordered to attack. Men in the other sections had not been so lucky, and the deaths of more than half of them had been the outcome, shot by the Russian defenders as they were caught on wire intact and untouched by the shells. They dangled and hung there, dead or twitching, still struggling as they died, until the attack was done.

That awful morning was not Nettermann's only experience of battle. He had successfully defended, too, against the Russians. Yet that dawn assault was the thing that stuck in his mind. It prevailed over the Russian attacks, and over the steady, weekly attrition from sniper fire, reconnaissance patrol and trench raid, over death from simple disease, too. That dawn attack prevailed over all other things. Perhaps it was its scale and the losses on the wire that made it difficult for him to remember the names and faces of those who had died there, for all but a few of them had lost their young lives in just ten or fifteen minutes of mad scrambling through the Russian entanglements, trying to rip and tear their way through the drag of the barbs as others died trying to cut a path, and the rest of the dead – those few who somehow first got through – succumbing to bayonet or bullet on the position itself when they reached it, their energy spent and insufficient for the desperate hand-to-hand fight of the trench. The men killed on that day were now gone from Nettermann's mind. He could not find them. They had been erased from memory as effectively as the machine guns and rifle fire of the Russian defenders had done for them physically, so that Nettermann could now remember only the attack itself: the thunder of the preliminary barrage with its spectacle of terrible force, the very earth itself heaving and exploding into huge gouts of clay and stone, and shells of shrapnel bursting above here and there in the murky sky, frightening split-second puffs of orangey brown-black that then melted into gentle smoke to drift quickly away on the stiff breeze, belying the death and awful mutilation that they dealt out below.

How many, then? How many dead as a total for the eastern theatre? Some said half a million, others reckoned more. Nobody knew, because there seemed to be deliberate obfuscation of the overall casualty count. The number of dead and missing was never mentioned in the newspapers, and somebody had told Nettermann that this was probably to prevent further, unnecessary damage to morale already sorely tested, and tested often, too. One of the men in the *zug* reckoned more than a million had gone forever in the east, this on the authority of a friend who served food to the officers' table at regimental headquarters, and who had overheard discussion of the numbers one night over dinner.

More than a million …

Unbeknown to Nettermann, the place to which they were now being sent was suffering casualties higher even than this. Though actual numbers were never made public, that there were casualties was not being hidden by those authorities who defined the limits of what people did or didn't need to know. Apparently, it was crucially important that the general population understood quite clearly that the Western Front was a life-or-death struggle with the French and the British. Germany absolutely had to defeat them on pain of terrible reckoning if the end of Germany itself should come, this Germany which history had consolidated into a single nation a mere forty or so years before. With this imperative of the Western Front revealed, with the consequence of defeat admitted and indeed emphasised, the nation continued to rally behind the fight, continued to send the best of its young men to the trenches to face the two allied enemies. Now, a third was busy arriving and assembling. Soon, this fight would be against the Americans too.

Nettermann refocused on the pages in his hands, on the meaning of the words. The overall message, simply but clearly delivered, was one of despairing determination to carry on. He visualised his sweetheart. How she had changed his life! How she had brought meaning and direction to his young years! How he loved her, wanted her, needed her! He was unable to express these emotions even to himself, for though he did understand the fact of them, he lacked the words. Yet he grasped clearly enough his need to be with her, to make love to her with a passion so hard and vital – so intense – that she might pass out with pleasure. Probably she was thinking the same, Nettermann hoped. As for him, this physical and emotional imperative that he felt had been matched only once during his nineteen years, equalled by the imperative to survive that terrible assault uppermost in his memory of battle – to live through it – while the enemy who were somehow still alive after all the earth had erupted about them under blistering shellfire, and who had somehow survived the pellets of red-hot steel flung at them from a pockmarked sky so prettily puffing death from above, had begun to go about the business of killing all on the wire to the left and right of Nettermann's own assault, while Goettner screamed encouragement and orders to him and the others as they breached their own gap, bellowing at them over the harsh, discordant sound of it all, firing down into the trenches as he reached them, and leading the charge as his men burst through.

Only that urge to survive – to live – had been as strong as Nettermann's love for his sweetheart. He knew that he needed her with every nerve and sinew of his being, with every fibre of his earthly existence.

The battalion, when it arrived at the field which would be its camp, stripped and prepared to bathe. A virgin meadow became a matted, trampled carpet of damp grass and ooze under the bare feet of hundreds of soldiers standing naked and shivering in the weak afternoon sunlight, some pretending immunity to the chill air, all arranged into orderly queues shuffling forward to the hot, cleansing water of the battalion bath vats set out in steaming rows. Other equipment had been set up in adjacent farmland: laundry tables for the newly bathed and cleanly uniformed to wash the filth from their battledress. That would happen later. Right now, the *feldwebels* from the brigade hygiene unit were urging the men to hurry:

'Three minutes only! No more than three minutes! Don't use all the heat, now!'

'There are others to come! Stew and coffee at your *kompanie* lines in forty minutes!'

Fifteen kilometres behind the front, out of range of British artillery but still within earshot of the rumbling, unhappy thump and crash of the guns doing battle around Cambrai thirty kilometres distant, the newly arrived battalion had earlier that day reached the small French village designated as its billet. This village, like most behind the German lines, was home to a handful of local men and women still clinging to livelihoods wrung from the occupying army. Germany's soldiers might well be the invaders, but they supplied welcome income to any villager able to offer rest, food, drink or other services as temporary escape from the harsh realities of the trenches. They offered conversation in broken German or simple French, and sex in the village brothel. An equal value was placed on all these things by the soldiers in field grey rotating back for a few days of precious leave from the constant hardship and occasional terror of the fighting. Everything on offer was greatly anticipated and gratefully received.

Goettner's *zug* and the rest of the newly arrived battalion were not now being permitted these pleasures. Disembarked from the train, they had marched to the village, then through it, this time in step as a display to the French populace of disciplined infantry – more infantry – on its way to the front: strong men, fit men, able and ready for battle, and with their morale high … this was the idea. Two kilometres beyond the village had come the meadow with its bathing vats. Now, revelling in the soapy water, the men from the east knew they must wait a while yet for the pleasures of the village. First would come a day of laundering and cleaning weapons and equipment, then four or five busy days of refresher training, and after that a spell in the line: the reserve trenches for perhaps a week, then an equal period in the forward positions at the cutting edge of the German defence. The men understood this. It was part of the routine. First though, before anything else as they halted on the track beside the meadow with its vats, there was a reunion with individual kitbags stored behind the line all the time they had been manning the trenches in Russian Poland. These bags had been pre-loaded by the supporting echelon onto the train for their journey west. Now, located once more, there came a grateful shedding of personal webbing, rifles, helmets, packs, boots and filthy uniforms, all of it left in small, individual piles beside these kitbags watched over by guards while the men moved to the vats eyed with such eagerness: hot water from the horse-drawn bowsers of the brigade's hygiene *kompanie*, arranged and spaced for rapid throughput, and to be followed by obligatory powdered de-lousing of the armpits and private areas of their newly washed bodies. Next, a donning of the spare uniform each man stored in his kitbag – clean, if he were properly organised – then hot food and a solid night's sleep.

So arrived this battalion newly withdrawn from the East to face the undefeated British sector of the western theatre; in this way arrived these reinforcements for the new and thoroughly constructed German defensive line – the *Siegfriedstellung* – shorter, stronger, deeper and more concentrated than the positions recently and deliberately abandoned. This new line had been deeply dug and carefully camouflaged over many months, and it was very well sited, with many of the trenches situated on reverse slopes to limit the effect of British bombardment.

Thus arrived Goettner and Nettermann among the battalion's eight hundred, one of nine battalions in this division pulled back from Russian Poland. Still to come, still aboard the trains rumbling across the railways from the east, still to arrive were yet further divisions released by Russia's collapse. And they were many. When all had arrived, when all was ready, there would be sufficient numbers for Germany to attack in great strength, driving the British once and for all time into the sea before the Americans, still organising, could make any difference.

Within the eight hundred, the *kompanie*, and within that the *zug*. Within the *zug*, Nettermann, the words from his sweetheart overshadowed by the memory of one terrible dawn assault. Within the *zug*, Zimmermann, König, Bauer and Old Man Schäffer with his bandaged head and a wife at home. Within the *zug*, Goettner, still mulling the contents of the handwritten orders – now read – passed to him by the *Herr Hauptmann* in the cold half-light of dawn of the previous morning.

CHAPTER THREE

Peake's uncle was as good as his word. He usually was. Peake could not remember a single promise or commitment that his uncle had failed to keep. Monday's working day completed, Wainwright returned home to collect Peake and walk with him through cold streets to The Duke, as he had said he would. He did not bother to change: as he worked in a government office, there was no need. He paused at the entrance to the pub to press coins upon his ward.

'There'll be no discussion about this, please, Simon,' was his instruction. 'You're here at my pleasure, and you know the law.'

Wainwright's manner was kind but firm, and brooked no argument. By recent bureaucratic proclamation, it was now an offence to buy another man a drink in any English tavern, the idea being to increase national productivity by reducing excessive drinking – the war effort was everything. Peake followed his uncle into The Duke, a tinkling bell at the door announcing their entry. They hung their coats upon wooden pegs screwed onto a bare brick wall, then moved to the bar.

The Duke was a plain, straightforward place possessed of a convivial atmosphere. Its patrons were folk from similarly plain and straightforward homes, and predominantly men. The arched entrance to the public house held a door of varnished wood fitted with two small, square viewing panes. Passing through it, customers were welcomed by a bar counter of dark wood mounted on bare brick, and backed by shelves fixed to the wall behind, one above the other. On two of the shelves were glasses arranged by type and size, while the third supported bottles of liquor. The bar itself, with its taps and serving space, was not too long, leaving enough room at either end for customers to wedge themselves between counter and wall, standing and conversing or leaning and pondering, according to mood. The floor was flagged, with a sitting area making up the rest of the room. This was arranged with three small tables equipped with three or four chairs each. A fireplace in one corner granted warmth. Aiding the serving area was a single electric lamp which, though dim, bore mute testimony to the city fathers' attempt at electrification, now paused for the duration of the war or, some thought, abandoned entirely. The remainder of the room was lit by the uncertain flames of oil lamps and candles. Overall, the effect was one of welcome and warmth despite the uneven lighting. The room was certainly not dark.

Peake's uncle placed the order:

'It'd be a wonderful thing to return to a brew of decent strength, Mrs Winterman, and that's a fact. There's no bite at all in just a half anymore. Two pints, if you please. We'll pay separately.'

'Two pints it'll be, Mr Wainwright, and a pleasure too, I'm sure. But the law's the law regarding strength – the German submarines, you know. A scarcity of grain an' all. Not likely to change, either, so the brewers tell me. Sober production in the factories is what Minister George is after, so I hope that he gets it.'

'Aye, production is what he wants all right. Well, I'm not at all sure how you manage, Mrs Winterman, what with weak beer and reduced hours.'

'It's not easy,' she agreed with a smile, pulling on the tap handles and switching the glasses now and then to limit the head. 'I've heard rumours there'll be food rationing come the new year … It's not only grain for brewing that's short. Anyway, gentlemen, you've a few hours yet until nine. People're drinking more to try to compensate for the ale's weakness, though I don't think that'll be your good selves, now, will it? I'd give you a long pull, too, if they'd allow me, but there's a hefty fine for it and Mr Jarvis over there is a constable off duty.'

Peake's uncle, watching her draw the two pints, asked:

'Have you given Thomas the night off then, Mrs Winterman? He's nowhere to be seen.'

This drew a hearty laugh from the woman at the taps. 'Make jokes if you will, Mr Wainwright. Make jokes if you will. And where might Mrs Wainwright herself be this evening?'

Peake's uncle had ready riposte: 'At home preparing our dinner, where every good wife should be at this time of day.'

Mrs Winterman snorted behind her bar counter, but she was smiling. She set the glasses before her two customers and smoothed down her apron that hung in white contrast to a darkish, ankle-length dress buttoned to the collar. She observed Peake and his uniform keenly. 'You've filled out, young Simon,' she offered. 'Seems to me there's more about you, though you're certainly still lean enough. Must be all that army food, though my John complains about the quality of it.'

'It's a treat to see you again, Mrs Winterman,' was Peake's reply. 'Do you have any news of him? I haven't seen John since he finished school.'

'He was home last month. A sergeant now, y'know. Had army business up in Stafford – Brocton, I think it was. Then he came home for two days. He's well enough, I'm sure.'

Peake wondered if he had detected any unusual degree of worry behind the reply to his lie. He couldn't be sure, for anxiety was certainly the way of any mother with a son in France. Or was there something more? Had she, too, seen him weep? Had Sergeant Winterman wept at home? Peake tried to study her face, but just then the bell above the entrance tinkled new custom, and Mrs Winterman moved away along the bar to serve new arrivals from the cold street outside. Wainwright changed the conversation:

'Padre Burke was certainly on form yesterday, wasn't he, Boy?'

'He was, Uncle. He was.'

Peake watched his guardian over the rim of his pint. Wainwright was a portly man of medium height. He was almost bald, but in a way that complemented a cheerful face that seemed always to be looking for an excuse to chuckle. People tended to brighten immediately in his presence. What remained of his hair was curly and still dark.

The conversation began to flow around the Sunday service. Peake's mind was not fully focused on the topic, though he was careful to maintain an attitude of polite attentiveness, cheerfully answering any question from his uncle and laughing when appropriate even as he remembered Christine and what had passed between them in the park. The wonder of this young woman and the delight of her kiss was with Peake still. That kiss had been an exquisite experience for him: long, tender and of sublime honesty. At first, he had tried to control it, had tried to manage that kiss as something mechanical, his inexperience leading him to try to project himself onto Christine in the manner he had imagined she might desire, something he had rehearsed mentally throughout the years of his adolescence using a construct fabricated from what little he had been able to glean from ribald friends and fellow recruits laughing and joking crudely about their knowledge of such things. Because of this, Peake had watched and studied Christine's face as they kissed, analysing the moment and prepared mentally to make adjustment exactly as he might have done with the aim of rifle or fall of grenade. With a little shock, it dawned on him that this was entirely inappropriate. Christine's own eyes, closed in the sweetness of the moment, had opened briefly. Reading in them a degree of questioning alarm, Peake closed his own and let go a little, surrendering to this most natural of acts between man and woman and allowing her to lead him, teach him, show him the way. Now, reliving in the The Duke's warm glow the intense happiness of that kiss, he thought that his surrender to the inevitability of Christine's lead had been the correct thing to do, the utterly natural way of things intended. She was older than he and therefore more experienced. While becoming in no way submissive, and indeed so powerfully aroused that he felt certain Christine must have felt him despite the layers of their clothing, Peake had permitted himself, finally, to allow their initial, tentative exploration of one another's passion to simply happen, to simply be.

It had been a most beautiful and wonderful thing.

Afterwards, she had clung to him, emitting a soft, shuddering sigh of seeming contentment as he embraced her. Peake hoped this was signal that his efforts had been successful, the kiss as wonderful for her as it had been for him.

'You all right, Boy?'

'Yes. Yes, of course, Uncle. I'm sorry. I was distracted for a moment.'

'The young lady at Mrs Brooke's, perhaps?' There was a twinkle of amusement in Wainwright's eye.

'Yes, Uncle. The young lady at Mrs Brooke's. Her name is Christine.'

Christine, too, was remembering the kiss, though it brought to her mind something besides recollection of their intimacy. There was in addition an uncertain questioning of her motives and emotions, and the nagging worry of Peake's imminent departure for France – now mere days away. She wondered at his restraint after he had abandoned his initial, awkward attempts at control. She worried at the brief time remaining to them. Would there be sufficient for their romance to fully blossom? Perhaps she would have to hurry things along a little.

Peake's first kiss it may well have been, but it was not so for Christine. Neither was she any virgin. Yet she was not to her own mind wanton, lewd or unrestrained.

When she examined her motives, Christine had the honesty to admit that the driving forces behind her encouragement of Peake were confusion and a simple physical need. Her fiancé had left her empty and she wanted a man – not any man, she corrected herself quickly, but one acceptable to her own moral code and to society's prevailing mores. She needed physical satisfaction and release, but she also needed to be sure that her partner was capable of discretion and public restraint. He needed to be able to control desire, managing its consummation as something that of necessity had to exist in parallel with the demands, conventions and drudgery of daily life, and not dominate it. Above all she sought a balance between passion and respect, one that would permit pursuit of ecstasy without afterwards leaving her feeling cheapened.

She believed Peake to be such a man: discreet and publicly modest despite his very clear attraction to her. That other attribute on her list, the ability to separate lust from the necessary drudgery of daily routine, was at the moment impossible for Christine to ascertain. She thought, though, that Peake might just manage it. He seemed to be an opportunity heaven-sent by Penelope Brooke, that most wonderful friend of her mother's, who had arranged introduction and left the rest to Nature's guiding hand, and perhaps a little to Christine's experience and natural drives, too. Mrs Brooke seemed to have sensed very clearly Christine's need for acceptable sexual substitution even though she had never spoken directly to her about it. Perhaps Penelope suffered similar unspoken urges. Perhaps the two women shared a common need …

Of course, before her introduction to the lean, fair young soldier fresh from Brocton's training, Christine had kept her options open in the way that any healthy, well-adjusted young woman would keep them open. She could either accept the advances of potential suitors or reply with polite rebuff. Yet Peake had made neither overt pass nor any careful, more cautious overture. These had not been necessary. A clear mutual attraction had taken care of progress from the very beginning, sweeping aside any need for withdrawal or rejection on her part, and encouraging an advance of her own.

Now she tried to define her passion for him. Penelope had made casual mention to her that Peake was younger than she by a full two years, something of a chasm at their very young stage of life. Yet Christine had found him to be mature enough in manner and outlook, a result perhaps of time enduring the rigours of Brocton, and she was honest enough to admit to herself that she was now experiencing an urgent and strengthening desire to know him physically, to teach him passionate love and, within the act of it, to reveal the unaffected ways in which it might be given and received. More, through consummation of their attraction, she hoped to bestow upon Peake a memory of something potent enough to serve him in France, something sufficiently powerful to carry him through. For in France, though she had no notion of the realities of the war, Christine understood well enough from her brother's letters and the government's casualty lists that a sufficiently high number of young Englishmen were being killed for Peake's young life to stand a good chance of being snuffed out.

Christine's instincts, pressured by a shortage of time and by conscious worry over the danger Peake would soon face, presented the thought to her that she might need to take charge of their romance with greater energy, becoming the driving force behind the relationship and imparting to it subtle direction toward natural climax. She would have to continue to encourage and coax, yes, but at the same time she would have to be prepared to corner Peake if necessary – to take him – leaving him no option but to make love to her before the army swept him away to join her brother in that awful struggle across the Channel.

She wanted Peake sexually, of that there could be no doubt. She wondered if this was how she had felt about him even at the moment of their meeting in Penelope Brooke's parlour.

They made love for the first time three days before Peake's return to Brocton Camp.

Their rendezvous was again the park, where Peake waited for Christine on the same bench as before beside its gated entrance, remembering the wonder of their kiss, his heartbeat quickened by both this memory and an anxious anticipation of their reunion. He could feel within his chest the steady beat of his heart, its rhythmic pulse of affection and desire the very core of his life. Yet Peake was unsure of the next step, uncertain of what to do when the moment of greeting arrived. Passion too overt might cause Christine embarrassment, but to greet with the public decorum he had seen pass between his uncle and aunt might confuse or, worse, disappoint her. It was a quandary, and Peake was very aware of his inexperience and ineptitude in the matter of women.

The winter's day was overcast, grey and cold. Though there was not yet any wind, low clouds were rolling in across the sky with considerable determination from the east, heavy-looking and threatening rain. Glancing behind to the park, Peake could see only a few visitors, something that would make it easy for him to find seclusion for them in the spinney but, if he did contrive to lead her there on a day as drab as this, would she be as eager as before to passionately repeat their embrace? Or would she hesitate, doubting him? His intention might be too obvious, it might cool the fire that Peake hoped still burned in her own heart.

43

Christine, when she arrived, was deft in her rescue of him.

Approaching directly, she did not slow her pace but moved in gracefully, quickly and without hesitation to kiss him fully on the mouth even as he stood up from the bench. She laid her body lightly against his, the palms of her hands raised outwards and upwards to rest gently against his chest within the spread of his shoulders, a caution against too tight a public embrace on his part. Her touch made it a simple matter for her to pull away when their kiss was done, yet maintain light physical contact.

'Hello, Simon,' she said softly and little huskily. 'Let's not walk in the park today.'

'Well … where, then? We'll have to walk somewhere.'

'Yes, we do have to do that. Come. Come on – I know a route.'

With that, and smiling encouragement, she took his arm to lead him away from the park, chattering gaily to distract and reassure. He seemed pleased to be with her – content – and this made her happy. To the few strollers braving the chill, Christine and Simon were a couple quite obviously in love as they walked Camden's streets between the rows of plain brick terrace houses under the gloomy winter sky. Yet they were insensible of this dull scene, oblivious to every sense except the touch of each other, the patter of their simple conversation, the pleasure of one another's company. Christine was finding it hard to keep her tone light and gay, for the plan that she had very carefully formulated was at the forefront of her mind. She felt heat within the pit of her stomach, though its glow was marred by cold worry at what his reaction might be to her intentions, once she revealed them.

After some minutes, the direction of their route dawned on Peake, who felt a little prickle of disappointment:

'We're not going to Mrs Brooke's again, are we? I'd … I'd rather not. We'd have to make polite conversation.'

But they were already at the door. Turning in to him, she reached up for his kiss, which was instantly there, urgent and insistent in the way of the young man encouraged. She pulled away, smiling up into his eyes to reassure. She took his hand in place of his arm and, squeezing further encouragement, turned slightly to unlock the door and enter. Closing and securing it again behind them, she moved in hard against him, offering kisses overflowing with fervour and passion, yet all the time alert for any hesitation that he might display. But there was none. It was clear to Christine that he wanted her. She heard him whisper:

'What about Penelope? She'll hear us.' His voice was hoarse with desire.

'She's not here, Simon. And I locked the door. Didn't you notice?'

And she giggled, then smothered his protest with another kiss. Now his hands were exploring, reaching up for her breasts, and moving down, too.

'Where?' he managed.

She broke the clinch to take his hand and lead him to the bedroom beyond the parlour. They undressed awkwardly, trying to rid themselves of clothing while maintaining the heat of their passion with kisses and touches between the shedding of their garments. Peake's puttees were the worst. She had to kneel down before him to help, and in doing this she was beautifully naked. She unwound and removed the long, broad bands of military cloth, and pulled off the heavy boots.

On the bed, she had to lead him, had to show him the way while all the while coaxing and whispering words of gentle encouragement. She was prepared for this and, though she wanted to conceal her experience she could not, because he so clearly had none at all. She worried that he might think her cheap. For Peake's part, he was eager to please, yet found himself self-conscious and embarrassed at a potent erection at odds with his lack of knowledge of this beautiful female form with which he now found himself entwined. He had little idea of what to do, and none at all of what performance might be expected of him. He penetrated her with help; he did his best; he paced himself with tender concern for this woman who had enveloped him with such softness and love. Eventually, when the pleasure and passion became too much to bear for both, Christine commanded him to let go, to lose control. Only by losing control could he reach climax and satisfy them both, she whispered. This Peake did. Afterwards, while still strongly inside her, he held himself raised on straightened, muscled arms, intelligent green eyes brimming with joy as he gazed into the amber of Christine's own, which were lovely to him. Then he lowered his head to smother her with kisses of happy gratitude.

For Christine, the memory of this encounter became quickly special. Peake had combined excitement and ardent fervour with an innocent affection and tenderness such as she had not before experienced. He had not been as her other lovers. He had not been selfish, instead seeming to rate her own delight as more important than his own. She remembered the muscles of his shoulders and arms, strongly defined. Though he was a thinnish man, those indications of his strength had rippled and changed shape as he pushed and pulled, in and out, all the while holding himself above her, a film of sweat forming on his skin: she had felt it beneath her hands and fingers as she clasped him to her. She had had to suggest less effort: 'Relax ... Relax, my angel.' Afterwards, when they were done, she whispered a request that he place his full weight upon her. She liked that. 'Rest against me, Simon. Come down to me. Rest upon me a while.' Now, in memory, she could recall the shallow, valleyed line of his spine as she gentled him with her fingertips in the aftermath of their passion, his full weight upon her as she had asked. She wondered whether or not she had achieved climax. Despite her experience of two men – three, now – Christine did not fully understand what climax was, and indeed her upbringing had been such that she was not at all sure whether climax existed for women, or whether she ought to seek it: she did not want to cause embarrassment to herself. Yet there had been sufficient pleasure for her in this act of making love with Peake, of giving herself to him. She had found satisfaction in his sharp intake of breath – a hiss between clenched teeth – as he entered her, and she had experienced her own form of ecstasy in the short, sharp cry forced from him by his orgasm – a violent, uninhibited curse appropriate, she thought, to the moment of his first time and the gush of his semen.

For Peake, the memory was one of elation mixed with anxious preoccupation as he analysed his performance and worried at her motive, and his own too. Christine's clothing, designed to indicate nothing of her figure below the waist, revealed once removed the delight of hips and legs perfect in every way to his young eyes. He had wanted to take her, possess her, devour her, yet in this first encounter he had lacked the confidence to initiate. Christine had had to show the way, encouraging him to kiss her wherever he wanted, to let go, cradling and caressing him all the while to inflame his ardour. He remembered details of her loveliness, the softness of her breasts, their creamy skin tipped with pink circles puckered and as proudly hard as he was himself; a gentle swell of stomach between the jut of her hips, and the perfect triangle of soft thatch below – his ultimate prize. Throughout the increasing heat of their foreplay, she had kept her eyes fixed on his, closing them only when he kissed her and he closed his own in the way she had first taught him. Peake thought he could read desire in those eyes when they were open, hazel but glowing with an amber heat quite apparent to him in this expression of love. At last, when neither could any longer bear the pleasure of the tease, she had opened herself to him in readiness, still caressing, still cradling, encouraging and enticing, and only withdrawing her hand when he was almost completely buried within her, and wanted to complete his thrust.

She had been libidinal and sensuous, winding herself wondrously about him, pulling him into her with the strength of all limbs. Later, with Peake recovered, she had exhibited an eagerness the equal of his own to repeat the act.

Peake realised that he was now entirely infatuated with Christine. His waking hours were spent in a daze of recollection. He was scarcely able to think of anything other than the feel of her lithe, womanly body beneath his own on the covers of the bed, enveloping him and pushing back eagerly with a rhythm perfectly matched to his own. Yet there was something in his recollection of their encounter that troubled him. It was not her experience, which he had suspected from the beginning and indeed welcomed as a necessary foil to his own ineptitude. Nor could he find any source of doubt in the way she had planned his seduction, the widow Brooke her obvious accomplice in its consummation – and thank God for the Penelope Brookes of this world!

Unable to locate the source of his worry, he attributed it finally to his tendency to overanalyse all things. He put the doubt aside, burying it beneath the pleasure of memory.

'Are you going to tell him about Luke, Christine?'

'No.'

'Good … It's not as if you're married to the man.'

'No, Mrs Brooke.'

Christine, replying to Penelope's question, gave silent thanks to this close friend of her mother for being a realist in matters of love and sex. Yet she recognised the worry in her own heart despite the confidence of her reply. Luke was her fiancé. She was betrothed to him. Yet here she was, sleeping with another man while Luke and her brother held the line in France. Well, she reasoned, Simon Peake would be holding that line too, soon enough, surely sufficient justification for her behaviour. Simon would very soon leave England to face the greatest of all dangers, and the widow Brooke, whom she trusted greatly, had encouraged this tryst – she had arranged the meeting and offered up her home for its consummation.

The two women, Penelope Brooke and Christine, were taking tea in Penelope's parlour, Christine remembering the bedroom beyond, still in wonder at her seduction of Peake upon the bed there.

'What will you do? When Simon goes to France?'

Christine eyed Penelope, considering the question. To Christine's eyes, the widow Brooke, now well into middle age, remained slimly elegant, and had been that way for as long as Christine could remember. She still presented an enviable figure, her unlined face attractive beneath auburn hair pinned up. Christine weighed her reply. Emotionally, she knew that the widow Brooke was often of more help to her than her own mother, and especially in the matter of men. Christine's mother had never broached the matter of sex, leaving it to Penelope to give instruction when the latter had insisted that Christine must be taught at least a rudimentary knowledge. Christine's guess was that probably her mother had been happy to pass responsibility to Penelope, because that way she had been able to maintain her own façade of prim abstinence. It was during Penelope's instruction that their friendship had begun, despite the difference in age. Penelope, sensing Christine's strong sexual drive, had encouraged her not to suppress it. Control was necessary, she taught, but not suppression. The urge was natural. After that, an honest friendship and mutual understanding had developed between the two women.

The widow Brooke, of course, had orchestrated Peake's introduction to Christine, after Christine had tearfully confessed the surprising revulsion that had come upon her during a home leave granted Luke by the British Expeditionary Force, brief and unexpected. Her initial joy at Luke's sudden return from the trenches had given way to dismay when she had found him to be a different man from the one who had left her to go to war. Much had changed in the personality of this soldier newly returned from the front. He was radically altered, and by what she could not comprehend. Though she tried hard, she could not imagine – could not fathom – what he might have seen, suffered, done that had changed him so. Luke had become not only distant – the horror of the thing, she supposed – but also cold in manner and attitude, seeking often the company of fellow soldiers back from the fighting instead of spending as much time as possible with Christine. She could not understand why he would do this. Worse, when she had been alone with him, she found their conversation strained. He seemed not to want to talk, his eyes often blankly unfocused and his attention somewhere other than the immediate present. On the two occasions when they had made love – and there had been only two – he had stared unseeingly through her, beyond her, eyes open and his soul emotionally detached and apparently uninvolved, his face blank and unreadable while he tore into her body as though she were something to be taken and then discarded, as though this were some task that he had to complete but did not want to. It had been almost an attack, she thought, something more like rutting than lovemaking. The man had been unable to achieve climax, losing his erection and rolling away from her in angry disappointment at himself. They had not tried again. There had been no third attempt.

Now there was Simon Peake, this young draftee who had aroused in Christine something akin to renewal, for he was as Luke had been before France.

'What will you do when Simon leaves?' repeated Penelope. 'And what will you do when he returns?'

'There's nothing I can do, Mrs Brooke. I shall pray. I shall pray for him as I pray for Luke … I shall pray for both of them, every day. I won't have to choose until the war is over.'

In the plain brick terrace house that was Peake's home, the kitchen was silent but for the sound of cutlery on plates. Warmed by the wood stove, the Wainwrights and their ward sat at table, dining on thin stew. The window was closed against the cold, so that the room smelled pleasantly of their dinner. Outside, a November wind gusted through damp streets, chasing the last of autumn's stray leaves into piles stacked haphazardly against corners found between wall and doorstep, or sending them cartwheeling onward in leafy semi-flight.

The silence around the small table was not intentional, nor was it the result of any disagreement. It was the natural consequence of knowledge of Peake's imminent return to Brocton. This night and one dawn only remained to them, and the stew upon their plates they knew would be their last dinner together for an unpredictably long period of time. All were well aware that Peake's mid-morning train back to his barracks would signal indefinite separation. At Brocton, this young soldier and his fellows would draw rifles and equipment, then move as a newly trained entity – a single body of men – to the coast for embarkation. The port had not yet been named.

The three at the kitchen table were informally presented. Peake's uncle was as he had returned from his office, wearing trousers and the same work jacket that Peake could remember even from his years as an early teen: Wainwright was always dressed thus for dinner. The aunt, too, wore clothes that were comfortably correct, her long, neck-to-ankle dress of dark grey – far from new – brightened by white collar. Unusually, Peake himself was not in uniform, for after that afternoon's final farewell to Christine he had changed into civilian clothes last worn when presenting himself at barracks for enlistment, almost four months before. He had brought these back with him to London, to be left behind with other things he would not need in France. Tonight he had decided to wear them to this last supper, the term matching the occasion's solemn mood. From the following morning onward, he would need only his uniform.

At the head of the little table, Wainwright's thoughts were on Cambrai, an almost unknown French town now thrust upon British consciousness because of the battle raging there. It occupied fully all the front-page space of every newspaper under headlines suited to the drama: WAR'S FIERCEST FIGHTING … GERMAN ARMIES IN FULL FLIGHT. More than one thousand British cannons had pounded and blasted the German line in a brief dawn bombardment unanticipated by the Germans and affording them no time to organise before they had found themselves facing eighty thousand British infantry supported by four hundred tanks, the whole, massive force advancing behind a creeping artillery barrage. Wainwright by now knew what a tank was. Most people did. It was a British secret weapon developed under the guise of a mobile water reservoir, hence the name. These clumsy, awkwardly moving gun platforms, tracked and armoured, had surprised everyone when they had been revealed a year ago, and especially the Germans. Their cover name – tanks – had been intended to deceive any spy who might have been observing their development, but the epithet had stuck. At Cambrai they had helped the infantry achieve spectacular initial success: a localised victory and perhaps even a breakthrough. Church bells had sounded – were still sounding – throughout England in celebration. They had not been heard since August three years before, when war had broken out.

Seated to one side of her husband, Peake's aunt faced her ward and listened to the embers settling in her stove, the only sound beyond those of knife on plate. She ate with her head down, avoiding the eyes of both men, her mind also on the British attack, and suffering a conflict of emotions as her thoughts chased one another like the abandoned leaves beyond the window shut tight against winter's chill. She wondered about casualties. Would they be as terrible as those of other, previous battles? Or would this victory herald that most unimaginable of all possibilities – an end to the war? Could it mean that Simon, whom she loved as her own, might be spared the horrible task which lay in wait for him across the Channel?

Peake himself was thinking neither of Cambrai nor of his probable involvement in imminent battle. He could think only of Christine and his wonderful romance with this woman, beautiful to his eyes. She had granted him an experience that combined both the erotic and the emotional. His mind could still recall the feel and taste of her: the smoothness of her skin, her scent, the soft resilience of her flesh and the small, semi-muffled gasps and moans of pleasure she had uttered. But it was not only the physicality of their lovemaking that Peake was remembering. There was also love's sweet intangibility, a thing he found difficult to define for he had no words to adequately describe the peace brought to him by the simplicity of Christine's smile and her welcoming acceptance of him, her joy at his presence shining always in her eyes. The combined effect of all these things had been joyously devastating to him. He was, he realised with some surprise at the kitchen table, utterly in love.

'This battle,' began the uncle, interrupting the thoughts of all including Peake, 'this battle around Cambrai … It may not be the end that some are predicting. Might not be the end of the war at all …'

'Then why the bells, dear? The bells are ringing. They can't be for nothing, surely?'

The aunt's eyes were as gentle as her voice, her round face calmly solemn. She seemed less ready to smile than was her wont, though she was not challenging her husband.

'Because it's the first significant breakthrough. There hasn't been one up till now. This is the first. But I fear it may not signal any imminent end to things.'

Wainwright directed another fork of food to his mouth, chewed thoughtfully, swallowed, asked:

'What d'you think, Simon?'

'About Cambrai, you mean, Uncle? Yes, well, I don't really know. We never exercise at Brocton in numbers bigger than a battalion. And no artillery. I've never seen a tank. The 'papers are talking about multiple divisions with this Cambrai business. A massive attack. I really can't imagine it. It's beyond me. A huge thing.'

'And dangerous too, no doubt. Now listen, Simon. I want you to promise that you'll do your best to get through things over there, d'you hear me? That you'll focus on what they've taught you about staying in one piece and do your utmost to come back to us.'

The uncle's tone was kind, his voice steady and quieter than was usual for him, and his words were deliberately measured. His request was all the more powerful for this, impacting the sombre atmosphere as a small pebble might fall upon the still surface of a pool of brooding worry to shatter its superficial calm. These words demanded consideration. Wife and ward sat unmoving for a moment, watching carefully this man of usually cheery countenance – less so at present – all their movements paused because of what he had just said, their forks halfway to mouths, jaws frozen in their chewing. Peake overcame his slight shock. He tried to reassure:

51

'There'll be a wait in France when we get there, Uncle. For more training. They won't send us straight in. We'll train first. Probably at Étaples. And I have to go. You know that. No choice, really. This thing is my duty … You mustn't worry.'

'Yes. Well, come back to us, Simon. That's all I'm asking. Do your duty, as of course you must. But finish this thing. Get it over with, and get back home to us here in one piece, please. Come home to England.'

Brocton Camp … The gloomy mid-morning, damp and darkening with the probability of sleet, carried a cold embrace that enfolded the assembling soldiers of Peake's company to chill them even as they worked. Returned from leave the previous afternoon, these men had finished cleaning their barracks while the new day was still dark, emptying the wooden structures that had housed them, scrubbing everything in readiness for new men yet to arrive. Now, they drew personal equipment, the same equipment they had trained with and stored before their leave, and which they would carry with them onward to their designated port, then across the Channel and into France: webbing, small and large packs well-worn and minutely adjusted for fit during their training, and now adorned with gas masks and water bottles, and stuffed with mess tins, spoons, spare clothing and other essentials. Most important of all, they checked and then signed for the short-magazine Lee-Enfield rifles that each man had zeroed on the range, and bayonets too.

There were no helmets yet: these they would receive in France.

While the men moved through the stores and armoury, collecting this and signing for that, Brocton lay around them as a familiar, second-nature sprawl of roadways and paths dividing hundreds of prefabricated wooden barracks – huts, really – a few clad against the weather with extra corrugated iron or asbestos sheet, but most just bare wood. The majority were long, narrow, single-storey boxes of slatted wooden plank, creosoted black and topped with angled roofs interrupted by the jut of ventilation channels and narrow iron chimneys leading up from the coal boilers and burners within. Forty thousand men slept, ate, washed and were sheltered in these serried ranks of huts at any one time. Barrack rooms, lecture rooms, hospitals, kitchens and offices: all were of the same shape, form, size and structure. Only the interior arrangements differed. The result was a fenced inland sea of military identicality that stretched in any direction for more than a mile. The forty thousand, sorted into individual intakes by date of arrival, were in continual flux here: enlistment, basic training, advanced training, embarkation. This was the cycle, and about it there was always noise, always sound permeating everywhere – even the open spaces that ran further on through the firing ranges, grenade pits, exercise trenches, parade squares and sports fields. Yet this noise was not the random, humming murmur of a commercial street, not the shouted greeting of residential lane or happy schoolyard. No. This noise, some of it distant and other parts close at hand, was principally an assemblage of barked commands and answering chorus: masculine voices issuing instruction or responding loudly as one body of many men. Around it, embracing it, the sound of marching was everywhere – the booted feet of young men coming and going in disciplined squads, hob-nailed heels crunching in practised unison as they passed on gravelled path, or ringing out as steel on paved parade square as they about-turned, wheeled, advanced or retired at their instructors' bellowed will. Yet further sounds, less obvious to the ear but ever-present during the hours of daylight, could be heard as a distant backdrop: the irregular, snapping crackle of rifles from the firing ranges, and the crump of grenades hurled from within and without the mocked-up training trenches. There were horses whinnying, too, and the loud intrusion of occasional clattering lorry to complete this symphony of sound bidding farewell to the young men of Peake's intake.

Peake himself was oblivious to the noise. Probably all of these soldiers drawing kit were immune to it. They had suffered Brocton for three and a half months, a long and difficult period for them, a time to be endured, a time to get through. Yet perhaps this time had not been long enough for their instructors, their NCOs who had been allowed just one hundred days to forge into soldiers the raw material that these young men once had been, toughening and even brutalising them to the necessary limit. The instructors were themselves not much older than the conscripts they trained – just two or three years, mostly – and few, very few, had experience of the army before war had broken out, even though they were now considered the equal of any who had. That original army – the professional regulars of 1914 – had been destroyed within the first year of the fighting, many dead or invalided out. Farmer's nemesis from the Somme notwithstanding, the instructors who had trained Peake and his companions were mostly new men who had themselves trained in this very camp, and had then gone on to attend courses specific to the purpose of qualifying them in the training of others, so that they could temper the raw material and instil in the individual conscript the discipline and toughness necessary for his survival in battle, drilling and regimenting him, and coaching him in the skills of shooting, bayoneting, stabbing, bludgeoning, blasting and throttling to death his enemy.

The British Army had had to expand so rapidly to meet the needs of this new and enormous war on the Continent that few of these instructors had been granted any time at all to experience battle themselves. Farmer's veteran from the Somme was an exception, for most had not witnessed the reality of their enemy. Yet the system was thorough. It had efficiently and completely transformed Peake and his fellows from schoolboys to infantrymen. Those now drawing stores for France were not the same individuals they had been three months before. They had been changed and, even though they understood and could acknowledge among themselves that noticeable differences had clearly taken place in terms of physique and soldierly skills, they were not at all conscious of the extent of the mental and psychological alterations that the system had wrought upon them. The accumulated tradition, experience and knowledge of the British Army's two hundred and fifty years of existence – every single useful skill gleaned from a hundred wars fought in a hundred different places – all these things had, for one hundred days, been brought to bear and thoroughly taught. All instruction had been carefully moderated. Brocton's attentive teachers, those trained corporals and sergeant-instructors of Peake and his fellows, had themselves not only been carefully taught the skills of instruction, but had also then been supervised from discreet distance by captains and majors – even colonels – throughout these hundred days to ensure that the fine line between, on the one hand, dangerous destruction of the morals of a civilised people instilled in youth by home, family, church and school, and, on the other hand, a mindful overlaying of these values with the essentially tough and protective tissue that would permit instinctive killing without it becoming in any aspect the way of the psychopath – these higher-ups and the syllabus of instruction had ensured that this fine line, so carefully defined, was never crossed. Only a few would become terminally psychopathic because of the experience still ahead. Only a very few … Now, therefore, when the moment of greatest personal danger and overarching national need arrived, the system could depend upon the fact that each man would unthinkingly and unreasoningly kill. Peake and his fellows would do it without question. Their instructors and the greater institution of which they were a part had seen to this. The officers who would command these newly trained men could be sure of compliance with their orders. Obedience was a given. Yet those drawing stores in the mid-morning gloom at Brocton neither knew of this fact nor were consciously aware of the very high degree to which their now instinctive skills and discipline had been honed. Though they worried about their personal moment of truth yet to come, they need not have done. For when it came – that moment to kill –

they would do it, and efficiently, too. They would neither examine the death that they would deal, nor would they hesitate in the moment of its dealing, for they understood well enough that to hesitate would mean losses in their own line, and perhaps even their own deaths.

The whole point of their training had been to move them, when the time came to kill, beyond any doubt or hesitation caused by moral value. And the training had been very thorough. It had succeeded in its point.

Thus prepared, thus trained, Peake and the others drew stores, donned trench coats, webbing, packs and gas masks, shouldered rifles, formed up and marched through the damp, cold air of that day to the open wagons of the train waiting for them on the short, dedicated line that serviced the camp. Entrained, they hunkered down against a strengthening drizzle while their train negotiated the sharp descent through woodland to Milford and Brocton Station, where there was pause for transfer to the standard coaches, covered, of a troop train of the London and North Western Railway. Once within, they waited, grateful to be out of the wet, while their empty wagons returned to Brocton for the remainder of the draft. When all had boarded, the powerful locomotive of the LNWR, gleaming a shiny black in the wetness of the day, belched smoke, snorted steam and whistled shrilly as it rushed them along the steel rails of the line south through Birmingham and on to London, and from there still further to the port of Folkestone. They were aboard their troopship before dusk.

For the duration of this journey, Peake's thoughts were constantly on the three people most important to his young life: his uncle and aunt – constant and sure throughout his memory – and Christine, for three days his lover. He was remembering their farewells …

On the Euston platform where Peake had departed London for Brocton only the morning before, these had been wrenching.

The uncle had been steady and in control of himself, though something of sadness had refused to release its grip upon the usually blithe face of this man who was the only one in the whole world whom Peake loved. With both hands firmly clasping Peake's – no embrace – Wainwright, Peake's unshakeable example throughout his eighteen years, had tried to smile, though the effort had emerged as more of a grimace because of the emotion of the moment: 'Be sensible over there, Simon. Nothing stupid, please. No heroics.'

Peake's aunt had been tearful, smiling bravely but dabbing at her eyes with lace handkerchief already wet. She had held Peake tightly, breaking down into sobs that shook her as she held him close. 'Come back to us, Simon,' she said. 'Come back.' And she had wept openly, turning away from him to seek comfort in her husband's chest, burying her face. Peake had boarded, found his seat and moved quickly to a window to see them waving from the platform as the train pulled away: two figures – one taller than the other – as familiar to him as his own soul, each with an arm raised and the other about partner's waist as they had always been at farewells for occasional school outing to distant derby or seaside resort. They were a solid couple, were Peake's guardians, a shining example to him of correct living, and he loved them dearly. He had felt the physicality of the lump in his throat as he turned reluctantly from the carriage window to take his seat, and had himself dabbed at the wetness of his eyes.

Christine had not been at the station. 'Not fair on you, my angel,' she had whispered in the afterglow of their final lovemaking in Penelope Brooke's bedroom, beautifully naked and nestled against him in the dim light reaching them through closed curtains, both of them weighing the gravity of separation. Peake had run a finger across the flawless skin of one cheek, the line of her jaw, the soft depression on the side of her neck.

'But I want you there,' he whispered, almost pleading. 'Who knows when I will see you again?'

'No. It wouldn't be proper. Your parents wouldn't like it.'

'They aren't my parents.'

'They are your parents in more ways than you realise, Simon. They love you as I do, and they'll be heartbroken to see you go, as I shall be heartbroken when you leave me to go to them after this.'

And with that, she had rolled over onto him, smothering his face in the mass of her fragrant hair as it fell forward, and placing delicate, gentle kisses – so sweet – onto his closed eyes, his forehead, cheeks and chin, the full weight of her body, softly firm, upon his. They made love again, and then again after that, until no more physical love was possible. Then they dressed. It was awkward. At the door to the street Peake lingered, holding on to Christine as he faced the terrible impossibility of further delay. Though Christine would remain at Penelope's house until she returned, he himself could stay no longer.

'Go now, Simon. Please go. I cannot bear this anymore. I feel pain.'

He kissed her tenderly one last time, and she shut her eyes tight against the tears. Pulling back, when he saw her open them, he could read in those eyes both love and the agony of parting. He asked for reassurance.

'Yes. Yes, my angel. I will write to you, Simon. I promise. Be safe, my love. Please be safe, my angel.'

'Will you wait for me?'

'Go now. Go before my heart breaks. I love you, Peake.'

'I love you too.'

He hesitated a moment, wanting to repeat the question, needing reassurance that she would wait and remain forever for him as she was at that moment. He was determined to return to her from France. Instead he said nothing, releasing her and allowing his hands to fall uselessly to his sides. He turned, descended the three steps to the street and walked quickly away. Abandoning the still open door, Christine ran to the stairs and up to the high window of the house's second bedroom, now weeping the tears she had somehow managed to suppress while still holding him. On the tiny landing, the dam of her control – this well of heartbreak filled by love torn apart – this thing broke. She sobbed, shoulders shaking as she wiped condensation from the window in time to see Peake's soldierly silhouette disappearing into the gloom of late afternoon. She watched the lean, tallish frame until he was lost to her sight. Then her strength gave out and she sank to the wooden boards of the floor, sobbing uncontrollably, broken in the anguish of separation, broken in the anguish of her loss.

CHAPTER FOUR

'That was quite a speech today, eh, Nettermann? What d'you reckon? I mean, what Goettner had to say – what d'you think?'

It was König asking the question. Nettermann did not answer immediately and knew that König would not expect him to. It was not his way. When anybody spoke to Nettermann, he preferred to digest the words for a few seconds irrespective of who it was addressing him. The only exception to this rule was his sweetheart, for he understood that his habitual pause in the reply, so much a part of his nature, could sometimes offend. Not so König, who was already with the *zug* when Nettermann arrived fresh from training. The two had formed an immediate liking for each other. Now, after a year, they understood one another quite well.

Nettermann thought about König's question. He was wiping and oiling his rifle, the parts stripped and set before him in a neat row on a square of cloth upon the tent's groundsheet. It was a tent for six. Two of the other four were Zimmermann and Bauer, also with the *zug* for longer than Nettermann: some said that Zimmermann had been with the unit almost as long as *Oberleutnant* Goettner himself. The fifth man was a replacement whom nobody yet took seriously enough to trouble themselves by trying to remember his name – too much bother. Schäffer was temporarily absent from the group, placed on light duties in regimental headquarters until his head wound healed. He had not yet been replaced, and they hoped to have him back before this had a chance to happen.

Beyond the canvas, grey-black clouds had begun emptying a cold mid-December rain that drummed steadily upon the tent's tautly stretched roof. It drained away in unseen rivulets, running off the sides of the shelter into a shallow drainage ditch dug around the groundsheet's immediate perimeter and arrowing out and away from its lowest point. Like Nettermann, König was cleaning his rifle. Both were dressed as warmly as possible: the same fatigues they had worn all day while training, but now with trench coats donned as well. They were sitting cross-legged facing one another. Their coalscuttle helmets they had removed, placing them on the groundsheet where their heads would be when they slept, marking in the manner of all soldiers the individual bed-spaces. There were no beds.

The tent in which they sat was one of about a hundred – all identical – allocated to the battalion. The rectangular canvas shelters were pegged out in rows of dark, dirty green across adjacent fields just outside the hamlet of Pronville near the village of Quéant, which was itself midway between Cambrai and Arras in the far north of France, quite close to the border with Belgium. The battalion had marched to Pronville on the second day after their arrival by train from Russian Poland, to pitch camp, and these tents now formed the unit's base while the men trained and prepared to move to the frontline a dozen or so kilometres to their southwest. The tents were low affairs. It was possible to sit but not to stand, and the soldiers slept directly on groundsheets without any mattresses. Nobody complained. To sit or sleep on a groundsheet out of the rain and the wind was good enough – cold and dry was better than cold and wet. If the rain eased long enough for the fields to dry, they would forage for hay as comfort.

Nettermann looked up at dumpy young König, who to Nettermann's mind could at times be irritatingly slow in understanding things which had already been carefully presented and explained. The *oberleutnant* had told them as much as he knew during his talk. Nettermann replied at last:

'Which part, König? What didn't you understand? Cambrai? Or what Goettner told us about the tanks?'

'The tanks. This new tank unit. Everybody knows about Cambrai.'

Everybody knows about Cambrai …

Well, that was certainly true. Everybody did know about Cambrai. In and around that town, twenty kilometres east of the Pronville encampment now receiving a steady drenching by the cold December rain, the biggest German counter-attack in three years had nullified all the spectacular initial successes achieved by the Tommies of the British Expeditionary Force attacking with massed infantry and tanks the Kaiser's new defensive line, the *Siegfriedstellung*. Seventeen days of intense fighting eventually pushed the British all the way back to the very trenchline from which they had begun their advance, leaving a battlefield littered with thousands. And there they stayed, those dead. The bodies were in direct view of both sides, scattered across ground able to be fired upon, so the corpses could not be recovered. Fortunately, they were decomposing only slowly because of winter's cold, and thank God for that. In summer they would quickly have begun to putrefy, bloat and stink, those

59

bodies. About them on the battlefield, the messy aftermath of conflict included as a new ingredient the scattered hulks of British tanks here and there. Some of these machines were untouched, abandoned victims of mechanical failure, but more were blackened wrecks, disabled, set ablaze and then destroyed even as their crews tried to get out but were shot or bayoneted in the attempt, or slashed and smashed by knife or spade in the rage of battle. The closing phases of this enormous struggle had still been playing out when Nettermann and König's battalion had arrived by train from the east. The Kaiser's Army lost fifty-five thousand men killed, wounded, taken prisoner or missing in the engagement. The British suffered this number and twenty thousand more.

Cambrai … Yes, everybody certainly knew about Cambrai …

Nettermann looked around the tent, taking in the five small clumps of damp laundry beside each man's helmet and piled webbing, and the empty place – the sixth – where Old Man Schäffer should have been. When it wasn't raining, they hung their laundry outside on guy-ropes, or draped it over the canvas of the tent itself. Right now, with the other three away on various duties, König and Nettermann had brought the washing inside. Mostly it was shirts and socks. Not everyone had spare trousers even when reunited with their kit behind the lines, and none carried anything spare at the front itself.

'Light the lamp, will you, König? Getting dark in here.'

König struck a match and set it to the tent's hurricane lamp. It guttered and flickered somewhat, but they were happy to have the light it provided. In the line there were only candles for the private soldiers, and these were always going out because of the draught. But you could rely on a hurricane lamp. König adjusted the flame, which set about casting silhouettes of their profiles upon the canvas. Nettermann reassembled his rifle, deftly fitting together the newly-cleaned parts with practised ease. He looked up and said:

'I think the change could be good.'

He was referring to Goettner's address, the one where their *zugführer* had informed them that a section of tanks was soon to be attached to the battalion so that it could develop ways of working with the new armour. The *zug* was to undergo training with these new machines, working out how best to attack together, tanks and infantry in combination. The *zug's* job would be to protect the new, mobile fighting platforms as they punched through the enemy lines, even though neither side yet knew how to do this. An offensive of their own was certain to come soon – probably in the spring when it was warm enough for the killing to begin in earnest once again: winter offensives were not popular with the generals, and even less popular with the troops themselves.

After training earlier that day, the sergeant had formed up the *zug's* four sections in front of their tents, Goettner observing this procedure from a respectful distance in that calm, reassuring manner of his, until he was given the go-ahead to present his update. Their *oberleutnant* told them that the British were still licking their wounds after Cambrai. The enemy was short on men, he said, even as their own army was being strongly reinforced by divisions released by the Russian collapse. Though these new arrivals from the east were as war-weary as they themselves, they nevertheless numbered in the tens of thousands, and Goettner emphasised to his assembled men that the build-up was therefore inexorably tipping the scales of frontline strength in Germany's favour. Ammunition, artillery shells and stores were being stockpiled as quickly as possible. When all was ready, a great offensive would begin.

'I have no details of this offensive as yet,' Goettner said. 'I don't know where we will strike first – from which sector – and I don't know when, but it seems obvious it will be a very big attack, and probably in spring. I also cannot tell you who will spearhead the thing. But I do think that we will be closely connected with whatever plan is eventually handed down, because all of us – this particular *zug* – are to be attached to a new unit currently being formed: a tank group. We are going to use the new British tanks against the British themselves.'

Goettner had paused to look at his men. He was a strongly proportioned man, powerfully built without displaying obvious muscle, his strength concealed by an exceptional height. The eyes below the fair hair possessed a piercing quality. They complemented a generally stern aspect that helped him come across as a man to be taken seriously, someone to pay attention to. People tended to listen to Goettner without him really trying. Addressing his soldiers, he continued:

'It's quite a wonderful thing, this new British invention. I say wonderful because our soldiers have destroyed a wonderfully large number of them!'

A low rumble of nervous laughter from the *zug* acknowledged this attempt at humour: news of impending combat always made edgy those who would be involved.

'Anyway,' Goettner continued, 'our units at Cambrai were apparently able to capture some of these new contraptions – generally breakdowns that had to be abandoned. The main cause was overheated engines. Our mechanics are busy repairing them, making improvements to the cooling systems and so on. We have a small number restored to workable state at the moment, but obviously any tank is useful.'

Another pause while Goettner examined the men. Perhaps he had been seeking reaction.

'Has anybody seen one of these things, by the way? Anybody seen a tank?' Heads shaking here and there among the assembled men. No nods. Nobody had yet seen a tank. Goettner continued:

'The *Herr Hauptmann* received word about our new attachment as we were pulling out of the line back in Poland. The signal came through then. But there was no detail. There's a bit more information now, and I can tell you that these new weapons will be grouped into a special unit to be used as a shock-weapon. However, the tank is going to need close infantry support when it is used, and that's where we come in. Why? Because, at Cambrai, our fellows learned that it's entirely possible to knock out a tank. It's difficult, but with a bit of cunning and a lot of determination it can be done. The crew's field of vision is limited, so if a man can get close enough, the tracks can be broken with explosive, or a grenade can be chucked inside, and so on.'

Goettner looked at his men again, then glanced down at his feet, grinding with the toe of one boot the butt of an imaginary cigarette into the damp earth. He looked up again.

'Quite a good way to earn a medal, I would think,' he suggested, face expressionless.

This observation drew guffaws of genuine laughter. Though none had yet seen a tank, the men had heard from other soldiers who had, and the word was that it was a formidable weapon, terrifying to face and difficult to stop. It was something to be feared.

'So, this is why we are going to be attached to the tanks. Our *zug* – us – we are going to be the infantry moving with the tanks. It's going to be our job to prevent any heroics by the other side. It's going to be our job to eliminate any British soldiers the tanks themselves cannot eliminate.'

Another pause. Another penetrating glance by Goettner at his men. Now, in the tent, remembering the address as he sat with König, Nettermann had a clear recollection that the assembled soldiers had received the news quite well – if not with overt cheerfulness then certainly without any grumbling. The mood had been one of interest and anticipation rather than worry. It was easy to grasp the logic of combining infantry with armour and, at a personal level, the chances of surviving an attack with the support of one of these large, mobile, armour-plated machines seemed better than attacking without the thing, something they had always had to do until now, and suffering always the inevitable casualties.

'There's more, and this is particularly good news,' Goettner had continued, picking up the thread. 'New tanks are arriving from Germany, specially designed around battlefield conditions here in France. I'm told that they are bigger than the British tanks. They have more firepower and bigger crews. Generally, our tank is a much better killing machine. At the moment, I have no more information than that. In particular, I don't yet know when exactly we will begin training with the tanks. We will have to wait for the order. But I think it's going to be more than interesting when we eventually do it, preparing to work with these new machines. So, over the next few days we will continue training as normal with our *kompanie* and the rest of the battalion, after which we'll move closer to the forward positions with them – as a reserve only, to begin with. We'll be rotated forward in the usual way. Do you have any questions?'

There were none, so Goettner nodded to his sergeant to have the men fall out for afternoon fatigues and personal administration.

Now, in the tent, rain drumming on the canvas above their heads as they sat cross-legged on the groundsheet in the yellow light of the hurricane lamp, Nettermann capped his tin of gun-oil and replaced it with pull-through rope and a tiny piece of greasy cloth within his cleaning pouch. He looked at König and repeated:

'I think the change could be good. I don't think we should worry about attacking with the tanks or whatever else the brass hats are cooking up for us. We should worry more about the size of this offensive, when it comes. It's going to be much bigger than anything we ever saw in Poland.'

'Why? How do you know that?'

'I know because this morning they made me a runner and gave me a dispatch to take over to the *kompanie* on our right – Twelfth *Kompanie* – when we were rehearsing our battalion attack formation. You know those lines in powdered chalk? The ones on the ground showing us exactly where to stand; showing us how far apart the sections and platoons need to be, and where we can expect *kompanie* HQ?'

'*Ja*, of course. Go on.'

'Okay. Well, when I was sent off with this message for Twelfth, I found their headquarters well to the right of centre, so I could see even beyond the last man on the extreme right flank. And guess what?'

'What?'

'Those chalk lines extended for at least a kilometre further on. I could see them because they went on down the slope of the ground where Twelfth

Kompanie was, and then further on still, up the side of the rising ground beyond. I could see the chalk marks quite clearly.'

'So then it'll be a regimental attack,' König countered. 'All three battalions. We know this already and we've done it before. What's new about that?'

Nettermann reverted to form and was silent for a while. Then, eventually, he replied thoughtfully: 'Nothing. There's nothing new unless you look at what's going on around. Unless you think about what Goettner himself told us about all the divisions arriving from the east. This is going to be a big do, König, bigger than anything we did in Poland. It's going to be bigger than our brigade and probably bigger than the division. Huge. It's going to be a massive attack.'

König's simple, roundish face, appearing almost ochre beneath its shock of dark hair in the light from the lamp, frowned in worry. He seemed to be about to say something, but at that moment the tent flap opened to reveal the face of their section leader, wet and dripping.

'Nettermann, you're wanted. You too, König. Over by the *kompanie* stores. Work detail. Rain's not too bad now, so let's go, let's move!'

Nettermann had developed some respect for his *unteroffizier* during their time in the east. The man had earned his rank. So he picked up his reassembled Mauser without question and followed the corporal out into the rain, König following.

The battalion moved up the line. From its tented Pronville camp, it moved out after dark three days later as a column of two files to begin the three-hour march to its allocated sector. Within the *zug*, Nettermann and the others marched together, König and Nettermann side by side, and behind them Zimmermann, Bauer, and then the new man – the replacement whose name none had yet taken the trouble to remember. Goettner marched, too, though he was at the column's head, right at the front, leading the eight hundred through the night.

Time in their tented camp they had used both carefully and well. The men were rested and acclimatised, and re-trained too, all their essential skills re-honed. The battalion had received replacements for men lost in the final days of Poland, and all had recovered for a while, but not for so long that any deep consideration of the war – America's growing army and Germany's deteriorating domestic condition – could take hold and damage morale. Their officers had made sure that all were too tired by the end of each day's training to think of much beyond food and sleep.

Their training had hammered home the latest tactics being used by the French and British in the attack. This theory internalised, attention turned to the practicalities of how such attacks could be repulsed by the *Siegfriedstellung*, Germany's recently prepared and deeply layered defensive front. Here, enemy assaults could be repelled in the manner of a broad elastic band – thick and very strong – absorbing the impact of a heavy steel ball fired directly at it: stretching, stretching, stretching under the momentum of that ball, then tightening in the stretch, slowing and gaining resistant energy before snapping tightly straight again, hurling the ball back whence it came. The days of stubbornly defending to the last man a single trenchline or two were over. The *Siegfriedstellung* was designed to absorb any assault over multiple, mutually supporting trenchlines sited in great depth, and then throw the attackers back as the British offensive at Cambrai had been absorbed and thrown back, and their tanks with it.

Finally, when the practicalities of such defence had been mastered through repeated exercise, the battalion practised their own attack tactics, honing unit skills and rehearsing coordinated battalion and regimental manoeuvres so that all were ready to execute an assault in brigade strength as part of an even greater force. They had trained both by day and by night until, refreshed, replenished and retrained, it was time to move, time to fight.

To avoid harassment by aircraft and artillery, Regiment had ordered their battalion commander to lead his men into position by night, the regiment's other two battalions moving up simultaneously to the left and right, some kilometres distant. To pathfind the way, Goettner had been sent forward on horseback to carry out a solo reconnaissance of the best route to take. It was therefore Goettner who was now leading the battalion through the darkness, on foot, leaving the *zug* in the capable hands of his sergeant as part of the general column.

It was raining. The wet weather had continued on and off through the three days since Nettermann and König's speculation in their tent. It was also cold. There was no snow as yet, but it was expected. The chill, steady rain soaked the land and tried to soak the soldiers moving westward, too, as they tramped along the muddy roads and farm tracks through the night toward the front. But they were seasoned, these men, and even the replacements were by now fully accustomed to wet conditions. Ignoring the weather, the soldiers withdrew physically and mentally into their coalscuttle helmets, trench coats and boots. They turned their minds away from discomfort and ignored the icy water trickling down face and creeping beneath upturned collar. Some had experienced all four winters of this war. They were reconciled to rain, welcoming it almost as a friend because of the rarity of attacks in such weather.

There was some excitement within the battalion as it marched, but it was not the prospect of the task ahead that excited. The soldiers knew from their orders that their immediate mission was to relieve a unit in the rearmost trenches, taking over as reserve troops a two-kilometre section of this part of the defence. Their two sister battalions would be in front of them holding one of three lines of fortifications each, with several kilometres between each line, while they themselves would be a further few kilometres to the rear, beyond the range of most British artillery. Therefore they could expect a relatively safe time of things for a week or so, until they rotated up to the middle trenches, and then again up to the frontline itself after that.

So, the source of the battalion's excitement was not the task itself. Rather it was because this move into position would afford them their first glimpse of the new and much talked about Siegfried Line.

The *Siegfriedstellung* was an engineering and military marvel. Relatively new, it was one hundred and forty kilometres long, five to seven kilometres deep, and garrisoned by fully twenty divisions – one division of about eight thousand soldiers for every seven kilometres. It had been deliberately constructed without pressure of enemy proximity, something unheard of in this war where frontlines usually began as shallow trenches dug for self-protection under fire, and which were then deepened over time, strengthened and improved once some wire had been thrown forward and machine guns established to keep the enemy at bay. But not here. Here, the new line had been carefully planned and painstakingly built with the express purpose of facilitating deliberate withdrawal from what had been a large existing salient – the Noyon Salient – that had been jutting dangerously into ground held by the enemy, inviting attack at the flanks to sever it and create a pocket to be annihilated at leisure. The generals wanted no such pocket and no such annihilation. So they built this new line while the salient could still be strongly held. Besides eliminating the jut and any possibility of a pocket, withdrawal to the straighter and much shorter line had also freed up the manpower of many divisions sorely needed elsewhere along trenches stretching from the Belgian coast all the way to Switzerland.

This deliberate fortification of land thirty kilometres to the rear of the Noyon Salient took place over five months during the winter of 1916-17, and employed the skills of private construction companies from Germany using a hundred thousand labourers, mainly Russian prisoners of war. The result was a formidable system of trenches, strongpoints, barbed wire, machine gun posts and artillery emplacements built around the existing natural obstacles of ridges, hills, rivers and canals. There were steel-reinforced concrete bunkers of uniform design for infantry, similar protection for artillery observers, and there were wooden panels of standard dimension and strength manufactured *en masse* to hold up the walls of the newly dug trenches. These could be replaced at will when repairs were needed. The sentry trench at the extreme front – the trench facing no man's land – was relatively lightly built, but the second line two hundred metres behind incorporated reinforced pillboxes and bunkers enough to shelter all men of whichever battalion was holding the forward area. Behind this frontal defence of two lines of trenches – and well back from it by several kilometres – lay a second, similar defensive position of wooden-walled trenches and reinforced concrete bunkers and pillboxes, and behind that yet another – the third line now about to be occupied by Nettermann, Goettner, Zimmermann, Bauer, König and the rest. Carefully laid barbed-wire entanglements higher than a man covered the ground for fully one hundred metres forward of each of these three defensive lines, and they were zig-zagged to channel attacking troops into killing zones covered by machine guns.

The idea, radically new, was not to stubbornly hold the front trenches come what may, but rather to fall back as part of a deliberate plan, initially just two hundred metres to the concrete defences, but, if necessary, all the way back to the second line up to four kilometres behind, forcing the British artillery to move up in order to bring the second line within range. While this was happening, the reserve battalion in the rear – Nettermann's and Goettner's battalion – would counter-attack in strength, its fresh troops catching the by then exhausted British or French off guard as they regrouped without artillery support, and throwing them back or even eliminating them.

It was a new concept and a successful one, because it had worked very well at Cambrai.

Withdrawal to the *Siegfriedstellung* took place in March of 1917. Now, nine months later and just before Christmas, Goettner was leading the way through a cold, wet winter's night to the trenchlines of the regimental reserve. When they reached them, the exchange of troops – one battalion for another – would be a routine affair carried out without fuss, for there would be no enemy fire there at all. The middle position would be similarly occupied. Only the regiment's third battalion moving all the way into the forwardmost position would have to negotiate the perils of British harassing artillery fire, the shells of which could be seen and felt detonating as muffled thumps and thuds now and again, glimpsed in the distance through the drizzling darkness as flickers and flashes of occasional grey-white violence that froze for split seconds the rain falling vertically upon the pale faces of these marching soldiers, tramping forward in weary resignation while the shells exploded among the distant concrete and wood revetments of the extreme front, hurling their splintered shards of white-hot steel hither and thither in search of unprotected flesh.

'Hey, you!' Zimmermann prodded the sleeping form roughly with the knuckle of one finger. 'Yes, you, New Man! Wake up! Tommy's about – he might sneak up and cut your throat. Wouldn't want that now, would we? Your mother wouldn't like it.'

The replacement awoke. He groaned and sat up, eyeing his tormentor warily, face slack and expressionless.

Three weeks had passed, Christmas somewhere among them – just another day. The medical orderlies had returned Old Man Schäffer to the *zug* on Christmas morning, a gift from regimental headquarters where he had been on light duties. Head bandage removed, he was almost his normal good-looking self again. Everyone was glad to have him back. A few days before that – before Christmas Day – the battalion rotated through to the forward trenches closest to the British lines.

The replacement was uncertain how to manage Zimmermann's taunt.

'We have sentries posted,' he tried at last. 'We're allowed to rest, Zimmermann.'

'Yes, we are. But not you, New Man. Not you.' And the lanky, biggish Zimmermann guffawed at the nervous reaction of the object of his fun. He had no intention of physically abusing this replacement, but the man did not know it. The replacement feared him, and Zimmermann understood this. So he laughed.

There were other new men in the *kompanie*, and in the *zug* too, but the object of Zimmermann's provocation was in the same section as the provoker himself and, unluckily, had slept in the same tent at Pronville. This made him Zimmermann's likeliest target.

Zimmermann was the *zug's* bully, though he would have taken offence had anybody openly labelled him thus. He did not view himself as a bully, seldom administering more than a light slap to the back of a man's head if he thought it was deserved, yet his manner was unconsciously that of the bully. Taller and bigger than most in the *zug*, it was fear of ridicule that had made Zimmermann the way he was. The son of a farm labourer, he lacked education beyond the most basic of literary and numerical skills. Plenty of other soldiers in the *zug* were similarly poorly educated, but in Zimmermann the lack was combined with psychological scarring from a difficult childhood. His coping mechanism was to pick on anyone he deemed weaker than himself, and to address them in a sneering, aggressive manner. When alone, Zimmermann tried hard never to dwell on the hurts of his childhood, and he never spoke of them publicly. Privately, he suspected that he might break down if he were to even try.

Zimmermann drew on the cigarette he was smoking, then gave the replacement's shoulder another prod with knuckled finger.

'Tell me, New Man, where's the closest communication trench? Point it out – show it to me.'

'Ten metres in that direction. I'm not stupid, Zimmermann.'

The replacement indicated an intersection in the wooden walls of the trench, some metres further up from the group. All along the length of the trench, men smoked, or chatted quietly, or chewed tobacco, or dozed, sitting with backs propped against the wooden planks, or lying huddled under their blankets on the fire-step.

'Not stupid.' Zimmermann repeated, seeming to ponder the statement. 'Well,' he sneered, 'not completely stupid, anyway. But up here you know nothing, New Man. Nothing. Not yet.' Zimmermann took a pull on his cigarette, looking hard at the replacement. 'Stay awake's all I'm saying …'

A shell exploding close by put an end to this exchange. The cold, muddy earth beyond the parapet erupted noisily upwards into a gush of mucky clods mostly unseen by the men in the trench, but near enough to deliver a physical blow of loud, intense sound that smacked the ear all the way inwards to the drum, and shook the ground on which the men stood, or sat, or lay. All flinched involuntarily, and tensed as dirt and mud showered down around them, ears ringing from the blast. They glanced anxiously up to the sentry on the fire-step. The wood of the trench wall beside him had snapped and fallen with the force of the explosion, spilling damp earth onto the platform upon which he stood. Now, the man cringed in a crouch, for he had been closest to point of detonation. Removing his hands cautiously from his ears, he uncoiled himself carefully to raise his head and peer tentatively through a narrow gap between the parapet's sandbags. It allowed him to watch the land sloping away toward the British lines. He searched for any sign of movement. Finding none, he used one hand to make a calming motion to the others: no troops and no assault, just another shell intended to unnerve.

No other shells followed.

The trench lapsed into silence.

* * *

The replacement, New Man, was listed on the *kompanie* roll as *Gefreiter* Winkler. The son of a Hildesheim policeman, he was the opposite of Zimmermann in almost every imaginable way, emotionally as well as physically. Winkler's average height forced him to always look up whenever taunted by the taller Zimmermann, a disadvantage compounded by a lack of any obvious strength. Whereas Zimmermann was tall and big, amply filling his uniform in the fashion of a recruiting poster-boy, Winkler's slight frame was barely discernible under the folds of his field grey, his tunic seeming to hang upon him like an ill-fitting cloak. Even his standard-issue helmet was too big for his head, which was so swallowed by the thing that his roundish face had to peer out from within it, like a mouse timidly assessing the ground beyond the entrance to its hole. Zimmermann's face was an utter contrast, handsomely framed by the pressed steel with ginger hair pushing out cheekily from beneath the brim. Yet Winkler was no weakling. He had proven strong enough for the infantry during his military training, and those months had developed and honed in him all the characteristics needed by a good foot-soldier: resilience to current discomfort, mental agility, physical fitness and the ability to endure. Winkler had been toughened to the required degree. Now, his only obstacle to managing a steady, even existence within the environment of the frontline was an inability to develop any useful defensive technique against Zimmermann's ridicule.

Perhaps it was simply Winkler's obvious sensitivity that so irritated the bully within Zimmermann, who hid whatever his own fears and worries might have been behind a mask of indifference to the shared circumstance of imminent danger and death. Winkler had formed a dislike for the man even before the very first jibe, becoming wary of him from the time they met. Days spent in Zimmermann's presence had intensified that dislike, deepening it and transforming it into resentment. The differences between the two ran deep, and Winkler knew that. In his own view, Zimmermann bordered on the unforgivably ignorant, avoiding all things written whereas Winkler was fully literate, reading as often as possible and pulling a book from his pack whenever he had a moment. Indeed, it seemed to Winkler that Zimmermann could barely read at all, and neither had the man any appreciation of music or art, an understanding actively encouraged and developed in Winkler by his mother as a boy. The big German – Zimmermann – additionally appeared to have no obvious love of nature, a fact incredible to Winkler given that the man had grown up on a farm.

Winkler's personal diary had posed an additional problem during his initial days with the *zug*. He had kept one since the day of his conscription, updating it whenever he could, whenever there was a lull in training or, lately, a lull in the line. But Zimmermann had ridiculed those efforts too, of course, so Winkler had given up, abandoning his notes to some indeterminate time in the future. Only his reading continued: he was reluctant to quit that.

Now, flinching with the others under the force and sting of the exploding artillery shell, Winkler's round face was sullen as he covertly observed the similarly cowering Zimmermann. At the sentry's signal of the all-clear – no British attack – Winkler moved from his crouch to sit on the fire-step, slapping at his trench coat to rid it of the shower of dirt and soil tossed over all by the detonation. Risking a covert glance to his tormentor who had inexplicably not immediately resumed his goading, Winkler was surprised to notice that the man's hands shook a little as he re-lit the cigarette he had dropped. That fact was somehow intriguing to Winkler. It was his first sign that Zimmermann might be human after all.

A few metres along the trench from where Winkler slapped at his grey fatigues, *Oberleutnant* Goettner, too, had noted the tremor in Zimmermann's hands. He watched the rigidity flow gradually out of the man's physically imposing frame as Zimmermann realised that there was no further immediate danger. Well, thought Goettner, size counted for nothing against the jagged, red-hot steel of an exploding shell. Neither did it count for much against a bullet, though height and weight were certainly useful in close-quarters fighting involving bayonet, club and entrenching tool. Zimmermann had unconsciously stiffened and ducked like everyone else against the crash of that explosion. Now, he stooped to recover the cigarette he had dropped. It had gone out, and Goettner watched him trying to re-light it with those big, slightly shaking hands. He pondered the man's unfailing capacity to tease and belittle despite the shared danger, wondering what he expected to gain by it. Zimmermann seemed to direct his cruel teasing toward any and all who were new to the *zug*, probing for weakness. Goettner had seen it many times, and he had observed that only a strong retaliation in kind, or actual physical confrontation, provided an effective response to the bullying. He wondered how long it would take the replacement to realise this. Zimmermann always backed off when confronted, unless it was by the enemy. Under attack and under fire, his nerve was as good as any man's. Goettner did not like Zimmermann, but he respected his ability as a soldier.

71

Beyond the trench's parapet, the battlefield stretched away under a sky of blanket-grey as far as the eye could see. There were patches of snow here and there, startlingly white and only a few millimetres deep, but they were not melting because the day was too cold, though in the trench itself the soldiers' boots had turned it to slush that was now draining away into the shallow ditch beneath the duckboards. Goettner was thankful for that drainage ditch. He sat on a ledge, smoking and killing the last hours of daylight before the orders group set for three hours from then. It would take place in the concrete command bunker, their *kompanie* nerve centre where maps plotted the ongoing battle, and where signalmen and field telephones linked them to *kompanies* left and right, and to battalion headquarters itself, centrally located to their rear. At the O-group, the *Herr Hauptmann* would provide more detail on the reconnaissance patrol Goettner was to lead that night. Earlier, the man had visited the *zug* in person, casting a steady but eagle eye over the state of readiness in this part of the forward trench, then squatting down on the duckboard next to Goettner:

'Battalion wants another recce tonight, Goettner. Same task: plotting gaps in the Tommy wire. They want us to find more of them and it's your turn tonight. If you can find just one it will be good enough to keep them happy. I don't want any casualties, you understand. So find one – you have to do that – but call it a night when you've done it. One will do. Clear?'

Goettner had nodded his acknowledgement.

'Detailed orders at twenty hundred hours. Pick four men and bring them with you when you come.'

Four men …

He chose Zimmermann and Nettermann. The replacement, Winkler, would go too, to gain experience. He needed one more. Not Schäffer – the man's wound, though healed, needed as much rest as possible to fully restore him. That was a pity, because Schäffer had all the necessary skills. Goettner chose a fourth, then passed on to all of them such information as he had. They understood that detail would come later, in the bunker.

Reconnaissance …

It was never as bad as a trench raid, but it was bad enough. Dangerous. They would have to move in complete silence if they were to avoid being fired upon by the British, and maintaining that silence would be difficult, because they would be crawling across the wet, rocky ground alongside all those steel barbs just waiting to sing out a warning as clear as any plucked musical string, should a man accidentally hook himself on even one of them. Broken silence was not the only risk. Of equal danger were trip wires and the possibility of bumping into a British patrol on its own mission in the misty darkness, repairing or extending their entanglements, or embarking on reconnaissance as they themselves would be doing. Well, Goettner, thought, he had led patrols before, many times. Tonight would be no different.

In the relative silence that followed the explosion of the bursting shell, Goettner rehearsed the patrol as a picture within his imagination. He would have liked to take the men behind the line to practise movement and formations, silent crawling, action to be taken on pauses, on flares being sent up by the British, on bumping into the enemy, on being fired upon … He would like to have rehearsed all these things and more, but rehearsal was not possible and they had practised it all anyway during the Pronville training. Their time in Pronville would have to suffice. But it would have been nice if Regiment had picked the patrol from the second line, where nerves were not stretched as taut as they always were here in the sentry trench. Goettner wondered about that for a moment, then remembered that the second line was several kilometres to the rear – much further back than they had been used to in Russia – and that this distance would unnecessarily tire any patrol starting from there even before they could begin the passage across no man's land. No, the men had to be selected from the forward line, and it was their turn tonight. Too bad. Somehow he would get them all through.

Goettner tried to relax. Within the trench it wasn't possible to see the battlefield beyond the parapet, so you had to trust your men, you had to trust your sentries to guard and warn of enemy activity. Still, he had to force himself not to worry. Over the years he had developed an array of mental tricks to help him drift away whenever there was a lull in the fighting. You couldn't worry all the time. Although none of Goettner's methods worked completely, all were useful. Today, he stared at a spot in the buttressed trench wall facing him, until his mind no longer registered its wooden planks and supporting uprights, so that he gradually floated away to happier times in happier places. He could see a girl, now, and his home in Graudenz. His family. His favourite food. Sometimes, when he was really tired, all of these things melded into a continuous semi-dream of fantastic recollection: dining on a proper meal with the lady of his dream world, then strolling with her along the Lindenstrasse with its fine buildings, treed pavements and modern tramway running down the middle. Home … Often, the young woman would segue, phantom-like, into his father, who would hold him by the hand on the same street even as he became a young boy again, then lead him along that path beside the Weichsel where he was suddenly in his early teens, fishing rods in canvas cover slung proudly across his back, and his father carrying their small wicker basket for the catch. They would head for the spot that his father liked, upstream from the arched steel spans of the main bridge resting on piers of brown brick sunk into the riverbed. His father had taught him how to fish at that spot, and Goettner could not remember any other that they had tried. Mostly, they caught catfish and perch, but it was the elusive pike that they always hoped for though never quite managed to tempt. So good to cast into the Weichsel. So good to be with his father, waiting patiently for a bite at the end of his line, and sometimes distracted by *Der Gesellige*, the newspaper his father always brought with him in case the fishing was poor. So good to watch the firm, swirling flow of the Weichsel – an eddy here, a log or branch there – heading steadily north to the Baltic at Danzig and Elbing. Some said that the river had flooded once, hundreds of years before, but Goettner could not relate to things that might have happened such a long time ago. His life could be measured only by two decades plus a year or three, and these were the years of his dreams. *Ach*, the Weichsel …

Goettner dozed, seeing the river waters and the familiar figure of his father on the bank beneath the trees even as he drifted away from this sentry trench in the *Siegfriedstellung* that had become his new life, this forward trench with its reeking chemical toilet and shivering soldiers often filthy and wet, who smelled bad and were always hungry because there was never enough food, carried up to the line as it was in pots to arrive cool or cold and sometimes containing grains of grit if the carrying party had been forced by shellfire to crouch and quake, dropping their load in their scrambling fear and perhaps abandoning the toppled lid. Goettner dozed. He drifted away beyond the reality of these things, floating back in time to be with his father, fishing line disappearing hopefully into the wide expanse of the Weichsel as the man read his newspaper, hoping for something to boast about over a beer at the local *kneipe* near where they lived. Perhaps a pike one day …

Nettermann, too, was drifting, using skills similar to Goettner's to escape the trench, though neither knew it. The exploding shell had left him trembling and wanting to empty his bladder. He did not bother to do it. He knew the sensation to be temporary, induced by fear. It would fade in a minute. So he sat down on the duckboards instead, using the movement to hide shaking hand and trembling knee. Most men experienced something similar after such a close encounter with an artillery shell, concealing it from others as best they could. Propping his back against the trench wall, Nettermann closed his eyes, glad of the blessing that the shell had at least ended Zimmermann's tiresome goading of their replacement. Nettermann was not a man given to introspection and did not question why he himself had never been Zimmermann's target, even when new to the *zug*. He was unaware that Zimmermann had been immediately wary of his solid, steady gaze and the way in which he paused before reply, characteristics that hinted at strength – mental as well as physical. They tended to dissuade provocation.

Sitting, drifting into his twilight world, Nettermann's mind went home. His imagery was different from Goettner's. There were no fine streets where Nettermann lived, and not many trees, no fishing trips beside any river, though he had of course visited the waters of the Emscher and the Ruhr, not too far away. No, home for Nettermann meant a skyline of grim smokestacks and angled industrial roofing beyond the massed dwellings of the Krupp housing developments where he had grown up. It meant polluted skies and grimy factories like those in which his parents and brother laboured to churn out the cannons and rifles, the shells and other ammunition needed here at the front.

Only the face of Nettermann's sweetheart softened the harsh landscape of this twilight semi-dream. Only her gentle half-smile, never full but always inviting; only her tiny, upturned nose so appealing, and the almost level brow above the clear, brown eyes that saw always through his defences – all of these features framed by her glorious raven hair that he liked to think she loosened for his pleasure alone – only the face of this young woman whom Nettermann loved; only this had the power to overcome the drab starkness of the city he called home, and the miseries of the cold trench about him now.

Dozing, head resting against his cap within helmet tilted back against the trench wall, Nettermann fancied he was watching her writing one of the letters that still gave him reason to live. He could see her dressed in one of the practical, full-length working dresses she wore when she cleaned the houses of the rich. She had released her beautiful hair to flow naturally about her shoulders as she wrote to him not of the harsh realities of food shortages, weary citizens, war amputees and widows mourning in black, their fatherless children clinging. No – she was writing instead of an Essen of plenty, an Essen at peace, with larders stocked and time to walk to the market together arm in arm while she gazed lovingly into his eyes in admiration of him as her husband, her hero husband come back to her from a war that had ended in victory at last. And he revelling in the glory of that new, hard-won peace, that time with his new bride. *Ach*, how that would be, to marry his lady of Essen. How that would be, to live with her in peace for the rest of his natural days …

* * *

'So, the gap in the wire you found. You think it is here?'

It was Goettner's *kompanie* commander, face taut and strained in the light of the bunker's trench lantern.

'Yes, *Herr Hauptmann*. Just one gap ... in that particular part of the line, anyway.'

'We need to be sure. And this place where you've marked the Tommy machine gun – that location differs from what we know, from the gun we already have plotted. Here.' He tapped the map with the tip of a pencil.

'Well, maybe they have moved it, *Herr Hauptmann*. Or perhaps there is a second gun. And another gunner, too.'

The *hauptmann* looked up sharply from the map he was studying. It was set on the table beside Goettner's sketch for comparison. He looked directly into his *oberleutnant's* eyes, assessing tone and seeming to wonder momentarily if there had been any attempt at sarcasm. But Goettner was merely stating things as he saw them, and the *Herr Hauptmann* knew all about the difficulties of making sketches at night without a torch or any other source of proper light, using only the reflection of a watery moon filtered by heavy mist hanging damply over the battlefield. The mist could be a friend to muffle the sound of close-in reconnaissance, but it could also be the enemy of any attempt at unlit sketching. Last night it had been the latter as Goettner attempted to draw in darkness what could not be seen but only guessed at during a pause in their crawl along the edge of the British entanglements.

Now, during this debrief in front of his *hauptmann*, Goettner's mind went back across the cold expanse of no man's land to the British wire ...

They had frozen into instant, terrified immobility when that machine gun – the one in question – had opened up without warning from a point ten to fifteen metres behind the last man in the silently crawling line of five.

All had hugged the wet, crunchy coldness of the snow. All had held their faces sideways to it while the British weapon belched death into the darkness behind them: two long bursts of perhaps three or four seconds each – a seeming age – the muzzle flash clearly visible beyond the wire in the split-second before all buried their faces in the snow and waited. Firing at what? God alone knew. Just firing, and an enemy machine gun so close and positioned where none was expected, was enough to make any man foul his pants and bellow out his fear.

None did.

When the abominably noisy stammer of the gun ceased, all in the patrol remained silent and still, waiting for Goettner's instruction. The seconds ticked by – three, four, five, six … Through the darkness came low voices, just two, speaking briefly in English that Goettner could not understand. He judged them to be fifteen to twenty metres away, for his patrol was quite a bit past the gun emplacement, and wire defences here, like their own, were deep. Then came the report of a single shot – sharply loud – splitting the silence again and causing each of the five to give a nervous start as they lay there, immobile, on the snowy ground. The shot came from the same point in the enemy line, but its sound was flatter and not as hard as that of the chattering gun, and it was followed by a hissing sound and a trail of showering sparks climbing quickly into the night, then a pop as the flare flooded the battlefield with an eerie, silvery white glow.

Goettner had been looking behind him, over his shoulder, when that flare went up. Now, as the darkness turned suddenly to translucent, phantom-like day, he froze in his posture as would a man turned to stone, completely still and with his men similarly struck, all hoping that the trick of stillness would combine with the thick wire entanglements to conceal them from the British soldiers searching this ground, all praying that the five of them might appear to tired Tommy eyes as just five more lumpy irregularities within a landscape characterised by rocks and giant clods of earth thrown hither and thither across the ground by the shells of both sides. The flare sank slowly earthwards, swinging and turning as it dangled beneath its parachute, casting shadows upon the ground that lengthened, then shortened, then rotated in unsteady patterns, now broad, now narrow, now seguing one into another with the swinging, descending light.

Steady …! Steady …! Hold your nerve! Don't even breathe! Movement is your enemy … Movement will betray you …

Immobile, feigning petrification even as he had been caught in the awkward pose of glancing back over his shoulder, Goettner found himself able to look into Nettermann's eyes as the man hugged the snow immediately behind him. Somewhat ridiculously, Goettner experienced the urge to wink. He succumbed to it, and saw Nettermann smile grim acknowledgement just as, with a final pop and hiss, the falling flare extinguished itself and the artificial day surrendered to the dark again, silent and still in the natural manner of things …

In the bunker, Goettner's *kompanie* commander startled him out of the memory:

'All right, I accept the gun. A Lewis, you say?'

'Definitely a Lewis, *Herr Hauptmann*.'

'Okay. And the lie of the land as you describe it confirms it as being here.' He marked the assumed point of the Lewis upon the British defences where they were drawn in a thick line of red across his master map, the weapon becoming an arrow in pencil black crossed by a single, short stroke drawn through its centre. There were many of these. 'Now, the routes out and back. And the gap in the wire. Let's go over that again.'

The route out …

They had scrambled from the trench one hour after midnight, then navigated in a cautious half-crouch along one of the zig-zagging passages left clear through their own barbed wire for work just such as this, and leaving behind them the other soldiers of their *zug*, stood-to on the parapet with rifles and a machine gun ready to give covering fire if the Tommies should open up at this critical moment. But the night remained silent. Only occasional, distant small-arms fire from here and there within the line, normal and reassuring, came to their ears.

They were lightly equipped, all but one carrying pistols and only sufficient ammunition for a brief skirmish, nothing more. This was not a fighting patrol or trench raid, they would use the darkness to flee if serious trouble found them. Three of the five carried two grenades each, just in case, and the man assigned the patrol's only rifle carried that weapon in case they got trapped – God forbid – and had to pass the next day in a shell hole somewhere in no man's land, defending themselves at distance until they could attempt escape the following night.

Reaching the edge of their own entanglements, which were deep, Goettner stood up to glare suspiciously through the night toward the British trenches some six hundred metres distant. Feet planted on the cratered earth, he tested with nose, eye and ear the chill air for signs of threat, seeming as some wild creature standing stock-still in the darkness on the edge of this forest of steel wire, trench coat flowing out from under his belt with gas-mask holder clipped to it where it crossed his back, strap removed. He seemed a man unhappy with this dangerous blackness all around. He was alert for danger. Satisfied that all was well for now, he signalled with his hand that the others should stand. Then, slightly stooped and with pistol drawn, he began the long walk forward at a determinedly steady pace to close the distance to the British line. The others followed in single file, each man sure to keep the one in front always in sight. The distance between each soldier was perhaps five metres.

Sometime later – a seeming eternity to each of the five and with a mist beginning to descend over the battlefield – Goettner crouched and motioned that the others should close up. The man behind, Nettermann, passed on this signal in complete silence until Zimmermann in the rear had received it, the four shuffling forward until the group became a single body with all in easy physical contact of one another, able to use touch or grip to caution or alarm. Then, Goettner lay forward onto the ground and began to crawl forward across the thin snow, the others following.

The first defences to show themselves through the gloom were the thick trusses of wood and steel that supported the British wire, principally in the form of connected crosses. There were many of these, braced and joined one to another by horizontal beams, and cocooned with the vicious barbs of the wire itself, difficult to see in the blackness. These framed, braced, connected boxes of wire lay on their sides, edge to edge across the land as a formidable obstacle to assault, with others stacked behind so that they were deep and very strong against even artillery fire, for an exploding shell could only toss, twist or upend, and the elongated boxes with their cruel barbs would then topple back upon themselves, impenetrable still.

Arriving within sight of this barricade, Goettner lowered himself fully upon his stomach, readying himself to leopard-crawl using elbows and knees. The patrol would move in this way along the edge of the entanglements across the cold ground. In careful silence, he withdrew from within his trench coat a pencil-thin sprig, green and still as flexible as it had been when he had plucked it from the remnants of a tree behind their own trenches. It was about fifty centimetres long. Holding this ready in his left hand, and with pistol clenched tightly in his right, he began to move, slithering awkwardly, deliberately and steadily forward to begin his search, positioning himself as far as possible from the wire without losing sight of its outermost trusses. It was slow work, physically tiring because of the need for stealth, and very dangerous. From time to time, whenever he thought the shape and angle of the trusses indicated possibility of a deliberate gap to allow Tommy movement to and from their trenches, he probed the air in front of and to the side of his body delicately with his stick, holding it between thumb and forefinger to achieve greatest sensitivity, arm raised to shoulder height, searching for any invisible line of taut, thin wire rigged to warn the defenders by means of tin cans or bottles tied to it. The British did not usually rig their wire with explosives, which were difficult to disarm when embarking on their own patrols – protection of their access and exit gaps by sound alone was good enough for them. To Goettner, whether the wire was rigged with explosive or tin can was really of incidental interest only, for the machine gun covering it would be as deadly as any booby-trap. His thin green branch probing delicately forward in the darkness had as its sole purpose location of any such wire – he would feel its resistance and then skirt around it, the probability of a gap in the entanglements confirmed.

The patrol of five moved perhaps a hundred and fifty metres in this fashion; a difficult, tiring, dangerous crawl with their enemy very close by as they slept in their trenches, sentries posted. Goettner and his men prayed that these sentries, often positioned in shallow saps slightly forward of the line, might similarly be dozing, for those saps would be considerably closer to the patrol than the trench itself. Over the ground they crawled, rocks and pebbles poking and biting into elbow and knee, and the snowy earth so cold and damp beneath them. That hundred and fifty metres took over an hour to cover. Then, Goettner's twig supplied the warning he was looking for, coming up against something tautly invisible and less resistant than barbed wire: a thin Tommy line of alarm strung tight across the black night. He paused, peering through the darkness, trying to distinguish the wooden and steel stakes one from another. There were so many that he couldn't be sure of any gap. No matter, his dedication to this task was not so great that he was going to dare any closer approach to those entanglements. He fished in his trench coat for pencil and sketching pad, a small square of hardboard with paper glued on, already marked with the principal rises and depressions of the land and with a thick line across it as the forward British trench. In the dark, difficult night Goettner squinted at this paper and drew upon it an X as accurately as he could …

Now, in the bunker while his debrief continued, the hardboard square with its pencilled record of what Goettner had found was lit by a trench lantern serving also as paperweight for the *Herr Hauptmann's* map of this section of the battlefield. He had spread it upon the trestle table for comparison and plotting. The lamp provided a yellowish, flickering light that seemed to Goettner like a reflection of his own unsteady nerves. He bore down on them, determined to project an image of calm control. The tension of the patrol had not yet subsided.

His *hauptmann* said:

'So you think we should adjust your mark a bit. You reckon the gap was closer to the dead horses. Here?'

'Yes. It was very dark, but we caught the stink. So probably a little bit further this way.' Goettner indicated, using the map. 'Where you have the gun is right, but we should adjust the point of the gap.'

The *kompanie* commander nodded, stooping over his map to mark it.

'And the machine gun opened up after that?'

'Yes. We were ten or fifteen metres further along. It fired from behind, but not at us. It was random.'

Again the *hauptmann* nodded, this time massaging his chin in thought. 'Yes, we heard that, of course. And we tried for direction because there were no other guns firing. But it's difficult at night, as you know.'

Goettner knew.

'And the Tommy patrol?'

The Tommy patrol …

In a mist thick enough to swirl and eddy about the five Germans who had by then put a few extra metres of distance between them and the machine gun, they were preparing to start back to their own line when they heard a sound, faint at first but growing quickly louder. With alarm, all recognised it for what it was: the approach of British soldiers, their boots picking a way over rocks and the thin snow covering the land, eager to get back to their trenches and tea, their task over, whatever it might have been.

What to do? Scramble away from the direction of the approaching English? Make a dash for it? Open fire? Or bury your head in the damp earth and simply pray for an end to everything?

There was no need to decide. The four who were with him had rehearsed in Pronville the drill for this situation and knew precisely what to do. Without any instruction, all lay completely flat and as still in the thick mist as they had been beneath the glaring illumination of the flare. They would open fire only if discovered. Behind him, Goettner knew that someone would have placed upon Winkler's arm or leg a tight grip of cautioning reassurance – Zimmermann, most likely. Though by nature a bully, Zimmermann could be counted on to look after the new men whenever there was danger.

The Tommies passed by behind the five, unseen in the mist and heading for their gap. The five heard one man curse as he stumbled, and they heard, too, the British patrol stop to locate the entry point when they reached the defences, and negotiate a careful passage around the wire with its tin cans. This would be the appointed hour of the patrol's return, a time pre-designated so that none in their line would open fire at the sound of the returning men's footfalls. Goettner suspected that the hour would be varied each night, but he made a note of it anyway: zero-four-fifteen. It might be useful, one never knew …

In the debriefing bunker, the *hauptmann* repeated his question:

'Goettner, the Tommy patrol?'

Goettner dragged his mind back to the present.

'*Jawohl, Herr Hauptmann.* Yes, five or six men. We did not see them in the mist. Back from a reconnaissance of their own, probably.'

The *kompanie* commander stood up from where he had had his arms braced either side of the map. He stretched, seeming to examine Goettner's face. He made no comment of what he might have seen there, offering instead a brief, tight smile of praise. 'You did well,' he said. 'A good patrol. Well done.'

Goettner understood what he meant. If there had been a skirmish, then the British would have known that the gap in their wire had been discovered. They would close it up and open another in a different part of the line. But there had been no skirmish, and therefore they did not know, and that was a good thing. It would help the attack, when it came. It made worthwhile the whole patrol and all its associated risk and danger.

The *hauptmann* led the way out of the bunker, Goettner following. Outside, standing on the duckboards in the thin light of a dawn just past, everybody bar sentries already stood down for the routine of another day, the commander lit two cigarettes and passed one to his *oberleutnant*. They smoked, the aroma of tobacco helping to disguise the smell of stale sweat and a latrine further up the trench. A couple of hundred metres away, a shell struck the ground close to the line, forcing a plume of earth many metres into the air before the clods and rocks fell back in a shower of dirt and filth. Smoke drifted away in the breeze above the parapet. The shell had been fired by one of the heavier British artillery pieces, close enough to make the officers flinch instinctively, but not so close that they tested the air, or weighed the probability of further shelling. They listened for screaming. None. Nobody wounded. The *hauptmann* drew on his cigarette and said:

'There are orders, Goettner. From Regiment. The ones we've been expecting. Came through just before you got back. Your *zug* is to be withdrawn from the line. This afternoon. You are to march back to Pronville to link up with that new tank unit we spoke about. To begin training.'

The first soft flakes of an early January snowfall drifted down upon the trench. Goettner was thinking about the thin, patchy snow over which the patrol had walked and crawled: it was not thick enough to betray their passage back from the machine gun and gap. Still, any new fall would help complete concealment.

'Goettner …?'

'Yes, *Herr Hauptmann.* The tanks. I'm sorry. Back to Pronville this afternoon. I will tell the men.'

'Now listen, Goettner, you must make good use of this time. You have been through a lot. More than most, and almost continuously since the beginning. You're still alive ... So, you'll be better off in the rear working up with the tanks for a time. And resting. Out of the line, I mean. Safe for a while.'

Goettner watched his *hauptmann*, who seemed to be examining him more closely than this conversation and mutual enjoyment of a cigarette called for. He said nothing.

'This place is different from Russia, Goettner.' The *hauptmann* drew on his cigarette. 'France ... it's very, very different. It's worse, and I think it's going to deteriorate further in the coming months. Something big is building. All these new regiments arriving from the east. Artillery as well. Now tanks. And they're stockpiling shells to the rear. There's going to be a big push from our side. I think it will happen before the Americans plug more divisions into the line. They have two now, but Intelligence reckons another million men will arrive through the ports by August. That's right, Goettner – one million, and all of them fresh ... They have no idea what they're in for. But we will have to attack before they can organise. So, when that attack comes – ours – they're going to put the tanks right at the front, you can be sure of that. And you with them ...'

Goettner kept his silence, wondering. Away to his right, another shell burst. Different place. Harassing fire only. Again, no screaming – nothing to worry about.

'Use your time well,' continued the *hauptmann*. 'Rest, but co-operate as much as possible with whatever people you find manning the tanks. Work with them. Put aside any differences that crop up. Arguments, inter-unit squabbles. That sort of thing. Nobody knows how to use these machines properly. The tanks. If you are to survive this war, you should try to be the first to work that out.'

The *hauptmann* chuckled grimly and quietly at his own joke, finished his cigarette and tossed its remains onto the duckboards, where the little cylinder of paper and leaf rolled to the edge of the wood and dropped into a small puddle of melted snow and muck, extinguishing itself with a hiss.

'Report to me here at the bunker when you're ready to leave. There are some letters you can carry back with you. I'd like to say goodbye, too.'

CHAPTER FIVE

'**P**eake! Zero-seven-hundred, Seventh Battalion.'

'Yes, Staff! Which regiment, Staff?' Peake's reply was strongly delivered. It was expected of him. He was standing rigidly to attention, formed up with the rest of his platoon before the staff sergeant.

'The Lancashires, lad! Have I read out any others?' There was an impatient edge to the staff sergeant's voice.

'No, Staff!'

'Well, pull your head through then, Peake! Wake up, man!'

'Yes, Staff!'

Peake took the rebuke lightly. He liked the staff sergeant, a tough, experienced soldier who had been posted to a training battalion after contracting trench fever at the front. When he'd begun to sweat and shiver in the line, they'd put him in a dugout to lie down a while, throwing a blanket over him and hoping for the best, but the staff's temperature had risen alarmingly quickly. After just one day the man was wracked with eye and muscle pain, drenched with sweat and exhibiting a pulse that had frightened even the company medical orderly when they'd called him. Stretchering him to the rear, they found space in a lorry packed with battle casualties heading for a military hospital rear of the lines. He was in that hospital for two weeks. When he was eventually discharged, the staff was so weakened by the loss of more than a stone in weight that they'd posted him to a training role, first at the base depot in Étaples, later Rouen where he now trained draftees arriving from England, Peake and the rest among them. The idea was that he fully regain his strength there.

All things considered, Peake reckoned the staff had been hard but fair on the new arrivals, organising, drilling and instructing them in the manner of Brocton, but also sharing with them the hardships of field exercises, something he was not obliged to do. He had dug in with the trainees in the sleet, the drizzle and the snow, sleeping rough and cold alongside them in the mud and slush on exercises, where he'd assumed the role of platoon sergeant or lieutenant as required, to make the training realistic. This had earned him the respect of all. More, he had gone to great lengths to pass on important practical pointers and tips he'd learned the hard way before he had fallen ill, anything at all that he thought might help preserve the lives of these draftees. The whole idea was to stay alive, the staff had repeatedly told them. In fact, it was the only idea. Their training under him lasted for twelve weeks through the worst of winter.

The posting order the staff sergeant was reading out signalled an end to things, an end to the training. An end – and a beginning. It was time to fight. Peake's draft was being broken up, a random scattering dictated by casualties at the front. Replacements were being sent to whichever units were most in need. For the three months since their arrival by troopship at Le Havre, Peake and the others had nervously anticipated this day. Right now, it was the Lancashire Fusiliers that needed men. A full half dozen of the Lancashires' many battalions were currently in the thick of the stalemated front, the past week costing more than a hundred soldiers dead or admitted to field hospitals behind the line. Replacements were urgently needed in this month of February 1918.

The Lancashire Fusiliers …

To even think of that name sent a wave of sharpened anticipation surging through Peake, for the regiment bore a battle history going back two hundred years. All his senses experienced a heightened level of awareness, as if a small electric charge had suddenly shocked each and every nerve to maximum activity, provoking a new and strange response in him, a surge of emotion stronger than any other he had known, surpassing even the ever-present pull of Christine's memory. Fear was certainly a part of it, but mostly it was knowledge of being on the threshold of something greater than the individual, something of real consequence. Peake knew that he was about to enter a new world over which he had no control, something quite rare in his young life. He could recall a similar but less intense impression seven months before, on that summer's day when he had reported, raw and unsure of himself, to the depot on the fringe of Camden for transport to Brocton. Yet this new sensation at Rouen was many times keener and more acute, manifesting in racing heart, shallow breathing and a mind alert to all things. He felt as a coiled spring waiting for release, and this feeling remained with him while he gathered and checked his gear, donned webbing and service cap, shrugged on his pack with steel helmet strapped behind, shouldered his rifle and formed up with the others for the march to the railway station.

The day was cold, the sky offering only hints of blue through a spreading sheet of grey holding promise of rain to come. Yet they were singing:

If you want to find the private
I know where he is
I know where he is
I know where he is
If you want to find the private
I know where he is
He's hanging on the old barbed wire …

The staff sergeant led the men in song. Marching with them, he was in fact the only one with experience of anybody hanging dead on any wire, but he nevertheless encouraged a robust rendering of the ditty's bitterly cynical chant, for he understood that the words would make all feel as veterans of battle, something that they would become soon enough. Singing would help the transition, he knew. The staff sergeant himself would board the train with his conscripts and accompany all as far as the front's railhead. Recently assessed fit enough by the doctors to return to the trenches, he was leaving Rouen for good, and after the journey by rail he would leave his trainees, too, and make his way alone from there to re-join his particular unit.

In the carriage, when all had boarded, the staff made himself available for conversation:

'Glad that little lot's behind us, eh, Peake? No more drill and playing soldiers now. Very different at the front. But don't you worry, Peake old son, because all that practice's been good – all those exercises we did. They were as close to what goes on in the line as we could make 'em. Not like that nonsense they dealt out at Étaples.'

'You were there, Staff?'

'Aye, Peake, I was. Sent me there for a while straight out of hospital. To retrain a bit. 'Orrible place. Very 'ard. Things were overdone in Étaples. I was glad when my posting order came. To Rouen. Was only there a few weeks.'

Another man in the railway coach moved to join the two. He was 'Quiz' Earnshaw, the moniker awarded for his endless stream of questions. Earnshaw was a burly individual of nondescript height. Possessed of eager manner and analytical mind, quick eyes beneath a shock of black hair made plain his underlying intelligence: many thought that he should have tried for a commission. Certainly he had a knack of correctly assessing situations in the moment, but Earnshaw professed contentment as a private soldier. "Don't want the responsibility", he would explain with a shrug. Earnshaw's questions were sometimes an irritant to his fellows, but none needed to ask anything at all when he was present.

Peake eyed the man's approach and waited for the inevitable enquiry.

'So wot 'appened exactly, Staff?' Earnshaw was not Cockney, but his manner of speaking sometimes suggested that he might have been.

'There was a revolt, Earnshaw. A mutiny.'

A pause. Perhaps the staff sergeant was remembering. It was difficult to tell. Others moved closer to join the conversation. Somebody said:

'People can be shot for that.'

'Aye, lad,' countered the staff. 'And they were, too. Two were shot.'

The staff sergeant's growing audience stood dumbfounded. They had not heard of the deaths. British soldiers executing their own? Surely not!

'Were you a part of it?' Earnshaw again.

'What? Étaples? The mutiny? No. But I was there. I wasn't involved, but I was there. An' I agreed with the reasons for it.'

There was another pause. It was filled with the rhythmic clattering of the wheels of their carriage passing over the rails, the soldiers swaying in unison with gently rocking passage of the train.

'Well, come on, Staff! Don't leave us dangling!'

'Just count yourselves lucky you were still on the water from Blighty when they closed the place an' diverted you to Le Havre,' said the staff sergeant, appearing to weigh his options. Should he leave it there? In training, definitely. But now, perhaps not, for all in the carriage shared the burden of heading for the reality of battle itself. The personal reserve demanded by rank could ease a degree or two, now. But not too much. He should still be careful. He continued:

'There was a scuffle,' he explained. 'With the Redcaps. A soldier'd been unfairly disciplined – or that was the feeling, at any rate. He'd been AWOL, but not in the sense you'd think. Didn't desert, or anything like that. He'd entered a part of the town that was off-limits, looking for an officer's woman. A prostitute. Fancied a bit of classy tail, I'd say. So 'e was arrested for being in a part of town banned to 'is type. Fair enough in a way, but the problem was that 'e was over-punished. And some thought it unfair that parts of the town should be kept apart for the officers, especially when most of 'em were there in a training role. They'd never been to the front, those officers, whereas quite a few of the NCOs at Étaples had been, and they'd been wounded for their efforts, too. Anyway, a mob gathered – angry and looking for a fight – and the Redcaps couldn't control it. Shots were fired. One man was killed – a Gordon – and so the game was on. It became a riot.'

The staff had quite an audience now. All within earshot had moved closer. They had heard about Étaples, but this was the first time they had encountered an eye-witness account, and none had heard of the executions.

'It wasn't about the scuffle, you understand. Or the Gordon. It was because the whole camp was fed up with the rotten treatment being dealt out. Too much unnecessary punishment. Bad grub an' not enough of it. Those of us who'd been at the front an' in the line itself, those who'd been wounded and sent to Étaples for retraining an' to re-gather their nerve – we especially 'ad 'ad enough, because none of the instructors 'ad ever seen action. Canaries all.'

The staff paused, remembering, weighing his young audience still inexperienced and unbloodied. He had to decide whether to continue. He did:

'Thousands refused to obey orders. Thousands. They simply put down their rifles, like a strike. They downed tools, so to speak. Wouldn't carry their weapons an' refused to train. There were massed gatherings in the town – men abandoned the depot and went walking. The brass brought in troops from outside to regain control. Took 'em a week to do it. A whole week before things were more or less back to normal. It was chaos. Things were still not right a month later. They closed the place, eventually.'

'Punishment?' This was Quiz again.

'One man got the firing squad. They shot him – executed him. An' the instructors made sure that the whole camp knew about it. His charge sheet an' sentence were read out at muster. Thirteen more got jail time. Ten years, most of 'em. Another thirty-three got Number One field – strapped to a wagon wheel for two hours a day in full view of all, an' 'ard labour for the rest of the time. They spread the wagons around the camp so that everybody could see the punished upon the wheel.'

The group waited for more, a sense of awe hanging over them. They waited for Earnshaw's next question, but the staff's tale silenced even him. The carriage lapsed into silence, the train rumbling steadily on towards the front.

Étaples … Peake considered this revelation of executions and field punishment. The facts were shocking to him. Obviously savage and brutal, the repercussions of mutiny had nevertheless proved effective, the whole ugly episode neatly tied off by the brass hats closing the depot and dispersing all within. Peake felt troubled by the story. It didn't fit with his view of a war which, despite arduous training and rigid discipline – perhaps even because of it – he still visualised as a glorious struggle of right versus wrong, good versus evil, fought by a British Army united with its allies in the single goal of giving Germany a sound and solid thrashing. Peake didn't like to consider the possibilities of flawed leadership or unhappy rebellion, and he found himself wondering whether the recent rise in pay for private soldiers might have been prompted by this mutiny; something to pacify and assuage, perhaps …

He moved away to a window, lit a cigarette. It was a habit he had picked up at Rouen. Pulling on the lighted tobacco and inhaling, he watched the passing countryside: pastures with animals huddled in groups against the chill, and fields bracing for the plough a few weeks from then.

For Peake, this story of Étaples was on the same level as the moment he had stumbled upon Sergeant Winterman weeping silently and alone upon the Stafford bench. That had been a shock, too. Sergeants were the backbone of the army, and infantry sergeants the backbone's backbone: tough, experienced men able to inspire others under the most extreme conditions. The sight of Winterman – his senior at school – weeping while on leave from France, had been deeply disturbing to Peake.

And now the mutiny at Étaples …

The train moved on, and with it Peake's thoughts. Christine was never far away. He had so many memories of their time together, and these drifted in and out of the urgencies of his new life like the thread of a tapestry still under weave. She was never far from his mind, no matter what he was doing. He could see and feel her face, her hair, her hands, her body. He could feel her at the door to Penelope Brooke's, clinging tightly to him in the agony of farewell. He loved her. His need for her was at times a physical ache, an urgent pull at him so strong that he sometimes thanked God for the army's rigid discipline – firing squads and Number One field punishment – for without it he would surely have been tempted to desert … Peake dragged his mind back to the present, to the train, wondering at its very slow speed. Rail routes from France's ports to the front were in continuous use day and night, with very long trains of munitions, food, supplies, replacements and wounded moving up and down the lines in both directions, one every twenty minutes in an unceasing cycle of replenishment and evacuation. Peake understood all that, but still he found their slow rate of progress unnerving. It hinted somehow at the scale of things to come … Anyway, he thought, better to place your faith in the system, snail trains or no. Better to keep faith with this vast machine that was the British Army and forget about Étaples and weeping sergeants. Better to forgive John Winterman; better to allow the man his private moment of weakness.

Pull your brain through, lad, and stay focused …

He wondered what Christine was doing.

The train reached Méricourt, the men disembarking as a sea of khaki. They were a blur of trench coats strapped about with webbing and pouches beneath young faces anxious under visor and cap, indistinguishable one from another. Arranging themselves, they were as a mass of uniformity varying only in individual height, any difference accentuated by the protruding steel barrels of many hundreds of rifles slung upon many hundreds of shoulders. Now, their chorus was no longer the verse of ribald disdain for dangling death, but rather the ringing and crunching of a thousand hobnail boots traversing concrete and gravel, the shouldered pack of each man containing all permissible possessions necessary for the trench, and the bowl of his steel helmet strapped centrally behind. Dangling from the belt of each was a gas mask in canvas container, a water bottle and a scabbarded bayonet. Nothing more.

Military Police – Redcaps – received these soldiers fresh from the train. They worked with a handful of NCOs from the destination battalions, veterans possessed of the calm authority born of battle. Watching their replacements so neatly turned out for arrival, they knew that all spit-and-polish correctness would vanish soon enough. Without ceremony they herded the men to prearranged assembly points for the march to the different unit transports – London 'Old Bills', mostly: double-deckers pressed into service and repainted army drab to cover the bright red of peace. There were field trains, too, depending on sector – to carry the lucky to points just behind the gun lines, where sat artillery supporting the defence. Ultimately, though, all would march the final miles to their designated battalions and the trenches themselves.

Everywhere in this sea of khaki, there were shouted farewells and the jocularity of the unbloodied:

'See yer, Ronnie!'

'Good luck, mate!'

'An' you! Pints in Germany when we get there!'

'A knock-shop'd do me better!'

'Blimey! I'll tell yer muvver.'

'Yer'll be lucky – she finks I dunno what ter do wiv it!'

'See you in Blighty, then. When it's all over!'

The draft was breaking up.

The tank, *their* tank, was stuck. Its driver had inadvertently allowed his machine to lurch into a particularly large shell crater, and could not now get it to climb out. The soldiers whose job it was to protect the tank gained some amusement watching him try, one of his mount's tracks slipping uselessly in the mud of the pit while the other, finding purchase somewhere, repeatedly heaved its own half of the huge machine up the side of the depression until gravity threatened to overturn everything, forcing the driver to give up and allow the vehicle to slide heavily back to the bottom. Now, it sat uselessly like some giant, angular steel turtle within the crater that had trapped it, its commander looking helplessly around from his perch on top – no turret – until he spotted the officer, the *Herr Major* overseeing the exercise. The tank commander raised his arms, crossing them repeatedly in a gesture of impossibility that led the officer to call a halt to the mock advance, his order passed on along the extended line of soldiers and tanks by whistle-blasts and hand signals.

The shouts of officers and NCOs still exhorting their men to hold formation within the forward movement of the exercise died away. The drivers of the other tanks switched off their motors. On the ground, soldiers shouldered their rifles or placed butts upon the earth, holding barrels loosely within clasped hands and looking about, resigned to the hold-up. Silence returned to the shell-pitted field they were crossing, broken only by birdsong that could once again be heard as a bright counterpoise to the constant, perpetually unhappy rumble of artillery fire reaching them from the distant frontlines.

The soldiers moved to rest while the problem was overcome. They gathered in small groups, some swigging from water bottles, others chatting or cracking jokes. Most removed their coalscuttle helmets and set them aside. All lit up, cigarettes mostly, but with a pipe here and there. They wondered what the next change in tactics might be.

The battlefield over which the tanks – a detachment of five machines – were labouring had been the site of deadly contest some months prior, but no enemy guns were firing on it now. There were no angry bullets or exploding shells, no British soldiers resisting the advance. Instead, the tanks and supporting infantry were exercising peacefully and undisturbed on abandoned fields and pastures outside Cambrai, trying to develop usable tactics for this latest wonder-weapon, the tank.

The soldiers had been exercising for some hours, and they were glad of the rest. Nettermann, spotting a patch of grass, moved across to it and, after setting his rifle upon some carefully selected clumps to keep it free of dirt, sat down. He did not bother to shed small pack or webbing, nor did he remove his helmet. The late winter's day was cool, so sweat did not dictate either effort. He simply sat down fully equipped, lit up and inhaled deeply, savouring the tobacco smoke as it reached his lungs. Looking about, he spotted

Oberleutnant Goettner moving across to join the *Herr Major* beside the tank within the crater.

It was a monster, that tank, a huge machine newly delivered from Germany. Though the British and French had been using their own armour in offensives for more than a year, this German machine was new to the war. It was bigger than its counterparts – almost half again as big in volume and with a greater vertical dimension twice the height of an average man – and it was dramatically different in both configuration and layout: a rectangular box of armour plate bolted together and fitted with angular, full-height prows at front and rear, imparting a boat-like appearance. At the front was the tank's main gun – a centrally mounted, forward facing 57-millimetre cannon – and at the back two heavy machine guns jutting through angular armour plate. Each of these weapons was manned by two soldiers. The remainder of the crew – commander, driver, two mechanics for the engine and soldiers to man standard machine guns poking out through slots in the armoured sides – contributed to a total complement of more than fifteen. Nobody was yet sure of the crew's optimum number; the officers were still trying to work that out, but they thought it should be not less than fifteen. Despite its height, the beast rested on caterpillar tracks situated low upon the chassis rather than rotating about the circumference of its profile in the manner of the British design. This made the German tank appear to waddle like a duck when it moved, especially during the turn.

Nettermann smoked steadily under the grey overcast of the day, watching the driver and his commander clamber down from atop the tank. Both men wore asbestos suits as protection against the heat of the engine immediately below their seats. After a while, the rest of the crew emerged, too. They knew it would take time to get the brute out of the hole – another tank would be needed. All removed the chainmail they wore to protect their faces against steel splinters flying about the tank's interior after an enemy strike, and they wiped away perspiration. Some moved a little distance away to rest. All opened tunic buttons to cool off, for it was hot inside that tank. The month was March and spring was threatening to arrive early. Well, if they were feeling the heat on a day as cool as this one, then God alone knew how the inside of that machine would feel in mid-summer. The crew would surely bake. They stood about or sat and, like the infantry, lit up.

Nettermann watched, and smoked, and considered things. The five tanks with which they were exercising comprised four British machines – captured – and this new delivery from the Ruhr. The idea was that their *zug* – Goettner's *zug* – would provide protection and support during the assault, covering the tanks' blind spots and killing anyone brave enough to try to get close-in and push a grenade through gun-slot or under the tracks. The *zug* would also look to suppress any fire from field guns sited in the trenches, for armour plate was proof only against small-arms, and any hit from a light artillery piece would certainly kill crewmen within, though not all. Tanks could generally survive a single hit, but two spelled the end of the contest. The generals believed that, protected by a small number of well-trained infantry, the tanks should be able to breach the wire when they reached the enemy trenches, trampling it underneath to clear a path for the main body of men following up.

The problem, though, was the shell craters …

Footfalls approaching from behind him broke into Nettermann's train of thought. It was Zimmermann, his large frame stooped, rifle carried at the slope and a cigarette already lit and clamped firmly between thin lips. Probably looking for company, Nettermann thought – the man was too loud and aggressive to make any real friends. Uncompanionable and looked upon by none in the *zug* as a chum, Zimmermann often sought out Nettermann when he needed someone to talk to. Now, arriving, the man sank to the ground and placed his rifle beside him, removing his helmet to reveal gingery hair that seemed to accentuate the shrewd, piercing eyes. He appeared tall and solid even when sitting down.

Neither man spoke for some minutes. They smoked, each in a world of private thought, surveying without really seeing the activity around the crater with its stranded tank and soldiers standing about. The major was despatching a man to summon one of the British machines halted some two hundred metres distant, its crew also at rest and lighting up. When the man had left, the officers, too, lit cigarettes and moved a little distance away from the problem to smoke.

'We need to bring these monsters closer in … closer together, don't you think?' The suggestion was Zimmermann's. 'It would concentrate the firepower a bit more.'

Nettermann thought awhile, silent in his usual way while he considered. After some time he said:

'The problem is we don't have enough of them.'

Nettermann watched Zimmermann. The man expected elaboration, but he did not feel like explaining to him that to close up the tanks would only make it easier for the Tommies to get a field piece into position and score hits. He drew on his cigarette instead, hoping that Zimmermann would permit him to drift back to his sweetheart with that wonderful half-smile of hers. How tight he would clasp her to him when next they were together! Taking a deep pull, he held the smoke for a few seconds then exhaled, trying for a smoke ring. It was a trick that he had never quite mastered, and the circle in the air eluded him once again. Eventually he said: 'Plus, we have so few, Zimmermann. We have to spread them out to make gaps in the wire far enough apart to give everyone a chance to get through. The rest of the battalion following behind are going to need big distances between those gaps. Too close together and it'll be slaughter – they'll be perfectly channelled for the Tommy gunners.'

'Well, I don't like it. And I don't like the pace of the advance – it's too slow.' Zimmermann felt the need to expand when Nettermann kept his silence: 'That is, when the damned things aren't stuck in craters … I can walk faster than our drivers can force those tanks to move.'

'Well, of course you can, but you'd be killed doing it. We'll have a better chance grouped behind and around the armour.'

Zimmermann grunted, unable to counter Nettermann's logic.

'Anyway, I don't like it,' Zimmermann repeated, shaking his head in emphasis. 'I don't like the slow advance. And rifles – there are too many carrying them. I don't like that either.'

'The spade, then?'

'Yes. Or the club. And lots of grenades. Like we used to do it in Russia – move up behind the barrage, throw the bombs and just move it. Get the job done. A rifle is fine for defending the line, but a spade is better for attacking.'

Nettermann said nothing, remembering and trying to forget all at the same time. The attack did something to a man's mind, and that was a fact. You killed in a frenzy of self-preservation, without thinking, and every time you did it something in you changed a little more. Something became a little darker and slipped a little further into the void. And what Zimmermann had said was true. The entrenching tool was a good weapon to have when storming a trench. It was light and easy to swing this way and that – no need to repeatedly chamber a fresh round, or heave on a bayonet stuck fast between somebody's ribs or jammed in their spine or pelvis. Just leave your rifle behind, take the spade and simply swing and hack your way through. The edge of that tool could cleave a chest just as easily as it could smash a face with the flat. Both actions disabled a man as effectively as any bullet, and you could switch targets very quickly. A club was almost as effective, too – many preferred it. He changed the subject:

'Why aren't you away baiting our replacement?'

'New Man? Don't need to. Or not as much anymore. He did okay on that reconnaissance, I thought. I've eased up on him a bit.' Zimmermann grinned, cigarette dangling from one side of his mouth.

'Yes, Winkler did all right,' Nettermann agreed, choosing to use the replacement's name. 'A close one, that, when those Tommies returned. Very glad he held his nerve … But why do you do it, Zimmermann – bait the replacements? Did somebody do it to you? Older brother, perhaps?'

Zimmermann pulled on his cigarette a while, thinking. Nettermann did not push the point. More than a minute later, when the cigarette was almost finished, Zimmermann said:

'My father.' Examining the butt between his fingers and deciding that it was finished, he flicked it away into the field, then began to scratch at his leg through the cloth of his uniform. 'My father,' he repeated. 'He did it to me. He used to ride me all the time. Told me once he thought it would make me stronger. "You need to toughen up, lad," he used to say. "You're not tough-fibred enough." There were beatings too.'

The honesty of this answer did not call for a direct response. It was too open, too genuine, too raw. Changing tack, Nettermann asked:

'Where're the others?'

'Bauer and König? Over there. The new fellow too, the replacement.' Zimmermann pointed to a tank on the far side of the machine summoned by the runner for the tow, whose crew had restarted their mount. Fumes belched darkly from exhausts, melding into a stream of grey haze as the driver gunned his motor. With a lurch the tank began to lumber awkwardly forward across the uneven ground to help, tracks flicking clods of mud this way and that behind its passage. The smell of hot fuel and burnt oil spread out from the lumbering monster across the torn-up heath to reach even these two in conversation.

A deep, shuddering sigh came upon Nettermann suddenly. He was not sure of the reason, and to cover it he said:

'I'm glad Schäffer's back,'

'Ja. A useful man to have around, that Schäffer. Steady nerves. We should share a bottle with him tonight. He still has some that he brought back with him from Regiment. Scrounged.'

'All right.'

'Just look at Goettner over there. Always busy, that one.'

Zimmermann jerked his chin in the direction of the stranded tank. Their *oberleutnant* had found some stout branches of wood from among the detritus of the old battlefield, and dragged them across to the shell hole. He was busy forcing the pieces under the fronts of the tracks, ready for when the tow arrived. Two of the crew were using spades to help him do it.

'I swear, I don't know where he gets the energy.'

'Also a good man,' offered Nettermann. 'Really cares about us, I think. And brave with it. Quite a rarity, the *Herr Oberleutnant*. We're lucky to have him instead of some of the other officers I could name. Uses his head and leads from the front, too. I trust him.'

Zimmermann nodded agreement. He lit fresh cigarettes, and the two smoked in peace, the conversation petering out.

In London, Wainwright bought a newspaper on his way home, but there was nothing on the front page to warrant pause at The Duke for further study. The world had dragged itself through another day of war with neither advance nor withdrawal, nor new offensive significant enough to make headlines. Instead there were summaries of scattered, smaller battles – skirmishes really – here and there along the Western Front, and of gains against the Turks in the Middle East. There was a separate piece about diminishing Allied shipping losses – good news, but detailed reading of it could wait.

Wainwright felt irritable as he walked. He could not identify the underlying reason, so he exercised caution as he entered his street, for it certainly had nothing to do with his wife and he did not wish to upset her. She hurried to greet him as soon as she heard him open the door, a light kiss of welcome upon her lips. She took his coat to hang.

'Penelope's here,' she announced brightly. 'There's fresh tea and toast.'

In the sitting-room, he helped himself to a slice, buttering it while his wife poured. There was rumour that butter and other staples would soon be rationed, but it had not yet happened. They sat, Wainwright chewing steadily, eyebrows raised in query while he glanced from Penelope Brooke to his wife, and back again. He strove for calm appearance.

'Penelope's brought news, dear. Of Simon. It's from Christine. She's received a postcard.'

Wainwright grunted, not impolitely and partly out of jealousy for this young woman – Christine – whom he had never met and who had taken precedence over him and his wife as far as their ward was concerned … they had yet to receive any news from him. Penelope rose from her chair to pass the card across.

'It's good of her to share it.' Wainwright's voice was sincere as he examined the missive from France.

'Well, she feels it should be shared,' Penelope interjected. 'And it's good news, really.' She sipped her tea. 'Christine would like to meet you both quite soon, if that's all right.'

Wainwright grunted again and looked at the postcard, which was plain and carried no photograph. The words *Field Service Postcard* were printed in black above Simon's handwriting on the address side, and there was a postmark announcing processing by Field Post Office 129, wherever that was. He turned the card over and read carefully. There was not much that Wainwright could not already surmise: The boy had arrived in France (no mention of the port) and moved directly to his camp – a "bullring", he called it – for further training. He was writing on the eve of departure by rail for the frontline, said the card, and news of whatever regiment he was to join would come next morning. After that, there would be no time to write again until he reached his new unit, if indeed at all. The closing words on the card were touching: 'Take care of yourself, my love. We will be together again soon. Please wait for me. I love you. Always yours, Simon'.

Wainwright felt a mixture of embarrassment and gratitude at being privy to the card's content; embarrassment at his ward's endearments and open affection for Christine, and gratitude that she had thought fit to share her postcard with them. He said:

'Would you be able to bring her over one evening, Penelope – Christine? Would she come for dinner? I'd … We'd like to meet her.' Wainwright directed a glance of apology in the direction of his wife. 'And will you thank her most sincerely? From both of us?' He rose to hand back the postcard.

A silence descended upon the three, the steady ticking of the clock upon the mantelpiece the room's only sound. Wainwright fished for his pipe, found it, then searched another pocket for tobacco and matches. He filled the briar bowl, tamped down the shredded leaf, struck a match and applied flame with the stem between his teeth, sucking softly until he could hear the crackle and see the glow within the rim. Inhaling, he looked across to his wife, whose inquiring eyes and the hint of a smile upon cheerful face showed that she had recognised his irritation. Penelope, when he glanced to her, he could not read. He liked the widow Brooke, yet sensed in her a suppressed impropriety. Well, he had never identified its direction, and her behaviour was always proper when in this home. Even so, there was something there, he was sure of it. Perhaps the younger woman – Christine – had become an outlet of sorts for Penelope, a conduit through which to vicariously live out her own concealed needs and desires.

'There's an offensive brewing,' he announced. 'I can feel it.'

His wife countered at once. Lowering her eyes to cup and saucer to avoid those of Wainwright, her light smile vanished and her tone became one of disappointment, though not of disagreement:

'Really, dear. Must we talk about the war?'

'Well dammit all, woman! Would you rather I pretend to feel no worry for the boy?' Then, immediately: 'I'm sorry. I apologise. To both of you. I'm sorry.'

It was Penelope who rescued him, perhaps recognising his need for angry release:

'There's always an offensive come the spring, Mister Wainwright. 'Twill be nothing new.'

Penelope never called him by his first name. Wainwright wondered why.

'Aye, Penelope,' he agreed. 'Always. But who will initiate the thing this year? Us? Or them?'

'What difference can it make, dear?'

Wainwright thought that the difference could very well be in which side incurred the greater losses, but he said nothing. With a sharp glance to his wife, he let the idea trail away. But she continued:

'Simon is adamant that he's ready. Trained. That's what his postcard says, dear. We've discussed this – both of us – many times. We've discussed the danger. He had to go. It's the right thing ... the only thing.'

Wainwright nodded. Penelope, watching, wondered what might be passing through the man's mind. Was Wainwright remembering all the trials, frustrations and difficulties of raising as his son a boy who was not his own? Or was he experiencing something else, a natural jealousy of Christine, perhaps? She had heard that mothers commonly experienced jealousy of their sons' lovers. Yet the emotion seemed to be coming from Wainwright himself, and not his spouse.

Christine ...

Penelope felt contentment that there had been time for consummation of the romance, and she felt satisfaction that she herself had encouraged it. To her mind, the couple deserved their chance at happiness, Simon for the possibility of his young life being cut short before he could fully live it, and Christine because of the interminable absence at the front of her fiancé, Luke, and the cold distance that had developed between them. She had had just a few, short days together with Luke in almost three years ... How was it possible to sustain love during such a long absence? Or rekindle it? And Christine's brother, too – he was in France – two men to worry about, and with Simon moving to the front there were three, now. And for how long? When Simon came back – if he came back – would Christine find him altered by his experience, as Luke had been altered? Whom would she choose – Luke or Simon? Well, perhaps neither man. Perhaps she would take another lover, though Penelope knew that she herself would not encourage it. There had been good reason to push Simon upon her, because of the heartache and frustration of Luke, but two were enough.

Penelope looked across at Wainwright sucking on his pipe. He seemed to be taking no contentment in the act, his face still reflecting frustration and irritation. She thought that probably it was because of the utter helplessness all felt when faced with the fact of the war, an inability to influence in any way its complete absorption of so many young lives. Then she glanced to her friend whom she knew was happy in her marriage despite the need to cede ground to her husband during any disagreement. Her eyes switching between the two, the widow Brooke felt a twinge of regret at the loss of her own husband to illness years before. Christine might yet achieve happiness in a marriage of her own, she thought. And Christine herself would choose her man when she was ready.

The room became silent again but for the ticking of the clock, mute witness to the identically intense wishes felt by all three, wishes frustrated by the fact that none could take action to satisfy them: that the war might become a thing of the past – something done with, an object of memory.

In the air over the forward trenches of the *Siegfriedstellung*, the three aircraft of the British photographic reconnaissance patrol met resistance long before they reached their objective. Anti-aircraft shells began to explode in violent flashes of yellow-red and black, pockmarking the sky as they sought airframe, engine and crew with unseen shards of ragged, red-hot steel. The pilots climbed, then dived, then climbed again, desperately changing altitude in an effort to throw off the aim of the German gun crews. They were only partly successful. The gunners were used to this tactic and made sighting adjustments, re-priming their shells to throw an explosive box around the anticipated extremities of the manoeuvre. Yet they scored no kills. Shockwaves buffeted the small machines, and shrapnel tore holes in wing and fuselage, but the pilots pressed on doggedly until they were through the defences into calmer skies that they hoped would stay that way until they reached the anti-aircraft positions protecting the Germans' second line.

Of the three aircraft, only one had the job of capturing images on film. The other two were fighter escorts. All were biplanes, flimsy designs of wood and cloth, glue and dope, mainly. Their clattering piston engines, one to each machine, powered two-bladed wooden propellers while at the same time causing considerable vibration throughout the airframes. The biplane crews took no notice. Motor vibration meant that their aircraft were still flying. It was a noisy business, flying, and exploding flak made it noisier still.

This flight of three was not the only photographic sortie that day. A score of similar patrols were simultaneously being made all along the one hundred and forty kilometres of the *Siegfriedstellung*, and not only on this day, either. Every day for several weeks now, weather permitting, missions had been ordered into the air by the British generals. They knew that their enemy was increasing his strength and preparing to attack in force. The burning question was where; at what point in the line, precisely? Nobody knew. So they sent out their aircraft to photograph the area rear of the German line, because exact knowledge of where the vast quantities of artillery shells, mortar bombs, small-arms ammunition, grenades, flares and fuel were being stockpiled – food, too, and fodder for the draught animals – photographs of these dumps and depots would help predict on which part of the line the German hammer would fall.

Besides flinging high explosive at the British 'planes, the Germans had their own aircraft patrolling the *Siegfriedstellung*. Two of these found the British flight of three over the second line of defences some four kilometres to the rear of the first, and a dogfight developed: an evenly matched two-on-two affair that played out while the third British machine – the camera-equipped reconnaissance aeroplane – pressed on toward its target.

On the ground below the aerial tussle, a thousand pairs of eyes followed the spectacle playing out in the early spring sky. Yet for the soldiers it was entertainment more than grim observation. There was no grinding of teeth or worried stares as they craned to follow the aircraft twisting and turning one upon the other, the notes of their engines rising and falling, and sometimes straining as the four pilots twisted, dived, climbed and spiralled in desperate attempts to out-turn and outmanoeuvre each other. Those four were trying for the kill, those pilots, and trying to survive the killing, too. But for the watchers on the ground, sitting, lying, or standing in attitudes of general disinterest, the outcome was academic. They knew all about killing in a much more personal way. Bets were placed, little more. Occasionally, as one combatant found the other, there were bursts of firing, the slow staccato clattering reaching the watchers like distant firecrackers, but louder and steadier, and with solid rhythm. The sound was sharp and dangerous.

'Good way to fight the war, eh, Bauer?'

It was Goettner. The *zugführer* had found his six from the tent in Pronville – Nettermann, Zimmermann, Bauer, König, Schäffer and Winkler, the replacement – while they were distracted by the dogfight. Bauer, recognising the voice, snapped to attention even as he was addressed, but Goettner waved away the display of discipline with a smile and signal to relax.

'*Ja*, Bauer. A nice clean cockpit with lots of fresh air, dodge a few bullets here and there while you sit on your leather seat, and then back to base for sausages and some sleep in a proper cot. Not a bad way to pass the hours.'

The others of the group, still watching the dogfight taking place a kilometre or so from where they waited in their holding area, could quite clearly make out the shapes of the aircraft: fuselage, wing and tail. When they heard the machine guns, the rattling chatter reached them in a note higher, clearer and faster than the dull, distant pounding of the artillery of both sides at the frontline, which was slower and steadier, and backed by the sharper crumping of the exploding shells. What they could not easily discern was to which side the individual aircraft belonged, and the pilots they could not see at all, which was why the dogfight had value only as entertainment to these men on the ground. Nobody really cared who might win the contest.

'Nowhere to hide up there though, *Herr Oberleutnant*. No shell craters.'

This was Old Man Schäffer, watching his *zugführer* dubiously.

'No parachutes, either,' added König. 'No parachute if you lose.'

'*Ja*, they are right, *Herr Oberleutnant*.' This was Nettermann, who in his usual manner had been momentarily silent before passing comment. 'But at least they don't have to worry about barbed wire. Not up there. No wire to stop them in their tracks while the enemy takes a clear shot. A cleaner fight, I think.'

The clattering of the winged combatants' firing stopped abruptly as two aircraft broke off the fight to fly away, parallel to the German positions.

'Must be ours,' Zimmermann said.

'*Ja*. Short on fuel, probably.'

The British fighters did not offer pursuit, instead accelerating to catch up to their camera 'plane. They took up position above and ahead of it, one either side, shepherding the mission on its way. The buzz and drone of their passage faded until it was overcome by the booming, distant artillery.

No barbed wire …

Goettner wondered about that. Together with their tanks, this *zug* had developed and perfected as far as they could the tactics to trample and smash that wire. All were confident now of being able to give the armour its best possible chance of success in that task. All believed that they could break through the British defences. Now, therefore, Division had moved the detachment forward of Cambrai and beyond the rearmost of the three lines to a crossroads just behind the second. From here they could be ordered either directly forward, or moved along the front along prepared routes allowing maximum ease of movement to the tanks, which could manage walking speed at best. All were ready to move immediately the order came.

The other armoured detachments available to the *Siegfriedstellung* had similarly been pre-positioned at suitable crossroads. The massive attack so carefully prepared and planned by the generals was imminent. Around Goettner's *zug*, Germany's build-up for the biggest spring offensive she had ever mounted was nearing completion. Fifty divisions freed by the Russian collapse in the east were now in place along this point in the Western Front – half a million extra men. Briefly rested upon arrival, they had been brought up to strength with replacements, then retrained to work once again as cohesive units. Most of the fifty were in place along that part of the *Siegfriedstellung* where the attack would take place, facing the River Somme. It was in this area that the British had lost more than 400,000 killed or wounded during their own offensive of the previous summer and autumn, and Germany 100,000 more than that. Germany's generals hoped to fare better this time. They were almost ready to give the order to attack, and all along the line were anticipating it. Along with those divisions already manning that sector, the new arrivals brought available manpower to three quarters of a million soldiers. The rest of the fifty were located further away, reinforcing flanks facing the French to the south and yet more British to the north. Artillery along the entire length of the Western Front – from the English Channel to Switzerland – had been thinned to make available as many guns as possible for this breakout across the Somme. Around Saint-Quentin, the point in the line designated by Germany's supreme commander for the attack, there were now six thousand six hundred artillery pieces in position, and more than three thousand mortars. All had been stocked with ample supplies of shells and bombs, with yet more ammunition held at depots to the rear. Some three hundred and fifty fighter aircraft had been assembled to support the attacking infantry.

Goettner looked at the group, assessing mood and morale. The six knew what was coming, though they appeared relaxed enough in the shade of camouflage netting struck over their tank, sitting or lying, or leaning against supporting poles. The replacement, Winkler, was chewing lazily on a grass stem, Goettner saw, lying back on his elbows, legs stretched before him and seemingly more at ease among the others than before. Those night-time dangers he had shared with them as they crawled along the British wire appeared to have helped the man fit in, Goettner thought. The others were similarly casual, and he preferred them this way, for there would be abundant opportunity for displays of nerve when they were ordered forward. His eyes roamed the men: young König, squat, slow and of simple appearance, yet steady enough when needed; Bauer the translator, reliable and steady no matter what; Zimmermann, ever alert to every nuance of individual behaviour so that he missed no chance to prod and poke lesser men to a state of higher efficiency (perhaps a stripe for him, if the man could just find it within his psyche to encourage rather than bully to achieve this end); married, handsome Schäffer, older than them all and who used to be quietly cheerful, but who now said so little after that Russian shell splinter had smashed through the side of his helmet to furrow scalp and skull. And silent, dependable Nettermann from Essen, one of the *zug's* few dead shots. Apart from the replacement, these five had been with him for at least a year now, and one or two for longer than that. They had survived the fighting in Russia that had claimed so many; more than half of the *zug* by Goettner's reckoning, the majority so badly wounded that they had been invalided home, the rest left behind in the graveyards of Poland.

Goettner looked at these six. He knew the attack would come soon. It was imminent – within the week for sure – and it was going to be an all-out affair, Germany's last throw before the arriving Americans could organise in strength. A swift victory now would stem brewing revolution at home; people could only be expected to stand so much, and the young men of so very many small villages had already been killed – in some villages every young man – while their parents and siblings were close to starvation. Victory would avoid revolution, rendering worthwhile all the sacrifice of four long, hard years of war, and securing Germany its rightful position as the vigorous nation state it had become since unification under Prussia in the time of the grandfathers of these six in the group, and Goettner's too. Germany was yet a young country. To lose this war was unthinkable.

A swift victory …

So, now, here in the *Siegfriedstellung*, all that remained was for those three quarters of a million soldiers of the attacking divisions to receive final orders. They were poised and ready. As for the *zug* itself, they had only to move into position alongside their tank and execute their part. They were experienced, most of them. Even Winkler now had experience. And all were trained and motivated too. Goettner hoped with all his heart that Germany could win the war in this way. The country had been through so much pain, so much sacrifice. More than hope, Goettner prayed. He prayed for victory. And he prayed that these six would make it through the cauldron to come.

* * *

They debussed at the gun line, about thirty men, Peake and Earnshaw among them. Replacements for thirty lost. The trucks drove away, the Old Bills too, and the men looked about them. Close by were the guns of an artillery troop: four cannons spaced about twenty-five yards apart, two forward and two back, staggered, dug in, sandbagged and netted against aerial observation. Their crews were in attendance and stood-to, one in the process of reloading.

The new arrivals were nervous. None spoke, but you could see the anxiety in eyes brightly alert to any hint of danger. The sergeant who accompanied them from the railhead said:

'Right, lads, listen carefully. Welcome to the Seventh. We're happy to have you. Very happy. First things first, and important things first of all, so pay attention. All that nonsense at the Bullring? That's over now – finished with. What was done there was needed and necessary. You've learned the lessons. Now it's behind you. Past. Over. Here, things are more relaxed. There's discipline, sure, but you're going to find that we're more like a family here at the sticky end of things. So do your jobs as best you can, do what you're told, and the way of the family it will remain.'

The sergeant had a rough appearance about him that bore little resemblance to the turnout of the NCOs at Brocton and Rouen. His boots were scuffed and muddy, and the khaki of his uniform, though correctly arranged, was creased and dirty. There was a short tear in the sackcloth cover of his helmet. The man had not shaved for at least two days, yet he stood erect before them, the rifle slung over his shoulder outstandingly clean, its steel bolt-handle, foresights and the single brass band about its wooden stock oiled and wiped clean, so that they gleamed in the patchy sunlight of mid-afternoon. The man had a cheerful, confident manner about him as he spoke to his new arrivals, and he made no apology for his lack of ablution. His voice was clear and firm, just loud enough to carry to all of the thirty over the sounds reaching them from the distant trenches: the uneven crack of rifle and popping machine gun, and the crump of a single shell. He was quite calm as he addressed the arrivals. He was a comfort to them, for his bearing and general manner indicated that whatever danger there was, it was not so close that they need worry.

'From here ...' A detonation, loud and very near, interrupted him – one of the artillery pieces had fired. The shocking sound drove fully a quarter of the men flat to the ground. Others crouched or ducked. All had taken fright, so that now they looked about them nervously. The sergeant said nothing. He had not flinched at the bang, remaining solidly on his feet before them. He waited while the prone picked themselves up to brush dirt from trouser and trench coat, the shouted commands of the gun crew and the brassy ring of the ejected casing and slamming breech a backdrop to their embarrassment.

'Just doing what we pay 'em for.' The sergeant kept his face impassive, observing the hurried retrieval of peaked caps by those now standing up, and pleased to see that none had fouled the barrel of his rifle. 'They fire about one round every two minutes – and they rotate the guns so they don't overheat. Be ready for the next one when it comes. Nothing to worry about.'

He reached into his tunic for a cigarette, found one loose and pulled it out to examine it, apparently pleased to find the thing unbroken, though it was certainly bent and flat. Unbothered, he lit it with a match, inhaled and continued, his words tossing tobacco smoke into the air about his face:

'From here I'm going to take you to the closest communication trench, just under a mile that way.' He gestured with the cigarette, but there was no need. The sounds from that direction were plain to all, and once or twice fountains of pummelled earth thrown skyward by exploding shells could be seen even from where this group were assembled at the gun line. 'At the communication trench, you'll be met by corporals from your individual companies. They know your names – they have lists – and they'll call you out. Work with them. Co-operate. These are not bullring canaries. They know the game and they'll be as elder brothers to you. Listen to them. Learn from them. They know exactly what they are doing. Your corporals will take you up the communication trench all the way to the line, and from there to your company positions where you'll be led to your individual platoons. Clear so far?'

'Clear, sergeant!' came the reply as one voice.

'Good. So – again …' Here the sergeant repeated the order of events, just to be sure. Then he said: 'Don't worry. Things are quiet at the moment. Under control. Stay alert but stay calm. Any questions?'

There were none. Another gun in the troop took its turn to fire. This time nobody fell flat, though all flinched at the very loud explosion of sound. Again there were the commands of the crew as the casing was ejected and a fresh shell rammed home. In the two-minute pause before the next interruption, the sergeant called out a list to physically divide the men into four groups, one per company.

'All right then,' said the sergeant, when they had sorted themselves out. 'Caps off now, lads. Pack 'em away. You'll not be needing those. Tin hats on.'

They did it, stuffing caps into packs and donning helmets against possible air burst.

105

'You …' The sergeant pointed without malice to one of the men. It was Farmer the squad joker, still with Peake all the way from Brocton. 'What's the state of your weapon, son? Loaded or unloaded?'

'Unloaded, sergeant.'

The reply was delivered respectfully, with none of Farmer's expected attempt at humour. These days Farmer made fewer quips, and he had never again mentioned the Somme after that tirade in the Brocton training trenches. It had left its mark.

'The rest of you? Unloaded too?'

Nods and murmured assent from everyone.

'Okay.' He raised his voice, but not too much – just enough to indicate that what would follow was not advice, but an order:

'With two clips of five rounds each – Load!'

The men unshouldered their rifles, retrieved ammunition from the pouches about their chests, used thumbs to crank ball ammunition from charger into magazine.

'Ready!' ordered the sergeant.

Each man chambered one round.

'Good. Now, safety catches on, lads.' He waited, keen eye roving to make sure that it was so. 'Right, let's go. Follow me.'

They went, nervously shouldering their rifles and shaking out into single file to follow the sergeant.

For Peake, this move up the line was something he would never forget, though he did not know it in the moment. So much was new to him, and his place in the file following the sergeant was just one novelty more. His world contracted into bobbing tin hats, shouldered rifles, stuffed packs and flapping trench coats; the things that filled his vision to the front. To left and right lay open fields and pastures, some bordered by poplars swaying elegantly in the breeze under a hazy afternoon sky. At the gun line, all had been evenly overgrown and fallow, but after ten minutes on the march the first shell crater appeared. It was an ugly blot upon the land, and the signs of battle increased in frequency after that: more craters, broken and blasted trees, the wreck of an abandoned vehicle thrown onto its side, and an overturned wooden wagon, its team of dead horses still harnessed to the wreckage. The horses were decomposing skin and bone, legs broken into unnatural angles beneath and about their bodies. Their ruptured fur, now hardened with blood, was coated in a thick mess of buzzing flies, iridescently green.

The day was warm and the pace quick. Peake perspired. He would have liked to quit his trench coat, and knew that all thirty would be feeling the same.

106

But there was no chance for that, and they were well used to sweat and discomfort. None complained, not even to themselves.

After twenty minutes they bypassed the ruined village of Foncquevillers to their left, the booming of the cannons from the gun line still reaching their ears every two minutes, though fainter now as the column came upon the entrance to their communication trench where it reached the weeds, grass and level ground of the fields. Four corporals were waiting there, crouched within the shallow cover afforded by the trench mouth, for there were shell holes about, and even the replacements knew that just one hole alone was reason to be cautious.

'A Company, over 'ere!' bellowed one, moving out of the trench with his fellows.

'C Company on me! Make it snappy, like!'

'D Cmp'ny, 'ere! Look lively, lads. Fritz is about!'

'B Company with me! Move it, now, lads! Move it!'

Peake, allocated with seven others to C Company, jogged with them to their corporal, who examined the group with a quick, all-encompassing glance from under his helmet, then read quickly from a dirty scrap of paper in one hand:

'Earnshaw!'

'Here, Corporal!'

'Watson!'

'Here!'

'Farmer!'

'Present!'

'Peake!'

'Present, Corporal!'

When all had answered similarly, these nine were the first to descend into the gradual slope of the trench, the corporal leading. The world that they had known ascended surreally into some unremembered space above, and their comrades of the shared months at Brocton and Rouen, they vanished with it. The nine were swallowed by this steadily deepening slash in the earth that was the communication trench so that, after thirty yards, nothing remained of the world they had known since the day they were born. Now, there were only two walls of damp, chalky earth, one on either side of the moving column, and a slash of sky above, darkening with the clouds of a gathering storm. The breeze had vanished too. Where was the breeze? Oh, it was there, of course, but it was above them now, unfelt as they descended deeper into the trench. Peake felt a worrying sense of foreboding. He realised that he had become a creature of the earth, now – a creature existing in a place where worms, centipedes and other unmentionables lived and bred – and it had happened so quickly that he had not had time to savour any last view of life at ground level.

At a junction in the trench, an offshoot to the left was signposted by a single wooden board painted in large red letters above an arrow in black: TO C COMPANY. Without pausing they left the communication trench, entering another dug more deeply.

Now the walls of bare earth became sheer cliffs of wooden planks held in place by uprights hammered irregularly into the base of the trench. Some were poles of creosoted gum already showing signs of rot. Others were of rusty steel. The place seemed to have been hastily constructed as and when time had permitted. In some places the planks had burst, spilling earth, and unknown shovels had thrown as much of the spill as possible up and over the rim of the trench to clear the path again. Beneath their boots now was mud and water. Here and there duckboards helped their passage forward.

Another sign: DANGER – SNIPER!

The corporal paused before this sign. He glanced behind at the eight. 'Get down nice 'n low now, 'ere,' he told them. 'You – Earnshaw is it? Get yer bleedin' 'ead lower! Stay as low as you can through this part an' do *not* get above a low crouch if you wan' ter live ter enjoy dinner. Clear?'

They nodded, crouching and shuffling through this interval in the line where some or other shell had obliterated the trench walls, opening much of the passage to an unseen enemy marksman watching from higher ground for any glint of steel helmet passing through.

Back within the protection of undamaged trench walls, they came upon an intersection, with the company orderly room just past and to one side, a rough dugout with an entrance framed by sandbags and a piece of Wilson canvas with blackout blanket serving as a door. A staff sergeant emerged to hurry them along:

'No paperwork today, boys – we'll sort things out later. Earnshaw, Farmer, Watson and Peake – identify!' They did it by snapping spare forearms – the ones not clasping slings – smartly forward. 'You four go with Corporal Tozer here. He'll take you on to your platoon. The rest of you'll be split up a bit, so stay with me until the others've gone.'

He nodded to Corporal Tozer, who led the four further along into a well-maintained stretch of trench, deepened so that the parapet reached a full eighteen inches above even a tall man standing. It was equipped with a wooden fire-step along all its length, and the walls were of hessian sandbags carefully stacked, though ruptured or broken open in places along the top row where something had burst them, and others – newly filled – had been cast hastily into the gaps. The whole length of it was manned by soldiers, standing, sitting, or lying and attempting sleep, and there were sentries posted at short intervals along the fire-step, their rifles with bayonets fixed and ready.

The four were able to walk with comparative ease through this stretch of the trench, and they felt quite safe. A minute later, their guide halted.

'Sergeant'll want ter meet you,' he announced. 'An' the lieutenant later, after dinner, I 'spect.'

They stood, nervous and uncertain. A shell bumped angrily further up the trench, perhaps seventy yards away, but nobody reacted beyond an instinctive ducking, quite pronounced – that spell in the gun line had served them well. Nevertheless, all cocked an ear for more.

'Nuffin' ter worry abaht,' Tozer reassured them. 'Nobody yellin' for 'is muvver, so nobody 'urt.'

A man approached from around a corner of the trench, the three broad chevrons on both upper arms announcing his rank. With a start of surprise, Peake recognised the solid stature and full face of Sergeant John Winterman, hair poking forward from under his helmet above the dark eyebrows. It had been five months since the Stafford meeting, and Winterman was as surprised as Peake at this one.

'Well, I'll be buggered!' he said. 'A face from Camden High!' And he grinned a tight smile of welcome. It was brief and somewhat grim beneath eye sockets dark with fatigue, the grey eyes themselves moving constantly as though seeking the arrival of something imminent.

'Names, please?' He examined the replacements as they replied:

'Farmer, Sergeant!'

'Watson, Sergeant!'

'Peake, Sergeant!'

'Earnshaw, Sergeant!'

'Earnshaw … There's a rumour they call you Quiz. That right?'

'That's right, Sergeant!

'Well, all right then, Quiz.'

Winterman nodded, examining the four and measuring each man, seemingly memorising their faces and attaching names. The constantly roving eyes were shrewd. Then he spoke quietly and calmly, like the NCO at the de-bussing point beside the gun line. His tone carried friendly authority. It was a voice to obey, but it sounded tired and in need of rest.

'You've joined us at an interesting time, lads. We are Eleven Platoon. Our lieutenant is Mister Williams – you'll meet him later. The other four of your group have gone off to join Ten. Nine and Twelve've taken no casualties these past weeks, but here in Eleven, three of those you're replacing took shrapnel – lucky, really, 'cause they're all only in field hospital for a spell and they'll be back with us in four or five weeks. A sniper got the fourth lad. Found him in that patch you've just come through. He was tired and he got careless – forgot to crouch, so he died. Don't make that mistake.' The note of his voice had risen a notch for emphasis as he spoke the last instruction, and now he looked into their eyes, one to another. He continued: 'The dead man was careless, pure and simple. So stay alert, read the signs, and listen to the men you're with because they know the drill around here. Try to stay alive. You're more useful to me that way.'

Another pause. Winterman was weighing his words.

'So, what's happening around here? Well, the good news is that almost all work parties have ceased for the time being. Units to the rear are carrying 'em out.'

The four glanced one to another, pleased at this – it meant no hauling of ammunition boxes or barbed wire and the iron poles to peg it, or the heavy bundles of wood for trench wall repairs, all of which they knew made up a large part of life in the line.

'The bad news is the reason for the good news.' Winterman smiled grimly at the old joke. 'Fritz is preparing to attack. A big one. A proper offensive. And he's going to come at us all along this part of the line. You'll hear his lorries as soon as dusk falls to queer Arty's aim. There's less shelling at night time. When the wind's right we can hear his trains reaching the railhead – his build-up. When he does come, the attack'll be something to see, you can count on it. And we'll be here in the forward position for a full week yet, so there's a good chance we'll have to face the thing down.'

The four were in some awe at this announcement. Winterman, recognising the underlying fear, sought to reassure:

'In a way, we're better off here than waiting further back to counter, because we're well organised and we have our guns properly registered to break 'em up as they come. Our wire's deep, too. The machine guns are well sited with good fields of fire, and we can aim as well as any, so we're ready, and I'd rather face 'em here than be chucked in as part of the counter-attack. Counters can be messy, take it from me.'

They took his word for it.

'So, I'll be with you when they come, and so will Mister Williams. We'll make the bastards pay for every inch all the way to the wire, and we'll kill the rest when they get to that. We'll hold here and we will not fall back.'

A pause.

'Questions?'

There were none.

'Right. You're all on one of the box periscopes for your first hour. Corporal Tozer,' he indicated the wiry, ferret-like man who had guided them in, 'Corporal Tozer will assign you someone experienced to show you the ropes. The periscopes'll give you a chance to get to see how the land lies up as far as Fritz on the higher ground in front. Take a good look at it and commit it to memory. Take note of the direction of the main towns – Foncquevillers just behind us, Bapaume and Douliens – Arras, too – so you can orientate when you have to. After that, you'll be shown your sleeping positions. Peake, you and I'll catch up on home news some other time, when there's an opportunity. We'll do it over a cuppa. I'll tell you when.'

'Yes, Sergeant.'

Winterman grunted, shot a last cursory nod at the four and moved past them into the trench beyond, to check on the rest of Eleven Platoon.

CHAPTER SIX

To the front of the *zug*, where the fallow fields and abandoned pasture fell away under a warm April sky all the way to what remained of the little village of Foncquevillers one kilometre distant, the land was calm and quiet. But just forward of the village it was angry, the ground heaving and boiling and erupting skyward in gouts of tortured soil and clay. There, where lay the British trenches, German shells rained down as fast as their many cannons could fire them, and all was fiery explosion and violent turmoil, shuddering vibration and ear-splitting noise as the ground recoiled and trembled and belched clods of earth into the air under the thunderous power of the attacking artillery.

Nervous and fearful, waiting and watching from their own trenches this work of the guns, Goettner and some others – not all – sensed the awful waste of what they were seeing: good farmland being torn up by the shellfire. They could feel, too, the pain of the village, battered into broken walls and blackened roof trusses by four years of war. Incredibly, most of the church tower still stood to point a mute finger of vertical admonition, as if affronted by the violence. And what of the trenches themselves, target of that bombardment? The men of the *zug* tried not to imagine, for they knew only too well the awful suffering of soldiers under bombardment. Most had been through similar.

The shelling of Foncquevillers was just one part of a far grander plan that had been in progress for some days. Codenamed Operation Michael, it was a massive German attack of unprecedented scale across a wide front centred on the town of Saint-Quentin. The role of the German artillery in this plan was to deliver a pounding of staggering proportion. More than one million shells hammered into the British lines in just the first five hours of the first day. Infantry followed, striking north toward Arras. The intention was to drive the British Army toward the sea, encircle it and force surrender, or destroy it should the British choose to fight. This would compel the French – their own army weakened and lacking any remaining ally other than the Americans still organising at the ports – to seek armistice. Victory would belong to Germany.

Today it was the turn of Foncquevillers. Today, the British lines defending that town were to be broken.

Goettner's *zug* watched the spectacle of the barrage, wondering at its fury as they waited for the order to advance. Despite the distance, they could taste the air they breathed, rent and blasted and pummelled as much as the erupting earth itself. That air was acrid, tainted with the odour of spent high explosive carried to them upon a warm afternoon breeze promising rain after nightfall. The smell mingled with the fumes from the engine of their tank, which was ready and protected by a dozen of the *zug* crouched in a group around it behind the trenches where sheltered many hundreds of infantry, waiting. The tank was a monster, pregnant with firepower. It looked like some nightmare alien attack ship bolted to caterpillar tracks, poised to move forward, engine idling noisily and belching black fumes.

Above the soldiers, the air was alive with shells of many calibres arcing unseen towards the enemy, searing and sundering the sky with their noisy passage. They could be heard as a continuously loud, hissing type of saw, hoarse and unsteady, something just short of a diminishing whistle, but rougher, coarser, more threatening. Each was a susurration of unhappy search that marked a projectile following its invisible path towards the beaten ground of the target trenches. This ominous noise, very loud, added to the awful clamour of the detonations themselves, the sky above spitting its own language and hissing its own code, each tearing sigh above the crouching soldiers a steel packet of high-explosive death hurled at the British.

Within the line of men ready to attack, Zimmermann grounded his rifle, cradling the barrel between neck and shoulder to free his hands for a smoke. There was still time. He lit two of the stubby cigarettes, passing one to the replacement – Winkler – beside him, who nodded his thanks and drew deeply on the tobacco, face drawn and tense around dark eyes wide with fear, his round head dwarfed by the oversized helmet. Zimmermann shouted encouragement above the thunder of the barrage:

'Listen to me, New Man,' he yelled to the boy, 'You stick close by me and everything'll be just fine. You stay very close to me, d'you hear? On my left and a little behind, like we practised. You see anything that's not grey like us, you kill it, understood?'

'Okay,' came the reply from the face within its coalscuttle helmet.

The hand holding the cigarette was trembling noticeably. Zimmermann saw it. He offered more reassurance:

'This tank thing will keep us all safe, New Man, don't you worry.'

'Okay.'

Nettermann, readying himself on the other side of Winkler, overheard the conversation and felt a moment of rare affection for the *zug* bully, who had taken their replacement under his wing ever since the patrol by the wire. Shared danger often made good friends of strangers. Nettermann wondered who was going to keep the rest of them safe. Who would do it? Who would watch over Nettermann himself? Who would watch over the others? He tried to draw comfort from the fact that most were experienced soldiers. They had done this before. The thought brought scant consolation, so he reached across to tap the new man's arm in a gesture of request. Winkler passed him the cigarette, and Nettermann took a deep pull, inhaling gratefully. He nodded thanks and handed back the roll.

Beyond Zimmermann crouched Bauer, dumpy König and Old Man Schäffer. These men and five more were loosely grouped around Goettner who, pistol drawn, waited in a crouch beside the tank. Apart from their *zugführer*, all carried rifles with bayonets fixed. There had been some debate about this, a few among them wanting to take club or entrenching spade in place of the Mauser. Yet the tank they were protecting was simply too slow to allow effective use of hand-held weapons, which needed pace to be effective: a sprint to the objective so that they could be used to smash and batter.

Nettermann examined his officer, watching for nerves, but Goettner was in control of himself, as cool as ever, the eyes in the face below the helmet supplying no hint of emotion as they assessed and measured the route to the British line. König, too, was steady, the fleshy face revealing nothing. The man seemed his usual unflappable self, open to the fate of the day without passively accepting it, determined to survive. Next to him, Bauer cradled his rifle in a manner equally inscrutable. He was carrying several extra stick grenades stuffed into his webbing. Schäffer was not so poised. He started and blinked with each crashing explosion that reached them from the village. Perhaps the *zug's* only married man had not fully recovered his nerve, but Nettermann hoped that Schäffer would be as valuable in the fight as he usually was. They would all have need of each other.

The artillery continued its pounding of the enemy line, the earth rippling and heaving like lava under the hammer-blows of the artillery. A haze of drifting smoke, quite thick, developed. Through it, Foncquevillers came and went as a ghost of spectral devastation, a battered remnant of the bucolic farming centre it once had been. Forward of the village, the British line could not be seen.

Goettner looked at his watch and stood. It was time. He glanced to his men left and right, managing a tight smile and a wink to those whose eye he caught, his habit of steady fortitude in the face of madness. The soldiers rose with him. Using a whistle, Goettner blew three long blasts, emptying his lungs with each one. Within the tank, the driver engaged gear, his steel monster coughing and belching a noisy stream of dirty black into the air as it lurched forward, lumbering onto bundles of timber thrown into the trench by engineers as a ford across the slash that was their line, leading the way. Nettermann, Bauer, König, Schäffer, Zimmermann, Winkler and the rest followed, rifles at the carry, bayonets fixed, spreading out a little beyond the timber ford to group loosely around their lumbering responsibility like shepherds with a single sheep. Their pace across no man's land would be a quick walk, for the tank could manage no more. Within the trench as they crossed, a thousand eyeballs bright with anxious fear peered up at them from taut faces waiting one minute more. After that, all would heave themselves up the scaling ladders to shake out into the line of attack behind the tanks. Goettner's men were unreasonable in their disdain for these watchers in the trench as they moved to begin their slow advance across no man's land, for the greatest danger was with them. Only when they and the tanks at the point of the attack – just four machines within the attacking regiment – only when these had smashed a way through the British wire could they pass the baton. Once through that wire, it would be over to the main body now safe in the trenchlines to finish the thing.

In the trenches held by the Lancashires, rum eased the terrible trial that was the shelling, but only a little. The weight of the barrage was such that the regiment's every soldier now cowered and trembled in dugouts along the line, sentries pulled in as soon as the bombardment began in earnest. They waited for the pounding to ease, and some prayed for actual attack – anything to end this violent hammering of the ground above and the fearful sawing sound – those scratching, tearing fingers of high-explosive destruction – seeking out their trenches with tips so carefully primed, and each exploding in a thunderclap of sound to fling red-hot steel fragments slicing horizontally this way and that, other shards thrown vertically to return to earth some seconds later as frightening smacks and slaps upon sandbag and duckboard, clearly audible within the dugouts.

Yet the men were steady enough under this terrible assault.

In Peake's dugout, Lieutenant Williams and Corporal Tovey did their best to calm the men by stoic example. Peake watched them, trying his utmost to emulate their behaviour within the damp burrow, looking at nothing at all and uttering no word, simply waiting it out and bearing down on an almost overpowering impulse to scream aloud his fear and outrage at this onslaught of high explosive and flying pieces of ruptured steel. His lieutenant and the corporal showed little sign of nerves beyond tightened faces below their helmets, their determined resignation an inspiration. Peake, Quiz Earnshaw and some one third of Eleven Platoon were in the dugout with them, about a dozen soldiers crouching or sitting with teeth set against this test of their resolve. The hole in which they sheltered, their dugout, was their protection: a dark place reached by half a dozen steps cut down into the earth, and with a ceiling of wooden poles, corrugated iron and planks held in place by props. Above those, solid earth to a depth of many feet was supposed to render the shelter bombardment-proof. It was a place excavated many yards below ground level and then buttressed against collapse in the manner of a stope. The engineers thought it could withstand all but a direct hit by the heaviest of enemy shells, and perhaps it would survive even that, they said, but who really knew? So the men crouched, or squatted, or sat, eyes burning with a hard brightness beneath the rims of their helmets, the light of guttering candles making them brighter still through the dusty air. Sergeant Winterman was with others of the platoon in a similar dugout further along the trench. Another NCO had the remaining men in a third.

Packed earth protection notwithstanding, everything shook under the tremendous buffeting. Wooden poles and planks shed rivulets and sometimes stronger falls of dusty soil, each exploding shell a juddering blow to feet and hands and buttocks, as if some nightmare giant of unimaginable size were trying to break in with a sledgehammer. Some of the men covered their ears against the deafening blasts. Others turned their minds inwards and smoked steadily, nursing bent cigarettes between dirty fingers. Peake licked dry lips with a tongue that was dryer still. Tozer, seeing this and understanding what it meant, reached behind to a hay-box of mixed tea and rum jammed into a corner of the dugout. It was still warm, and he dragged an enamel mug through the contents and thrust it at Peake.

'Pull on that!' the wiry corporal shouted above the din. 'An' pass it along! Don't you spill any, now – nowt more fer a while.'

Peake drank and passed the mug to Earnshaw. The lukewarm liquid was fiery with liquor, bolstering his determination. Quiz bellowed something unintelligible above the racket, a question probably, then passed the mug to the next man. Peake shook his head in mute reply, but Earnshaw's eyebrows remained raised in query above his quick, brightly alert eyes. Peake pointed to his ears in non-committal excuse, shaking his head. He didn't want to hear Earnshaw's question, anyway; he was remembering another mug of tea, one taken with Winterman's brandy and the sergeant himself just a few hours ago, immediately before the bombardment began. It had been the sergeant's idea …

'Set up some tea, will you, Peake old son?' the sergeant had said. 'Need to catch up on Camden.' And Winterman had disappeared among the men further along the trench while Peake filled a mess-tin from the platoon's non-fortified urn and reheated the sweet, milky brew on a brazier. It was brought forward twice a day from kitchens at the rear, already pre-mixed with milk and an arbitrary load of sugar. Take it or leave it.

Winterman returned. He sat, propping his rifle carefully against the wooden revetment.

'One cube or two, Sergeant?'

Winterman smiled at the joke, accepting Peake's proffered mug and rummaging in his tunic. He retrieved a hip flask of polished steel, an object of quality on which Peake could see some engraving – a gift from somebody special, no doubt. Peake watched his sergeant splash a generous tot from the flask into both mugs.

'Local brandy,' Winterman explained. 'One of the few good things about this place. Wish I'd bought more last time we were rear of the line. Better than our rum ration.'

Peake eyed his old school senior, glad of this break in the nervous monotony of another day spent in anxious anticipation of expected attack. It had to come very soon, for the flanking sectors had been on the receiving end of grave assault for some days now. Nobody was quite sure why Foncquevillers had been spared, but everybody was certain it wouldn't last.

Peake and the other replacements had now been in the forward trenches six days. Peake himself felt as though he had been there for months, accustomed as he now was to the grimy routine of a fire-trench eternally on the receiving end of desultory artillery and machine-gun fire directed at some or other point. It never ended, but the constant booming of that much more determined bombardment now reaching his ears from distant flanks – something very different and clearly serious – was very troubling. Where he sat with Winterman, it was a continuous background to conversation.

Winterman was eyeing his flask, seeming to remember something or someone as he examined the curve of its steel.

'Tell me about the football, Peake.'

'The football, Sergeant?'

'Yes. Camden Secondary. We do okay this season? Before they sent you to Brocton?'

'We did okay, Sergeant. But you would've been useful in the derbies. They were difficult. Nobody quite had your touch.'

'Ah. I thank you for the compliment, son.'

Winterman scratched at a fleshy cheek. He had somehow found the time to shave, but his dark jowls remained patchy with traces of beard. Perhaps he had shaved without water. Peake examined the man surreptitiously, trying to decide from the number of tiny nicks whether there had been water or not. To his eyes, the sergeant appeared solid in manner and attitude, every inch of him exuding subtle confidence, that intangible *je ne sais quoi* possessed by all those who had been through the mill and excelled under an almost insupportable weight of nervous pressure. He was to Peake a quietly self-controlled man, and Peake felt nothing but confidence in his leadership. Stafford didn't matter, really.

As if reading his thoughts, Winterman looked directly at Peake and said:

'I went home after I saw you. In Stafford, I mean.'

Peake held the other man's eyes, though it was difficult. Between the two, there passed a moment of tacit acknowledgement of that difficult encounter in the village square, and an understanding that it held no relevance to their current situation.

'I'm engaged to be married when this mess is over,' Winterman continued. 'Visited my fiancée when I was over there. She gave me the hip flask.'

A pause.

'Do you have anyone special, Peake?'

'Yes.'

'Good.' The word carried empathy. 'Hold her memory close. She will help you through this thing.'

She will help you through this thing.

Sitting on the fire-step with his sergeant, Peake looked into the depths of his brew and considered this proffered wisdom, ignoring as far as he could the activity and sounds of their uninteresting section of the line: here a machine gun, rattling brief acknowledgement of some temporary threat somewhere, there the crump of a single shell exploding four or five hundred yards away. Christine had not come to the railway station to bid him farewell. And she had avoided reply to his insistence that she wait for him, her amber eyes veiled and cast down as he held her close in final farewell at Penelope Brooke's. Those eyes were wonderful to Peake. He felt that he could spend the rest of his life gazing into them. Why hadn't she come to say goodbye? Why, why? Was it because of his implied demand of fidelity?

She will help you through this thing.

'The attack, Sergeant …'

'What about it?'

'You said it would come soon … the day we arrived. But nothing's up.'

'And thank God for that, Peake. Be glad of it. Maybe they'll hold off till we get reserve duty, not that there's any real advantage in that.' Winterman paused, considering for a moment before continuing: 'They'll shell us first. Heavy stuff and lots of it. We'll be okay in the dugouts, so don't worry. But when they do that – and you can stake all seven bob of your week's wages that they will – when they shell us, well, the attack'll come right after they stop.'

A little more than one hour later, tea done and the sergeant gone about his duties, that prediction came to pass. Without preamble, the routine, sporadic irritation of the enemy's harassing fire increased in intensity over a period of just minutes to become shelling that was fiercely violent. It became a storm, a powerful force of almost irresistible strength, a living thing, angry and malevolent, the high explosive raining down all along the line around Foncquevillers to force the men of the Seventh to abandon trench and fire-step, and seek shelter below ground. Fritz was coming …

Now, within Peake's reinforced dugout seemingly so fragile under the battering of that shell-storm, all waited, nerves stretched taut by this barrage which assaulted all senses, and their minds as well. It was an obscene onslaught, a massive, flailing hammering on eardrum, skin and flesh while, on the open ground above the parapet, the world was an all-enveloping hell of high explosive, flame and smoke, searing steel and loud reverberation.

Without warning the lieutenant – Williams – cocked an ear, head lifted and body tensing as he tried to make out something beyond the roaring of the Germans' shelling. The Welshman appeared to be testing the air for danger in the manner of a pointer close to its quarry, his expression one of worried expectation. Peake fine-tuned his own senses at the lieutenant's unspoken warning, but it was impossible to hear anything over the clamorous shellfire, though the terrible shaking and quaking of the ground about them appeared to be easing by a degree or two, subtly shifting centre and focus.

Williams clambered to his feet. Drawing his Webley, he ran up the steps from candlelit darkness into the day, blinding himself and becoming ensnared for a moment in the heavy blackout canvas. He leaped to the fire-step and took a quick and careful glance over the sandbags into no man's land.

'STAND TO…!' he bellowed. 'STAND TO, BOYS! MACHINE GUNS IN PLACE! QUICKLY, NOW! GET THOSE GUNS READY …! '

They did it. All scrambled to their feet, clutching rifles to follow Williams out of the dugout, cursing the Wilson canvas that clawed at them until somebody paused to hold it aside. They jumped to the fire-step, peering nervously out over sandbags tossed hither and thither like so many weightless leaves by the shelling. The boxes and coils of barbed wire had been similarly upended and thrown about. Searching the land in front of the trench, the soldiers hurried to pull bayonets from scabbards at their waists, sliding them with an oiled clicking into position below the muzzles of their weapons, becoming suddenly as men made instantly more dangerous by those long, wicked steel blades extending their reach. Adjusting helmets and checking ammunition pouches, holding themselves close to the damp wooden shuttering of the trench walls and aiming their rifles through the tangled barbs of their upended wire, they knew that the fight was upon them.

Remarkably, apart from scattered sandbags and chaotically blasted wire entanglements, the trench was largely intact, though in two places it had partially collapsed under the shock of near misses. Thankfully, no high explosive had found the trench itself – or not C Company's part of it, anyway – but further away there was the screaming of wounded men. Peake and the others closed their ears to the frightful sound; it was coming from the direction of company headquarters and was not their problem. Peake checked the readiness of his rifle, thumbing the safety forward to 'fire'. He glanced about nervously, glimpsing Quiz to his right making ready in similar fashion, beyond him a machine-gun crew struggling to re-position their heavy Lewis among the chaos that was the lip of the trench. Some of the barbed wire frames had been blown backwards upon the sap set for the Lewis, and one of the crew was lunging and hacking furiously with his entrenching tool at the broken box-frame of the springy wire, pushing it away to clear his arc of fire.

The smell of cordite mixed with the reek of smoke and blasted, ruptured earth.

Another officer appeared from somewhere, one hand holding unfastened helmet upon his head and the other his Webley. It was Pearson, the company captain.

'Williams!' he bellowed against the noise of the shells still crashing and tossing earth into the air, but falling further away from the line now, closer to the village behind the position. 'Williams, I need two of your men as runners – now, Williams, now! Two men, Lieutenant, and quickly!'

Williams pointed:

'Samuels! Jackson! Both of you – runners. Go!'

'Yes, sir!' They scrambled to quit the fire-step. Hurrying to their captain, they listened intently as he spoke to them urgently and hoarsely. He was panting, voice cracking slightly with effort and strain:

'Listen, lads. Our wires are cut. We've no communication to Guns or Regiment. Nothing. Can't talk to 'em. I want you to move back to the reserve. Keep moving back until you find someone with a working line – could be as far back as the village, I don't know. Tell 'em we're okay up here, but we need artillery between us and Fritz, and we need it now! Tell 'em to bring down everything they've got on registered targets in front of our lines – gas, HE – whatever they have. I want the lot. Got that?'

'Yes, sir!' This was Samuels, an experienced soldier. 'Gas and high explosive on no man's land to our front. Registered positions.'

'Good man. Go now! Quick as you can, lads. Get going!'

They went.

Above the din came the unmistakable voice of Sergeant Winterman walking quickly up and down the trench, exhorting the men on the fire-step to readiness, his simple presence steadying nerves shaken and made unsteady by the shelling, and fortifying resolve. Already, three or four had taken aim and begun to fire through the wire. Winterman put an end to it:

'Cease fire! Hold your fire!' His bellowed command was hoarse. 'Hold your fire and reload! I want full magazines in all rifles. Full magazines, lads! Check and hold your fire – do *not* shoot! There's time yet – wait for my word!'

Peake, fingering his trigger and checking his magazine, licked dry lips and peered out through the chaos of tossed sandbags and ruptured wire. Away towards the German position, something was not as he remembered it from his time on the periscope. Something had changed. Something was moving. Narrowing his eyes, squinting and peering through the smoky haze, seeking to identify the difference, he was shocked to make out several long, staggered ranks of soldiers advancing steadily upon them. They wore field grey, and he could make out jackboots, bucket helmets and the long, bayonet-tipped Mausers they were carrying. The Germans were already midway across no man's land, about four hundred yards distant and closing steadily, walking determinedly forward.

But why on earth were they walking? Were they mad?

Peake's incredulity was cut short by something in the line of grey that coughed loudly – he wasn't sure what or where it was. Then a high explosive shell burst off to his right among the wire. It was almost as nothing after the nightmare of the artillery bombardment, and Peake was surprised to find himself searching quite calmly for its source. There it was! Some kind of moving steel contraption – very large – had fired a shell at them from a position ahead of the line of advancing men. It had its own group of infantry about it.

Peake identified the thing. Tank!

Holding his fire as ordered, Peake watched the monster tilt crazily into a crater, then crawl up and out of it to continue its unsteady passage forward. The cannon coughed again, but the gunner's aim was off because of the machine's lumbering, shuddering gait. The shell passed harmlessly overhead.

There was a lot of noise still. Shells from the enemy barrage were bumping and crashing further back among the reserve positions around the village. No small-arms fire, though. Not yet.

Somebody bellowed:

'ELEVEN PLATOON! SIGHTS AT THREE HUNDRED YARDS! WAIT FOR MY WORD! RATE RAPID! REPEAT, THREE HUNDRED YARDS, RATE RAPID! WAIT FOR MY WORD! WAIT NOW, BOYS … STEADY … WAIT FOR IT …'

Peake adjusted his sights to three hundred, eased his rifle into his shoulder, waited. He tried to place the voice: Sergeant Winterman, probably, or maybe Mister Williams. Tozer and two other corporals bellowed back a repetition of the order as confirmation, and this had a further calming effect on all. They were ready, now. There was discipline here. This was no different from the range work of Brocton and Rouen. They knew exactly how to do it.

Peake checked his rifle for the umpteenth time. There was time to examine all his senses: vision very clear, ears pulsing with blood, and he could feel his own sweat. Somebody was panting heavily, damned fool. With a little shock, he realised that the fool was him, the panting his own. Suppressing it immediately, he fought for self-control as he squinted along the sights of his rifle. It'll be just like Brocton, he told himself. Just like at Brocton range: Single slow breath in … Hold for the shot … Fire, work the bolt and fire again … Then breathe out quickly and repeat: Slowly in … hold for the shot … Fire, work the bolt and fire again. Breathe out. Nothing to worry about … Winterman was close by and there was still no firing from Jerry's side. Or not yet, anyway. Wait now! Wait for the word! He placed his foresight squarely on the chest of an advancing German soldier, trying to estimate the distance. Couldn't make out any facial features. Were they at three hundred yards yet? Must be, surely. Must be there by now …

'RAPID FIRE! RAPID FIRE! FIRE, FIRE, FIRE …!'

They did it. Each man in the line fired at his target, worked the bolt of his rifle to chamber another cartridge, took aim and fired again – two shots in just less than one second. Four hundred rounds from the men of Peake's company alone slammed at high velocity into the advancing Germans. The other three companies of the Seventh fired an equal number of shots, and the companies of the other battalions, too, and there were also the Lewis guns … The soldiers in grey, that line of determined Germans closing steadily upon the trenches, disappeared – something of a miracle to Peake's mind – leaving only the lumbering steel machine that was the tank, now turning its flank to them and stopping uncertainly, hammering back at the British with broadside machine guns.

That first British volley tore the advancing Germans apart. It stopped them absolutely. Many of them thought they were under machine-gun fire alone – no rifles – such was the speed and fury of the Lancashires' discharge.

Not all the British rounds found their mark, for the men in the trenches were far from steady. Shelled for three hours before the German artillery shifted its aim, they were stunned and very badly shaken. Most were suffering from a degree of deafness, and some could not hear at all. Many – especially the replacements – experienced extreme fear as they viewed that line of enemy with bayonets fixed, long blades glinting wickedly in the afternoon sun, closing to kill them. They trembled at the sight. So, when the British opened fire, hundreds of rounds went high and hundreds more wide. Nevertheless, many of them – especially those first shots most carefully aimed – these found their target, and the effect was devastating.

Around the tank, Schäffer went down like a brick, collapsing as if his legs had been cut from under him, and perhaps they had. Dropping his rifle, he fell, gurgling and clutching at his throat. He was dead in seconds.

The rest jinked and zig-zagged forward into cover. Bauer, Zimmermann and Winkler found the same shell crater at the same moment, rolling or tumbling into it and staying well down.

'Schäffer …!'

'SCHÄFFER …!'

It was Goettner bellowing from another hole not far away, but there was no reply.

Bauer was groaning, holding his thigh, blood oozing between fingers, his face a mask of pain. Above the shell hole, the air over the battlefield had become a thing alive and venomous, the British fire hissing, buzzing and whip-cracking through the space where the German soldiers had stood. After some seconds – a seeming lifetime to the men being fired upon – the rate of fire slowed as the British realised there were no more targets, and took time to pause and reload. Sensing the lull, Winkler the replacement tried to edge carefully up his side of the crater, readying his rifle to return fire. Zimmermann caught an ankle and dragged him back into the watery ooze that was the hole's centre.

'Let go of me, Zimmermann! Let me go …!'

Zimmermann said nothing, the sharp, assessing eyes in the helmet-framed face set hard against current circumstance. Those eyes spoke volumes as Zimmermann moved to shift his hold on Winkler, now gripping the replacement firmly by his tunic, head cocked, listening intently and questioning the air for answers while he held his charge down in the safety that was the crater's depression.

The tank, its protecting half-ring of infantry now either dead, wounded or in cover, found itself the only target remaining to the British. A hail of fire hammered into its armoured sides with a loud metallic banging and clattering as the fire intensified again. One or two rounds found the rectangular firing slits, causing a terrible screaming to begin from within the machine. It manoeuvred to present again its armoured prow square-on to the British, then began to reverse, cannon barking defiance, exhaust spewing fumes, gears grating and with engine roaring at maximum effort as it began to back away from the hell that was the battlefield. In the shell hole, still holding Winkler down, Zimmermann chanced a glimpse over the rim in time to see a door open in the tank's side, a wounded crewman with bloody tunic clawing his way through it in a bid to escape. The British rounds found him immediately, and he fell forward to hang half out of his machine, legs trapped within the tank and the heavy steel door he had opened slamming repeatedly into his now lifeless body as the driver negotiated his uneven path in reverse, not always managing to avoid his own wounded, and crushing or maiming several.

The noise was now awful to hear. Carrying above even the angry snapping and buzzing of the British bullets, the three in the shell hole could hear a terrible groaning and, from several directions, screaming. Some of those in cover were still calling out to the missing, trying to assess the situation, trying to assess losses. Goettner had stopped trying; he had stopped shouting for Schäffer. Zimmermann hoped the *oberleutnant* had not attempted any kind of rescue and been killed himself. He tried to think. At ground level, all around the shell hole, the air remained alive with the desultory crack and snap of enemy fire. To skirmish forward would be impossible, the advance was pinned

124

down. Zimmermann glanced to the man he was holding, measuring Winkler and assessing whether he realised that any attempt to leave the hole, or even to return fire, would be futile. Satisfied that he did, he released his hold, the replacement's face immediately becoming a mix of anger, fright and thankful relief that he had been held down within the crater's safety. Zimmermann managed a few words of reassurance, his voice as grim as his face:

'We stay where we are, New Man. We stay in the hole. We do *not* move. Got that?'

There was a nod of understanding. Zimmermann crawled over to Bauer, who had stopped groaning and was concentrating on trying to stem his own bleeding.

'Where does it hurt, Bauer?'

'Here.' Bauer used his chin to indicate a leg.

'Nowhere else?'

'No.'

'Sure?'

'Yes.'

Working quickly with pocket-knife, Zimmermann cut away the trouser leg and examined the wound as best he could. It was difficult because Bauer refused to let go of his own thigh, the flesh and trouser about it slick with blood, so Zimmermann tore and cut at a dry part of the uniform until he had a strip sufficient for a tourniquet, which he wrapped loosely around the leg above the wound. He looked directly at Bauer and warned him: 'This is going to hurt, Bauer. Just for a moment. Can you take it?'

Bauer nodded, bracing his boxer's shoulders. Zimmermann yanked the tourniquet tight. Bauer gasped, passed out and slumped back against the damp earth.

Now came a whistling, feathery sort of sighing, growing louder in the air.

'Shell …!'

Zimmermann shouted the warning.

The thing exploded somewhere ahead of their crater to hurl soil at the sky. Shrapnel sang overhead. Clods of muck thumped and splattered the hole and the three soldiers sheltering there. A second shell arrived to detonate in similar manner, then a third, over towards where they had heard *Oberleutnant* Goettner shouting for Schäffer.

The replacement was wiping sausage-like slime and filth from the sleeve of his tunic, now suddenly bloody.

'You hit?'

'No. It's from … somebody else, I think … It's … It's a piece of someone.' Winkler's face was contorted with revulsion, and he began to shake and tremble as he flicked and wiped at torn innards that were not his own.

'Stay calm! Calm down, boy, calm down! No shell ever lands in the same place twice! It never happens. We'll be all right. Nothing's going to hit us. Calm down and get your gas mask on. And stay low. Over there.'

Zimmermann pointed, and Winkler abandoned his rifle to crawl into the muddy bottom of the shell hole. He dragged the mask and straps over his face and head, dark hair wet with sweat, rammed his helmet back on and went about trying to put hands over his ears, but found he couldn't because of the helmet. He gave up, instead glancing at Zimmermann's efforts to tug and drag Bauer's unconscious form lower into the depression. When Zimmermann had done that, he scrabbled for Bauer's gas mask, strapped it over the sagging face and replaced the man's helmet in case the Tommies started using air bursts. Satisfied, he wrestled his own mask and helmet into place, very aware of the need for speed. He pulled the straps tight, and the three hugged the muddy earth almost as one, two with eyes bright and fearful under the rims of their helmets as the shelling began to intensify, the third oblivious.

The British artillery did not use gas, but Peake didn't care. Neither did the burly Earnshaw beside him. None of the British soldiers cared. Shells of any kind were good enough: anything to hold the Germans back and keep the attack broken up and stopped.

'HOLD YOUR FIRE! CEASE FIRE!'

It was Winterman bawling the order. Further away, Lieutenant Williams was also yelling:

'CEASE FIRING! CEASE FIRE!'

Peake chambered a fresh round but did not trigger it. He leaned against the parapet, alert beyond description but at the same time tired – fear and nervous tension, he supposed. His will to live was stronger than his exhaustion, though. It called forth reserves of determination that made him carefully search the ground of no man's land through his rifle sights. There were no targets. Peake was astonished: No standing or kneeling targets at all – only grey lumps and bundles, shapelessly sprawled and mostly motionless. The dead and gravely wounded lay scattered everywhere over the ground, but they were too distant for Peake to make out detail. He wondered if some might be shamming, then recognised the thought as irrelevant; they had been ordered to cease fire. Now something new caught his attention: fountains of earth erupting without warning from the tortured battleground, the first of the British shells finding their mark. Beyond these artillery strikes he could still make out the German tank continuing its slow reverse, almost back within its own lines and no longer firing at them, out of effective range.

The smell of cordite filled Peake's nostrils, acrid and strong. It overpowered for a while the usual pungency of the trench with its chemical latrines and unwashed men. It made less obvious, too, another new kind odour, strange to Peake. He spent a moment trying to place it, then recognised the scent of newly turned earth – soil overturned and upended around the trench by the German bombardment, like a field put under plough.

Peake gave up his search for movement among the enemy scattered across the ruined land, lowering his head to rest a cheek against the stock of his rifle. The wood felt cool against his skin even as the weapon remained ready, still in place upon the remains of a sandbag, still aimed through the wire. Oily smoke rose in wisps from the snub end of its hot barrel. He found himself tugging at his helmet – some part of it was catching uncomfortably against the torn hessian of the sandbag. He gave up, pushing the thing back and loosened the chinstrap. He began to pant in short, shallow breaths. He was trembling, too, as reaction set in, but this time he did not bother to try for self-control. Instead he waited, hoping for it to pass and looking at nothing at all. He was surprised to find a sudden, vivid image of Christine passing across the ragged edge of his mind.

Corporal Tozer appeared from further up the trench, distributing clips of ammunition and checking for casualties. Around Peake there were none, but Lieutenant Williams was shouting for stretchers from his part of the line. Tozer exuded a steady, determined type of calm resolve as he worked, coaxing and encouraging the men to remain alert. His firm, reassuring Cockney had a steadying effect:

'Reload, boys!' Tozer told them. 'Full mags – reload an' wait! Stay wivvit, nah!'

Peake glanced towards Farmer and Watson beyond the corporal. Farmer had removed his helmet. The squad's joker was alternately sipping water from a canteen and splashing it upon blond curls against the heat of the afternoon. Next to him, Watson was wrestling with the bolt of his rifle, trying to clear a jammed round.

'Easy wiv that wawter, Farmer. An' git yer 'elmet back on. Fritz 'asn't s'rrendered just 'cos yer've arrived ter fight 'im!'

Tozer's reprimand was friendly but firm. Peake half expected Farmer to attempt humorous retort, but there was none, the man remaining silent and doing as he was told. Reaching Watson, Tozer helped clear the stoppage:

'Steady nah, boy, an' 'ead down still. Weapon ter me – quick like, there's a good fellah!'

He took the rifle, expertly clearing the jam. Checking the weapon, he returned it. 'Empty chamber, Watson. Reload an' stay wivvit! This fing ain't over yet. More ter come.' And with that the corporal moved further along the line.

The afternoon was cooling towards its end. Sunset was perhaps ninety minutes away. A broad stretch of cumulus had moved in, mostly grey but becoming a beautiful, shining gold where the sun had slipped behind to edge it, casting angular shafts of bright, shining silver radially across a narrow band of clearer sky to the horizon below. The sight was spectacular to behold, though few in the trench noticed, for they were mostly facing the other way, and for them the gun line rear of Foncquevillers held more urgency and importance, especially since its rate of fire was not increasing to hoped-for intensity. They watched the detonating shells falling uninterestedly in and around the place where the Germans had gone to ground, flashes that blinked red-black for just a split-second, then hurled gouts and clods that spun and danced skyward before slowing and falling back the way they had come.

But surely there should have been more shells ...

Samuels and Jackson, the runners sent back to the guns, reappeared, out of breath and sweating from their exertions. Winterman and another soldier moved to greet them. The sergeant was anxious for news, but he allowed the two time to recover. Halting, the runners were quite obviously exhausted, one stooped with hands on knees, the other using his rifle as a prop. They panted heavily, chests heaving. The soldier with Winterman offered a canteen, and the arrivals gulped gratefully. All waited until conversation was possible. Winterman lit a cigarette, then used it to light three more, passing one to each of the men about him.

'And ...?' he enquired of the two, smiling thinly and exhaling smoke. A hint of humour was always Winterman's way.

'We 'ad to go all t' way back to Reserve, Sergeant.' Samuels managed. He was still panting, but considered the tobacco a priority and filled his lungs anyway. The effort cost him a coughing fit. Jackson took up the thread:

'No communication ter Guns before that.' Breath. 'No lines. Not even right at the rear.'

'Nothing at all? No field lines?'

128

'Nowt, Sergeant. Shelled out. Regiment says they've men tryin' ter lay new cable for'ard.'

Winterman nodded, pulling on his cigarette, considering the announcement.

'Why no gas? Perfect wind for it.'

'Guns said they'd give what they 'ad, but Brigade told 'em no gas. Savin' it. A bloke at Regiment told us Jerry moved 'is bombardment t'the gun line after it lifted 'ere. Art'y took casualties. Bloke said ter expect only about 'arf the guns ter fire. An' no gas.'

'Okay. Get yourselves off to Company, sharpish. Report to Captain Pearson there. He'll want detail, so try to remember exactly what you saw and heard. The Major's dead. Captain's running things now.'

The two runners registered a moment's shock at this news, then sloped off down the trench. Winterman called after them:

'And, you two …'

They stopped, turning for the additional instruction.

'Well done.'

The cloud thickened, the cumulus roiling and rising, stacking steadily upon itself and changing colour, chameleon-like, to become an expanding brown-pink that darkened half the sky. A sun tired of the day cast a swipe of red across the narrow gap between horizon and the cloud bank's base. Evolving and mutating, the cloud continued to build until it could deliver rain to the battlefield and to the battered, broken buildings of Foncquevillers.

The first droplets fell just as it began to grow dark, little more than a gentle drizzle at first, but it meant that gas would not work. Understanding this, the soldiers in the shell craters tugged off their uncomfortable, constricting, goggle-topped masks, and took time to gulp gratefully at the clean air. They packed away masks and adjusted trench coats and webbing, a difficult thing to do while remaining below the rims of the relatively shallow craters. With Zimmermann's guidance and help, Winkler managed it well enough. He retrieved his rifle, then lay prone and tried to withdraw into his coat as protection against the wet. Zimmermann did not trouble himself. For him there seemed no point in the effort. He had experienced worse in Poland, so instead he set his mind against the drizzle and hunkered down next to Bauer, who was conscious again but in obvious pain. From time to time, Zimmermann checked the tourniquet. He knew he had to loosen it periodically, but every time he did this, Bauer's bleeding began anew. He persevered with the routine for a time, stemming the flow of blood with his hands whenever the band was loosened, but eventually he gave up. The flow of blood was too great and the tourniquet would have to stay in place, the only way to keep the bleeding in check. Zimmermann was not a religious man, so he gave vent to a stream of torrid profanity against every god he had ever heard of, blaming them for placing him and Bauer in this predicament – and the replacement too – and hoping against odds that his efforts to save the life of his friend would prove successful. Bauer, a devout Catholic, prayed fervently for the same thing.

Centimetres above the rim of their hole, red-hot shrapnel whined and burned through the air whenever a shell fell. There was occasional rifle fire from some parts of the British line.

The rain strengthened and steadied to become a shower that soaked the land and all fighting to win it. Some three quarters of the attacking Germans had survived the British volley, though a significant number had been wounded, and any of these who had not found the shelter of a crater were now not far from death. In Zimmermann's crater, semi-prone against the earth, Winkler sought to huddle further into his trench coat, adjusting the big helmet in a struggle to remain damply wet rather that become entirely soaked. Zimmermann simply sat there, knees drawn up and forearms dangling upon them while he kept an eye on Bauer beside him. The wounded man was leaning back against the crater's side, legs stretched stiffly out in front like a mannequin. Zimmermann watched the replacement with neither comment nor observable expression. Bauer looked without seeing anything at all, in a haze of pain. Of the three, Zimmermann was the only one to make good use of the rain, occasionally holding his hands out with fingers spread to wash them of Bauer's blood.

The British shelling was not heavy.

'You'd think they could do better than this, eh, New Man – the Tommies? With their guns? You'd think they would try harder.'

Winkler, still visibly shaken, starting with every detonation and trying to hold himself closer to the earth, did not reply directly. He asked:

'What now?'

'We wait,' Zimmermann answered, patting his tunic for cigarettes until he found a crumpled box, and managing to light one in spite of the rain. He drew on the roll until its tip crackled and glowed red, then held it out towards Bauer, who gave a weak shake of his head. He passed it to Winkler instead. 'We wait,' repeated Zimmermann. 'Can't re-start the attack … Can't withdraw either, or not at the moment anyway … So, we wait for the shelling to stop, then we pull back. They won't keep this up all night. Can't. Plus, it's not possible for them to observe and correct their fire in this rain. That's if they can still talk to their guns.'

At the rim of their hole, the last of the light was failing. Beneath it, details of wet rock, mud and the three men themselves – all of these were beginning to blend with the darkness, losing shape and form, becoming indistinct. The definitions of face, helmet, rifle, webbing and boots were melting into shadowy nothingness, ready to meld with the night when twilight was done.

With full darkness came flares from the British lines. Soaring into the night like comets, they popped over the battlefield but failed in their mission to turn night into day, for the rain blurred and weakened the illumination, rendering them ineffective halos of nothingness. They fell prettily through the darkness, lighting little. Eventually, the British gave up.

All were exhausted, German and Briton alike, but none slept, especially not the Germans, soaked and exposed as they were in no man's land, muddy holes their only cover.

Around midnight, the shelling stopped as it had begun, decreasing in scale over several minutes before ending completely. Within the crater, Zimmermann cocked an ear to the night. He could hear almost no small-arms fire, though occasional shells from German artillery continued to whistle-hiss overhead, their crashing detonations harassing and distressing the British line. In the shell hole, rain drummed and splashed upon the wet earth and central puddle, while from nearby came a new sound: the weak moaning of a wounded man. Schäffer? Zimmermann hoped against hope that it might be the Old Man, still alive.

Now a heavy, slithering sound: a stealthy crunching and sliding from somewhere near at hand in the darkness, approaching their hole quite quickly. Zimmermann placed one strong hand in silent restraint on Winkler's arm, signalling him to make no noise, then readied his rifle with long, wicked steel bayonet ready to thrust. A hoarse whisper came to them from the black:

'Zimmermann … Bauer … Can you hear me?'

It was Goettner.

'Over here, *Herr Oberleutnant*!'

Goettner appeared at the rim of the hole as a helmeted outline of head and shoulders completely black against the actual night. There was a forearm and hand too: he had his pistol drawn.

'Is everybody all right here?'

'Bauer has a bad leg wound, *Herr Oberleutnant*. The bone is splintered, I think. He needs a medic.'

Goettner was silent for some seconds, thinking before deciding:

'Okay. We must get him back to the lines. I'll send somebody to help you.'

'Not necessary, *Herr Oberleutnant*, I have one of the new men with me.'

'Good … All right, both of you go now. Take him while we still have the rain. Do it quickly, Zimmermann. Get it done.'

Winkler moved in the darkness to help with the load that was Bauer, but Zimmermann passed the man his rifle instead in a gesture clearly indicating that no assistance was needed. There was no rancour in his voice:

'Take my weapon, New Man. Bauer's too. And stay close.'

Zimmermann's tone offered no possibility of debate. The big man turned in the night to place a hand under each of Bauer's armpits and heave him out of the hole, Bauer gritting his teeth and grunting against the pain, then passing out again. Zimmermann was thankful for that loss of consciousness. He hefted his wounded comrade across his back and prepared to leave, then turned briefly to the black shape that was Goettner, still at the crater.

'What of Schäffer, *Herr Oberleutnant*?'

'Dead. Back where the tank was. About fifteen metres.'

'Who's that groaning?'

'Don't know. Nettermann and König've gone to find out and get him back to the line. They'll be around, so watch out for them. Others, too, so don't fire at anything at all. There'll be no Tommies about. Now go – get it done while there's still rain to hide you. The rest of us will come as soon as I've located everybody.'

'*Jawohl, Herr Oberleutnant!*' And Zimmermann set off, Bauer upon his back and Winkler by his side encumbered by their three rifles and the wounded man's webbing. Goettner watched them set off in the direction from which they had come that afternoon. He pondered for a second the waste of it all: so many good men dead. Then he resumed his crawl to craters where he remembered seeing others of his *zug* take cover when the British volley had torn apart their advancing ranks.

Dawn. It crept upon the land with dull reluctance, lacking beauty as if acknowledging what had happened, how many had died.

In the forward trenches of the British line, rent sandbags, collapsed walls and a mess of barbed wire mangled by the previous day's shelling emerged from inky nothingness to assume identifiable form. Everything, everyone, became damp silhouettes under an overcast sky revealing itself in shades of lead. Later, it would rain again. The air was calm and still – no breeze at all –

and the temperature a chilly low that painted rifle barrel, helmet and all things steel with brushstrokes of dew.

Within their part of the line, the worried eyes of the Seventh – the entire battalion stood-to as always for first light – peered with a kind of determined anxiety over wet, hessian-covered bags and through the yards of barbed wire into no man's land, everyone very tired. They had not slept, yet their apprehension delivered sufficient energy for careful examination of the battlefield. They sought any change revealed by the strengthening light. They sought sign of attack, or preparation for one. The Seventh was a seasoned unit, and it watched, prepared and ready for any kind of first-light German trickery.

In Sergeant Winterman's view, an attack was unlikely. There was no barrage to warn of it – only the harassing fire of a front returned again to inactivity, the artillery of both sides unpredictable and their firing infrequent: perhaps one shell falling randomly every ten or twelve minutes somewhere up or down the line – though in the distance and from both directions the sounds of heavy bombardment continued as ominous sign of the greater German breakout. Where stood the Seventh, however, there was a temporary lull, both sides passive, licking their wounds. Winterman thought that probably Fritz had used the rainy dark of the previous night to pull back – it was what they themselves would have done. Glancing up and down the trench, assessing the state of the platoon, his eyes rested longer on the new men: Watson and the ever-eager Earnshaw – Quiz – and Peake and Farmer. The sergeant was measuring them still. To Winterman's eye, these four were noticeably twitchier than the rest, though they had held up well enough under yesterday's attack, their first. He would make a point of chatting with them later. He'd deliver a quip or two to make light of things, and maybe coax some humour out of Farmer. Further away, he could see Lieutenant Williams holding binoculars to his eyes, scanning the torn fields now scattered with lumps of field grey, none moving. Winterman glanced to Williams' hands, reassured to see that they were steady. He was okay, that Welshman.

The light increased. Word came to stand down and they did it, posting sentries and allowing the level of tension to ease a little for the first time since the bombardment and the attack, though none relaxed completely. How many hours ago had that been, exactly, when the Germans began their shelling? Had it been midday, or later in the afternoon? Winterman couldn't recall, and with that realisation came worry, because he knew that he needed to function – it couldn't have been the morning, surely. Why couldn't he remember?

He was tired, that was all. He needed to sleep.

133

The communication trench disgorged a new arrival: a runner, out of breath and looking about. Orientated, he headed for the dugout that was battalion headquarters – written orders from the rear, probably. The shelling must have severed his most direct route forward, Winterman reasoned, or the man would not have come via C Company. After him came carrying parties bearing awkward loads of heavy boxes that forced them to walk semi-sideways like crabs. The boxes were from the company kitchen to the rear: steel hay-boxes with stew, the first hot food to arrive in the forward trenches since the start of the shelling. Winterman shouted to Tozer and the other section corporals to direct the newcomers. The carrying party was enthusiastically greeted.

While the food was distributed there was little for Winterman to do, so he propped his rifle against a nook in the wall and sat down on the fire-step to rest. He found a cigarette, bent and flattened – it had been a long time since Winterman had seen any cigarette that wasn't. He lit up, cupping the glowing tip to warm his palms against the chilly dawn. The ritual gave his hands something to do. He held the roll in circled thumb and forefinger, switching from left hand to right and back again as he smoked. He let his thoughts wander:

Some attack, that one. Never known shelling like it. No casualties – or not in this platoon. Definitely wounded beyond Mister Williams, though, among Ten and Twelve. Some of the other companies must've copped it, too, judging by that screaming just after the shelling. Why on earth had Fritz come on so slowly? Why hadn't he been closer to his shells when the barrage lifted? Must've been because of that tank – probably ordered not to out-pace the bloody thing. And their artillery'd lifted way too soon, leaving 'em exposed to the volley. By God, if that enormous armoured bugger'd reached us it would've wreaked havoc … we've nothing to stop it. So, what now? What next? They'll re-organise and come on again, of course. But when? No shelling at the moment, though it sounds pretty bad away to the flanks, maybe three or four miles. Seems to have moved rear of us. Maybe Jerry's broken through everywhere in the sector except here … Hope we hear something from Mister Williams when he comes back from OC's briefing; it'll be Captain Pearson now that the major's gone. Sad that. A good man, was the major. He'd been all right. Captain's briefing could take a while, because Williams and the other officers'll wait until everybody else has had food before they eat their own. Bloody officers! They get theirs first but they eat it last, cold. Always trying to set a good example, silly buggers. Just as well, probably. So, maybe an hour before we get briefed on what's happening on the flanks. Maybe more than an hour … Must organise a team to help clear that collapsed wall over there.

And the other one, too. Must remember to tell the lads to put up extra shoring if there's time … Won't shave today – maybe tomorrow, and it'll have to be dry: I hate that, but it'll be a while before any water comes up and it won't be for washing when it does … Lots of dead Germans out there. They'll start to stink if we get warmer weather. Hope we got that sniper. I hope he's one of those dead bundles out there … Bastard … Wonder how things are back home …?

And Winterman touched the outline of the engraved hip flask through his tunic, thinking of his fiancée and the peace that was Camden.

The company sergeant-major came into view, pausing briefly here and there as he approached, casting an eye of expert examination over this and that within the trench. He had two soldiers in tow, rifles slung and carrying a large, heavy wooden ammunition box by rope handles. All three were still wet from the night's rain. Everybody was.

'Over there, lads,' he instructed, pointing to the fire-step next to Winterman, who stood in greeting. 'And bring another one. Sharpish.'

They dropped the heavy box and went back the way they had come.

'Ammunition, John,' announced the CSM somewhat redundantly. 'For when they've eaten.' He looked about him, taking in the burst walls. Winterman caught the glance. He gave reassurance that repairs would be promptly effected.

'Good, John. Good. When your corporals distribute these clips, have 'em inspect weapons too, will you? We'll need 'em clean and oiled, ready for the next lot.' A pause. The CSM pushed his helmet back a bit on his head. 'So, no casualties here in Lucky Eleven, eh, John?'

'No, sir, not this time. How many in the others?'

The two men locked eyes briefly, faces grim in mutual understanding of losses and what they meant, but there was no resentment on the part of the company sergeant-major at the direct inquiry; these two had been together since Winterman had arrived as a private straight out of Brocton, the CSM then still a junior sergeant.

'Fifteen, John. Twelve during the shelling and three in the attack. All wounded except the major. Dead. The trench right outside headquarters dugout copped a hit. The major killed an' prob'ly two of the other blokes won't make it beyond the aid station. Haven't heard yet about the other companies.'

Winterman drew on his cigarette. One of the platoon orderlies approached. He was holding a mess-tin. Stew.

135

'Mornin', sir!' the man greeted his sergeant-major cheerfully. 'This 'ere's for Sergeant Winterman, but there's overs if you'd like. It's good grub.'

The CSM mustered some or other quip about kitchen cooks and rear echelon bottle-washers, declining the offer. To Winterman he said:

'Well, I'll be off, now, John. There'll be a company briefing after Battalion's passed down the word to Captain Pearson and the other OCs. I've told Lieutenant Williams I'll send word of the time. Make sure as many of your men as possible get some kip until Mister Williams gets back from that. No doubt he'll work some kind of roster with you, but keep the first rest-spell short. Or the first two, if he'll allow it – everyone's tired an' needs a chance at shut-eye. We can make 'em longer later. And be sure to get some rest yourself.'

With that, the CSM applied a firm and friendly grip of encouragement to Winterman's shoulder, then turned and moved further along the trench. Winterman watched him go, marvelling at the indefatigability of the man, and wondering when the company would get replacements for the fifteen lost.

Winkler led the way, plotting a path around craters and other obstacles, sensing more than seeing these in a night made almost completely black by cloud and rain. He tried to avoid the bodies. There were many in the area where they had all gone to ground, stopped by the British volley. Once he tripped on an outflung limb, falling forward across the corpse. He displayed no reaction; it was just one more bad experience in his new life at the front. Clambering to his feet and rearranging the load that was Bauer's webbing, pack and helmet, and all three rifles too, he drew down a mental curtain of self-protection to envelop and seal off his revulsion at death's touch, compartmentalising the nightmare feel of newly lifeless flesh beneath blood-soaked tunic, and burying the memory as deep as he could. Winkler had taught himself to lock away awful experience. Though he disliked the army and hated everything to do with the war, his training had taught him very well how to cope with battle's challenges. Now, he summoned one further reserve of resolution and focused again on the task at hand, something quite difficult because of his fatigue, his shock and the rain-soaked night. He stumbled often. Behind him came Zimmermann, Bauer draped heavily over his back, the wounded man's good leg and one arm clasped tightly to his chest. Bauer's head lolled and bounced, his boxer's nose dripping rain. From time to time Zimmermann ordered a correction of their general direction, but it was not too often that he did this. He himself was unsure of their precise position and orientation – no compass – and the replacement seemed to be doing the difficult job of navigation as well as anyone.

Around them, all was blackness in a night filled with rain that had become lighter but remained steady. It hissed on the soaked earth and it drummed on their trench coats and steel helmets, and on the back of Bauer's lolling head. They could not hear even their own unsteady footfalls across the puddled, uneven ground. From time to time came machine-gun fire from some or other point in the British lines behind them, a steady staccato aimed at who knew what, for none could see. To their front, their own line was silent.

Then a voice from close at hand – it reached out to them through their fatigue and fear, and it spoke in German:

'Over here!'

The voice was urgent, more a hoarse whisper than spoken summons, and pitched just loudly enough to overcome the drumming and splashing of the rain. Zimmermann thanked God for that voice. Ahead of him in the wet blackness, he sensed the replacement turning towards it, so Zimmermann followed just a pace or two behind, exhausted under Bauer's unconscious weight, and disorientated because of that exhaustion. Before the voice, he had been fretting over how to find passage through the wire without inviting fire from the men covering it: How would they safely make their presence known? How would they find a gap? What if they bumped other survivors, nervous and trigger-happy? Now, this voice from the darkness ended that terrible worry. It was the voice of a man from their own lines.

A crouching blur materialised from the inky wetness ahead of the replacement: a soldier kneeling with rifle aimed at them.

'Don't shoot! Don't shoot! We have wounded!'

The shadowy shape lowered his weapon, said:

'Gap's beside me on my left … Here … That's it, that's it … Right there. Keep going straight but watch out for a turn after about ten metres. One turn only. We've marked it for you. Dead straight after that – no more corners. There are medical orderlies waiting in the sentry trench.'

Zimmermann managed a word of thanks, stumbling past the soldier at the mouth to the passage. Tangles of wire thick and barbed reached out crazily from left and right to snag them: walls that were scarcely visible, hints of denser black in the rainy darkness. The hazard of the wire forced Zimmermann to call forth a final reserve of determined concentration so that he would not slip or stagger, or snag Bauer on the wire. Then came a large square of wood painted white to indicate the corner … They turned into a new eternity of struggling effort, staggering on and then on yet further, until the deeper black of the entanglements morphed without warning into human form, two shadows appearing through the rainy darkness to their front, friendly strangers prepared and ready to receive survivors of the failed attack. These took control, relieving Zimmermann of Bauer and lowering the unconscious soldier carefully into willing arms waiting below within the trench.

'Okay … Okay, we've got him. Let go. You can let go. Easy, now … Careful, careful. All right, onto the stretcher and straight to the aid station. Go, *brüder*. Go!'

Zimmermann was too exhausted to speak. Winkler did it for him, calling after the stretcher:

'There's a tourniquet on his leg. Maybe twenty minutes …'

'Don't worry. He'll be with an orderly before he knows it.'

'Where are they taking him?' This to the soldiers who had received them.

'Second trench. There's an aid station there. Here, drink this. Not too much, now. Strong stuff.' The stranger pressed a water bottle into Winkler's hand: warm coffee laced with something – schnapps, probably – and quite potent, as the stranger had warned. He took a pull and passed it to Zimmermann.

'Move along now,' the soldier urged. 'Follow the stretcher party down the communication trench. Go now … Quickly, go! There'll be others coming in. We need the space.'

A short jog along the duckboards until they caught up with Bauer on his stretcher, feeling all the while the close presence of soldiers stood-to on the fire-step. Stood-to? For God's sake, was it nearly dawn already? Then a turn away from the sentry trench toward the rear, and they kept going for quite some time until they reached the careful engineering of the main trench itself, all concrete bunkers and neat walls of wood, unseen in the dark. Strong hands, firm but friendly, grabbed an arm of each man to restrain the two from further progress. Another proffered more laced coffee. The brew was in a mug this time. Winkler mumbled thanks and sipped gratefully, then passed the mug to Zimmermann who declined, sensing his wounded friend being borne away in the darkness. Zimmermann began to shout:

'Where're you taking him? Where's he going?'

'Hot food this way. Come, man, come. Your friend is in good hands.'

'No. I must go with him.'

'Don't worry. You can see him in the morning.'

'FUCK YOU! I WANT TO GO WITH BAUER!'

'Well you can't. Here, drink this,' replied the voice calmly but with a note of caution against Zimmermann's bellow, recovering the mug from Winkler and insisting that Zimmermann drink. Strong hands held him by one arm in a clear gesture of restraint. Zimmermann submitted, mumbling apologies. Someone lit cigarettes, match flaring in the darkness to show a face and helmet made yellow by the flame held in cupped hands. All smoked a while, until the two survivors appeared ready to go where they had been directed. All considered apology, but none was needed from any. There was tacit understanding of what had been endured, of what had been lost. Only two of them understood completely, though.

Somewhere along the trench, food was offered. They tried to eat, but could manage only a mouthful or two. After, they stumbled to a bunker lit by the unsteady illumination of a trench lantern. The soldier guiding them placed the unfinished food carefully on a shelf and left. They shed their equipment. They checked rifles like automations, making them safe, Bauer's weapon too. Then they looked tiredly at one another, each man seeking affirmation and reassurance of life from the other, and appearing to see his fellow *gefreiter* as though for the first time. They were wet through, filthy with caked mud and blood, exhausted. Each looked into the other's face, thinking it gaunt and haunted. Zimmermann nodded to the stacked rifles:

'Can you believe it, New Man? I did not get even one shot off. Please tell me you did better?'

'No, not one. Bauer's magazine is also full.'

They fell silent and sat, Zimmermann proffering a water bottle to the other, who declined with a shake of his head.

'It's laced coffee, New Man. I kept their bottle. It is still warm.' And Zimmermann laughed softly at the other's grateful surprise, passing the bottle and watching him sip. But it was only a very short laugh.

They slept, two survivors side by side who did not wake even when others from the attack dribbled in as twos and threes: Goettner, Nettermann and König first, then more from their *zug* equally intent on rest. All slept the deep sleep of the truly spent, seeming in the darkness left them by the expired lantern much like the dead they had left behind.

In the late morning of the following day – around eleven o'clock – they did eat, consuming ravenously the bully beef and beans, now cold, that none had wanted when fresh and hot. Zimmermann and the replacement ate their ration together, side by side on the fire-step outside the bunker.

'Time I learned your name, New Man.'

139

The replacement looked at him, round face reflecting weary suspicion. He was uncertain of Zimmermann's direction.

'You do have a name, New Man?'

'Winkler. It's Winkler.'

'Winkler,' acknowledged Zimmermann between mouthfuls, chewing and considering. 'Well, Winkler, good job last night – guiding us back.'

Winkler kept his silence, unsure how to respond after so much bullying by Zimmermann over the weeks before the patrol. The latter, swallowing, changed tack:

'They broke a lot of rules here last night, Winkler. Must've considered our situation most serious.' It was a judgment.

'How so?'

'The man by the entrance to the wire. Him for a start. And the other soldiers out of the trench, on the parapet waiting for us. Never seen that before. It's dangerous, against orders. One shell would've killed everyone. I heard this morning there were other parties out between the gaps, too – guides looking for stragglers. We took a pasting, that's for sure.'

'Some of us are missing. Four or five at least.' Winkler was looking around.

'Probably more, Winkler. Probably more. Poor old Schäffer …'

Both glanced down to their food, remembering the groaning man beyond their crater and wondering who it might have been. Well, not Schäffer. Schäffer was dead.

A *wachtmeister* approached, seeking Goettner. Finding him, there was brief conversation. Then the *wachtmeister* left. Goettner announced casually that all should finish their meal. No hurry, he told them – they should eat their fill. But afterwards they must prepare to leave. The *wachtmeister* had brought orders. All survivors were to pull back to the third line four kilometres to the rear and reorganise.

CHAPTER SEVEN

'Our part in Operation Michael, Dieter, our attack at Foncquevillers … Why did it fail?'

'The British have placed additional machine guns in this part of their line, *Herr Generalleutnant*. We did not know about them.'

'No. I do not believe that. The intelligence that we have does not point to any extraordinary machine gun concentrations anywhere along the British front. What I do believe is that there are determined infantry defending the line where we attacked, men with excellent fire discipline.'

'There was also the matter of our artillery, *Herr Generalleutnant*. They lifted the bombardment too soon. The first wave was still four hundred and fifty metres short of the objective when our guns moved on to targets rear of the Tommy line.'

'Yes. That I do believe. There have been similar reports from other units, though they pressed ahead anyway and took their objectives as planned. But not our own attack at Foncquevillers … Not your own men.'

The *generalleutnant* – the divisional commander – was standing with his back to the man with whom he was in conversation, the *oberst* whose regiment of two thousand five hundred had been one of two beaten back by the British defence. The *generalleutnant's* other regimental commander had already undergone a separate debrief. Now, his second *oberst* – Dieter – was sitting with legs crossed on a chair at one of the general's planning tables. His face was taut, lips compressed into a tight slash by the strain of self-control, but he was prepared for this interrogation and sure of his case. There were no other men in the room.

The general, a lean man of nondescript looks and height, was pacing now, a short riding crop of braided leather held up and pressed to one cheek in the manner of someone determined not to speak unnecessarily. Deep in thought, he interrupted his pacing from time to time to examine a battlefield map mounted on one wall of what had once been the drawing room of this double-storey mansion, his operational headquarters. The mansion was situated on the outskirts of a small town a few kilometres behind the rearmost positions of the *Siegfriedstellung*, one of many such headquarters along the one hundred and forty kilometres of that heavily fortified line. Back in 1914, artillery covering Germany's advance through Belgium into France had fired upon this place while it was still being defended, destroying one wing of the mansion and forcing its occupants to flee. Later, when the advance bogged down and deteriorated into the static defence adopted by both sides, realisation dawned on High Command that this new form of stagnant warfare could last a long time, so the general had pressed into service local builders to effect rudimentary repairs of the mansion walls and roofing, and he occupied the place. Since that time – three years ago now – the abandoned mansion had served as the *generalleutnant's* operational centre, its one hastily re-constructed wing of bare brick an ugly reminder of the fighting that had briefly raged here. From the mansion's attic windows it was possible to actually see the rearmost fortifications of the *Siegfriedstellung*, something which gave the general a sense of connection with his soldiers. Other sections of the division's headquarters – staff, supply, administration – occupied houses on both sides of the street leading back to the town centre.

'Why did we not manage it?' mused the man at the map. 'How is it that we did we not take Foncquevillers? We had the numbers. Why didn't it happen …?'

His words carried neither threat nor menace. Rather, they were a soft murmur for his own benefit, uttered as if to help his considerable intellect deliver a solution to the problem that was as much the successful British defence of this tiny French village as it was the failure of his own division in the attack. Soft though the general's words may have been, they nevertheless prompted a response:

'But, with respect *Herr Generalleutnant*, if we …'

The general interrupted his *oberst* mid-sentence:

'No, Dieter. I cannot deal in "ifs". We must ask and answer the "hows". We must define the reasons for this failure, and make adjustments so that there is no repetition. There is no witch-hunt here, you understand. But we need solutions. And quickly, too.'

Choosing not to resume his pacing, the general turned from the map to face his colonel.

'What news of casualties?' he asked.

'Twenty to twenty-five percent, *Herr Generalleutnant*. We are still assessing. Some *kompanies* are not yet back in the third line.'

The general repositioned his leather crop behind him, clasping the device in both hands and staring down at his polished jackboots of gleaming leather. That crop was part of him. Without it he felt ineffective – naked, almost – for his background was cavalry, and the mannerisms and character of those regiments of horse through which he had progressed remained an integral part of his personality and outlook. Half a dozen years before the war, ability and intellect had propelled him to a post too senior to confine his leadership to the cavalry alone. Now, promoted yet further, he commanded units from all arms of the German Army: infantry, artillery, engineers, supplies and signals as well as cavalry, and he commanded this new thing too – the tank – predicted by many to replace the horse entirely, given time. In the view of the *generalleutnant*, this was a dangerous prediction, but perhaps the soothsayers were right, for the cavalry formations that were his passion had so far had little part to play in this new type of conflict, being kept eternally in the rear in hope of exploiting some unfolding advantage that never quite managed to materialise.

The general half-turned to his map so that the other man, too, could see it. He used the crop's leather tip to indicate specific points marked upon the thick paper.

'On both sides of Foncquevillers – here, and here – on both flanks of the British infantry that held firm, our attack is now some four to five kilometres deep,' he announced. 'The other divisions continue to push north and west every hour, perhaps two hundred thousand men on either side of this single British regiment holding this single village. On either flank the advance continues. But at Foncquevillers the British hold firm. And they are doing it with just three battalions as far as we can tell – no more than a brigade at any rate. At Foncquevillers and at one other objective the wider push has been dented.'

The general was deliberate in his avoidance of the word 'stopped'. Another word – 'failed' – came just as easily to his mind. But he was very well aware that the colonel in discussion with him was an officer possessing an excellent record of success in battle, even though it had been earned in the east against the Russians. Well, it was just too bad that here in the west things were different. It was a different front, a different enemy. The *Herr Oberst* was going to have to try harder.

The crop moved short distances across the map, pointing:

'There is another village – here – where the greater operation also did not gain the objective. It means that we have the makings of two dangerous bulges in the line of our advance. If those bulges develop to become definable salients, then the British might reinforce the units defending them. They might make use of them to mount a pincer attack to cut off our troops advancing across the ground in between. Should they do that and do it successfully, then the British would have a very broad dagger thrust deep into our advance, with the bulk of our forces well to their rear, left and right. There would exist the possibility of the British breaking through.'

'But that would surely open them up to encirclement themselves, *Herr Generalleutnant*.'

The general did not deem this observation worthy of reply. It was correct, of course, but it was irrelevant to the current situation, and he was not prepared to debate the matter. The point was that Foncquevillers had to be taken, and taken soon. There was enormous pressure coming down on him from Seventeenth Army Headquarters, where phrases like 'last chance' and even 'last hope' were rumoured to be in surreptitious use. Not surprising, really, given the situation at home: critical food shortages, the people weak and exhausted. Revolution was a heartbeat away, swift victory the only way out.

'Dieter. You wanted to make some suggestion about how you might have succeeded?'

'Yes, *Herr Generalleutnant*. I wanted to say that we need more tanks. If we had had more, we might have done better. There were just four in my entire regiment. What of all the British machines we used for exercises prior to the assault? What happened to those?'

'The general staff think it would be bad for morale if we were to use enemy tanks in any of our assaults. They forbid the use of enemy weaponry other than for training purposes. Simple as that.'

'I see …'

The *oberst* waited, passing no further comment. He sensed that his general already knew what the next step would be. He watched the cavalryman cross to a trolley that had been wheeled in with coffee and cups ahead of their meeting. The general poured for two, setting one before his colonel as a gesture of friendly respect, commander to subordinate.

'Cream, Dieter?'

It was not real cream, of course, so the *oberst* declined; he was not fond of the substitute, too gluey for his palate. The general returned to the trolley to bring sweetener – local honey from some or other farm – then fetched his own cup and saucer, stirring the dark liquid for almost a full half-minute before placing it upon the planning table, untouched.

'Your regiment will attack again, Dieter, at dawn tomorrow.' Even as the *oberst* opened his mouth to voice objection, the general held up his hand to request patience, to request silence. The gesture was a plea for time to explain. 'Wait, hear me out. Your men will not lead the assault. A fresh regiment, the Fifth, will lead. Your own and the other from yesterday's attack will support it from one hundred metres behind. Additional battalions will be attacking on the flanks. Three regiments plus the flanking units should break the British defence, I think. The attacking ratio will be four to one. It is sufficient.'

The *oberst* was silent. The news was not all bad.

'You will want to know about replacements,' continued the general. 'I do understand that your casualties are heavy and that your men need rest. But the danger of a British pincer movement is very grave. It carries a more pressing threat than the men's need to recover, and you are to explain this fact very clearly to your battalion commanders when you issue your warning order. You have the remainder of the day to rest your men as you might. No move before twenty-three hundred hours tonight, when you will move up to the first line in readiness. I am reinforcing your regiment with replacement *kompanies* fresh from the reserve. It will give you a command slightly over-strength, given your casualties. There will be motor transport as far as the second line. Detailed orders for the attack will be delivered here at nineteen hundred hours.'

The *generalleutnant* paused, measuring his man, watching for reaction and assessing the state of his nerve, looking for any sign of unwillingness to undertake the task. Seeing none, he reached for his cup, sipped, replaced it delicately upon its saucer, and continued:

'Now listen, Dieter, we are not going to blindly repeat what we did yesterday afternoon. There is not complete madness here.' A tight smile. 'The planning staff are preparing a different and much more careful fire plan for the guns even as we speak. There will be gas, given the correct wind, and I want Fifth Regiment within two hundred metres of the Tommy trenches before the artillery lifts – closer if possible. There will be more detail at the orders group tonight, but what I want is for the Fifth to be able to get through the wire and rush the trenches before the enemy can reorganise, even if we ourselves have to take light casualties from our own shells in order to be close enough to do that. They will have the tanks, too – the Fifth, not your own troops – and I will press upon them the need to move quickly forward using fire and movement over the last dash. The tanks will have to catch up as best they can. You will press upon your men the need to exactly match the rate of that rush to the British line until you reach the tanks. Ideally, you will move onto the position with them.'

145

No reply to the general's words was necessary, so the *oberst* held his silence, sipping at his coffee to mask his feelings and wondering if the general had passed him the brew precisely to allow that mask. He felt deep relief at not being ordered to take the point of the attack; others would have to overcome the British wire when they reached it – if they reached it. That the Fifth would lead was a Godsend: it would make tomorrow's assault easier for the *oberst* to sell to his battalion commanders, especially after the casualties they had so recently suffered, and after such a brief period of rest.

Wainwright was preoccupied. Entering The Duke, he barely noticed the tinkling of the little bell announcing his passage from the street. He had a folded newspaper under one arm. Closing the varnished front door with its misted viewing panes, he removed the 'paper, hung his jacket and removed his scarf.

It was early evening. At the bar, Mrs Winterman watched him. She was an experienced publican with instincts honed over many years regarding the mood of her customers, and straight away she began to draw Wainwright's pint, surreptitiously examining him between pulls at the varnished tap handle. She watched him move to a stool at one end of the bar, and she noted the absence of any greeting.

Under the dim light of the bar's single lamp, she approached him cheerfully, but with caution.

'Here you are then, Mr Wainwright. A pint of bitter's been my guess, and I've given you a long pull – no off-duty constables here tonight.' She smiled her welcome as she placed the glass before him, then chuckled at her own jest. 'There's better light closer to the taps, if it's the newspaper you'll be wanting to read.' She studied Wainwright's face beneath its widow's crown of shaggy curls. The man's normally cheerful expression was absent tonight. He seemed not himself.

'What news of young Simon?' she tried, wanting to relax him. 'Any postcards or letters?'

Wainwright thanked her for the pint, passing her the price. He spread his newspaper upon the counter. A banner headline carried dark news of the German offensive taking place in the British sector of the line.

'The light's fine here if I might borrow a candle, Mrs Winterman.' He tried for a smile with limited success. 'I just want to see the front page before I go home. Dinner's waiting, or will be when I get there. We have guests.'

146

She recognised in the oblique reply his need to be alone, so she pushed a lighted tallow toward his newspaper and let him be, moving away to serve another. A friend had already told her of the German push, and her own cheeriness was forced – she was more worried about the war today than was usual for her.

Wainwright sipped, reading, oblivious to the patrons around him, small groups of three and four seated in huddled conversation at tables arranged across the flagged floor. There were two men standing at the further end of the bar, but they seemed to be doing more thinking than talking – sons at the front, too, probably.

The front page of the newspaper was more headline than detail, announcing a German breakthrough at an unspecified point. There were no hard facts within the terse lines of the official communiqué from the Committee of Imperial Defence. That took up most of the space, and the next two pages carried only vague reports and speculation telegraphed through from various sources who, though present in France, were well to the rear of the fighting. They weren't witnesses. There were no photographs and no casualty figures to suggest scale; the press had long since stopped listing names – too demoralising. Now, you had to buy a weekly booklet specific to detailing war casualties if you wanted to gauge the intensity of the fighting.

Wainwright read rapidly through the reports. They ran to three full pages, but it was impossible to guess at either the depth or breadth of the German successes. He gave himself over to speculation, trying unsuccessfully to picture a war about which he knew very little. It was difficult. The young men he had met on home leave preferred light anecdote to detail, deftly deflecting questions even about general living conditions, let alone the actual fighting. Yet of one thing Wainwright was absolutely certain: this war had become something both terrible and unprecedented. British soldiers had experienced nothing even remotely like it before.

He re-read all the reports, sipping steadily at the weak wartime beer. Then he put aside the newspaper to ponder what facts he had. His view was that the stalemate along the front would continue as before. This attack would be stopped, and the status quo resumed. Almost four years, now, and the damned thing just kept dragging on and on: an advance here, a withdrawal there, but only a mile or two gained by either side before whatever push had been mounted fizzled out ready for the captured ground to be lost again, leaving thousands more to be buried. Until today, that was, for the newspaper had hinted at an offensive on a grand scale, and with considerable success too. Was Simon involved in this latest fighting? If not, would he become so? Was the breakthrough grave enough for Simon's battalion to be repositioned in support of a broken defence, or was he already part of a general retreat? Or even a prisoner? There were no answers, so Wainwright gave up. Draining his glass, he bade Mrs Winterman as cheerful a farewell as he could muster, donned scarf and coat, and left. He did not take the newspaper with him – the first few pages had been enough. No point in upsetting his wife or Penelope Brooke, or Simon's young love whom he was going to meet for the first time over dinner.

Outside The Duke, a muffled, throaty growl came from the night sky above. Wainwright looked up, questioning the darkness. Must be a 'plane of some sort – those were aero-engines – hope to God it's one of ours and not a Zeppelin. He shut his mind to the possibility, continuing along the darkened street as he made for home, thinking deeply about this war that had no end. He was so deep in thought that he barely noticed the chilly night, his progress through the stark streets automatic, his mind a churning turmoil. After a while, he forced upon his imagination the more pleasant picture of his wife and home, and the dinner soon to be enjoyed with her and with Penelope and the girl, Christine. He was looking forward very much to meeting this young woman.

Above, in the gloom, the lone aircraft that Wainwright had heard continued on its course. It was a very large, multi-motor machine – German – a *Staaken* bomber of the *Luftstreitkreitkräfte*, one of eighteen such aircraft built to take over night-bombing missions from the gas-filled Zeppelin airships withdrawn because of their vulnerability to British incendiary bullets. The *Staakens* were new-technology biplane bombers, enormous machines with wingspans of forty-two metres, powered by four motors mounted back-to-back in push-pull fashion within twin nacelles fixed between the upper and lower wings, one nacelle on either side of the fuselage, and a mechanic seated in the open centre of each. Besides ensuring that the propellers kept turning, the job of the mechanics was to man defensive machine guns.

On that particular evening, there was only one *Staaken* flying across the vast expanse of nothingness that was the London sky. It was the single source of noise in a night otherwise silent and unusually clear, and it flew unseen and unopposed. The bomber had taken off from Scheldewindeke Airfield outside Ghent, in Belgium, navigating by dead-reckoning on a single bearing across the English Channel until the line of solid darkness that was the enemy coast interrupted the reflection of moonlight off seawater. Now, the aircraft commander spotted reflection once again: the unmistakable shape of the Thames. This was not only his navigational marker, but also his objective. He could order the bombs to be dropped, orientate where the river flowed in meandering curves through the capital city, then chart a new bearing home.

When the crew toggled their bombs, the high-explosive canisters fell as a single drop, a single cluster. They were small affairs – two-hundred-pounders only – but there were twenty-one of them and, the *Staaken* being a slow aircraft, the bombs arrived within a small footprint just one hundred and fifty metres long. They exploded as a condensed packet of destruction that demolished two terrace houses, killing or maiming all within those two, and damaging a further five dwellings. The first bomb to leave the *Staaken's* internal racks – the first explosion of that strike – impacted twenty yards in front of Wainwright as he walked home from The Duke, his thoughts still transitioning from the worry about Simon and the new German offensive to more pleasant anticipation of dinner with the three women waiting for him. The road was cobbled, so the bomb did not penetrate and caused only a small crater, its steel case instead disintegrating into red-hot shards of flying, scything death, and it was one of these that found Wainwright's head, slicing it in two even as he was hurled backwards by the blast, and turning his thoughts into a millisecond of blinding white light and pain before his life was ended.

Across the Channel, many kilometres east beyond the armies slugging it out in and around the trenches of France and Belgium, other battles were being fought in the heartland of Germany herself. These were different struggles, personal, unpublicised and out of sight. Fought at the level of the individual, these contests were being fought alone. But they were battles nonetheless. Taking place throughout Germany's cities, towns, villages and hamlets – places ostensibly still at peace – their objective was food. In Nettermann's Essen and Goettner's Graudenz, in the Hildesheim of Winkler and the hometowns of König, Winkler, Zimmermann and the wounded Bauer – Schäffer, too, his body lifeless and now stiff in no man's land – all across Germany people were starving. Most did not know this truth. Most were aware only of a perpetual, nagging ache in their bellies, understanding only that there was never enough to eat. Subconsciously, they resisted acknowledging any possibility of starvation, for that was too stark a reality to face without going mad. Yet each and every day was a struggle to find something, anything – food of any kind – in quantity sufficient to prepare a meal. It had become a task to which most were unequal, yet few comprehended the possibility of death. Instead, the people bore down on the discomfort that was their hunger. They drank water in an effort to fill themselves, declining to acknowledge that they were in the process of dying.

The newspapers – Graudenz's *Der Gesellige*, for example, and the other broadsheets, too – these blamed Germany's food shortage on the Royal Navy and its blockade, carefully avoiding mention of the true cause of the shortages, which was the transfer of so very many men away from the fields to the slaughter taking place in the trenches, and the diversion of chemicals needed for fertilizer to the factories making high explosive.

Nobody in Germany had eaten bread – real bread – for three years. The rationed substitute was made chiefly of potatoes or turnips. Nobody could remember the taste of a proper morning coffee, drinking instead a morning brew of roasted acorns. Dried weeds had long since replaced tea. Butter, sausages and other staples were similarly substituted. The best of everything went to the soldiers at the front, or to the wealthy who could afford the outrageous prices of a flourishing black market. Rationing allowed each person a small piece of meat and one egg a week, but these were often unobtainable. Buildings had gone unheated throughout the previous winter, when the damp and cold had led to an epidemic of tuberculosis. Germany's working women – Nettermann's mother and sweetheart among them – tried their best to maintain efficiency during the long hours required of them, but they were hungry and it was difficult, and at the end of every day they had to stand, exhausted, in long food queues hoping to find something in the stores for which to exchange their ration cards. Daily existence had become a struggle for survival.

The change forced upon the individual by inadequate nutrition was gradual. Skin drew hard into the bones, losing colour and leaving the face appearing pale and bloodless. Eyes sank deeper into sockets. Colour left the lips. Foreheads became parchment. Hair hung dank and lifeless. Some half a million civilians were already dead of malnutrition by the time of the German Army's assault on Foncquevillers. An equal number were close to that fate.

But it was not only hunger that dominated German thought. Worry for sons, husbands and brothers bearing arms was ever-present. The malnourished at home were only too well aware of the terrible numbers of casualties at the front: one in four young men already either buried or blown to pieces – obliterated beyond any possibility of collection of body parts for proper burial. At home, the maimed roamed the streets for all to see. These were the survivors – an eye or part of a lower jaw gone here, over there a man's arm or neck bearing the purple-grey cicatrix of fire, or the narrower, neater gouge of bullet. Men who had lost a leg to shell shard stumbled about their business on crutches. Those who had lost both used wheelchairs. In their houses, safely out of sight, the families of the blind and the many unfortunates who had been paralysed forever, they hid their burdens from public view.

Still, some among the general population seemed to have more pressing concerns than the nation's wounded.

In Essen, Nettermann's sweetheart had often heard new mothers voicing a greater level of concern over their drying milk ducts and the deteriorating health of their babies, than over casualties caused by the war's progress, or lack of it. She herself did not share their priorities. She wanted only for Nettermann to return to her alive, and she prayed that he might still come through it, might still love her in spite of a mirror reflecting back a face that every month appeared more and more skull-like. Nettermann would not remember her like this. She knew that he would be remembering the face of that lively, attractive young woman she had been the last time they had been together, and this thought made her sad. She thought of Nettermann constantly. She prayed for him and wondered what he might be doing ...

Even as she wondered, the *zug* was preparing for renewed attack, Nettermann among them. The assault set for dawn of the following day, they made their preparations in a tented camp not far behind the *Siegfriedstellung's* third and rearmost line. The *zug* had received their warning order with the weary resignation that only the truly tired can muster. Well, it had to be done, and therefore they would do it. At least there would be trucks this time to take them as far as the second line – good news – and probably the march to the forming-up points just behind the forward fire trenches would leave sufficient time to rest a little before going in. Now, while yet rear of the third line, they were stripped down to underpants, their wet uniforms draped over guy-ropes, shrubbery and the occasional tree, whatever could be found to help them dry out under a sky that was clearing after the rain that had cloaked their withdrawal. They cleaned weapons and restocked on ammunition and grenades, they scrounged dry rations for the hoped-for breakthrough, and they washed themselves as best they could with water carried from a nearby stream. Bathing there was forbidden, the stream patrolled by military police to enforce that order – there were too many soldiers. Instead the men checked equipment, smoked, dozed when they could and prepared their minds for the attack to come. There was little conversation, and what there was avoided talk of home. They had enough on their minds without allowing too many memories of pleasanter places to add to an already heavy burden, especially since all were only too well aware of the changes wrought on those towns and villages by four years of war. All were conscious of the desperate plight faced

151

by their families. The lightly wounded sent home to recover brought back upon their return details of daily life in Germany, describing conditions so bad that it was better to avoid discussing the matter altogether. They did talk of Schäffer, though …

'He's still out there, you know.'

'Well of course he's still out there. Do you think because he's dead he might have grown wings?'

It was Zimmermann and Winkler, the *zug* bully and the replacement with the newly revealed name, or new to Zimmermann, anyway. A wary, semi-friendly sort of sparring had replaced the animosity between these two that had until the reconnaissance patrol been overtly hostile. Though their topic was macabre and the banter callous, both seemed to feel the need for continuation of their contest, albeit in milder form. Others in the *zug* voiced no objection to the subject of this bout, Schäffer. They allowed it. All had witnessed death and become immune to the thought of an end of life – its implication – whether the focus were Schäffer or somebody more remote. Death was all around. Even Winkler had seen death now, and he was risking it too, equally to the others.

'We should recover his body.' This was Nettermann, his contribution as always considered and delivered only after a pause of some seconds. He was sitting in his underwear on an empty ammunition box, dragging a razor with steady strokes over the stubble on his jaw. There was no soap, but he had set before him on the ground a tin of heated water to aid the ritual. Nettermann had correctly guessed Winkler's intended outcome on the subject of Schäffer: it was not right that the Old Man should be abandoned in death.

König was busy packing his pipe with tobacco. He was one of very few in the *zug* to prefer the device over issue cigarettes. Lighting it and sucking on the stem, he asked:

'Whose body? We lost eleven …'

'Schäffer's body, König – Schäffer's! Please try to wake up – we need you alert for when we go in!'

There was nervous laughter from the others at this exclamation from Zimmermann. And it *was* funny, given the way it had been delivered. Even though Schäffer's death and the deaths of the others were keenly felt by all of them, they held their pain within, a deep and very private thing. Losses were a part of life at the front. It was nothing new.

König grinned an apology around his pipe. 'Still two hours before orders,' he said. A pause, then: 'I'm glad the Fifth will be leading. We should be better off.'

'Poor bloody Fifth.' Nettermann.

'*Ja*, but better them than us. We've done it once. Shouldn't even be going in at all. Or not so soon, anyway.'

'Have you taken a look at the people they sent over as replacements?'

'*Ja*. Children, all of them. None a day over seventeen. I'd put money on it.'

'If that. Some just sixteen, I think.'

Zimmermann, who had been silent for a while but who was now remembering his father's beatings and the reasoning behind them, summarised what all were thinking:

'Well, they'll grow up soon enough. They'll be at least a year wiser after tomorrow, those that live. A bit like you, eh, Winkler?' Glancing to the replacement, Zimmermann's grin showed that he meant no malice. Not anymore. Winkler allowed himself a small smile. It carried through to the dark eyes in his schoolboy face, a face that seemed to the others somehow older after the experiences of the previous day.

Zimmermann continued:

'One day for a year. *Ja*, I think it's quite a reasonable exchange. Applies to us all, really. After tomorrow I'll be able to pursue some even older ladies I've had my eye on.'

And they laughed again.

The hours passed, but there were not enough of them to allow a visit to Bauer, though all wanted to do it. They had only arrived at this encampment in the early afternoon, having marched five kilometres rearward of the forward trenches. There wouldn't be enough time.

Just before orders, they queued for warm stew and turnip bread under a darkening sky. The sergeant had miraculously found four bottles of the local wine from somewhere – bought them himself, probably – enough for all to enjoy a good tot. They ate and drank and smoked as darkness fell. There were stars here and there. The weather was clearing.

The *oberleutnant* – Goettner – presented orders, explaining details of their part in the attack and taking questions without ceremony. This assault would be more of the same, he told them – same formation, same spacing, same rate of advance – the tanks would dictate their pace until the final rush to the enemy lines. But the armour would be moving ahead of them this time, with the Fifth, their own role being to follow up and reinforce. The only other change would be the fire plan, Goettner said. The artillery would use gas if the wind were right and, since there was no way to predict its direction, guns would switch to gas at the general's discretion. All would advance wearing masks. No exceptions. Also, the bombardment would lift much later than

153

before, and they could expect to be able to move right onto the British trenches, reinforcing the initial assault by Fifth Regiment. Oh, yes, one thing more: they were not to stop for wounded under any circumstance – they were to keep going until they had broken the line. Nothing and nobody was to allow the momentum of this attack to falter. Wounded would be attended to afterwards. Nobody was to stop for any reason at all until the Tommy line had been taken.

There were uneasy glances at this, the men weighing Goettner's order and seeking to balance their chances. They searched the tall *oberleutnant's* hawk-like face for signs of his own attitude to this new madness, for to know that none would stop to help a wounded man was to lower individual willingness to risk that wounding, and also determination to press home the attack. They searched the *zugführer's* eyes below that broad forehead with its mess of fair hair but, as always, Goettner revealed no emotion. Well, they were certainly better off than last time, they reasoned, what with the new artillery plan, the possibility of gas to further weaken the British defence, and the Fifth to take the brunt of things. *Ja*, definitely better than last time, at least until the artillery lifted, at least until they reached the Tommy wire, at least until the hand-to-hand fighting began.

Unless they were wounded.

'Wonder wot all're doin' back 'ome.'

'At supper, prob'ly. All 'avin' dinner an' off ter bed. Nowt else ter do. Not finkin' of us. Don't 'ave a clue wot we're up ter over 'ere.'

The whispers came to Winterman from further along the trench, past a Lewis crew crowded around their weapon. The day was ending, the Seventh stood-to on its fire-step ready for any attack by an enemy taking advantage of twilight.

The sky was beginning to clear. It had been cloudy all day after the previous night's rain, but now the stratus was thinning from the west. There, where the sun had already set, the remaining belly of cloud shone a beautiful pink edged in white.

'Looks jus' like my muvver's cottage pie, that cloud does. But upside dahn, like.'

'I could do wiv a spot o' pie. Sick an' tired of Maconochie. 'Orrible, disgustin' stuff.'

Winterman hissed hoarsely down the trench toward the conversation: 'Hey, put a sock in it, will you? Watch your front!'

He sensed the two offenders grinning as they peered over rifles in the gathering gloom. Winterman knew there would be no resentment or grudge. Eleven Platoon was a brotherhood. Months of fighting – years, for the unlucky – had made it thus. He listened. Forward and rear of the Seventh's section of the line, all was eerily and unusually quiet. There was no shelling and almost no small-arms fire. Winterman considered it odd. He wondered whether perhaps both sides were just too exhausted to properly engage. He mulled the thought. He mulled the years …

Winterman was one of the unlucky – or lucky, depending on how you viewed it. Standing on the fire-step in the gathering gloom, he permitted himself a wry grin at this observation. Three years at war now, and still alive – it was incredible. He suspected that his general demeanour reflected this unlikely fact of survival, for even when he shaved and scrounged a haircut from the platoon barber, smooth jowls and a short back and sides failed any longer to bestow upon his young face any appearance of youth. Nowadays, what stared back at him from the small rectangle of his shaving mirror seemed a face nearer thirty than the twenty years of its actual age. It was pinched and tired-looking despite its fleshy makeup, with deep shadows of grey around the eyes, and especially under them. They bothered him, those shadows, not for any reason of vanity but because they were reminders of what he suspected he might have lost forever. The last three years had changed him. He was doing his best to hold on to his humanity, but he suspected a part of it had irretrievably gone. He worried that he was losing the skill of empathy, an empathy that he knew had endeared him to the younger boys at Camden High back in his school days, because it had been such a contrast to the often overbearing arrogance of other seniors.

How much of his schoolboy innocence remained? Some, he hoped. He couldn't be sure. There had been too many days and nights in the rain, sleet and snow of winter, too many weeks without shade from summer's scorching sun. The grind of working parties and the dozens of night patrols had taken their toll, too. He had been shelled too many times, and too many times terrified, even as he did his best to hide the fear and show a confident face. He was still trying to do that, and he was still trying to be fair, too. It was a hard task, being platoon sergeant. He had to measure each newcomer and assess each man, guessing likely reaction and predicting reliability under fire. He had to watch for weakness and remain alert to signs of nerves about to crack. His guesses were mostly correct, but not always, not always … Sometimes he erred, and the result was a man's premature death, or the deaths of others if a soldier did the wrong thing at the wrong place and time or,

155

worse, broke under fire, the result of his faulty judgment. Because of that, because of these risks, Winterman trusted nobody anymore until proven – no one. And the only technique he had discovered to manage this enormous burden of responsibility was to withdraw into himself, bearing down on his doubts and worry and keeping them private, projecting in public only a cool, encouraging confidence with an occasional touch of humour. Winterman had become dependably secretive, and he knew it.

In the gloom, the sergeant put grubby fingertips to tired eyes and rubbed at them to ease his fatigue. Peering over the sandbagged parapet through the barbed wire, he searched the darkening, ruptured earth of no man's land, grateful that nothing appeared to be moving upon it. Yesterday's corpses still lay there as so many darker smudges upon the field. But there was no attack. Fritz had not come again this day. Soon they would get the word to stand down. Good. There would be tea with a spot of rum, and not long after that food coming up from the rear under cover of darkness. Sandwiches, probably. And with a bit of luck some bacon. Usually he ate just one strip of his bacon ration, and kept the rest to reheat come morning, provided the Hun left them alone. He could do with a bit of bacon. They hadn't seen bacon for four or five days now.

Winterman's thoughts drifted to Camden, to his fiancée, one hand moving unconsciously to touch the hip flask positioned snug within his tunic, the one she had given him engraved with her words of love: *Come back to me.* Sometimes he imagined he could actually see her, and hear her voice as she delivered that plea. Well, he had returned to her, once, hadn't he? But things hadn't been right – not even close. Why was that, exactly? Why hadn't they been right? Why hadn't he been able to make them right while they were still together? In the twilight, Winterman shook his head at these questions, not understanding, knowing only that there was now a rift of immeasurable dimension between them where before there had been only passionate love. His fault, probably. Not hers. He should have tried harder.

And Peake … Young Simon Peake. How does he view me now, I wonder, after catching me weak and vulnerable back there in Stafford on the bench beneath the tree? What must he be thinking? He would surely have wondered why I wept, must wonder more, now, because now he has to depend on my decision for his life. Well, if he could but know that I feared losing the woman I love that time on the Stafford bench, he would understand why I'd been weeping. It's as simple as that; it was fear of loss, fear of losing her. Because by then I knew I *had* lost her, during that visit to Stafford and Brocton Camp. Something – some force – had come between us, and there was nothing I could do to overcome it and restore what once we knew had been, what once we knew we had. Well, nobody would've seen those tears had it not been for Peake, and I hope he's kept what he saw to himself.

Still no firing from either side. No angry noise where we stand – the Seventh and the other battalions of this regiment of Lancashires – only that thumping, bumping bombardment coming from both flanks; flashes too, now that night is falling, barrel flashes from the guns and the brighter, more powerful, bright white of detonating shells, all of it well rear of us, all of it quite far away. A worry, that: the fact that it's to our rear. It means the Hun must be pressing on with his advance. Well, not here. Here we hold. He'll come again, of course. He'll mount another attack. It's impossible that the old routine of the line will return. Fritz will reorganise and mount another assault, perhaps in greater strength and probably sometime during the day to come. Mister Williams said we've been ordered to hold and not fall back with the rest even though we'll receive no replacements and no reinforcements – everything chaotic retreat left and right, the lieutenant said. Well, at least our own casualties have been light. It was the Germans who copped it yesterday. But they'll come. They'll come again …

The eastern horizon blackened completely, and after it the west. The torn and broken boughs of trees rimming the fields succumbed finally to darkness. After a time, night set in properly. Word came to stand down. They did it, a bristle of bayonets caught by moonlight reflecting as glinting flashes all along the line, the soldiers easing themselves gratefully back into the duckboarded trench. They set sentries and went about their business.

Beyond the Lewis gun, beyond the two chastened privates and further away from Winterman, Peake settled down with Watson and Farmer, waiting for Earnshaw to return with tea. They had sent him to fetch it. The four had scrounged a team pot which they used for the communal brew – easier than all of them queuing at the platoon's urn. Today was Earnshaw's turn. Beside them, weapons stood ready. They had taken it in turn to strip, clean and oil their rifles thoroughly during daylight, pulling the barrels through and checking them for rust, and the fore and rear-sights, too. Some days before, Winterman had divided up this group of newcomers, placing each man under the wing of a more experienced soldier, but the four regrouped whenever they could to enjoy a cuppa. Despite their having survived the attack of the afternoon before, none yet felt a true part of this battalion; they were still outsiders unequal to the veteran soldiers who had been through so much more. Waiting for the tea, their conversation was unfocused and noncommittal:

157

'Quiet, eh?'

'Too quiet. Not normal.'

'And since when did you become an expert?'

'I'm not, but there's hardly any firing at all, and no shelling anymore to mess up the food. We've not seen that before. Not until today.'

'Lots of noise from the flanks.'

'Aye, but a long way away and further back.'

'Bad sign.'

'Fritz is going to come on again, I reckon. He's saving his shells.'

'Ah well, the more shells the merrier, eh?' This was Farmer, trying for humour. Nobody laughed.

The three fell silent, mulling the likelihood of another barrage and its timing. During the day, their section leaders, the ferret-like Corporal Tozer among them, had passed down word from Lieutenant Williams: Brigade had ordered Regiment to hold in spite of the fact that almost all of the line on either side had been broken. Entire divisions there were now in full retreat. But the Seventh and its sister battalions had held, and the order had come that it was to continue to hold. Division had told Brigade to hang on to Foncquevillers at all costs.

Earnshaw returned with the tea and rum, placing their pot carefully upon the fire-step. He was a man given to care as well as analysis, not a drop had been spilt while he negotiated passage along the narrow duckboard with its continuous traffic of soldiers coming and going in the dark, no easy trick for such a burly man. Farmer and Peake held a blanket to shield their torch from enemy eyes while Watson poured the milky-sweet brew carefully into tin mugs. From above came the noise of aircraft heading for the German lines, impossible to see.

'Jerry reconnaissance,' suggested Peake. 'They can still see up there. Going home, I reckon.'

'Aye. But no guns to counter.' This was Earnshaw. 'Bad sign. Anti-aircraft's pulled back.'

For a while there was little conversation, the four sipping, all of them tired.

'I 'ave to say that attack yesterday really 'ad the wind up me.'

This observation – Earnshaw's – was devastating in its semi-Cockney honesty, and it took a while for the others to muster comment. They had avoided discussion of personal feelings, so great had been the intensity of their surprise at discovering themselves still alive after beating back an attack delivered in such overwhelming force.

'We all had the wind up, Quiz,' said Watson.

'Probably the whole bloody line had the wind up,' offered Farmer. 'It's just that nobody shows it. Probably even we didn't show it.'

'And still don't. That's the trick, isn't it?'

'Well, I don' mind admitting I was shakin' like a leaf in a gale fer a good five minutes after t'all stopped,' confessed Earnshaw.

'And me.' This was Peake. He could hear Winterman moving away on the other side of the Lewis, down the trench toward platoon headquarters, offering words of encouragement here and there as he went.

'It was damned good fire discipline,' said Watson. 'Winterman had it well and truly buttoned up. And Mister Williams. Waited until exactly the right moment.'

'We all did. We all waited. Nobody broke.'

'Well, 'e's delivered a right clobberin' to the rest of the line, 'as Fritz. What'll we do when they come again?'

'The same, Quiz, I reckon,' answered Peake. He could still hear Winterman, now in muted conversation with a sentry manning one of the trench periscopes. Night or not, the periscopes were always crewed in case of star shells or flares lighting the battlefield. Peake heard the sergeant deliver a cheerful slap of farewell to the sentry's shoulder as he continued on his way to Williams, their Welsh lieutenant.

Peake considered John Winterman, remembering how he had been at school, and making comparisons. At Camden Secondary, Winterman had been generally unknown to Peake apart from football, where he played for the first team. He'd been just another 'bigger boy'. In his senior year, when Winterman had gained the privilege of being allowed to demand fagging, he'd shown a preference for Peake to undertake those chores. These had all been pretty harmless: watering the seniors' vegetable patch, cleaning the common room, brewing the odd cup of tea, or carrying Winterman's boots and other gear to and from practice or match. Winterman had never used his authority to bully or unnecessarily coerce. Rather, he had displayed an easy manner with the junior boys, guiding and coaching them in the correct workings of the school's hierarchy. Winterman's fags had always held constructive purpose. They'd been something a lad could learn from. In those days, he'd been almost an open book, Peake recalled, a young man easy to trust and easy to like even if you were his junior by two or three years – no fear of random shove or clip from Winterman. Even in those days, he had been able to earn respect without the need to intimidate, never using size or age to enforce his seniority. Now, here in the line in 1918, nothing much seemed to have changed. To Peake, the sergeant seemed consistent, determined and fair, ideal qualities for his function, for all private soldiers looked beyond their corporals to their sergeants for true inspiration and guidance. Yet some of the platoon's old sweats said Winterman could at times be an unbending and obstinate taskmaster, something Peake had not yet witnessed. And they reckoned he was generally a loner, withdrawn and almost secretive when it came to interfacing with the other senior NCOs in the company. Even the CSM saw Winterman in this way, so it was said. Above all, the veterans' advice was never to cross the sergeant, for there was an angry side to him that could border on the brutal.

Well, reasoned Peake, this last was certainly something new – no sign of it during school days. Perhaps it was the result of too many years in the line.

Of course, Peake's peers in Eleven Platoon knew that the two had been at school together, because of the sergeant's obvious surprise upon recognising Peake the day of their arrival. But Peake had not allowed discussion of it, wary of arousing any suspicion of favouritism, and not wanting to mention the Stafford tears at all. They remained a worry to him though, those tears, for he judged them as signal of stretched nerves, even though Winterman's determined control of his men on the afternoon of the German attack had put to bed any doubt of effective leadership on his part.

'Wonder where the grub is?'

Rhetorical question. Nobody replied. It was dark and they were weary. The conversation dwindled and died. Food would come in its own time. They would wait for it, eat it and then seek sleep under blankets on the fire-step, or in nooks carved out of the trench walls as beds.

'It's wonderful that you could join us, Christine, dear. Penelope has told us so much about you. And Simon too, of course. I feel we already know each other quite well.'

'It's very kind of you to invite me, Mrs Wainwright. And Mister Wainwright – I'm looking forward very much to meeting him.'

Christine, nervous, strove not to show it, regretting the way she had phrased her response and wondering if she had been too forward in her reference to the absent host. She had been fretting over this encounter ever since Penelope Brooke had communicated the invitation. She was older than Peake by two years, and Christine knew that this gap was something many a mother would view unfavourably while inspecting for the first time the object of her son's fancy. Christine glanced to Penelope for reassurance, catching a light smile and barely discernible nod of encouragement.

'My husband will be here in ten minutes or so, I'm sure, Christine. I thought we might enjoy a small glass of sherry while we wait. Would you like that? Penelope, are you amenable?'

Without waiting for reply, their hostess turned to a tray already set with glasses and decanter. Conversation lapsed while she poured, the clock upon the mantelpiece ticking soothing reassurance, a gentle and unobtrusive rhythm entirely impassive even as it became the focus of this small sitting room with its two doors, one leading to a short passage from the front entrance, the other connecting with the kitchen where they would eat. The sound of that timepiece seemed to embrace the silence of the moment, making the three women somehow feel closer together in spirit, and aided in that by the pleasing aroma of dinner to come: a stew of sorts by Christine's guess.

Fortified wine distributed, they sat to sip, the two older women engaging in light chatter to put Christine at ease, and discussing the unpredictability of *The Landlord's Game*, which they would all play after dinner. Christine was glad of relief from direct question and answer, though she fretted still, and not only over age and careless reply. There was also her constant worry over Simon, already four months into his war, and Luke too, her fiancé who had endured it for much longer and who had changed so much, his gentle ways and loving ardour apparently vanished. When the war ended, when they returned – if they returned – what was she to do? Who would she choose? If she chose Simon, how would she excuse to Luke her unforgivable act of infidelity? If she chose Luke, how would she explain to Simon her engagement to him? She seemed caught in a trap, for she had feelings – different feelings – for both men. She needed both, and to imagine her life without them was to imagine a life deprived of breath itself. She had discussed the dilemma with Penelope, who had advised her to allow the problem to work itself out. Nothing lasts for ever, Penelope had told her, and even this war would pass in due course. Until the day came for these two men to return, who knew what might happen? No choice was necessary, for now.

Christine was not at all convinced of the wisdom of that outlook. She considered it too simplistic, and she remained confused by her feelings for Simon, feelings which seemed to be strengthening with every day of his absence. She felt herself to be in love with him, but she wasn't sure. And what was love anyway? Did she love Luke? Did she still have feelings for Luke? Again, uncertainty. Suppressing a sigh, she found herself wondering whether her acceptance of the Wainwrights' invitation to dine was not of itself an indication of a choice she had already made.

Above the steady ticking of the clock, something else – another, more intrusive sound growing steadily louder and emanating from beyond the home.

'Shhhh … Listen … Do you hear it?' This was Penelope, face alert beneath the auburn hair piled high, head cocked but still politely poised as though attentive to her hostess, though listening closely to something else as she shifted to sit forward in her chair, glass of sherry halted midway to her lips.

'An aeroplane.'

Then the sound of explosions, not too distant and very close together so that the loud, crumping thuds, felt as well as heard, seemed as one continuous sound of only a second or two. The source of these detonations was not so close that the women felt any personal threat, yet it was close enough it could not be ignored. They were on their feet as one, Wainwright's wife, sherry in hand, leading the way quickly from sitting room to the front door. They moved into the night, looking up into the clear, pure blackness of it, dotted with stars and streaked by feathery cirrus brushed as silver strokes across the western horizon where the quarter-moon was setting. There were no more explosions, only the sound of aircraft engines becoming steadily fainter, receding toward the coast.

Now another engine in the night. One more. It seemed to come from the north.

'Ours,' offered Penelope. 'Looking for him.'

Neither Mrs Wainwright nor Christine replied. The three stood for a while, searching the star-speckled dome that was the night sky above them, black as tar, for sign of either machine but meeting with no success until, over the Thames estuary, narrow needles of bright white light shot suddenly upward into the blackness, unbending and unwavering for some seconds, then beginning to move in an ungainly, juddering, stick-like fashion, fingering the sky in search of the exiting intruder. The sound of cannons came to the women: big guns firing in support of the searchlights. But there were no flames to indicate any target found. Eventually, the three returned to the sitting room.

Time passed. Ten minutes. Fifteen. After twenty, worry set in. Wainwright was overdue, and the sound of the bombs, distant though those explosions had been, had come from the general direction of his route home.

'We should do something. We should look for him. Do you know the road he would have taken?'

'Yes.'

They donned overcoats and scarves against the chill, leaving dinner to simmer on the hob, still hoping to enjoy it as four. Exiting the house, Wainwright's wife led the way. She carried a lantern, for the gas lights of London's streets were not lit – the city needed to hide from the Zeppelins and new German bombers. The three moved without talking, winding their way between dark silhouettes that were two and three-storey brick dwellings, angular shapes only half seen against the black night. From here and there came the orange glows of dimly lit windows: kitchen, living room or bedroom, vague suggestions of life continuing beyond the almost empty street. The women huddled into their clothing against the cold night air. All feared the worst without giving voice.

Now came the brighter, flickering light of fire, reaching them from around the walls of brick homes bordering an intersection and giving first warning of where the bombs may have hit. The shrill bell of a fire engine racing toward the site confirmed it. The women increased their pace. Rounding the corner, all became plain: emergency teams with organised lighting, policemen forming a cordon against the frightened and the curious, and a team of firemen directing water onto flames that had broken out in one of the damaged homes. A second fire engine – the one they had heard – arrived to manoeuvre a passage through bricks strewn across the cobbles of the street, its crew jumping from the vehicle to uncoil their hose.

The three women broke into an anxious run, unaware of doing so. They made for the nearest policeman, awkward within their constricting petticoats and long dresses, and lifting them quite high to help the dash. They searched as they ran, eyes roaming the small crowd braving the cold to witness this event. They sought Wainwright's familiar form and face.

The constable was politely assertive when they got to him:

'You shouldn't come any closer, please, madams. Crews're carrying people from their homes. There are injured. No further, please. We'll get the better yet of that fire, don't you worry.'

There were uniformed men bearing stretchers to a collection point, the jutting shapes of heads and feet recognisable beneath full coverings of blankets: occupants being carried out on their backs, the indignity of unexpected death hidden from view.

'And the street, Constable? What about the road? This one … Was anyone walking in the road?'

'Just one person, ma'am. As far as we can tell, the rest were all at home having supper.'

Just one person … The women knew at once who it would have been.

* * *

The *zug* moved up – Goettner's *zug* of König, Nettermann, Zimmermann, Winkler and the others still with him after the attack of two days before. Goettner usually counted thirty-six, but this night they were only twenty-five. The others were in the field hospital with Bauer, or missing, or known to be dead like Schäffer. Well, they had been replaced, of course, but the newcomers were beardless, fresh-faced youths – boys, really – and they were studiously ignored by the survivors as the *zug* moved up, part of three full regiments – seven thousand five hundred infantry. Their orders were to take Foncquevillers. With them when dawn came, on their flanks as they attacked, would be smaller protective forces defending against counter-attack so that the main thrust could concentrate on the job at hand. The assault thus planned, all moved forward to their forming-up positions and start-lines under cover of night. There was a quarter-moon to light their passage, a silver arc suspended in a sky of ink and stars. Trucks carried them as far as the second line, then returned for others. There were many convoy routes, the vehicles using whatever farm tracks there were to ferry the troops in packets, steering by moonlight and aided in their navigation by detachments of two and three soldiers detailed to indicate the way at gates and where tracks crossed or bifurcated, anywhere confusion might arise. At the second line, all debussed and waited in the assembly areas until the totals from the various *kompanies* and battalions tallied. With everyone present, the units marched the final kilometres to the frontline, where they waited, restless, apprehensive, fearful.

Around the area of their attack, the night was quieter than usual, though on both sides of them the distant rumble and thunder of artillery continued. There, to their west and northeast where the German attack had already broken through and the British were in retreat, the advance to the sea was continuing through the night, and these soldiers waiting to assault could see the cannon flashes flickering and dancing on the horizon, and hear the booming of the guns themselves. But at Foncquevillers it was quiet, with not even a flare sent up by either side to compete with the moonlight for detail of the dead still lying where they had fallen between the forward trenches of the two sides. It was as though the living were holding their breath ahead of the violence to come.

Across no man's land, in the trenches held by the Lancashires, the British were preparing for that violence, each soldier coping in his own way with the inevitability of a difficult defence, for they knew the Germans would come in greater numbers when they attacked again. Some wiped down weapons

164

already clean and oiled, or re-checked ammunition already prepared. They sought anything that might serve as distraction. Some used the power of their minds to escape the reality of imminent danger, remembering happier times in happier places with wives or lovers, or family. Many prayed. A few managed the escape of sleep. All had heard the sound of the German motor transport in the hours around midnight. Attack was inevitable. It would come with daylight.

Winterman managed his anxiety well, moving up and down the platoon trenchline to check a sentry here, a Lewis crew there, and offering words of cheerful resolve at random. Not a single man displayed any need of encouragement, but Winterman knew that they did need it – all of them – for there was nervousness and fearful expectation everywhere in the line. Once, he sought out Lieutenant Williams. Finding his platoon commander standing restless beside one of the trench periscopes, Winterman paused to chat, then, when he sensed unease on the part of the officer (probably the man wanted to be alone), he departed for the headquarters dugout to scrounge a mug of tea. He sat down to sip. He thought of Camden and his love, one hand moving as always to the hip flask.

Peake managed his worry less well. Memories of Christine were there, of course, but they failed to soothe. They failed to overcome the worry of certain attack. The memories were troubling to him that night. He tried to recall Christine's kiss and the feel of her breasts, those wonderful amber eyes closed in ecstasy and her long hair let down just for him when they made love. He thought of her touch, her scent. He brought to mind her voice, and he remembered her body's secret places hidden by the curtain-filtered shadows of that first afternoon on Penelope Brooke's big bed. But there was doubt for Peake, that night. He remembered Christine's silence before his final departure for Brocton Camp, her refusal to buckle under his insistence that she wait for him, and her absence from the railway station. Seeking her motive as he waited in the darkness of the trench, the extra burden imposed on him by these questions made worse the battlefield's oppressive tension. Peake was infatuated with Christine, his first and only love, but his desire for her was now tainted by the onset of doubt, and this added to the weight of his worry.

Around Peake, the others of the platoon seemed as halves, partly dark shadow cast by the silvery moonlight, and part seen more clearly as something grey. Watson dozed, sitting, rifle resting across his lap and the crook of one arm. Farmer slept completely, his weapon beside him. Earnshaw watched and observed, noting the familiar shapes of the men he knew, and the rifles and packs and webbing and helmets of others he did not: these were everywhere along the trench. He studied the forms of the soldiers lit by the moon and the vaguer shapes of those in shadow, silently questioning everything and everyone about him as was his wont. Like Peake, Earnshaw discovered no answers. Like Peake, he could find no positive distraction. A few yards beyond Earnshaw, in a darkened nook of the fire-step, Corporal Tozer tried for sleep but failed, so lay on his back, half a blanket underneath against the planks of the step, half of it over to cover him against the dew, examining the stars and wondering why some appeared to pulsate while others did not. Eventually, he resorted to counting them to lessen the dragging suck of his waiting.

Williams, the lieutenant, had the trench periscope. Through that tool, he probably had the best escape of all save sleep, for the rectangular, rough-and-ready box of wood and angled mirror afforded at least the distraction of a view different from the mundane, interminable parapets of sand-packed hessian, buttressed walls and fire-step. He applied himself to that 'scope from time to time, peering through the eyepiece at the moonlit landscape of no man's land, searching for movement. There was nothing to be seen. Even the dead had become indistinguishable now from rock and ruptured field as moon approached horizon. Well, thought Williams, there would be movement on that landscape soon enough. Jerry would come, but let him, let him … He would pay the price for that coming. The platoon was ready, as ready as it could ever be for the day soon to dawn.

CHAPTER EIGHT

In the Wainwright home, Penelope Brooke had not slept. She was awake even as dawn came to Camden. Now she lay restless upon a strange bed in a strange bedroom – Simon Peake's – tossing and turning, trying for an oblivion barred to her by the events of the previous evening.

When the women left the bomb site they returned home, shocked and in despair. There was little conversation. Christine seemed the worst affected, shaken by the sudden, devastating circumstances of a night yet young. What to say? How to help? How to behave? These must have been among the questions passing through the tumult of her mind after what she had witnessed, for she was just twenty.

Wainwright's wife, now a widow, remained calm, perhaps too calm. She was dry-eyed, too, preferring denial to acceptance.

For them all, how strange to return to the lounge of this house whose clock still ticked steadily from its mantelpiece perch, and where the aroma of dinner wafted stronger than before, when the three had left. It was as though nothing had changed, though there were only three to dine, now. Once inside, plump arms hanging limply at her sides, the widow said:

'I ... I'll need somebody to come with me. To the police station, I mean. In the morning to … to identify him like they asked.'

It was a cry for help disguised by tight self-control.

'I'll come.' Penelope did not hesitate. 'And I'm sleeping here tonight. Don't argue, please.'

The widow Wainwright began to wring her hands helplessly, uselessly, as the truth of things came upon her and she began to comprehend her loss. She protested, but Penelope understood the dreadful task of the morning to come: the widow would certainly need support.

'We should eat,' Penelope said, leading the way into the kitchen and deftly clearing Wainwright's place of its setting. She served the meal. None was hungry. The women picked at their food, staring down at their plates and

167

avoiding conversation. There were quick, occasional glances to the empty seat at the table's head.

Now, sleepless upon the bed in Simon Peake's room, Penelope remembered these details. At table, it had been as if Wainwright might still walk in at any moment. Really, the only thing to remind them of the fact of his death had been his very absence – the empty setting, the unoccupied chair – for by that hour he would always be home. Penelope had glanced to Christine. The young woman was prodding miserably at her plate, introspective and silent. What was she thinking? What were her emotions? Sadness? Distress? Perhaps there was even self-conscious embarrassment, a fear that any words of consolation she might offer could only ever come across as shallow, for Christine did not know the widow Wainwright at all.

'Twenty-two years …'

The words broke the silence of their supper, the widow sighing deeply as she said them. The sound of that sigh seemed to hang in the air like some invisible shroud about the three women, Penelope and Christine looking up from their plates for explanation.

A moment more of silence. They watched her, the bun of her tightly swept hair seeming greyer than before, and the round face older as she held her grief within. She said:

'For twenty-two years he's been coming through that door, never too late for dinner even after a hard day. And even if his time at work had been especially difficult there'd be no knowing it. He'd always have a smile for me. Always. Some days it was more genuine than others, but it was always there. He always tried, he was never too tired to try. It used to make my day, that smile. It used to make everything worthwhile, somehow.'

And then the widow Wainwright began to weep.

Dawn crept upon Foncquevillers as a slow progression, the sun seeming to hesitate, delaying the moment of its appearance, withholding for a while provision of shape and shadow. To the eyes of those soldiers willing to muster appreciation of beauty – very few – that coming dawn was indeed beautiful, though it held something of a reluctant quality within its advance, seeming not to want to bring upon the world the strength of full daylight, loath to surrender to the morning. Yet it did surrender, the sun clawing a new path into the sky above the rim of the land, and delivering light for battle. In front of the British and behind the German soldiers, the eastern edge of darkness surrendered. Where before the sky had touched the horizon with blackness, it now began to do so as a burnt orange mutating into a spectrum of colour that forced the night to retreat – an east-west arc of yellow, green and indigo melting into the dark blanket that still cloaked the British trenches. The day was dawning.

An easterly breeze blew gently from behind the Germans, bringing bursts of light cloud. These bursts, like the sky, were bronze where they hugged the horizon, but a multi-shaded grey higher up where they mutated into dirty puffs. There – higher up – these puffs were like the after-marks of artillery air bursts, though no artillery was yet firing and the puffs failed to shift and fade as did those of true detonation. Perhaps their intention was to warn. Perhaps they were an omen of death rather than death itself, pointing to the direction of attack, for the Germans were to attack from the east, advancing out of the dawn with the sun behind them. The British would be blinded.

As the topmost arc of the sun crawled over the battlefield's rim, the German barrage began. Guns roared and flashed and spat, filling the air with the hissing, sawing noise of shells hurled at the land around the British trenches, where they gouged and tore and churned and broke the earth, upending it to fling huge chunks upwards toward the heavens, quickly at first, then slowing to fall back again, passing on downward trajectory fresh clods tossed skyward. To the German soldiers watching these explosions, they often seemed different from one another according to the type of shell and point of impact. On harder ground they appeared to burst more suddenly than was the case in other places, the red-black of their centres asymmetrically flinging points of lighter colour instantly outward and upward, the two halves of the same explosion never mirrored. Some explosions shot out sideways, almost horizontally, while others were as a flat mushrooming, with little vertical force. Yet others – those on softer ground – were a coughing, upward spew of the earth, as though some giant reclining underground troll were projecting mucky vomit, a dirty yellow-grey spout that fell back directly upon itself.

The German gun line mounting that bombardment was dug in near the operations centre belonging to the *Generalleutnant* commanding the attack, the commandeered mansion where the man himself was now positioned to oversee execution. He stood there in his command centre, tapping crop to face or palm as he examined maps or monitored staff, face set tense and firm against a great weight of responsibility. The consequences of the outcome of the battle about to begin, victory or defeat, would be for him alone, and he could feel the pressure of his command. It was a pressure arguably greater than that borne by the attacking infantry themselves, for the *Generalleutnant* would not have the physical relief of action as an outlet for his tension. Indeed, he could not even see the battlefield – he was reliant on messages alone: verbal communication received through a network of field telephones leading from the forward bunkers, or scribbled signals brought in by runners from the point of the assault itself. His would be a battle fought virtually blindfolded, because only the rearmost fortifications of the *Siegfriedstellung* were actually visible to him with the aid of binoculars, and these were several kilometres to the rear of where the fighting would take place. He felt both frustrated and anxious. To mask these feelings, the general held tightly that riding crop of braided leather, kneading it and flexing it, or sometimes slapping it into the palm of one hand to emphasise a point made to aide or subordinate. At other times he simply held the tool in both hands, bunching his fists tightly around it and bearing down on the thing to ease the tension and turmoil of his mind. Were the attack to fail, hundreds of casualties – perhaps thousands – would have been sacrificed on his orders, and to no effect. In that event, Seventeenth Army Headquarters would very quickly summon him for reprimand and transfer, demotion a probability. His reputation would be ruined and his career over. Worse, he would have to live the rest of his life knowing that he had ordered men to their deaths for nothing.

Around him his operations staff. Around him, too, planning tables and manned telephone desks with jangling handsets and signallers holding paper and pencil ready to scribble and jot. On the walls, maps of the land to rear and flank as well as a central map of smaller scale marking the progress of the wider assault of Operation Michael: three quarters of a million soldiers sweeping the British toward the sea. One table in the room was bigger than the others. Upon it lay the most important map of all. This one was littered with wooden markers painted in different colours. It was the large-scale attack map, and around it stood the officers who had so meticulously pieced together the plan. They were ready to compare actual progress with theoretical reasoning and calculation, and their job was to coordinate armour, artillery, infantry and resupply – all by field telephone and runner – to execute the *Generalleutnant's* orders as he flexed his will to accommodate the unforeseen chaos that was the reality of every battle.

Thus stood the operations staff. Thus stood the *Generalleutnant* himself, though noticeably closer to one particular telephone table than to any of the others. This was the communications link to the headquarters bunker of the Fifth Regiment – a bunker at the very forward edge of the fortifications – and in that bunker among the other steel-helmeted men at the cutting edge of the battle was an officer from the division's meteorology department, his job being to measure the wind and, more difficult, predict it.

170

The phone upon that desk rang briefly, its handset immediately seized by the signaller manning it. Against the buzz of conversation around the planning tables, against the jangling of other telephones and the background booming of the artillery, this man scribbled fiercely upon the pad of paper before him. It was a short message, and when he had finished writing it down, he read it back to its sender to be sure of accuracy. Then, replacing the handset on its cradle of wood and bakelite, he tore the paper from his pad and passed it to a *hauptmann* to check and present to the *Generalleutnant*. But the general had heard the message even as it was being read back, and he was already crossing the room to his artillery liaison officer.

'Tell Guns to effect gas,' was his order to the artilleryman, his voice quietly resolute. 'They are to switch to the fire plan for gas with immediate effect.'

The artillery officer turned to his table of telephones connected to the gun lines. He began to pass the word.

The Germans had an observation balloon up that day, a fat, stumpy sausage made of fabric and fitted with horizontal tail stabilisers. It was filled with hydrogen and tethered to the ground in a slightly nose-up attitude. The rear, reinforced to accommodate the tether, looked from the side like the palm of a cupped hand supporting the sausage. Four times the height of a lorry and three times the length, the observation balloon was quite big. It was rigged with a one-man wicker basket suspended below to hold an observer equipped with binoculars and a field telephone communicating with the controlling headquarters by cable. At three points on the ground around the balloon were light anti-aircraft weapons to defend against attack by British fighters.

At first light on the morning of the attack, before sunrise initiated the artillery barrage, the balloon's ground crew let their charge rise into the cool morning air from a position one kilometre behind the forward sentry trenches, controlling its ascent by ropes until the balloon was at a height carefully calculated to grant a view of the objective while remaining safely below the trajectory of the artillery shells. The balloon was not in the direct line of fire of any cannon, but its height was calculated anyway, just in case. From that elevated roost, the observer could see the entire battlefield. His job was to report fall-of-shot and correct the artillery's aim until he received a flagged signal from the attacking troops ordering the barrage to lift. If gas were used, he would also be able to report its drift and direction.

The observer's task in the unfolding battle that day would leave him with an indelible memory of what he witnessed. At first he was preoccupied with correcting the barrage to maximum effect. Later, satisfied that the shells were on target, the entire British line erupting and boiling under the thump and thunder of multiple explosions, he lowered his binoculars to watch with awe the opening phases of the attack.

It was a noisy view, the shells rending the air with a harsh, tearing sound, very loud, their uneven chorus rising and falling in intensity and making him jump from time to time, but his view was spectacular: abandoned fields and pastureland, ruined farmhouses and the battered village of Foncquevillers itself, the tracks and paths and hedges and blasted windbreaks spread out below him like a patchwork quilt quite damaged – all of it eerily side-lit by the yellowish glow of a rising sun. He had the sensation of being a secretive spectator to some theatrical performance from hell.

The high-explosive barrage was spectacle enough, but then came tanks from behind the trenches. They emerged from patches of dead ground that had hidden them from enemy fire and view, and advanced to the infantry trenches. Upon passing over with their attendant clusters of shepherding infantry, other gas-masked and helmeted soldiers scrambled up from the trenches to follow in their wake – thousands of them over a line of almost one kilometre – shaking out into an attack pattern of three huge boxes of field grey, each one containing four rough rectangles quite distinct within the larger three. Thus the first ranks of soldiers advanced, one behind the other. This was the Fifth Regiment, arranged two battalions up and one behind, and within each battalion the smaller squares comprising four *kompanies* arranged two forward and two behind, one tank to each of the forwardmost *kompanies*, and the whole – all of the soldiers in their spaced ranks – presenting an attack in depth. The observer could see the tanks in some detail, and he could see the men too. He could make out their helmets and gas masks and forward-pointing rifles, and he could see the glint and sparkle that was the steel of their bayonets.

With the Fifth advancing, yet more infantry emerged to bring up the rear. These were the two reserve regiments so badly mauled during the attack of two days before.

The field telephone in the wicker basket jangled harshly. Handset to his ear, the observer was told that the artillery had been ordered to fire gas in addition to high explosive: he was to report direction and flow. The observer became alert, watching for first sign of the chemical. Yes, there it was – a poisonous yellow-brown stream unfolding from first one point on the patchwork quilt, then another, then another – not directly upon the British defences but about a hundred metres short – until there were multiple fingers of the evilly coloured substance drifting ominously toward the British positions. *Jawohl*, he affirmed to his handset. *Ja, ja*, the wind is good – the gas is headed for the enemy trenches – at a small angle, but the general direction is good.

Forward, forward strode the infantry, with here and there a tank crashing into ditch or crater, then clambering out with juddering wrench, each machine protected by a small huddle of infantry. They reached the first gas shells hissing horrible death from their canisters, ahead of them still the boiling, churning ground that was the line of British trenches pounded by noisy high-explosive barrage. Above those trenches but below the level of the observer's basket, the air was now erupting in yellow-red flashes mutating briefly into grey-black spheres of smoke that drifted away with the breeze. These were the airburst shells. The observer watched them for a while until he was distracted by what looked like men falling – German soldiers. The rate of advance faltered at that point, halted. Yes, there could be no doubt about it – those were casualties out there, half a dozen German troops felled by their own artillery. The advancing infantry stopped, the soldiers in grey kneeling or lying, appearing to the observer quite calm as they waited, for he was not close enough to hear the shouts and screams, or experience the fear. Binoculars to his eyes, he scanned the area around the centre of the ranks of men where lay regimental headquarters. A flag was unfurling – Germany's national flag – and the observer spoke urgently into the handset: 'Switch fire now! Switch fire now!'

The bombardment ended as suddenly as it had begun, the cacophonous roar of detonating shells giving way to an eerie silence while the artillery drew breath and recalibrated their guns to fire on targets rear of the British line. It took time. Now came another sound, a roaring sound, angry and desperate. It took several seconds for the observer in his basket to identify this for what it was: the enraged bellowing of thousands of soldiers giving vent to their terrified determination. It was the hoarse battle cry of infantry bent on delivering death as they charged the final hundred and fifty metres to the British line. Their dash forward was very quick.

In front of them there remained the barbed-wire entanglements. They would still have to overcome those ...

In their shelters and dugouts, the British endured the shelling with the same stoic resilience of two days before. Teeth gritted and with hands over ears, they waited. Most stared blankly at nothing. A few trembled openly as the air barked and whined and roared with noise of appalling intensity. About them, the earth bumped and shuddered and shook, soil trickling dustily through cracks between the supporting poles and planks. Peake was in the wrong dugout – a shelter allocated to others – along with Earnshaw and Watson who had also found the wrong shelter in their fright. Sergeant Winterman was with them, reliably in the correct one. Corporal Tozer was there, too, also finding the wrong place in the scrambling chaos caused by the detonations of the first shells to hit. Missing from the usual group was Farmer, who had somehow managed to get to his shelter with Lieutenant Williams and others of the platoon. It was a mix-up of note. The German artillery had found the target almost from the first round, catching the position by surprise just as tea was arriving after the order came to stand down. All had made a dash for the closest shelter, abandoning the allocation plan.

For most – for those not on the receiving end of a direct hit – the shelling was above all a clamouring noise of terrible fury, but the men could also feel the pummelling violence of those shells: strong, jarring thumps that reached through the trembling earth to physically shake each soldier. This was how it was for Peake, Earnshaw, Winterman and the others. One blast, very strong, came without warning to wrench at them from a point very near. For a moment all cringed and cowered, some dropping rifles to wrap arms about their heads in futile gesture of self-preservation as though the last moment of their lives might have come. A wall collapsed inwards, burying three soldiers. All was chaos until Winterman took control, calming the men with bellowed commands and urgent, gruff encouragement and reassurance, exhorting all to order. Tozer and another man dug and scraped at the pile of earth and splintered wood until they could pull free the buried men, who emerged coughing and gagging violently. None was injured.

Now came an easing of the barrage, gradual but noticeable. All were aware of it, and they glanced anxiously upward to their timber roof, and to the thick blackout canvas at the earthen steps to the exit.

'Gas masks!' bellowed Winterman, face taut with tension. 'GAS MASKS ON … GET THEM ON … NOW, BOYS, NOW! GET THOSE GAS MASKS ON!'

With shaking hands they struggled to obey. Watson fluffed it, trying to don his mask while still cradling his Lee-Enfield, and succeeding only in dropping both. Corporal Tozer, already masked, helped and steadied him for the fight to come. From beyond the dugout, further up the trench, came shouts and bellows of equally urgent command:

'GAS, GAS! GET THOSE MASKS ON!'

No shelling now. The barrage had stopped.

'Get out of the dugout! GET OUT, LADS! GET OUT, GET OUT! GET OUT OF THE DUGOUT AND FIX BAYONETS – THEY'RE COMING! FIX BAYONETS!'

And again came that sensation of raw fear as in the first attack, scratching at Peake's gut and constricting his bladder. Mustering his courage and pulling his rifle close in across his chest, he scrambled to his feet and stumbled with the rest through the dust-filled exit, up the steps into the bright light beyond. He blinked, blinded for a moment. He looked around, forcing his eyes to adjust to the light reaching his eyes through the goggles of his mask, and seeking a clear space on a fire-step that was everywhere covered in upended sandbags and clods of muck and earth. The step was wrecked in places, too. He reached behind for his bayonet, withdrawing the long blade from its scabbard and fixing it in place. Click. Chancing a glance along the trench to where the shell had hit – the one that had collapsed the dugout wall – he saw in that direction all blown inwards, the duck-boarded passage between fire-step and the shoring of the wall opposite now an impossibly chaotic mess of broken earth, torn wire, sundered sandbags and shattered wooden planks. It was where the entrance to the other dugout should have been – the one with others of the platoon. There was still a narrow part of the trench open there. Loud groaning came from the place, and there were two men trying to free themselves of the clawing muck that was the collapsed trench wall.

'Peake! Peake … PEAKE! ANSWER ME, MAN!'

'With you, Sergeant! Sorry, Sergeant!'

'Get up there!' Winterman pointed. 'Quickly, man! The fire-step – get to your weapon. They're coming!'

He did it, clambering up, weapon instinctively forward and ahead of his body, bayonet toward the enemy. Panting now and trembling a little, he was immediately blinded for a second time by a sun rising directly in front of the parapet, far worse than the bright light that had followed the dugout's darkness. Squinting, trying to shield eyes already hampered by the goggles of his cumbersome mask, he noticed wispy fingers of misty yellow probing the air about him. Gas! He checked the readiness of his rifle and sniffed warily, relieved that no smell at all came to his nostrils, not even the cordite of exploded shells. He lowered the rim of his helmet against the fiery orb in the east, peering over the long barrel and bayonet of his rifle into the restricted view afforded him by the gas mask. Searching the battlefield, his eyes opened wide in shock: the German infantry were almost upon them! Stalled only by the deep wire of the close-in defences that began just a few yards away, three enemy soldiers wielded wire-cutters while others pulled and yanked at the entanglements with hooked poles, all of them creating whirling whorls of yellow gas as they seemed to swim within the mustardy liquid of the poisoned air. Yet more knelt with rifles aimed toward the British trench, covering the work. One of them, seeing Peake, shouted in alarm, fired, missed. The round went wide and Peake took careful aim and fired back at the man, finding his mark even as his target worked his bolt. Chambering a fresh round, Peake selected a second man and fired once more, hitting his target in the shoulder so that the man spun like a top under the impact, weapon flung aside as he fell. Others were falling, too, sought out by the rifle fire of other soldiers left and right of Peake along the fire-step. The Germans wavered for a second, held, returned fire. They were monstrously grotesque, those men in grey firing bravely back, their faces made ugly and alien by goggled masks beneath their coalscuttle helmets.

To his left, Peake sensed the man closest to him slumping forward over his rifle, the rim of his helmet catching on the weapon and wrenching back what remained of his head and face beneath the mask, his lifeless body sliding back within the yellow, swirling mist that was the gas. Ignore him, Peake told himself. Ignore the sight of death! Ignore the fear! Ignore the gas! Work your bolt – chamber and fire – chamber and fire. He did it, aiming and shooting steadily, aiming and firing ... Germans were falling everywhere, but not enough, for there were many. Now, from one side, came the shouts and bellowed screams of men in hand-to-hand combat. Some of the enemy had reached the trench over comrades slumped dead or gravely wounded upon the wire, their bodies becoming ramps and crossing points for the living. More fell, becoming entangled in the terrible trap of that wire as they jerked and twitched, the British bullets finding them, finding them ...

But there were more Germans than the British could stop, and the attacking infantry were killing or maiming with their own fire more British than they themselves were losing, picking off the Tommies as they defended their parapet, now mere metres in front of the first troops scrambling over the bodies of their fallen comrades to reach the objective.

'*Vorwärts, kameraden! Vorwärts!*' their leaders exhorted them, even as fresh troops reinforced the attack from behind.

'*Vorwärts!*'

So close now ... They were so close ... Peake saw one hurl a grenade. It fell short of the parapet, exploding in a brief crash-bang of bright, flashing noise and dark smoke, and followed instantly by surprised bellows of pain. A

Lancashire close to Peake had been knocked to the duckboards, abandoning his weapon to clutch at his neck, rolling about in pain.

Now the noisy cranking and squealing of mechanical tracks, the grinding and grating of gears and the roar of a motor – very loud from somewhere to Peake's left. No time to look … Chamber and fire. Chamber and fire. The grinding and metallic clanking and scraping was becoming deafening. A cannon barked, forcing Peake to search for the source. Tank! – God help us! – The enormous, monstrous machine ground and clawed its way through the wire, chewing, crushing, destroying it, catching it in its tracks and dragging it in a tangled mess behind, exhaust fumes billowing from rear, gears grinding and grating, the soldiers within the steel cocoon firing out from behind their armoured walls, and half a dozen gas-masked enemy breaking through with the monster into the trench, some thrusting with bayonet, others swinging mallets or spades. The cannon roared again, and Peake sensed men dying where that skirmish was taking place. There was a lot of screaming. Winterman's voice came as a bellow over everything:

'Tozer! CORPORAL TOZER! Close off that trench! Over there! Quickly now, man, close it off! Simmonds! SIMMONDS!'

'Yes, Sergeant!

'Help Tozer with the gate. HELP HIM WITH THE GATE, MAN! DO IT NOW!'

The order was not for Peake, who continued working the bolt of his rifle, firing steadily until his magazine was empty. He moved to duck below the parapet and reload, scrabbling urgently for a clip from his ammunition pouches. It took time and he needed to focus on the task, yet he could sense Simmonds and the corporal hauling and shoving into place the big, buttressed frame of barbed-wire and wood, sealing off the trench and blocking passage to any approach from the direction of the ruined dugout and the tank that had now crashed forward onto what remained of the defences around it, grinding laboriously into a turn. Magazine recharged, he glanced to the obstacle. Simmonds was kneeling with rifle aimed through the wire of the gate-block, firing occasionally at the bend along the trench to discourage any enemy thinking of reaching around to chance a grenade. The gas was in the trench now, and the shouts and screams of men fighting for their lives were becoming ever more urgent, ever more intense as the gas found mouths and throats of men who had had masks torn from their faces in the close-quarters fighting. There was noise coming from the other direction too – the enemy were in the trench on both sides of Winterman and his men.

Peake chambered a round, steeled himself against his fear, mounted the fire-step, took aim and fired. The Germans were closer. He could make out the angry determination upon their gas-masked, helmeted faces. Unable any longer to gauge the scale of the threat – not wanting to comprehend it – he became a trained automaton, firing two more carefully aimed shots and felling another two enemy. But then the German rounds began to seek him out, forcing him to duck below the parapet's sandbags as canvas tore and sand flew about him, stinging his skin. He looked to Winterman for direction. Winterman must help them, must tell them what to do! Winterman must take charge!

'PULL BACK! PULL BACK! Peake – get down here! Get down here with us! WITHDRAW! LEAVE THE WOUNDED – LEAVE THEM! Follow me – LET'S GO!'

The surviving members of the platoon pulled back. They withdrew. They ran. Soldiers abandoned their posts to scramble from the fire-step down to the duckboards and follow Winterman away from the gate-block to a communications trench leading to the rear. They encountered others, some of them fighting a confused, running, rearguard action with aimed shots and occasional grenade, though few of the enemy seemed to be pursuing the fleeing soldiers with any determination: they had survived a terrifying assault through the wire – no point in dying now. The Germans had to consolidate, too, yet from behind Winterman and his men even as they scurried along the communications trench – single file – came shouting and bellowing and the desperate cries of men still in combat within the trench, and loud crumping – grenades – and the occasional unmistakable bark of the tank's cannon. There was single-shot rifle fire, lots of it, but very little automatic rattle from the Lewis guns – almost none at all – for the British had had no time to remount them after the bombardment.

Winterman, running ahead of his men, leading them, was of the opinion that at least part of the defence had held, but it was difficult to tell. He pressed on toward the rear.

Breaking out of the communications trench into the second line, the panting, frightened soldiers were amazed to encounter fresh troops readying themselves within it – about a hundred of them – bayonets fixed and gas masks donned, preparing to move against the flow. The officer in charge, a young major, shouted a query that rallied Winterman and the others as they emerged. He was calmly in control:

'Easy, lads! Easy now! Who are you? Identify, please!'

'Sergeant Winterman with Eleven Platoon, sir. About half of us …'

178

'Good. Well done. Keep moving back now … Gibson?'

'Sir!'

'Gibson, show them the way. You – Sergeant … Winterman, you said your name was?'

'Yes, sir. Winterman.'

'Follow Gibson here. There are more, further back. Keep moving. Somebody will reorganise you. We're going to need your help for the counter …'

Camden Police Station was a cold, impersonal building of unwelcomingly stark décor. It was sparsely furnished. The constables on duty displayed genuine concern for the newly bereaved as they arrived in dribs and drabs, but no amount of empathy could lessen the impact of the station's thoroughgoing drabness. The morning after the bombs fell, there was an atmosphere of profound grief about the place as all prepared for the dreadful task of identifying the newly dead. But they did their best, those Camden constables.

A sergeant appeared in the frame of the door from the passage leading into the main body of the building. His eyes were red-rimmed from lack of sleep, and his voice grated like gravel when he spoke, as though it might fail him at any moment. The man was exhausted.

'Anyone from the Wainwright family here, please? Is there a Mrs Wainwright here at all?'

She stood up from her seat, looking about numbly at the others waiting for summons to identify. So many of us, she thought. Beside her, Penelope Brooke stood also, but her help would not be enough, for Penelope was not family. How she wished for the presence of proper family to help her cope! How she wished for somebody very close – anybody – to relieve her of the awful burden of this task she was about to undertake. She yearned for the presence of their child – their ward Simon who had become as a son to them. Simon would certainly have known what to do. And what was he enduring at that moment? Everywhere this day the talk was of some new assault on the British positions: the biggest ever, folk at this police station were saying.

Unknowingly she clenched her hands into balled fists at her sides as she stood, then unclenched them with an equal lack of awareness. Her mind was racing:

Who would take care of things, with her beloved Wainwright dead?

Who would look after her? Who would provide? Who would oil a squeaking door or repair a window broken by football kicked carelessly from the street? Who would replace a worn washer or paint a wall in need of a lick? Who would carry out all the mundanities for which she lacked time as she dedicated her life to keeping house and looking after her husband, the man whom she loved more than life itself?

Who would love her? God, oh God! Who would love her?

Beside her as she stood, Penelope, that constant friend whose own husband had been lost to illness years before. How had Penelope coped? How had Penelope managed? The widow Wainwright wondered all these things even as the sergeant put an end to her companion's good intentions:

'Next of kin only, ma'am, if you please. I really am very sorry ...'

The sergeant's voice trailed tiredly away. It sounded like cracking sandpaper. Penelope took her seat again, and the sergeant turned to lead Wainwright's widow toward the passage and the room where waited her sorry task of identifying the pale, pitiful corpse. It was there for her, all that now remained to the world of this man whom she had loved.

In the wicker basket below the observation balloon, the artillery NCO continued his correction of the German guns onto their new targets – places of likely assembly in and around Foncquevillers, places where the British might regroup. But even as he did this, he was able to watch the battle unfolding before him.

He saw the leading waves of the Fifth falter upon the wire. Stalled by it, some men began to fire through the entanglements at trenches now very close, while others cut and hacked and pulled desperately at the thick, barbed strands, falling and dying under the British bullets. Those that lived pushed forward, using the bodies of their dead as bridges and ramps. He gawked at Tommies scrambling to organise their defence, pitying them in the haste and pressure of their scrambling, for there was not enough time – the Fifth were already upon them. He watched, hypnotised by the violence, the first tank successfully clawing its way through the barbed-wire barricade to fall victoriously and vengefully upon those defenders, and he could hear the sound of the bitter, hand-to-hand fighting that followed, angry and desperate. He saw the other tanks – all three – breaking through also with their clusters of gas-masked infantry crowded about the awkwardly moving machines.

All was noise. All was chaos. But the man in the wicker basket grasped that all was not success, for on the extremities of the attack the British were holding even as their centre fell back. This was where the German *kompanies* defending against potential flanking movements were positioned and, because it was not their job to actually attack, it was at this junction of German units – attackers and flankers – that the British were managing to hold, managing to organise, managing to lay down effective defensive fire …

Goettner was watching the unfolding battle, too. His was a different view and perspective from that of the man in the wicker basket, not only because he was on the ground, but also because he was more intimately involved, part of the advance to the fight itself.

Putting the fingers of one hand to a temple, he massaged it through his gas mask to ease the fatigue that threatened to overwhelm him. His body felt leaden and slow. There had been too little rest, too little sleep.

On either side as he walked cautiously forward with pistol drawn, the *zug* matched his steady pace in an extended line, brought up to full strength by replacements from the reserve. Yesterday he had made a point of meeting these newcomers. He would have liked to have met each man individually for a personal chat, however brief, but the pressures of battle preparation had been very great – scarcely enough time even for essential tasks – so he had had to settle for a group encounter. Now these soldiers, none yet nineteen and many barely past their seventeenth birthday, advanced nervously, each one a semi-trained packet of helmet, gas mask, pack, webbing, rifle and bayonet, each man bent into an undignified stoop that forced him to move forward unnaturally and with difficulty even as he hoped that this stoop might somehow keep him below the scythe of death. They were frightened, those replacements, scared by the noise of the shells whistling and screeching overhead, and by the erupting earth exploding in great gouts of mucky soil forward of the advance, around the objective. By contrast, the veterans – König, Nettermann, Zimmermann and the others – these men walked erect, their appearance almost proud, though none would have considered themselves so, their bold bearing and manner the consequence of a clear and selfish understanding that the three battalions of the Fifth, arranged in deep, extended ranks ahead of them, would take most of the enemy fire. Even Winkler seemed suddenly to have come of age in this new attack, his second – he walked erect too. The veterans were more confident in this advance to the fight than the replacements.

Thus moved the *zug*, Goettner with pistol at the ready, his men with bayonets fixed to rifles held at port or carry, each man difficult to identify, made almost alien by the obscene masks and goggles. The *oberleutnant* could pick out but a few: Nettermann's rolling gait was easy enough to identify, and there went Zimmermann, the man bigger than most. The broad frame of his sergeant and dumpy young König beyond were also obvious.

Ahead the Fifth, that regiment moving steadily forward, closer and closer to the boiling earth that was the barrage, huge clods of soil and clay, root and bark dancing upward to a sky dotted with the violent orange-red flashes of air bursts hurling shrapnel down upon the defenders. Closer and closer to this hell moved the Fifth.

Closer …. Closer …

Now a slight easing of the barrage, and then gas, some of the guns rearward switching ammunition and shortening their range to let the canisters fall just short of the objective. Goettner glimpsed the evil fingers of brown-yellow smoke colouring the air, spreading, spreading … drifting forward. The Fifth were in the gas now, the soldiers moving as ghosts through a cancerous mist. The *zug* itself would reach that horrible place quite soon.

A man at the forward edge fell, then another and two more around him, all within seconds and one torn so utterly that he collapsed into separate, bloody piles upon the earth. These were victims of their own shells. The Fifth wavered, halted, fell flat. Goettner shouted to his men, signalling a halt with left arm raised, but the instruction was superfluous. Most had seen these casualties at the point of their advance, they knew what to do. Pausing automatically to kneel, they held their rifles ready and adjusted their masks, watching, waiting, praying.

Goettner risked a quick glance behind, noting hundreds of men similarly halted. His attention was caught by something silhouetted against the sky above them – the observation balloon. It hung, suspended above the battlefield as an ungainly, bloated fish-like thing of dull cloth and silk, an inanimate monitor pasted against a sky so blue and peaceful, streaked with hints of cirrus, white and pure.

Turning again to his front, his eye spotted something at the Fifth's mid-point: a flag unfurling to flutter bravely in the breeze. The shelling ceased at the fluttered command. Now those men of the Fifth came quickly to their feet to dart forward, abandoning the tanks with their groups of foot-soldiers guarding them, and sprinting to gain as much ground as they could before the British mustered defensive fire. Goettner and the *zug* broke into a run, too, matching the pace of those men in the forward ranks, about them the rest of their *kompanie* and the soldiers of sister *kompanies* and all the men of the battalions of the greater regiments – more than four thousand running forward to support the two thousand five hundred men of the Fifth pouring themselves upon the British wire. It was a massive attack, determined and violent, and made thunderous by the roaring voices of all about to fight for their lives.

He was panting now, Goettner was, struggling to draw breath through the tight, sweatily constricting mask, struggling to keep an eye on the *zug* left and right of him through goggles that narrowed his view. It was difficult. He gave up, deciding to simply run on, and knowing the rest would stay with him if he led from the front, setting the pace for the necessary last dash forward. Leadership by determined example – this was the only way Goettner knew. Bodies came into his view as lumps of field grey upon the ground. Who were they? These were not the dead of the Fifth, so which was their unit? My God! My God! These were their own! These were their own men from two days ago when the first attack was halted – they were running through the same place! Goettner glanced to the uniformed corpses as he ran past them lying untended upon the battlefield, stiff and still in death, some broken into unnatural form by shellfire, most encrusted in the dried red-brown muck that was their blood. Could that be Schäffer over there? Was that the old married man of the *zug*? Yes, there could be no doubt. It was him, somehow still handsome at quick glance, even in the sprawled indignity of his death.

Goettner looked to his front. The *zug* was closing rapidly with the four tanks left behind by the forward rush of the Fifth. One machine was now only just ahead of them, while the Fifth itself was fifty metres further forward and already upon the British barbs, men struggling to breach those vicious entanglements now halting their rush, wrestling with the wire, wrenching at it, striving to cut a passage through even as they fell victim to the first British retaliation.

'Stay with the tank!' Goettner bellowed to his men, pointing with his pistol and hoping his command would carry beyond his mask. 'MOVE WITH THE TANK! STAY WITH THE TANK!'

He saw that some were breaking. Some of the newcomers were faltering, turning, running, faces twisted in fear, utterly terrified.

'LEAVE THEM! IGNORE THEM IF THEY RUN! MOVE WITH THE TANK … STAY WITH THE TANK!'

They did, slowing to match the pace of that clumsy, noisily awkward armoured box of steel as it lumbered and lurched unsteadily forward, engine roaring and belching grey-black fumes at the sky, guns coughing death at the enemy. Goettner's soldiers clustered about its armour-plated sides, encouraged by the tank's slowly stammering machine guns, and by the deafening crack of its cannon. Yet even as the machine advanced, men of the Fifth were falling wounded or dead ahead of it, while others of that regiment continued to fire steadily at the enemy trenches, or hack and pull at the obstructing wire. Everything appeared wrapped in clouds of yellow-brown. The Tommy positions had become as a hazy scar upon land glimpsed through a swirling, dirty mist of gas that was in places quite thick, like muck from a factory smokestack. Surrounded by it, swimming in it, the *zug* reached the surviving men of the Fifth as a stumbling, tumbling huddle of noisily terrified men, some trampling underfoot the outspread limbs of the fallen, or tripping over them as they strove to pass as quickly as possible through the obstacle that was the wire. Others hesitated, hoping to follow an easier passage carved by the tank.

A masked face appeared in front of Goettner – a soldier in brown with an upturned, rimmed steel dish upon his head – a Tommy. Goettner fired two shots at a place somewhere below the face. The Tommy sank to his knees, disappeared. To his right he glimpsed Zimmermann bayoneting another in the gut, then struggling to free his blade stuck fast in the bone of the spine. Even as Zimmermann put his boot upon the dying man's chest to fire a shot that blasted his weapon free but sprayed him with blood and gore, so the others of the *zug* were likewise falling upon the enemy, the tank crashing forward and down into the chaos within, and the attacking troops hacking, firing, smashing and bayoneting their way forward.

Simon's room … This was Simon's room!

The thought was Penelope's as she looked about the small space where she had spent the night. It was as similarly tiny as the one in her own home reserved for guests: just enough space for a bed with side table and small wardrobe – no more than that. Penelope already knew that she had left nothing behind. No need to check, really. She had brought no bag to dinner, yet still she looked the place over so as to humour the woman waiting in the living room, melancholy and maudlin after the identification just completed. Was there nothing more she could do to ease the widow's pain? Hard to tell, really. She had done her best to soothe the initial shock, and would have stayed to do more had her friend not insisted that she needed time alone. Perhaps that insistence was genuine. Wainwright's widow would certainly need time to grieve.

Simon's room … On impulse, Penelope walked the few paces from door to one corner, putting out a hand to touch a propped cricket bat. Now, as she looked around, she noted other boyhood milestones, the markers of growing up. There were dented, scratched tin soldiers – a gift bought second-hand, no doubt – arranged upon a shelf screwed to one wall, and a model locomotive crafted from painted wood and board. There were books, among them a school text left unreturned when time had run out in young Simon's haste to leave for the fight.

And where was Simon at that moment, she wondered? What might he be doing, the young man who had become Christine's lover? Shaking her head at the thought, Penelope left the bedroom to move to the lounge where sat her friend, damp handkerchief clenched tightly in one fist.

'What am I going to do, Penelope?' the widow wailed between sobs. 'What am I going to do?'

Breath was reaching her in wrenching, shuddering gulps. The woman was grief-stricken, desolate, afraid.

Penelope sat down opposite and looked down at her own hands, examining them so that she did not have to look at this friend whose grief was so intense as to make Penelope herself want to weep. Without looking up she said:

'Christine will keep you company, if you like. She's offered. She said she would come by anyway – later – to see how you are.'

'No, no … What can she do, Penelope?' More sobs, more dabbing. She was struggling to control the grief. 'What can anybody do?'

Silence for a while, nothing but the clock's melancholy ticking.

'How did you cope, Penelope? What did you do when Phillip died?'

'I wrote to him.'

'What do you mean?'

'I wrote to him. I wrote him letters – one letter every day, for months.'

Penelope paused in her simple confession, looking down at her hands again and wondering at the slight embarrassment that crept upon her. After a time she continued:

'They were love letters, those notes … They were my love letters to Phillip. And I think they helped me come to terms with losing him. I wrote down all the things that I wanted to tell him while he was still with me, but somehow never could. Little things – maybe big things … I don't know. I wrote down what was in my heart. I told him that I would have tried to take better care of him, given a second chance. I would have loved him more … physically, I mean. And I would have held his hand more, would have stroked his hair more – he liked that … So many things I would have done better, so many areas where I could have – would have – tried harder if I'd only known that our time together would be so short.'

The two women looked at one another in silence for some moments, listening to the clock. Their mutual honesty brought about by grief and confession was as an open wound: a raw thing, a fragile thing, a painful and momentary thing that was an impulsive, necessary consequence of Wainwright's death. It would not occur again, and both were conscious of that fact.

'I believe that Phillip knew what I wrote. My faith tells me this is so. And the knowledge that he knows what was ... is ... in my heart where he is concerned, well, it helped me get through things. It still helps.'

Wainwright's widow nodded, dabbed at her tears, said:

'If Christine comes, I'll ask her to write a letter to Simon while I write to Thomas. We can sit together in the kitchen ...'

'Christine will come. She said she would.'

The Lancashires were mauled. Most of their forward positions had fallen, though not all, and even in hasty retreat their junior leadership was solid and their senior officers determined. The colonel himself, the man in overall command, was not only resolute but stubborn, too. Battered though his forward three battalions most certainly were, there remained one dug-in as a tactical reserve several hundred yards to the rear. Apart from light casualties suffered during the preliminary barrage, this reserve battalion was relatively unscathed, and the colonel very quickly organised its eight hundred troops to counterattack while the fighting in the forward trenches was still going on. It was through a company of these troops readying themselves for that counter that Winterman, Peake and the others had passed after exiting the communications trench.

The colonel was aware that his reserve was greatly outnumbered. He estimated that between six and eight thousand Germans were assaulting, while his own troops had numbered just over three thousand before this attack, one fifth under-strength through losses – mainly wounded – incurred in the first attempt to take the line. The question now was how many more had been lost within the forward fire trenches. He himself reckoned up to a third, maybe more. Yet he also knew that the flanks were holding. Quite why that was he did not fully comprehend, but he was glad of the fact and, counting himself lucky, sent orders by runner: the flanking troops were to skirmish inwards along the line of the trench towards the centre, clearing it as best they could. Minimise casualties, he wrote – none at all would be best. The idea was not for them to retake the lost trenches, but to keep the Germans fully occupied defending a newly captured position unfamiliar and confusing to them. His hope was to force the Huns onto the back foot as they defended their gains against aggressive probes from both sides while the reserve battalion fell upon the centre even as the fighting continued. The colonel was gambling on the likelihood that his enemy would be unsteady in those places they had succeeded in capturing, having suffered many casualties crossing no man's land, and wanting to tend to them while simultaneously trying to suppress those pockets of British resistance that still held. In the captured trenches, the Germans would be busy consolidating and preparing their defence in a direction opposite to that for which the position had been designed and prepared, a difficult and time-consuming task not yet properly begun. With luck and determination, the counterattack might succeed.

The colonel had no artillery – it was being bombarded by the German guns after they had switched from the trenches. Even had there been access to artillery support, inability to spot the fall-of-shot meant correction would be impossible – the British had no observation balloon of their own, and no high point other than the village church tower in Foncquevillers, long since shelled into ruin. So the colonel had no alternative but to make best possible use of his trench mortars: three-inch Stokes tubes, mainly, toys when compared with pukka artillery, but effective in their own way, firing almost vertically their unstabilised, high-trajectory cylindrical bombs to fall within a pre-determined area, forcing the target to seek cover.

Such was the colonel's plan, and it was implemented very quickly. The crews manning the twelve mortars that they had – a mix of the Stokes and some smaller, two-inch tubes – achieved a rate of fire of one bomb every four seconds for a full two minutes, almost all the munitions they had. Three hundred and sixty bombs fell upon the forward trenches, a fierce barrage that allowed the reserve battalion to move forward unopposed. There were British prisoners in the target trenches, of course, many of them wounded, but the colonel considered the risk of casualties among his own troops acceptable, secure in his experience and knowledge that only a very small number of bombs would actually find the trenches themselves, most detonating close about them while the battalion mounting the counterattack moved up to a wait-line just short of the flying earth and grit to their front.

Now, the men of that reserve battalion charged with bayonets fixed, a spontaneous, vengeful roar erupting from their ranks as a battle cry terrible to the ear; fiercely hoarse and raggedly loud despite the masks. The fighting that followed was intense, merciless, brutal, the British wreaking death upon German troops already shaken by their awful assault. Attacking from their rear, these Lancashires of the reserve reached the trenches in seconds, for there was no wire to slow them. They had other advantages, too: intimate knowledge of the labyrinth that was this entrenched position, and they were relatively fresh. The enemy, by contrast, was exhausted. Their debilitating assault through the barbed-wire entanglements and the subsequent hand-to-hand fighting within the trenches had sapped their strength.

The attacking troops inflicted losses upon the Germans disproportionate to their numbers. The enemy began to fall back in confusion, scrambling out of the trenches and back into the wire in a scene reminiscent of Hades: chaotic, awful, bloody. Within the excavated defences, soldiers fought one another to the death, stabbing and slashing, bludgeoning, gouging, shooting. Beyond that place, and with the Germans once again caught in the wire so recently conquered, it became more a picking-off of individuals by the men of both sides as the Germans made short dashes hither and thither before standing firm for a second or two to aim and fire, and work their bolts and fire again. Some knelt, others stood, all tried to give cover one to another as they retreated.

Many of the Brocton replacements took part in this counterattack, among them Earnshaw, Watson and Peake, Corporal Tozer leading them. Away to one side was Sergeant Winterman with another group of stragglers assembled on the run. They joined the attack late and in separate pockets, having first assembled and reorganised after falling back from the initial German assault. Along with many others who had retreated under that pressure, these men now moved quickly forward across open ground between the reserve and the forward trenches, scrambling and stumbling, sliding and leaping into the fluid chaos that was the mortal combat along the floor of the trenches themselves, and within the dugouts.

Earnshaw killed for the first time at close quarters, saving a comrade by shooting a German from behind as the man swung his rifle left and right among the British.

Watson killed for the first time also: two men in quick succession, bayoneting one in the gut, then withdrawing the blade to free his rifle and swing it to bludgeon a second, smashing down repeatedly with butt at the man's goggles and mask until the face beneath collapsed inwards upon its own skull.

Peake did not kill, though this was not through any conscious choice on his part. Rather, he maimed, preferring to conserve his strength and move on to his next target when the first was already crippled by bullet, butt or bayonet.

The attacking British were everywhere in the trench, and they were savage. The fight was desperate. Within the melée, Goettner was one of many to realise that things were now no longer going the way of the Germans. What the devil was happening on the flanks? There was the sporadic crumping of grenades from both directions, not their own but a distinctly different sound – Tommy grenades – and there was a growing crush as their own troops began to be forced back from both sides. What was happening? What to do? Again he fired his pistol at a goggled British gas mask appearing suddenly before him, conscious of the back of the man's head exploding outward to the rear, spraying the trench wall red as the soldier's helmet adopted an unnatural tilt and the man collapsed in a heap of loosened rifle and disarrayed, uncontrolled limbs. He looked about to see where he could help, seeing in a single instant to his right Zimmermann, on his knees upon the duckboards and wrestling with a burly Tommy, winning the match as he snapped the Tommy's neck with an audible crack while behind him Nettermann was slashing left and right, using his bayonet as a dagger. Where was the man's rifle? Where was Zimmermann's? To his left several more of the *zug*, among them König, tunic red with blood (was he wounded?) and the slight frame of Winkler, on his knees like Zimmermann his mentor, smashing at a Tommy's masked face with his fists, his rifle also abandoned in the desperate combat.

The remainder of the *zug* were similarly engaged around the tank that had crashed forward with them through the wire. Several soldiers had fallen, wounded or dead – Goettner couldn't be sure which. The machine itself was now stuck fast in the trench, some of its crew firing out through their weapon slits, others beginning to spill out through the hatches. Goettner glanced behind, back toward the wire so recently conquered. He saw a *hauptmann* leading a retreat through the broken barbs, his soldiers trying to move backwards so that they could still face the British and shoot, but becoming caught in the wire once more, and some falling to the snapping, accurate Tommy rounds.

From somewhere, a bellowed order:

'Goettner! GOETTNER!' It was their commander's voice, their own *hauptmann*. 'Pull back, Goettner! Pull back! Withdraw!'

The Tommies were everywhere, attacking from the flanks and the front. On all sides was madness.

Ammunition was low and nothing was coming forward to replace it.

We are out! We are going to run out of grenades! This was Goettner's thought and realisation.

'GOETTNER …! Get your men out of the trench and pull back. Withdraw! Do it, man! Pull out! Pull out NOW!'

189

CHAPTER NINE

'Yes, yes – you are right, of course. But can they hold? Will they do it?'
'They have held until now, sir.'

The two in conversation were British officers: divisional commander and chief of staff. The defensive line at Foncquevillers fell within their sector. Around them, other headquarters officers – mostly majors with a sprinkling of captains – stood in tense debate or toiled steadily at trestle tables serving as desks in the big canvas tent, drafting plans, executing operational and logistical orders, checking execution or acting on messages arriving by runner or rider. Their mood was subdued. Grim. All were weighing the odds even as they laboured, aware of the awful decision that had soon to be taken: whether to pass the word to the Lancashires to withdraw, or order them to hold firm and die.

They have held until now …

The commander considered his chief of staff's reply, looking squarely at the man. Eventually, he gave voice to his own reasoning:

'Yes, indeed they have. They've held. But do they have enough men to continue holding? There must have been losses … Very heavy losses this morning ... Hundreds, I think.'

Over the previous week, the weight of the German attack and its catastrophically rapid pace of advance had twice forced this divisional headquarters to move. First had come an evacuation from the comfortable château that had been its base for months. The staff had withdrawn ten miles, only to be ejected a second time and forced back a further ten to this slipshod cluster of tents of different sizes erected in great haste and arranged haphazardly within a small wood. Some of the bigger tents spilled out onto an adjacent field, vulnerable to observation and attack from the air. It was far from ideal – just how was one expected to think properly in such a place? But it would have to do. It would simply have to do. No other choice …

The largest of the canvas constructs was the operations tent, the nerve centre for command and control of the division's ten thousand troops – fewer, now, because of casualties. This was where the two senior officers were in debate. They lacked much information. Forward communication by field telephone had been cut by shellfire, with many lines still being reconnected or relaid. The only reliable means of dispatching orders or receiving situation reports to and from troops digging in or miraculously still holding – as at Foncquevillers – was by rider on horseback or vehicle-borne messenger, or sometimes even a runner on foot. The situation was chaotic. There were units fighting fluid rearguard actions to cover other battalions in full flight. But where were they? And what was the precise situation? How many were left? And could they hold? Send a runner! Send a runner!

That operations tent this April day was hot and noisy, made more so by the incessant, thunderous artillery of both armies pounding away at each other without pause, the clamour of their firing rising and falling according to distance, always loud. Much louder still was the periodic crash-bang of the cannon dug-in on the edge of the coppice, the nearest gun of a troop of four. After the loud, sharp crack of each shell fired came the tinny, empty-sounding clatter of an ejected brass shell-casing falling to earth, and the shouted commands of the crew reloading to fire again.

The divisional commander, a major general, mopped perspiration from his pate with a handkerchief. He was a handsome man, but his hair had receded and what he had left was thinning. Sometimes he felt self-conscious without his crimson-banded cap of rank to conceal his loss, hence the gesture with handkerchief. The ops room headdress rack had been misplaced during the chaotic second move – complete with all the caps – and most of the officers were now hatless. Batmen had been dispatched to search for the damned things. Must be somewhere.

'Wonder what's happened to our dispatch rider,' mused the commander, his voice steady and revealing no unease. Self-control was vital at this moment, given the circumstances. People needed to keep calm. It was imperative that he set the example. He continued to face his chief of staff, continued to examine the man squarely. After another pause he said:

'I must know the numbers … I have to know what strength remains beyond the village.'

'Four battalions, sir.'

The chief of staff's reply was superfluous, for of course the general knew the number of units involved. Rather, it was the number of men still on their feet around Foncquevillers that was important to him; the number still able to fight. The chief of staff attempted to recover from his blunder:

'But I agree with you, sir. We need to know our strength. We should probably plan on having lost up to half. Two attacks in three days ...'

His voice fell away under his commander's keen stare.

'So, about two thousand men, then,' said the commander, 'Two thousand if we're lucky. Probably fewer, after this morning ... Very lucky to have pulled off that counter. Damned fortunate. What about ammunition? Rations?'

'We still have logistical routes in place. A bit tenuous, but we're managing to get essentials through.'

In the tent, the faces of those waiting on the general's decision were quietly anxious. Among these were two officers from the allied armies, American and French. They were half-colonels and their role was liaison. Now, the commander turned to the American.

'What about your men at the ports, Colonel? Brest would be closest. We need them, please.'

The American weighed the general's question, measuring the man and guessing at his nerve. Understanding the commander's stress, his reply was wary, its New England accent contrasting greatly with the general's clipped, Harrow-modulated tones:

'I think General Pershing might resist, sir. He won't want to give you what you need – still gathering strength. Lots of men still arriving. And he takes the view that American troops must be commanded by American officers.'

'Yes. Quite so. But we must ask him, must we not? Dammit all, man, we're fighting the same war – the same enemy – and they're going hell-for-leather for your landing ports!'

The general's fist rose and fell lightly upon the trestle table in emphasis of his words – a fist, not a palm. He continued:

'I'm sorry, Colonel, but I want you to get on to your General Pershing and I want you to do it now! We still have communications to the rear. I *must* have more troops! Request a brigade – more, if he can. He should be able to spare me at least one.'

The American turned to obey, his French counterpart looking on with some sympathy, feeling himself safe from the angry reprimand the New England man would doubtless receive from Pershing in reply to his dispatch, his function being to filter or, better still, completely stall requests such as this one. The Frenchman himself knew he would not be similarly asked, for his own army was already fully committed to the south. But the Americans – one million strong and so few actually in the line – well, the Americans had yet to join the fight in any real strength. The British general had a point.

'Who do we have at Foncquevillers?' the general queried. 'Which battalions exactly are they? Are they still as marked?'

He tapped the annotated map spread before him on the trestle table, one finger indicating four small, neatly marked rectangles identified by the crossed straps of the infantry. These four still stood defiantly between Foncquevillers and the Germans as a growing bulge within the marked line of the general retreat, each one clearly annotated by unit number, not a cohesive regiment but rather four battalions patched together into brigade strength. Elsewhere across the map, the chinagraphed markings of other units had been erased and re-positioned so many times and at so many points – always rearwards – that there was some uncertainty as to accuracy. The smudges of their erasures were everywhere. But these four had not been erased. These four were still clearly, neatly and carefully marked in their original positions. North and south of them, though, the British Army was being pushed quickly back toward the sea.

'Yes, sir. Those units are correctly marked. They are the Lancashires' Second, Ninth, Fourth, and Seventh Battalions – Lancashire Fusiliers.'

'They must hold. Whoever's left *has* to hold that salient. I need twenty-four hours to find reinforcements and get them up there. If they can do it – if they can hold on – we will relieve them tomorrow night. They *must* hold that salient.'

The General turned to a young major among his staff:

'Ian, draft an order around this wording, if you please: *Hold position until relieved immediately after last light tomorrow, April 6*. Do it now, will you?'

'Directly, sir.' And the major turned from the table to execute his task.

A brief silence fell upon the tent. There were other key decisions to be taken, all equally urgent, for the division contained two other regiments besides those Lancashires holding firm at Foncquevillers. But for perhaps ten seconds not a word was spoken. The thunder and rumble of artillery and that single, monstrous crashing of the cannon firing close by, these were the only sounds while all considered the inevitable consequence of that one decision just taken, that one order just delivered. All were relieved that it was not they who had been forced to issue the command, for those words now being expanded into detail for delivery by runner would certainly mean the deaths of many young men still able to fight. The Germans would come on again at Foncquevillers. They had to.

* * *

Schäffer's corpse was muddied and bloody; a filthy thing that barely resembled the man who once had been. The waist and crotch of his uniform trousers were caked and gummed with patches of dark red. Though it was the shot to Schäffer's neck that had killed him, he had been hit in the lower body too. Now, the cadaver was stiff and unyielding, heavy and awkward to drag, so that when they reached the sentry trench, the team of two hauling the corpse by its legs dropped their load gratefully, then repositioned and heaved it over the parapet, feet first. Schäffer's body slid down the wooden shoring to stand for a moment, stiffly propped against the trench wall and refusing to bend at waist or knee. Then it toppled sideways and fell over onto its front, face on the duckboards and boots caught upon the fire-step. The haulers jumped down into the trench to pull the corpse into a more dignified pose. They glanced worriedly to Zimmermann who had overseen their task, but Zimmermann only nodded his thanks. They could not read his mind.

The tall frame of Goettner appeared at a bend in the trench, approaching. His forehead and cheeks were grimy and still slick from the fight, but the greater part of his face was startlingly clean where he had worn his gas mask. The shape of the thing was clearly marked by an outline of angry red upon the skin, so tight had been the straps. He was still wearing his helmet. Goettner asked the nearest soldier for his field blanket. Shaking it out, he placed the rectangle of coarse cloth carefully, almost tenderly, over Schäffer's body, then straightened, eyeing and assessing his men, and fixing them with his penetrating stare. He said nothing.

'Couldn't leave him out there, *Herr Oberleutnant*,' offered Zimmermann by way of explanation. 'Didn't seem right. Not another night.'

'And the others? The rest we left in the Tommy line?'

Zimmermann shrugged, managing to look guilty and indifferent at the same time. All understood that to recover the dead only just lost in the British trenches had been impossible because of the fight. But Schäffer … well, the Tommy sniping had faded by the time they passed his body for the second time that day, the observation balloon once again directing its guns to fire upon those trenches they had conquered for so brief a time, then evacuated. The shelling had provided opportunity to recover the corpse. They might have picked another from the many scattered about, but they chose Schäffer. *Ja*, they really loved that old married man.

Goettner relented.

'It was the right thing to do.' He nodded. 'The noble thing. Leave him now, Zimmermann. The burial detail will take care of him. Get yourself back to the main trench. Find something to eat, and put something strong in your coffee.'

The big soldier turned to obey, a jerk of his helmeted head indicating to the others that they should follow. In the network of trenches to the rear, they searched for Nettermann, König and Winkler. They found them resting, Winkler prostrate and asleep beside the other two. He was snoring, mouth open, but flinching and twitching too – bad dreams, probably. His companions were conversing in low tones as they sat upon the fire-step. Round about lay webbing and packs, helmets and gas masks in untidy piles. Zimmermann examined his comrades. The front of König's tunic showed a deep red that glistened and glimmered dully as somebody else's blood dried in stages upon it. The mess was fully soaked into the cloth, horrible to see and attracting flies, but the man was evidently too exhausted to remove the garment. Some of Zimmermann's haulers were similarly bloodied, though König's uniform took the prize.

'We brought Schäffer back,' opened Zimmermann, indicating the other soldiers now departing along the duckboards to seek their own friends. They were moving in the manner of the very tired, and he wondered if his own movements betrayed similar exhaustion. He hoped not. The thought crossed Zimmermann's mind that Winkler was right to succumb to the escape of sleep. He examined the man for a moment, as if seeing him properly for the very first time. Then, unslinging not one but two rifles from his shoulder, he propped the weapons carefully against a recess in the boarded wall and sank heavily onto the fire-step. He indicated the Mausers with a tired half-wave.

'Found a spare along the way,' he said. 'Did you leave yours in the Tommy trenches, then?' His eyebrows were raised in query.

Silence. Zimmermann knew that the two sitting upon the fire-step would guess that the spare had been Schäffer's, but perhaps they were too tired even to speak. Eventually, Nettermann's careful consideration of the query led to a reply:

'*Ja*. Had to drop them while we were mixing it with the Tommies. But they paid a price, those Tommies. König still has his.'

König grinned sheepishly, trying to hide his pride at having held on to his rifle in the melée. He held out a dented enamel pot to Zimmermann.

'Here,' he said. 'Have some. It's coffee with schnapps. Quite good. Hot and strong.'

Zimmermann sipped, then passed the pot to Nettermann. For a while, nobody said anything. All drank, savouring the alcohol more than the brew.

195

It numbed somewhat the latest bloody memory layered upon all the others that rattled at the barred cages of their carefully guarded sanity, threatening to tear asunder that fine line between raw animal and civilised man, destroying all values taught by home, school and church.

Thou shalt not kill …

'It doesn't matter about the Mausers. Plenty of those.'

König looked at Zimmermann, said:

'That was bad.'

'What was?'

'The Tommy line. The fight. We were lucky to make it through … to get back.'

'*Ja.* Lucky.'

Winkler came to. Rubbing his eyes, he looked about him, sat up.

'Hello, Zimmermann,' he said.

'Hello, New Man. Glad to see you're still with us. It makes me very happy.'

Winkler grinned, then began to giggle and found he could not stop. It was an edgy, hysterical sort of laugh that made the others nervous. Observing him closely, König said to no one in particular:

'You know, I can't look at a person smiling or laughing anymore without seeing the skull.'

'What do you mean?'

'The skull … The jawbone beneath the smile … So many skulls, the flesh gone. All those teeth in the jawbone. I studied one, once. A skull back in Poland. It was quite rotten, almost completely clean. Or the outside was, anyway. Now it distracts me … from the living. The smile, I mean. I can't enjoy the sight of anybody smiling. I see only teeth and the smallness of the bite behind the flesh. Everyone seems to have the same size bite … So every time I see a person smile, I see only the bite. I see their skull … their jawbone with the embedded teeth … and that's all I see.'

'*Gott im Himmel.*'

There was silence for a while as the four considered this point. Eventually, Nettermann said:

'You need to focus on the living, König. You need to focus on life. Better some flesh that's still in one piece around proper, living bone than the grin of a dead man.'

Winkler nodded agreement. He had regained control of himself. Visualisation of König's thought had killed his giggling. He wiped away nervous tears, worrying that the others might see how utterly shaken he was from the ordeal of the British trench so recently behind them.

'*Ja*. The living … Well, I have to tell you I don't fear death at all anymore.' This was Zimmermann. They looked at him.

'No, really – It doesn't trouble me. I used to fear it, but I don't anymore. We've seen too much of it … too much death. We've killed too many Ivans and too many Tommies.'

To the others, it seemed that Zimmermann did not want to talk about their own dead.

'So now,' he continued, 'now I think that when my own time comes – my own death – I shall welcome it quite willingly. I will allow it to take its course. I shan't resist. It will be just another part of another day, something that will take care of itself like all the other things of my life before it … like all the other obstacles and calamities. It's not going to worry me. I don't fear it anymore.'

Silence. None replied. None wanted to debate the observation and none wanted to point out that, given current circumstances, perhaps Zimmermann's death was not going to be sufficiently peaceful to avoid resisting its arrival. Nettermann, remembering the man's confession about his father's beatings, felt pity for the big soldier. Winkler, having regained his composure, tried for a less morbid topic of conversation, though it was only slightly less so:

'What now? The rest of the day … what'll happen?'

'Well,' replied Zimmermann, 'König here would do well to change his tunic. The flies will certainly call their friends for all that blood. Schäffer's is available. He won't be needing it anymore. *Ja*, Schäffer's tunic is an option. But not his trousers.'

'Schäffer?' queried Winkler.

'Schäffer,' confirmed Zimmermann. 'We brought his body back.'

A solemn nod of understanding from Winkler at this news. After a time Nettermann said:

'We'll go in again.'

'Today? You think so?' This was Winkler again, his round face reflecting worry beneath the dark, sweaty hair.

'Not today,' offered König. 'But tomorrow for certain. They'll send us again. They have to.'

'*Ja*,' agreed Zimmermann. 'König is right. They'll have to send us in again. The generals need Foncquevillers. It's a problem for them.'

* * *

197

A new smell had come upon the retaken trench. Subtle and vague, it lay oddly upon the place, cloaking every part of that labyrinth and competing with the mundane and ordinary stink of stale urine, and the unpleasantness of faeces never quite overcome by latrine chemicals. There was spent cordite about, too – it caught at the back of nose and throat. The rank smell of sweat went without saying: the men had not washed for days. The gas had dissipated.

Sitting on the fire-step, Watson wrinkled his nose in disgust at this new layer set upon an already tainted air. The odour bothered him. Tozer, too, but he chose to make light of it. He tossed a glance toward the other man:

"'Ere, ain't you nevva smelt dead 'uns before, then, Watson?'

'What do you mean, Corp?'

'Yer nose … t'at smell … t'at's death, chum. Them's the freshly dead you can smell. Too many of 'em makes the air stink like t'at. I seen it at the Somme – smelt it. It changes after a while, t'at smell when they begin ter rot. 'Specially in wevver like today.'

Watson thought about a reply, but nothing suitable came to him about this whiff that came sickly sweet to all in the heat of the day. He nodded instead.

'Better get used ter it, Watson, t'at smell,' continued Tozer. 'There's more ter come. More death.'

'Cheerful bloke you are today, eh, Corp? You got any more like that?'

This was Peake, and the corporal rewarded him with a mirthless chuckle. Retrieving a crumpled pack of cigarettes from his tunic, he offered them around. What remained of the section accepted gratefully. Two of Tozer's men were dead and two more in a hospital tent rear of the village, wounded, but Tozer still had five with him, Peake, Watson and Earnshaw among them. Somebody produced a match and lit up for all.

Winterman approached from along the battered trench. The corporal reversed his cigarette and held it out. Winterman accepted. Dragging upon the thing, he said:

'Five minutes, lads. There's work to be done. Colonel wants the bodies cleared away before stand-to. All of 'em to be out of the trench. And it's not just the Colonel, either – I want this mess cleared up more than he does, and that's a fact. It'll rid us of some of the stink.'

Nods of agreement. They continued to smoke, watching him. Winterman handed back Tozer's cigarette, nodding his thanks. He said:

'Company Sergeant-Major says we're to take care of that dugout by the Jerry tank … the shelter that took the hit.'

'T'at was our platoon in there …' This was Tozer. It was more of a plea than an objection.

198

'Well, it's got to be done. And be thankful we were under strength to begin with. Some got out. Should be no more than five or six in there, and we're going to need that shelter when Jerry comes at us again – what's left of it. CSM says he'll lend us a work party to help. From Twelve Platoon.'

Nothing more was said for a while. The trench was quiet save for the chit-chat of others working wearily either side of the group. The German shelling of before – not too intense, just enough to keep everybody's head down while the Huns quit their attack and pulled back – had once more died away and finally ceased some hours previously. The British guns dug-in rear of Foncquevillers were silent, too. Once again, it was as though both sides in this battle had paused for breath. It was as though each had exhausted the reserves of energy necessary to engage the other, though from north and south came still the distant grumble and thump of German cannons helping the advance towards the coast, and the lesser, more disorganised British riposte.

The relative calm was welcome. Tozer rummaged again in his tunic, found a final, flattened cigarette in the pack and lit it from his own for Winterman. All smoked for a while, nobody speaking, each alone with whatever he was thinking. Mostly they were trying to remember who they might find within the demolished dugout. To left and right of them were groups labouring to drag away the battle's dead, one body at a time, making space: they would need it when the time came again to fight. It required great effort, this clearing away of bodies, needing two men for every corpse, each grasping a lifeless ankle as the generally preferred method of haulage. Where a body had lost half of a leg to shell splinter, or had the boot of a mangled foot dangling by sinew and broken bone alone, then the clearing party would use wrists instead, in which case the victim's head sagged back to bump sadly and unpleasantly along the duckboards directly between the draggers. If British, then that lifeless face beneath the gas mask was familiar. That was why they preferred the ankles.

There were many dead to clear after the fighting. Very many. They were dragged away to recesses within the defences where they were heaved into piles like so many sandbags stacked one on top of the other. The men recovering the bodies built these stacks in separate places, careful not to mix friend with foe. The two sides of the battle remained as divided in death as they had been in life, the heaps of German field grey set apart from the piles of brown British serge. It took four soldiers to heave each corpse onto the pile, sometimes five, and the unsightly body stacks grew steadily wider and higher, here a dangling arm, there a splayed leg or twisted head with gas-masked face staring blank accusation at those still alive.

199

'Some job,' said Tozer resentfully, watching the work, a proper complaint this time. He spat, then cursed foully. 'Some task, 'avin' to clear out Fritz as well as our own. The prisoners should do it.'

'Not enough of 'em. And what there're mostly wounded. Be thankful you don't have to haul Jerry's dead up the parapet tonight,' Winterman answered evenly. 'We've been spared that one. Colonel wants 'em all dumped in front of the trench after dark. Neatly, though, in rows and not any old way so they don't block arcs of fire. Have to show some respect. Says it'll demoralise the Hun. Reserve's pulled the job.'

'Thank God for small mercies,' somebody said.

They moved to the demolished dugout. The abandoned German tank squatted just beyond it, stuck fast, prow-like nose pointing down and tail in the air like some circus fat lady overbalanced in the ring. The hatches of the empty machine were open, the crew either escaped back to their lines, or dead and heaped upon a body stack further along the trench. Beside the hulk was the crater from the fluke artillery shell that had entered the narrow slit of the trench and demolished the dugout, killing most of the men sheltering within. It had obliterated the revetment. The trench's construction had simply disappeared around the point of that explosion, its walls serving to contain the blast and direct it back into the shelter and up and down the trench on either side. What had been a carefully built defence was now spilled earth, tangled wire, torn canvas sandbags, bits of shattered wooden shoring and splintered duckboards. The trench bulged slightly where the shell had exploded. The work party from Twelve Platoon was already filling sandbags for a new parapet. Yet more men were working to build a fresh fire-step and re-shore the walls with corrugated iron and whatever planks of wood they could find. They moved uneasily aside when Winterman's men approached, understanding their purpose. The newcomers would need room to dig.

Wordlessly, Tozer and the others applied entrenching tools to the point where they guessed the dugout's entrance to be. Physically, it was not hard work. The earth had been loosened by the shell's explosion, giving way easily so that the mouth of the dugout was re-opened in fewer than ten minutes. The men continued to hack at the soil and broken clods of clay until their work gave access to the cavity beyond. Holding a trench torch, Winterman ducked inside to shine the light around. After about half a minute he emerged, the group eyeing him cautiously and waiting for his word. They were anxious, grimy and dog tired as they leaned on their tools.

'There're five in there. Gone, of course, all of them,' announced the sergeant with grim expression, answering the unasked question he could see

200

in the eyes of the diggers. 'Peake, Earnshaw – you're up for the first one. It's Mister Williams. Show some respect, but get him out and take him back to the pile.'

They did it, Winterman following them into the dugout to shine light onto the lieutenant so that the two could work. Beyond Williams' corpse was Farmer's and three more. The bodies of all were remarkably intact, though blood trickled slowly from ear and mouth. One was sitting, chin slumped upon his chest as if asleep.

'Blast got 'em, poor buggers. Funny 'ow some got away wiv it …'

'Going to miss Mister Williams … his Welsh way.'

Peake gripped one of Williams' boots, Earnshaw the other, and together they pulled their lieutenant up the path they had cleared with their digging, from dusty darkness into sunlight and the shadow of the wrecked trench. But it wasn't Lieutenant Williams Peake was thinking about. No, his thoughts were of Farmer and the harsh reprimand the man had received at the hands of the sergeant-instructor that day in the Brocton training trenches:

God help you if ever they make you move forward in a charge like that, Farmer! God help you! There were dead and wounded everywhere …

Well, there were dead and wounded everywhere here at Foncquevillers as well, now. And Farmer had acquitted himself well enough in the charge that had been their counter-attack. He'd done that much. And God had helped him do it, too.

In the Wainwright kitchen, Christine watched the other two. The idea had been that the women should write, yet neither Penelope nor the widow Wainwright herself seemed to have managed more than a sentence or two. Upon their faces was a solemn sorrow, and sadness sat upon their shoulders. Christine herself was not writing at all. She had not even begun to write. She simply sat there, watching the others.

The mood in the room was sombre, a heavy, depressing contrast to the bright light provided by late afternoon sunshine arriving through the window. Nothing that day could lift the women's tragic burden.

Penelope looked up from the writing paper before her. She managed a hint of a smile.

'You should try to write something, Christine,' she said.

Christine nodded, pen in hand. Yes, she agreed. She should. But what? And to whom? A letter to Simon? Or to Luke? Of course, the expectation was that she should write to Simon, because this was the only relationship known to the widow Wainwright, who might enquire after her thoughts and who suspected nothing of her engagement to another. But what to say? What words? She wanted to set down what was in her heart. She wanted to tell Peake of her feelings, of her aching want for him. Was this love? Did she love him? She had felt attracted to none other since Peake's departure for France. She wanted only him, yet she knew she should not write down the detail of what she felt, this physical need to have him naked and pressing hard once more against her, in her. It would be an impossible breach of all accepted etiquette to put such a thought onto paper, even were Simon to be the letter's only reader. To reveal these feelings in such graphic manner was simply not acceptable, and perhaps should not be her purpose at all in such a moment of loss, his guardian and virtual father now gone.

So the paper lay blank before her on the table and she sat there, wondering … What did she want of Simon? Did she want a future with him? Did she want to spend the rest of her life with Peake? Did she want marriage? Yes, yes, oh yes! If the rest of her life could be spent in the sizzle of a love as intense as that which she had experienced with him, then she wanted it. She wanted marriage. And she had never felt that way about any other man, not even Luke. Certainly she had never felt as intensely about Luke as she now felt about Simon Peake, and neither had she yearned for him as much when he had left for France that first time.

Applying herself to the paper before her, she managed a salutation before pausing again, pen poised. She was remembering both lovers, considering both men. She was wondering how she had lost Luke or, more accurately, how he had lost her.

Christine had formed the opinion that women's greatest fear was abandonment, because of the emotional rejection it implied, a thing far more important, she thought, than the loss of mere physical love. The way Christine viewed the world, that emotional tie was the most important tie of all. She knew that for women it was absolutely vital, but she was not sure if this held true for men, too. In her experience, emotion was the thing at the core of her relationships, the thing that sprouted from initial physical attraction to grow into the strongest of all bonds. Abandonment meant that this emotional tie would be over – lost – all power of one partner over the other irretrievably gone. Abandonment was the final cut, the final slash, the cruellest wound of all. The loss of a partner's physical love could be managed, and from Christine's own observation it often was. But emotional abandonment was something more, something different and devastating. She recognised that she herself had inflicted such loss upon Luke, and that she had done it with little thought and almost no difficulty. After attraction for Simon had set in, she had simply transferred her affections from one lover to another. Would Luke feel it, when he found out, as deeply as would she, were the roles reversed? On the countless occasions she had tried for her own benefit to rationalise this switch of her affections, she had found no salve for her guilt, no oil for the troubled waters of her unease. No matter her reasoned excuses, the fact was that her emotional abandonment of the man had been brutal and, no doubt, destructive to him. Poor Luke … Christine felt sure that he now sensed love's death. His recent letters from France had hinted at it. Poor, poor Luke. She would have to break off their engagement. A formal end to things was necessary. She would do it the minute he returned to England.

What might his reaction be? Would he show anger? Rage, even? No, she thought. Luke was not like that. At Luke's core lay a gentle sensitivity. All else was mere camouflage, the layers of his social mask. He would be saddened and bewildered by the end of things, perhaps devastated, but he would not be angry.

She hoped that Simon, over there in France, did not suspect her betrothal. She hoped that he remained ignorant of it. The tie of her engagement to Luke was redundant, its love grown cold. She had merely to announce formal termination, and that to Luke alone. Simon did not need to know.

Stifling a sigh, Christine composed an opening sentence:

How I miss you, my angel! How I long for your return to me!

Then she paused again, remembering. She had not gone to the station to bid him farewell. Selfishly, she had avoided the wrench of that departure, though she knew Peake would have been hoping for her appearance right up until the moment of the guard's whistle and the locomotive's first hiss and chuff, tearing Peake away not only from her, but from his family, home and country.

And she had not been there …

Whatever words she wrote to Simon Peake, she knew that she could never send the letter.

Come back to me soon, my angel. Be safe and come back to me! I want you by my side, here with me to love me again. Return quickly, my angel!

The following morning, Saturday April 6, 1918, the Germans attacked again. Their pattern was the same as the previous day and the hour identical – dawn – with the rising sun directly in the eyes of the British. On this day the glare was reduced by mist that had crept upon the battlefield as an opaque blanket of pearl grey. It shrouded the soldiers in an ethereal murk, filtering the light so that individual men became as phantoms wreathed in wisps of whiteness. Above the fog was clear sky, the German observer suspended below his balloon waiting hopefully for his view to the ground to clear so that he could precisely direct the artillery's fall-of-shot.

In the tented British divisional headquarters, the major general had overestimated the number of men still able to fight. There remained some sixteen hundred, and these had regrouped into a single composite battalion of one thousand soldiers occupying the forward trenches, with the rest in reserve. They faced nine German battalions totalling seven thousand individuals.

The German commander did not delay because of the mist. He did not postpone his attack. The bombardment began as planned and the infantry moved forward under its protection, unhindered and unopposed all the way to the shrapnel line a hundred and fifty metres short of the Tommy position, the lead regiment arranged as before with two battalions up and one behind, and followed by the two reserve regiments in similar formation. No gas was used. There was no wind for it, and in any event the officers who had led the previous day's attack had very forcefully reported the diminished ability of their soldiers to see, move and fight in the constricting masks. Their generals had listened. No gas shells were fired.

The tank lost with Goettner's *zug* during the previous day's assault had not been replaced. There remained three machines, well forward with the first wave of troops, but today they were not in the *zug's* sector of the attack formation. Human casualties – slightly fewer than one man in every five – had been made up by two battalions conjured somehow and from somewhere by High Command. This time, the *Herr Generalleutnant* did not disperse these fresh troops among the very tired. Instead he ordered his three *obersts* to combine and consolidate their men so that he could allocate the fresh units intact and undiluted to lead the attack, fighting as cohesive battalions that would be the first upon the British wire.

As part of this consolidation, Goettner's *zug* had been brought up to strength by survivors from another. They had lost their *leutnant*, their sergeant, most of their *unteroffiziers* and more than half of their overall number. Now, Goettner's survivors and those who had joined them were arranged within one of the battalions immediately behind the regiment leading the attack.

During the initial phase, with the German guns pounding the British trenchline and the infantry moving up through the fog to the invisible outer reach of the exploding shells' deadly, red-hot steel shards – the shrapnel line

204

– the British secured one significant initial success. They had dispatched a flight of three biplane fighters to skirt the German shell trajectories and take the observation balloon by surprise. Approaching through the whorls of misty white at the very top of the fog, nobody heard them coming until it was too late. The aircraft fell vengefully upon their prey. Light anti-aircraft weapons fired at them from three points around the balloon as soon as they were heard. Despite the gunners' limited visibility, they found one of those three fighters almost immediately, the aircraft cartwheeling into the ground as a roiling ball of flaming fuel and bursting ammunition. The remaining two machines pressed home their attack, finding the balloon with incendiary rounds that ignited the hydrogen. The thing exploded into a fireball of fabric and flame that expanded briefly, then collapsed and deflated inward upon itself to become a falling torch, very large, that incinerated not only the observer still within his wicker basket below, but also one of the three anti-aircraft positions and its crew upon the ground.

It was wasted effort, that aerial attack delivered with so much determination. The German artillery was already firing quite effectively on the British line, using range and direction data recorded by each battery the previous day. The attacking battalions were already in position when the artillery observer burned and died within his wicker basket. There was no disruption to the attack plan at all.

At the prearranged hour, the German guns lifted their fire, switching to road intersections and artillery emplacements rearwards. It was the signal for the infantry to attack. Clambering to their feet, screaming out their fear and outrage as they began to run, their voices combined to become a hoarse and savage bellowing, a roar of desperate intensity as they charged, and it was heard by the British defenders as the battle cry of an enemy absolutely determined to take Foncquevillers, no matter the cost.

Thus began the third assault.

At the moment of the bombardment's lifting and switching, Winterman's instincts were mixed. As always there was the powerful urge to lead and show example. But he also needed to locate Watson, Earnshaw and others who this time had not made it into the dugout. The platoon had been on the fire-step at stand-to when the shelling began. He knew their allocated posts. He knew where to look. The problem would be time.

Jumping the shelter's steps, thrusting aside the blackout canvas and exhorting the others to follow, he ordered them to the fire-step, what was left of it. Chaos greeted his glance. Fog hung damply in tendrils and whorls about broken timbers, upended barbed wire barricades, and dozens of heavy sandbags tossed hither and thither as though filled with feathers. Bits of blasted equipment lay everywhere: trench periscopes, signal flares, some rifles.

The German artillery had been deadly accurate.

Winterman's men were in disarray, too, some with gas masks strapped, most without. Nobody knew whether Jerry was using gas or not, and fighting with a mask on was a nightmare. You couldn't see properly, and you had the terrible feeling that your enemy could. Winterman hated the mask. He wasn't wearing his.

Shouting orders, Winterman glanced around, assessing damage. He spotted Watson's form immediately through the murk of the fog, motionless some yards to one side of the dugout. He was slumped and twisted upon the dewy fire-step, bent knees skewed to one side with torso turned the other way, head cast back against the wall as though asleep, helmet wet and glistening.

'Watson! WATSON!' Winterman moved to him. Placing his rifle aside, he shook the man's shoulders, unsure of things and hoping against hope. But Watson was dead. Winterman let the body be. Grabbing his weapon, he bellowed encouragement to the others:

'MAN YOUR POSITIONS, LADS! MAN YOUR WEAPONS! STEADY NOW. STEADY … WE CAN DO THIS …'

They did as they were told, clambering onto the fire-step, heaving aside barbed wire entanglements blasted this way and that, and wrenching at sandbags tossed about by the shells. They needed these to better support their rifles.

Peake was as steady as ever – a good man, that – and through the mist Winterman could hear Corporal Tozer rallying his section and hurling Cockney abuse at one of the heavy Lewis guns, helping its team heft the cumbersome weapon into place.

Where the devil was Earnshaw?

Winterman peered into the dank greyness that was the fog, searching the spot that had been the private's post before the shelling began. The defences in that direction appeared entirely demolished, the result of a direct hit by a German shell. Both trench walls, front and rear, had fallen in to become a messy chaos of piled earth, broken timber and upended barbed wire that entirely blocked passage beyond.

Earnshaw must be under that! He's buried under the pile!

Then he saw a face poking through the clods and muck at the heap's surface, a head. Earnshaw's? Was that Earnshaw he could see?

Winterman's urge was to make a dash to see whether he could uncover Earnshaw's nose and mouth, clear them so that the man might breathe. Even to free the nose might be enough to save the man's life. But there was not time. The terrible bellowing of many thousands of angry men, terrible to hear, filled Winterman's ears – the German charge.

Watching. Waiting. Worrying. Nettermann's mind was a mixture of animal fear and animal readiness to kill, to do whatever was necessary to stay alive. He held no thought of anything at all beyond that and the absolute reality of the few hundred metres of ground ahead, those few hundred metres that held immediate threat to his survival.

Bent on one knee behind the lead battalions, right hand clenched around the stock of his rifle, the weapon's butt resting upon the damp soil of the shell-scarred field with muzzle and bayonet directed for the moment harmlessly skyward, Nettermann peered at the swirling fog from under the rim of his coal-scuttle helmet, trying to see through the silvery-grey mist even as he anticipated the order to advance. The roar of shells battering the British line was thunder in his ears. He could feel the force of the blasts slapping cheeks and forehead as the invisible shockwaves washed over. The din was appalling. Nettermann tried cocking his head in an effort to find sound and meaning beyond the irregular, clamouring crash of the high explosive pulverising the British line. He could see very little, and nothing beyond the second man on either side of him. The third was a mere wraith, a barely identifiable smudge shrouded in the grey-white wash that came and went and swam about them according to the fog's whim. His vision thus limited, Nettermann was forcing his ears to decipher any clue of what lay in front of him, but the noisy bombardment drowned all.

Nettermann reckoned the lead battalions would have lost more men to their own shells this time. More than yesterday, certainly. There would be no word going back to the gun line from an observation balloon made useless by the murky gloom of the fog. Whoever was up there wouldn't be able to see anything at all. No, the forward units would have again advanced until the first men fell to the flying steel of their own shells, but there would have been more this time because everyone would have been moving blind – each *kompanie* would have had to keep going until it took casualties, unable to look to units either side for first sign of the scything shrapnel.

Maybe that fog would hold some advantage, though, thought Nettermann. It might just help them get all the way to the wire – or even through it –

without the Tommies being able to shoot with any accuracy. The fog might yet prove an ally.

Now came the sound of aircraft, a higher note than the thunderous bombardment, barely audible but growing quickly louder. Nettermann looked up, then behind, unable to assess direction. A machine gun began to stammer and clatter, then another, followed by the monstrous tearing sound of a crash that could only have been the end of one of the airborne machines. Must be Tommy 'planes! They're going for the observation balloon! Nettermann listened to the rattling guns and the rise and fall in the nasal drone of the aero engines until the fog behind him coughed forth a *whoomph* that glowed an expanding coppery orange, quite shocking, like some kind of sky demon setting fire to the air. The balloon! Had the Tommy flyers taken the balloon?

There was no time to think. No time to find out. Shrill whistles screeched and warbled from everywhere at once as the gloomy, fog-shrouded battlefield became suddenly and eerily silent. The 'planes had gone and the bombardment had ceased, the guns switching because of the dead reckoning of minutes marked on their fire plan and not waiting any longer for word from their now non-existent balloon. The infantry got up, voices rising to a determined, self-fortifying roar as they made for the Tommy line. Nettermann could hear Goettner emboldening his men even above that roar as the sea of grey-clad soldiers flowed forward through the clammy, clinging, pearly damp. Beside him was König whom he could see, and on his other flank Winkler and Zimmermann, whom he could not. Goettner was similarly invisible in the fog, but he could hear the man exhorting his *zug* to continue forward.

Running now. Quite a quick jog. And not too many of those shouts and screams of frightened, unbelieving surprise – the wounded falling unseen here and there. A body appeared in Nettermann's path, prone and probably dead because it was not moving and made no sound. But only one this time, only one in the way. Yes, the fog had helped mask the charge of the lead troops. The Tommies' aim was off. The enemy couldn't see them. The fog was their ally!

On and on, a couple of hundred metres seeming as a marathon. Surely the wire must come soon? Yes, here it was, already cut and wrenched aside by the lead troops, the cost of their breach marked by half a dozen dead scattered about or hanging upon the barbs of this particular opening.

They poured through the gap, ignoring the bodies. He followed König into it, with somewhere behind them in the melée and mix of whirling white fog and shell-smoke Goettner and Zimmermann and Winkler and the reinforcing remnants of that other *zug* mauled in yesterday's attack, those men now joined with their own.

They were through! They were through the wire! They were into the Tommies!

This time, Winterman could hear no tanks, only a chorus of angry voices rushing to battle. The fog, though beginning to thin a little, was still managing to hide almost everything, swirling and whirling, and rendering ineffective any and all rifle and machine-gun fire, whether attacking or defensive. Throughout the British trenches, all discharged their weapons as fast as they could find targets, but their efforts were random, dispersed and disorganised. This was not the determined volley that had halted the first attack three days prior.

Such were Winterman's thoughts and observations even as he realised just how close the Germans were – they were already at the wire and might have breached it, something entirely possible because there had been neither material nor sufficient time to complete repairs to those entanglements during the night.

He glanced to Tozer, just visible through the swirls and organising his group as well as ever. He glimpsed the nearest man taking a chance and resting his rifle to remove his gas mask and throw it aside. It nearly cost him his life: a German materialised through the opaqueness as a rushing grey phantom in an oversized steel helmet, his ghostly appearance taking solid form and shape in a mere instant as the enemy soldier bounded to the parapet and stepped upon the sandbags, pausing to aim downwards. Caught unawares, realising his error, the British soldier seized his weapon and forced its full length desperately upward with all his strength even as the German took aim, his thrusting bayonet finding and penetrating the German's innards.

But others emerged from the swirling, whirling fog to replace that bayoneted first man. Dozens of them were coming on now, pausing briefly to fire – some standing or choosing to kneel as they did so – then darting forward again under the cover of their fellows. Tozer's man had eliminated the first to reach the parapet, but the rest would soon spill into the trench. The worst of the struggle was about to begin.

Winterman's view of the desperate battle that followed was coloured by his responsibilities. He needed to rally his platoon, wanted to rally them and was indeed doing so, instinctively bellowing orders and encouragement to those about him. But he still wanted to get to Earnshaw. Watson was already lost and he did not want to lose another. Not now. In an instant he weighed the situation. Around Corporal Tozer and throughout the section beyond, things were for the moment as steady as the chaos would allow. All were firing at a frantic rate, and many of the misty grey phantoms were crumpling and falling under the weight and impact of that fire. But there were too many enemy – perhaps the second wave of the assault had already caught up with the first – and the main weight of the attack would certainly be upon them in moments. Turning toward Earnshaw and the collapsed trench, Winterman could see nothing of the remainder of his platoon beyond the upended pile of soil, sandbags and smashed defences at the point where the shell had struck. His thought was that there was probably nobody to command the soldiers beyond that place – beyond Earnshaw they were cut off and on their own. He had to do something. Winterman made up his mind. Leaving Tozer to rally and coordinate the men's fire as best he could, he began his dash, intent on ensuring that Earnshaw might still breathe. He was determined to save one life at least.

Winkler moved into the gap with Zimmermann, eyes roaming where he expected the Tommy trenches to be. He could not yet see them, the tell-tale sandbags of their parapets still hidden by the mist and the tangles of wire, but he could make a fair guess at their location. Beside him was Zimmermann, the big man's presence reassuring where just a few weeks before it had been so intimidating – they were friends, now, and Winkler felt safer in the knowledge, moving into the breach with this soldier who was now his guardian, and perhaps always had been. It had been Zimmermann who had guarded his path into that first attack three days before, preserving his life, and it had been Zimmermann who had kept him safe in the shell hole even as he cared for Bauer who had been in danger of bleeding out. Winkler felt that Zimmermann would keep him safe through this attack also. He now trusted the man completely. He knew that his big friend would do all in his power to keep the manner of the immediate battle in similar equilibrium. Thus reassured, Winkler moved with his comrade into the gap in the wire.

Ahead, on the other side of the breach, he could make out the dance-like gait of Nettermann pushing ahead and fanning out with others on the further side of the gap. Obvious, too, was König's dumpy frame. On either side of Winkler and Zimmermann themselves, the dead of the Fifth lay scattered about like so many discarded toys. Winkler glanced at their crumpled bodies to left and right. How had they done it? How had those men won this gap, for now the corpses of those victors lay unspectacularly strewn about their

210

tangled trophy, a body crumpled here and two more over there, a fourth caught in his fall by the barbs so that he hung upon the wire with one elbow held unnaturally high by the angry tangle against the weight of his corpse.

Six or seven were like this. There were no wounded.

The two comrades were moving quickly, now. Winkler could sense that the other man wanted to run so that they might achieve the other side of the constricting channel as quickly as possible, for this was potentially a deadly place. But it was impossible. Their advance was more like a clamber through a low hedge of brambles, for even though there was a gap, not all the wire was gone.

Behind them, the others.

Then, from just ahead, a warning shout. It was König's voice, only just discernible above the general cacophony of battle. Through the mist and smoke, Winkler glimpsed Nettermann raising his Mauser into the aim and getting off a shot. He watched the drama playing out as if in some terrifying, slow-motion nightmare. Then he remembered that Nettermann was the *zug's* marksman – whomever was the target was most certainly done for. Winkler chanced a glimpse to his flank to check that Zimmermann had registered the danger of König's warning, but the big man had mysteriously disappeared. Winkler looked about, momentarily bewildered, then saw his guardian lying flat upon the ground.

'Zimmermann?'

No reply. And no movement either.

'Zimmermann! Talk to me!'

From just behind, Goettner's voice came through the mist even as Winkler moved to help his friend. The *zugführer* was exhorting and encouraging as always:

'Keep moving, boys! Keep moving! Don't stop! Keep moving forward!'

But Winkler could see that Zimmermann was making no effort to obey their *oberleutnant*. The man wasn't moving at all. Winkler knelt down beside him, grounding his rifle to free one hand to offer help. Realisation dawned.

And then Goettner's voice, this time beside him – the *zugführer* had caught up:

'He's done for, Winkler. Come on, let's go.'

Winkler said nothing. He felt dazed, shattered. To left and right, he sensed others of the *zug* scrambling past through the hard-won gap, some cursing loudly at him because he was blocking the way.

Winkler felt his *oberleutnant* shake him by the shoulder. It was not a gentle shake.

211

'Winkler! Let's go, man! Let's go! He's done for, don't you see? Dead. Now *get up*! And let's go!'

Confused, Winkler hesitated. He was troubled by the lack of any obvious sign that Zimmermann was no more, other than that he was lying so completely still. Winkler could not see the face and, to him, Zimmermann's big, imposing frame was as it had always been and as he expected it always to be: reassuring if only for the physicality of its size. Only the odd angle of the helmet, obviously uncomfortable upon Zimmermann's head with its ginger hair, only this and the utter stillness of the body gave the lie to Winkler's hope for life. That, and the fact that he made no effort at all to comply with Goettner's order, for all in the *zug* obeyed their *oberleutnant* without question, for they loved the man as a father.

A final, urgent tug at his shoulder. It was strong enough to break through the haze of shock.

'Winkler, get *up*! He's *dead*, d'you hear me? Come on – let's go, man, before we get hit too!'

He did it.

Earnshaw's view of the onslaught was as uniquely terrifying as any, but it was helpless, for he was trapped by the earth and could not escape it. Buried to his neck within the mess created by the exploding shell, he was nevertheless alive and unhurt, his head and one arm above the broken soil. He could breathe.

Clods of earth, broken timber and a mess of sandbags mixed with a tangle of wire; these things held his body tight within their grip, squeezing him like a heavy cocoon. His head filled with a shrill ringing from the blast that had blown in the trench, he experienced the numbness of hearing loss – neither shouting nor the cracks and banging reports of rifle fire came to him.

He had been trying to mount the fire-step when the shell hit. He had been trying to fight. Now he could do nothing. He was buried, trapped, terrified, deaf and struggling for air because of the press of earth upon his chest. Clearing his eyes with the hand that was free, twisting his head to peer through the lifting fog, his view was filled by a desperate British defence. He found that he needed to wipe his eyes again. He realised he was sobbing.

First to be overrun was Corporal Tozer's group. The Cockney corporal had four with him – two on the nearest side, two more farther away. He saw the wicked upward thrust of bayonet into the first enemy to reach the parapet, delivered by the man who had shed his mask. He saw the frenzied aiming and firing – not all of the five at once – each man hurrying to re-chamber and fire as rapidly as possible to lengthen the odds. But Tozer's four had been caught off-balance. They weren't ready. Their fire was haphazard and disorganised. He heard the corporal's exhortations turn suddenly to warnings, his voice climbing an octave under the pressure of the moment as a group of infantry in field grey broke through the wire to fall upon the men defending the parapet. They were led by an officer who promptly shot two of Tozer's men in quick succession – the German had the advantage of not having to reload, his pistol was designed for the close-quarters fight. Through eddies and swirls of grey mist, Earnshaw saw these attackers fall violently upon Tozer and his remaining two, one of the Germans swinging an entrenching tool, smashing its flat into Tozer's chest so that the corporal fell backwards, somehow managing to keep hold of his rifle and aiming at his assailant even as he recovered from his fall to the duckboards, firing and finding his target who sank to his knees, dropping the spade to clamp hands to his wound. Very quickly, the officer aimed his pistol at the danger and felled Tozer with a single shot. On the other side of the disabled corporal, another German put his full weight behind a bayonet thrust that pushed his steel blade directly through one of the group who had been scrambling, only lightly wounded, to retrieve the weapon he had dropped when falling backwards from the fire-step. The last of Tozer's four discarded his rifle to raise his arms high in surrender, but he was shot even as he did this, a lucky death, clean and quick. He sank to the trench floor and did not move, dead before he hit the ground.

Everywhere the trench was filled with similar scenes: men locked in hand-to-hand struggles, men firing into one another at point-blank range, men swinging rifle butt or spade, or smashing down with club. Some had resorted to the bayonet alone, detaching it from their cumbersome weapons so that they could more easily stab, gouge, or batter with the hilt. At the place furthest from Earnshaw's view, beyond Tozer's group and just short of an angle in the line where was trapped still that abandoned tank of the previous assault, two Englishmen were surrendering and the Germans allowed it, kicking aside dropped rifles and trying to cover the prisoners with their own weapons even as they cast frightened looks about them at the fighting close by. Earnshaw could see their mouths moving as they bellowed orders that he could not hear.

Earnshaw twisted his head a little, wiped again at his eyes, refocused.

His sergeant – Winterman – was making a dash along the duckboarding toward him. There were Germans in the trench beyond, but none in the space between.

The sergeant was mouthing something that he could not hear: 'Hold on, Quiz – hold on, son! I'm coming. I'll get you out!'

But then Winterman was knocked off his feet – some or other bullet had found him. He crumpled onto his side, skidding forward a few inches under the momentum of his run. For some seconds he lay still, then managed to drag his head with great effort to look at Earnshaw. His face was grazed and scratched – bleeding – and it carried splinters of wood from the boards. He was dying. Earnshaw recognised that fact immediately. He was dying, just a few yards from where Earnshaw himself lay buried still by the collapsed trench wall.

Earnshaw realised that he was shouting, his hoarse effort part pity, more a mix of alarm and terror. His cries went unheard and unheeded. The tough young sergeant was dying, chin resting awkwardly on the duckboards, jaw working and grinding uselessly from side to side in his pain, eyes losing focus until he seemed to be staring at nothing at all. Dead.

Now, everywhere Earnshaw looked brought the same view: soldiers in grey and soldiers in khaki locked in a terrible hand-to-hand combat among those who had already fallen, the wounded managing occasional screams of surprised fear, the dying managing only low, moaning groans and grunts, or making no sound at all. Those already dead were unmoving, like Winterman and Tozer's group, some slumped in a sprawling half-crouch against the angle between trench wall and fire-step, or hanging from it backwards onto the duckboards, most lifeless and some with their weapons still clutched in unnatural grip, as though defying death. Many were bloody, but some displayed no obvious sign of what had killed them, or who.

The German infantry continued to pour over the parapet into the trench, like a river of grey treacle reaching the short drop of a very wide cataract.

He saw Peake die as he fought alongside another Lancashire already wounded but still able to shoot. Peake died well, taking one German with his final shot before his barrel was thrust aside by the weapon of a stranger in grey. Holding on to his own rifle, Peake pulled and swung and hacked viciously with barrel and blade, smashing one steel edge into the face of the assailant below his bucket helmet, so that the man fell aside in great pain, clutching at the gash. Peake continued swinging and hacking left and right at yet other attackers coming on, causing grievous damage but unable to follow through with any truly telling blow or thrust. His defence was as desperate as it was valiant, but it was ended by a bayonet backed by the full weight of the soldier pushing it before him – a shortish man with broad build who lost his footing and fell forward over the parapet into the melée, his rifle held forward.

214

Peake sagged, screaming, the steel buried deep within him and the tip lodging in his backbone. He scrabbled and scratched weakly with both hands at the weapon that had stuck him, even as his attacker scrambled to his feet and placed a boot upon Peake's chest, attempting to tug his blade free. The German officer leading the charge shot Peake through the head in an act of necessary mercy.

König knew that he was nearing exhaustion. The fight-through from the barbed wire entanglements to the British parapet had been hard and vicious, the lead troops slowing in the face of stiffening defence until the weight of the reserve catching up – Goettner, König and the rest of the *zug* a part of it – delivered the extra momentum needed to gain the trenchline. But they had lost Zimmermann in the gap.

Now, with the sandbagged parapet just metres in front and half a dozen soldiers already fallen here and there, he was still running even as he prepared to jump. He could hear the crazed voices of fighting just out of sight within the trench, then felt something catch at his ankle so that he stumbled into a half-slide, half-tumble forward over the parapet. At the instant of his falling, he glimpsed immediately beneath him a Tommy slashing this way and that. König had his own rifle pushed firmly forward in a reaction of self-defence and protection against his fall, but his bayonet struck the wildly swinging soldier in brown, penetrating fully the man's chest as the entire weight of König's tumble followed through upon it.

The impaled enemy, grimy and muddied, let go his own rifle to collapse backwards into a half-crouch against the timber of the opposite trench wall. He was beside another Tommy already badly wounded and out of the fight. König's own victim emitted no sound except a hiss of breath as if punched very hard – almost a sigh, though it carried clearly through the shouts, shots and screams around – and the man clutched with both hands at the barrel above the steel now driven into him. His accidental thrust deadly and complete, König placed one hob-nailed boot heavily against the chest of his victim and heaved in a desperate effort to pull his Mauser free, an action taken more from selfish need to defend against British still in the fight, than from any impulse of training or aggression. He failed. The blade was stuck fast and seemed to pull at the man's heavy body even as he tugged and watched, horrified, those hands that scrabbled so weakly at the weapon's barrel. The German could sense the man's imminent death, yet still his bayonet remained firmly embedded. The body would not yield it. Goettner put an end to the struggle, turning briefly from his own part in the fight – dwindling now – to shoot with his pistol the dying man directly in the face, somehow providing the leverage needed for König to free his blade.

'Next time just fire, König, d'you hear?' bellowed Goettner. 'Just fire the damned thing to clear the blade – we don't have time for this!'

And with that, Goettner moved away to seek others he could help, only to discover that the vicious fighting up and down the trench was beginning to die out, the number of Tommies still standing now very few, and no reinforcements reaching them through the rearward communications trenches. Probably everybody was already committed, Goettner reasoned. Probably there were no more men to send. How hard and bravely these British had fought! How determined had been their resistance, even to the end.

His bayonet free, König chambered a fresh round and raised his Mauser, alternating his aim quickly left and right as he sought danger or threat. But there was none. Around him, most of the British now lay heaped and tumbled in the random attitudes of the newly wounded or already dead, here a limb moving weakly, there a man thrashing and calling out – looking for a friend or seeking aid, most likely – König couldn't comprehend the language. So few had surrendered! They had fought almost to the last man. König listened to the diminishing noise of battle. There was still some shouting coming from points further along the trench – places out of sight beyond the angles of its line – and the occasional loud retort of grenade. No chattering machine guns anymore, though; those had stopped as the attacking Germans – the lucky ones not hit during the desperate skirmish forward of the barbed-wire entanglements – had poured over the parapet into the depths of the trench, the British crews falling back from their cumbersome weapons that could not be brought to bear at such close quarters.

König heard Goettner shouting orders to move with Winkler along the trench to where the passage turned and disappeared around the angle of a bend. At the same time their *zugführer* sent others in the opposite direction to move to the part where the walls had collapsed inward from a direct hit. They were to pause at those points, Goettner told them, and wait for the units beyond to link up. No heroics.

König moved away with Winkler toward the angled turn. Reaching it, and being careful during his approach not to tread upon any of the fallen, König knelt to peer cautiously around corrugated iron holding back damp earth and mud, trusting Winkler to cover his rear. Beyond the bend, the scene was similar to that in their own part of the trench: dead or dying British, dead or dying Germans, and everywhere discarded rifles, expended cartridges and upended sandbags. Some of the lucky few were already receiving attention from others doing their best for their wounds even as the fighting died out.

An ugly chaos.

Behind König, Winkler realised they had done it. They had taken the British position, permanently this time. Amazingly, within the trench itself there were fewer German dead and wounded than there were British. Most of the casualties they had suffered had fallen during that final dash from the vicious barbs of the wire to the parapet, when the Tommies could finally see them through the mist. The enemy had hit Zimmermann firing blind, then, they must have. It had been a lucky shot, for they could not possibly have seen him; would not have been able to see the breach in their wire at all. Recollection of the big man sprawled so still within that gap brought a stab of sadness to Winkler. With sudden clarity, he now saw that all Zimmermann's earlier taunts and goading had had the sole objective of keeping them both alive. They had not been for Zimmermann's selfish protection alone. Without ever expressing it, Zimmermann had clearly understood that all in the *zug* would benefit if they could just work together, and that included the replacements who were mostly ignored. His taunts had been Zimmermann's way of goading newcomers to that end.

Zimmermann … How sudden his death, how unexpected. There had been no final words, no sign-off to the pages of his life. Indeed, Winkler could not recall his last conversation with his guardian. Well, it was the usual manner of things in this war: sudden death all around and ever present. What Winkler could easily remember, though, was his ultimate view of Zimmermann, the big man lying motionless in the gap, so still and so alone, and with his helmet uncomfortably twisted. The vision of that moment brought dampness to Winkler's eyes and he wiped at them guiltily, stealing a glance at König to be sure his stubby friend hadn't noticed. He would ask the *oberleutnant* for permission to join the burial detail and recover Zimmermann's body when things had quietened down a bit.

Zimmermann …

The mist continued to lift. There was relative silence and little firing. The victors knew that there would now be pause until British Headquarters understood that their position had been finally and properly overrun. When that realisation came, they could expect some shelling, but until it happened there would be time to breathe. Winkler did not think the British would counter-attack. He was quite sure that they had not had sufficient troops to properly man their second and third lines of defence, even before this latest assault. The German attack of the day before, though repulsed, had killed many British. Winkler felt that what few reserves there had been had already been thrown forward into the defence.

It was over.

Now, defending where Goettner had ordered them to, beside the bend in the trench, the two *gefreiters* felt an indescribably massive wave of relief wash over them, and with it fatigue. König glanced to Winkler, who nodded agreement at his companion's unasked question. There was a perfect understanding between these two in the moment, though not a word was spoken. They knew no enemy would come along the trench – only others from their own side feeling their way forward to friendly troops. It was time to rest. With Winkler covering him, König up-ended his rifle into the crook of a shoulder and sat back awkwardly but gratefully from where he knelt. Resting his back against the planks of the British trench, splintered and scarred clean where bullet or shrapnel had been stopped by the wood, he patted down his tunic, seeking pipe and tobacco. Finding them, he retrieved both and lit up. He looked about him.

While König was lighting his pipe, Goettner searched and examined the position, deciding what more needed to be done. There were a lot of bodies within the trench, most of them British. An edge of white paper protruding from a tunic caught his eye. The body was lying awkwardly on its side, one chevroned arm stretched out as though striving to reach something. Goettner moved to the dead sergeant, examining the body briefly before retrieving the paper. It was an envelope smeared red across the white, the letter's handwritten address made illegible by blood. In the same pocket as the letter, Goettner felt the smooth curve of something crafted from steel and tugged free a hip flask, also bloody. Glancing at the dead *Britischer* and pocketing both letter and flask as souvenirs, Goettner stood again to check on progress. Weak movement from the cave-in beyond the sergeant's outflung arm caught his eye. A Tommy was almost completely buried over there. The man was sobbing, tears streaking pale tracks across grubby cheeks that twitched and jumped in disbelief and shock.

'Nettermann!'

'*Herr Oberleutnant?*'

'Dig out the buried man.' Goettner pointed. 'Give him water and show mercy. Check for wounds and take him prisoner. Be gentle. No need for rough stuff.'

'*Jawohl, Herr Oberleutnant.*'

the others to eat and rest. The sergeant he ushered into the operations tent where, approaching the general and invited to speak, he saluted and presented the man who had been the patrol's commander.

They offered considerable contrast, the general and that sergeant. The general was impeccably turned out. Despite missing cap, everything else about him – bearing, grooming, manner, rank and speech – oozed authority and commanded respect. The sergeant, too, invited respect in equal measure, but for different reasons. His dirt and sweat spoke volumes of recent engagement with the enemy – the nasty end of things very foreign to the men of this headquarters – and the respect that it called forth was strongly reinforced by the three chevrons of his battlefield rank made grubby by the skirmish he had just survived, and by his rifle slung upon shoulder, obviously discharged. His hessian-covered helmet was still strapped in place. All in the tent made way for this man. They stood aside.

'Well, sergeant?'

The general's tone was frank but friendly. It carried empathy.

'I have to report that Foncquevillers has fallen, sir.'

'Fallen? Fallen, you say? But how so? We still have field guns in place … The gun line at the rear? They must still be defending there …?'

'No, sir. Not anymore.'

The sergeant paused, fearing his remark perhaps too bluntly delivered. He elaborated:

'They were spiking the guns when we got there, sir, those they hadn't had time to hook up … Then Jerry came on and sent us scarpering … We scrounged a ride back with one of the pieces they got out … sat upon the carriage. Further back we saw four-and-a-halves getting ready to go as we moved through.'

'I see.'

The general thought a while, considering. Then:

'And Jerry? Was he upon the guns in any strength?'

'No, sir. He's not yet there in strength, but he's there. We bumped him just t'other side of the gun line. Fritz had a patrol well forward. We fought our way out with the gun crew. Had to leave the gun.'

'Regimental headquarters?'

'Couldn't reach it. Couldn't get that far, sir … Sorry, sir.'

'No … Don't apologise.'

Another pause. Then the general again:

'And communications, sergeant? There at the guns themselves … Messages coming back by runner? Anything at all getting back from the forward lines?'

'No, sir. Nothing coming back. Nothing at all. Fritz has sealed it off. Overrun, I'd say.'

The general turned to his signals officer.

'What about birds, Peter? Anything by carrier pigeon? Anything coming back by bird?'

A shake of the head.

It shocked the general, that news. It appalled him that a position so resolutely held at great cost against overwhelming odds – and for nearly four days – could actually have fallen. With great effort he kept his face expressionless, but in fact the general was greatly shaken. He was remembering … remembering his battalion commanders and the regimental sergeant-major whom he had known personally along with many of the company commanders. A few captains, too.

His next words, a thought formed for his private mind alone, he whispered unintentionally aloud because of the state of his shocked disbelief:

'My God!' he said, 'A complete regiment … Four battalions … All gone. And for what?'

In the aftermath of the attack, when the Germans had moved through the fire trenches and taken the rear, and when they had established an aid station and begun to stretcher out the wounded of both sides for medical attention, when they had marched away their prisoners and brought forward a burial platoon to begin taking care of the dead – in particular the many bodies stacked forward of the parapet – when all of this had been organised there was time to rest.

Goettner did so. He sat upon the fire-step and stared without seeing along the battered trench, the dead sprawled motionless here and there throughout its length, and the gravely wounded being hefted one by one onto stretchers or, if less seriously hurt, supported by two men with an arm around each as they limped off to the medical orderlies. The collapse in the trench – the bit blown inwards – caused Goettner's eyes to pause and refocus for a moment. He saw that there was no longer anybody buried in the mess. They must have dug the Tommy out. Goettner hoped they had given him water and a cigarette before they sent him off with the other prisoners still able to walk – very few. Most of the British were either on stretchers or dead.

* * *

At British divisional headquarters, the staff officer in charge of organising runners to Foncquevillers was careful in the way he received men coming back. Relieving them of written dispatch, the captain went to considerable lengths to relax his arrivals, calming them before enquiring after personal observation – important situational details which he jotted down.

He was quite young, that junior staff captain – a man wounded six months prior, recovered and now posted to Division to complete his recuperation. As the battle around Foncquevillers developed, his duties had expanded to include organising runners as required, and debriefing them as they returned from the regiment in defence. His jotted notes added background to the dispatches. Brief and to the point, they helped the divisional staff, and especially the major general, form a clearer picture of conditions at the frontline. This morning, all news and formal signals coming rearward had been bad, and the captain's own experience of battle led him intuitively to increase the strength of the teams he sent forward. Since dawn he had been sending not the usual one or two men, but five or more as the reports dispatched by the commander of the defending Lancashires portrayed a rapidly deteriorating situation. Under the captain's guidance, the final group had been seven strong and led by a sergeant, more of a reconnaissance patrol than any mere dispatch by runner. He had sent these men forward by lorry, with orders to get as close to the line as they could on wheels, then make their way forward on foot, ideally all the way to Regiment. There were enough of them to give a good account of themselves if they bumped the Hun.

Now, receiving the returning patrol, the captain offered tea fortified to almost half its volume by rum, a brew he had ordered specially prepared in anticipation of what he expected the patrol to have been through. He asked no questions for quite some time, allowing the soldiers to recover a little. He watched them as they sipped. They appeared calm enough, but the captain had considerable experience of men who had encountered the enemy, and he recognised that they were shaken. Ostensibly quiet, the eyes of three darted about, while one stared fixedly and vacantly at nothing at all. The hands of another trembled. The patrol had returned two men short.

Eventually, in their own time and when they were ready, they began to speak, and the young captain listened attentively to a description of events delivered in phrases and sometimes comments of a single word, their sergeant supplying a thread of narrative and adding detail as necessary. When the conversation dwindled, the captain dismissed all except the sergeant, ordering

He patted down his tunic in search of tobacco, instead rediscovering the hip flask and letter he had taken from the dead sergeant. The man's corpse still lay upon the duckboards over there: the body on its side, open eyes dulled but seeming still to stare at the part of the trench that had collapsed upon one of his men. Those British bodies would be the last to be dragged away, and the sergeant's too. The burial team would take care of their own dead first.

Retrieving the letter and flask, Goettner sent a man to find the *zug's* translator. The new man not as good as Bauer, but he was better than nobody at all. Poor old Bauer – he would have translated quite well. There had been word that Bauer had lost his leg. Well, mused Goettner, at least the man still had his life.

Passing the letter to his translator, Goettner asked him to prepare to read it aloud. He took a cigarette and lit up, drawing deeply. Then he noticed that the hip flask he had placed beside him on the fire-step was still smeared a messy red. Putting down his cigarette, he picked up from the duckboard at his feet a handy piece of tattered Tommy serge. He used it to wipe clean the flask's burnished steel. When the blood was mostly gone, he passed it to his translator, eyebrows raised in query at the inscription's meaning. The man translated for him:

Come back to me. Christine.

Goettner took up his cigarette again. He smoked and listened as the translator began to read.

The letter was dated four days previously:

My Dearest Christine

The Germans have begun a really strong push over here. I feel sure that this will be headline news in London, so perhaps our censoring officer will allow me to reveal the fact that we are in the middle of this fight, and not cross everything out. I know he likes to do this – make crossings-out. What a sensation of power it must give him!

It is no secret that we are in the midst of a titanic struggle – the whole British Army is involved. At the moment we are dug in and waiting, but I feel the Hun will come soon. He must. I hope I can finish this letter before he does.

It's a very strange thing, this fight between us and Fritz. I have been in this war three years, yet I don't hate the Germans and I am sure that they don't hate us. We have all been caught up in a mess cooked up by politicians – the same thing seen through different lenses – and because of that we continue to kill one other in very large numbers. But I don't hate the enemy. When we capture a Hun, he seems normal enough to me: frightened and scared, just as we are. These are emotions that all of us feel, I am sure, when the fight is on. Jerry carries photographs of his family, too, just like us, and he has similar hopes and fears. Prisoners tell us they want the war to end, when we capture them. And we want that too – all of us. We want it to end.

Lately, I have given a lot of thought to this thing called hatred, because some of the men _do_ hate Jerry. I think this must be because they have lost somebody close to them in the fighting, whereas I myself have not. I have nobody here close enough to me to cause feelings of hatred, because I do not allow myself to become close to anybody here in the company. So I don't feel it as much as I might do when a man disappears. Perhaps if a brother or an uncle of mine had died (yes, some of the men's uncles are in this thing), then I would feel differently. But I have no brothers, and my parents are safe over there in Camden, at The Duke. So I cannot bring myself to hate the Germans. They attack us because they are ordered to, as we attack them.

There is not much news. I am not permitted tell you which part of the country we are in, and I would bore you if I tried to describe our daily routine. The only noteworthy event is that the platoon – my platoon – has recently been joined by an old school chum of mine – Simon Peake. He's a decent sort of fellow who is proving quite useful in the line, though I must be careful not to get closer to this man than we were at school. He was my junior and used to fag for me! I must not allow him to become my friend. Anyway, we talk about Camden now and then, and it does me good. He's an orphan with guardians – an uncle and an aunt who live in the same town as we do. His uncle apparently visits The Duke, and sometimes Peake's aunt as well. They know my parents quite well. I must remember to mention this the next time I write to them. What a small war we live in!

How I miss you, my dearest Christine! And how sorry I am that I brought you such unhappiness, such pain, when last we were together. Yes, I do know you were unhappy, my darling. You tried to hide it and you never spoke of it, but I knew. The blame is mine and mine alone, for I am not the same man you fell in love with. This thing over here has changed me.

Please wait for me, Christine. Only wait for me! I feel sure I will return to you, and let this be my promise: When the war does end, we shall marry immediately (if you will still have me) and I shall strive to be a good and faithful husband to you to the end of my days. That day – the day we marry – will for me ever afterwards be the happiest day of my life. So be steady and strong, my dearest Christine, and wait for me.

Just wait for me!

Your loving fiancé
John Luke Winterman

Dedication

A Salient in Flanders – written in memory of my grandfather, Captain Harry Thrush, late of the Lancashire Fusiliers, buried by shellfire forward of Foncquevillers, France, dug out and taken prisoner by advancing German infantry on Saturday April 6th 1918.

More novels by Alan Thrush:

A Cross for Two Graves: a compelling thriller with a strong element of PTSD and how destructive it can be. Read it here:
https://www.amazon.com/dp/B08P3JVYMT

Of Land and Spirits: critically reviewed as the finest piece of writing, novels or otherwise, on the fighting in the Rhodesian bush. Read it here:
https://www.amazon.com/dp/B083NDT848

Please take a moment to rate *A Salient in Flanders* (star rating), by scrolling down to **Customer Reviews – Review this product**, here:
https://www.amazon.com/dp/B0BC5NYNCZ

Want to drop the author a line? He'd be glad to hear from you and will reply. You can reach him directly (no gate-keepers or middlemen) here:
rhodius.pressoffice@mail.com

For more from this author:
www.amazon.com/author/alan.thrush